PLAYING PRETEND

WITH THE *Prince*

SIENA TRAP

Foreword

A comprehensive list of trigger warnings for those who need them can be found on my website: www.sienatrapbooks.com

This one goes out to all those girls with thick thighs and belly rolls. You deserve as much love as those sporting thigh gaps.

Don't worry, thigh gap girlies, I love you too.
But seriously, though, what's that like?

Prologue

Liam

NOW OR NEVER. IT was time to go.

Making my way through the maze of hallways inside the palace I called home, I reached the door to the suite of rooms belonging to my older brother's family. Not bothering to knock—knowing I was expected—I turned the doorknob, entering the darkened sitting room.

"Nat?" I whispered, not knowing if anyone was awake.

"I'm here," came a weak reply.

Turning on a lamp, Natalie, my brother's wife, became visible, curled into a chair in the corner of the room. On the floor at her feet—asleep in his car seat—was my youngest nephew, Beau, who was barely ten months old.

Glancing at the five suitcases lined up by the door, then back at my sister-in-law, I asked, "Are you ready? We only have a short window to get out."

I noticed her body visibly shaking as she stood. She was terrified.

Eyes wild, she asked, "What if he finds us?"

Gritting my teeth against the rage coursing through my veins, I shook my head exactly once. "Even if he does, he'll have to get through me first."

The *he* she was referring to happened to be my older brother, Prince Leopold Remington of our tiny alpine country of Belleston, settled in Central Europe. Charming by all appearances in public, Leo—as he was known to most—was depraved in private. Natalie had married him young, and he'd spent the last ten years torturing her with mind games and control tactics—most of which we hadn't uncovered until recently.

As a military man, I viewed tonight like an extraction. I was getting my brother's family out of harm's way so he could never hurt them again. The window was small. Leo had left this morning for an engagement in Spain and would be back by the afternoon tomorrow. If we were going to get them to safety, it had to be tonight, under cover of darkness so no one saw.

When my mother approached me, asking if I'd accompany Natalie back to the States, there had been no question in my mind. Only two years younger than me, Natalie had become a second little sister to love and protect—emphasis on the protection as she was married to my sadistic brother.

Together, we'd been planning tonight for a week, capitalizing on Leo being out of the country, and taking the necessary steps for security once we landed in Natalie's hometown of Hartford, Connecticut. Natalie had only been told of our plans once Leo was in the air this morning, so as not to show our hand. She already had one secret to keep from him at present—we didn't want to burden her with another and risk a leak.

Natalie was pregnant.

With Leo, Natalie had three children. My niece, Amelia, had just celebrated her seventh birthday a week ago. Then, there was Jameson—my nephew, who was six. They were two peas in a pod, not even a full year apart. The baby was Beau, but my brother had strongly contested the source of his existence. He believed that Beau was not biologically his, which was utterly ludicrous with how he had Natalie's every movement controlled almost down to the minute. We feared for her safety should he discover she was pregnant again. He'd never been physically violent but was devious enough to find a way to harm her—and the baby—that would leave him free of suspicion.

Driving home the point of our urgency, I looked directly into Natalie's chocolate brown eyes, bloodshot from days spent crying in private. "I can't protect you from him if you stay here."

Message received.

Nodding sharply, she moved toward the adjoining room, where the older two of her children were sleeping. Following her inside, I watched as she first sat on Amelia's bed, gently nudging her awake.

Amelia groaned into her pillow, but Natalie persisted. "Wake up, sweetheart."

Slowly, my only niece's eyes fluttered open, barely visible in the dark room. "Is it morning?"

"No, baby, but we're going on a trip and have to leave," Natalie explained.

"A trip?" Amelia's voice was still groggy, having been woken in the dead of night.

"Yes, darling. An adventure."

Amelia sat up slowly, rubbing the sleep from her eyes. "Like a vacation?"

"Sure, like a vacation." The white lie slipped from Natalie's lips easily. "But we have to go now. Can you go to Uncle Liam? He's coming with us."

"Uncle Liam?"

Calling out in the darkness, I beckoned for my niece. "Over here, Amelia."

Slipping out of bed, Amelia joined me in the doorway of their room while Natalie moved to Jameson's bed.

Jameson stirred, asking, "Mama?"

Natalie stroked his blonde curls. "Time to get up, sleepyhead."

Amelia spoke to her brother. "Jameson, we're going on vacation. Get up."

Jameson, always eager to be his older sister's sidekick, didn't require additional urging. He was instantly awake and ready for action. Finding me in the doorway, he looked back to Natalie. "Where's Daddy?"

Amelia stiffened at my side at the mention of their father.

Natalie swallowed so hard I could hear it, bravely declaring, "Daddy's not coming."

Believing they were indeed going on a short-term vacation, Jameson nodded. "Okay, we'll see him when we get back."

They weren't coming back. Not if I could help it.

As I led them both into the sitting room, my mother arrived to say goodbye. Deciding to send them away had broken her heart, knowing her only grandchildren would be an ocean away, but it had been deemed necessary. Staying here was dangerous. Protecting them required us to put our own feelings aside.

Throwing her arms wide, she called to Amelia and Jameson, "Come here, my darlings."

Without hesitation, they ran into her waiting arms, and she hugged them tightly, a single tear slipping down her cheek. Some might have thought royal families were cold and clinical, but not ours. My mother, Princess Adelaide, had always been hands-on, ensuring we understood that even though it was our duty to lead the country, we were a family first and foremost.

Before releasing the children, she whispered, "I love you both very much. Be good for your mom and Uncle Liam, and we will have a video chat soon."

Standing, she walked to where Beau was sleeping. Going to one knee, she smoothed a hand over his downy soft black hair. Rising, she turned to Natalie, pulling her into her embrace. "I hope you find peace."

"Mother, we have to go," I urged.

"Right. Of course." She picked up the car seat while Natalie and I grabbed a few suitcases, leading the children down the hallway to a back door where a black SUV waited to take us to the private airstrip. Mother had pulled strings to ensure there would never be a record of the flight we were about to take. The idea of Leo losing his mind trying to pinpoint how and where his family had escaped was deeply gratifying.

Another round of hugs all around while I loaded the bags, then Natalie began buckling the kids into their seats. My mother squeezed my hand, and I looked down at her from my six-foot-two height, promising, "I've got this."

"I have no doubt," she replied. "You're a natural-born protector. This is where you thrive. Just know that I'll miss you terribly."

Leaning down to drop a quick kiss on her cheek, I whispered, "I love you, Mother."

Hugging me close, she whispered back, "I love you too, Liam."

Climbing into the SUV's passenger seat, we waved as we drove off the palace grounds. Within fifteen minutes, we were seated inside the private jet while the crew stowed our limited luggage and did final checks prior to departure. Amelia was already drifting off in the seat next to mine—her head lolling onto my arm—while Natalie had Jameson curled in her lap. Beau hadn't stirred this entire time.

Looking across at Natalie, I noted how her cheeks were hollowed out—barely a shell of the woman she had once been. Her eyes had lost their signature sparkle, and even her golden hair seemed dull. Her smile once held the power to light up a room, but I couldn't remember the last time I saw it grace her lips. She was as fragile as she looked, and with how thin she'd become, it was a wonder she was still standing.

My brother did this to her. He'd always been different, but having someone to control brought out an ugly side he hid from the world.

Taking off, I watched out the window as my homeland faded away, not knowing when—or if—I was ever coming back. The country didn't need my presence. I was sixth in line for the throne behind my father, my brother, and my brother's children. It wasn't impossible, but it was certainly improbable that I'd ever take the throne—not that I wanted it. The concept of power had turned my brother into a monster.

Unsure whether that trait was inherent, I made a silent vow to never inflict this kind of pain on any innocent woman—or child, for that matter. The monarchy didn't need me to procreate, so I didn't need to take a wife.

As we fled to protect my brother's family from his own malice, I decided at that moment that I would forever remain a bachelor. It was the only way to ensure I never traveled the same dark path.

CHAPTER 1

Liam

Three Years Later

"More bubbles, Uncle Liam!" Beau screamed happily from the middle of the bathtub, his excited hands splashing water on my face. An afternoon spent playing outside had left him covered in dirt, requiring a pre-dinner bath.

The smile on his four-year-old face lit up my world. He and his siblings had become the center of my universe.

Backing away from the spray of water, I used my sleeve to wipe away the errant droplets covering my skin. Smiling—something only reserved for when I was alone with the children—I grabbed the bottle of bubble bath from the edge of the sink. Holding it up, I teased Beau, "I don't know. Who will your mama be mad at if you make a mess?"

With a devilish gleam in his dark brown eyes, he shouted, "You!"

It was a trick question. She wouldn't be mad at either of us.

After the trauma that had resulted in relocating her family back to Connecticut, Natalie adopted a policy of not sweating the small stuff. There were, of course, rules for the children and discipline when warranted, but minor offenses—such as a messy, wet bathroom—were given a pass. The main objective was to create a carefree, protective environment for them. They were free to enjoy their childhood without worry. At least, they were now.

Returning to the side of the massive tub, I reached an arm into the water to pull the plug to allow the water level to drop before adding more bubble bath. Satisfied that enough water had drained, I dramatically squirted the pink liquid in a circle around Beau before turning on the jets. He squealed in delight as more bubbles rose around his body, attempting to pop the few that escaped to free-float in the air.

"How's it going in here?" A voice from the doorway reached us over the roar of the jets.

Turning, I found Amy standing there. Amy was one of Natalie's two best friends, and had been the one to move into the house with us to help care for the kids. At that moment, Natalie was the one who needed more care, but she had been so worried about her children that we used them as an excuse to bring in additional help. We'd become an unorthodox family unit, sharing responsibilities and working together. It was routine, comfortable even.

Beau spun in circles but answered the woman who had become an honorary aunt. "I'm having a bath, Aunt Amy!"

Amy smiled. "I see that, but I think you might need more bubbles."

"Yes! More bubbles!" Beau demanded.

Beau was too young to understand the subtleties of sarcasm. Any more bubbles, and I feared losing sight of him, even from two feet away.

"Not so fast, little man. If I add more bubbles, you might float away," I cautioned.

He giggled at the silly picture my words painted.

Beau's giggles were infectious, causing Amy to laugh in response, adding, "I was teasing. Dinner will be ready in fifteen minutes. Make sure you're squeaky clean."

"Aye, aye, captain!" Beau called back. He was currently in a pirate phase, spurred on by the new treehouse in the backyard. The kids treated it like a crow's nest, pretending to be at sea.

Amy vanished from the doorway, and I turned back to Beau. His cheeks were shiny and pink from the warm water heating his tiny body. Taking a bottle of dual-purpose baby shampoo and body wash, I poured some into his dark hair, working up a considerable lather. Using the rest of the soap on my hands, I cleansed the remainder of his body before grabbing a whale-shaped scooper to rinse him off. Knowing the drill, Beau tilted his head backward to avoid any suds entering his eyes.

Just as I was about to pull the plug and remove Beau from the confines of the jacuzzi tub, my phone began buzzing in my back pocket. Grabbing a towel, I quickly dried my hands to see who was calling. Feeling my forehead wrinkle in surprise, the caller ID showed my mother's number requesting a video call. A quick glance at the time told me it was nearing midnight back home in Belleston, so this didn't feel quite like a routine check-in.

Sliding my finger across the screen to answer, concern laced my voice as my mother's face filled my phone. "Mother? Is everything all right?"

"Grandmama!" Beau called from behind me.

Brown eyes filled with love, my mother called back, "Beau Bear! Liam, dear, let me see my sweet boy."

The tension from when I saw her name—combined with the time—eased somewhat. Whatever reason for her call couldn't be serious if she was willing to talk to Beau first. Turning my body to lean against the wet tub, I angled the phone so they could see each other.

"I'm in the bath," Beau declared.

My mother's voice was warm. "Yes, you are, my darling! It's quite early. Were you especially dirty?"

Beau's face lit with a mischievous grin as his head bobbed up and down enthusiastically. "We were playing in the treehouse! I was a pirate!"

"That sounds marvelous! You have such a wonderful imagination. Can you be a good boy and play in the bath while I chat with Uncle Liam?"

"Yes, Grandmama."

"I love you, darling."

"Love you," he called back as I moved away from the side of the tub.

Turning the phone in my hand, I kept an eye on him while I spoke with my mother. Wasting no time, I asked, "What's wrong, Mother?"

Appearing offended, she huffed, "Does something need to be wrong to be able to call my son?"

Taking a moment, I surveyed the woman who had raised me and given me life. In her early sixties now, her hair—gone gray a long time past—was in its iconic French twist. Crow's feet appeared around her brown eyes from years spent smiling with her whole face. Even as a public figure, my mother had never been vain, allowing her aging to happen gracefully rather than turning to artificial means attempting to prolong the appearance of youth. Natural beauty at its finest, her eyes still shone like that of a much younger woman.

"Mother . . ." She wasn't fooling me. I knew something was up.

She raised a single eyebrow at my tone and softened. "There's a matter that needs attention."

Defenses instantly raised, I questioned, "What kind of matter?"

"It's something I'd rather not discuss over the phone."

Knowing exactly what she was implying but still holding onto a single shred of hope that I was wrong, I asked, "Are you planning a visit then?"

"Liam, I would greatly appreciate it if you could make a trip home so we can handle this in person."

Home.

I hadn't been back to Belleston since the night I helped Natalie flee the country more than three years ago now. There had been no reason to go back. My parents and my baby sister, Lucy, had made many visits to Hartford over the years. I'd avoided returning for one primary reason.

Leo.

My brother was my polar opposite, both in looks and temperament. Standing out in our family, Leo was the only child to sport blond hair and brown eyes, whereas Lucy and I had inherited our father's almost black hair and the famous Remington Blue eye color. Leo was slender and of average height, whereas I was broad and considered tall. Disgracefully, Leo had shirked his required military duty to our country, citing that he was too crucial to the continuation of our bloodline. At the same time, I'd embraced my duty, going so far as to enlist beyond my requirement. Leo used charm as a weapon—it was how he'd practically ensnared Natalie. Almost subconsciously, I'd hardened myself at a young age, remaining stoic for all outward appearances. The only ones who saw my softer side were the children.

"Please, Liam," my mother's voice practically begged.

Blowing out a sharp breath, my eyes were trained on hers through the screen. "What's the timeline?" Translation: how urgent was this matter?

"In the next week if possible." Translation: mildly serious, not life-threatening but also not insignificant.

"All right," I acquiesced against my better judgment. "I will make arrangements and reach out once I have them finalized."

A soft smile graced her lips. "Thank you, darling."

I nodded sharply once. "Of course."

Allowing her a moment to say goodbye to Beau, we ended the call, and my mind began to wonder what could possibly need my physical presence to discuss. I'd taken my role as a member of the Bellestonian royal family seriously all my life. That hadn't ended when I departed willingly to support Natalie and the children. I remained the chair of several local charities but now handled all business remotely. Some days, the time difference was a struggle, but I always made it work. I was duty-bound, after all.

Pulling Beau from the tub and wrapping him in a fluffy towel, I dressed him in pajamas. Even though we had yet to eat dinner, it was an informal affair at best. There was no need to create more laundry for Amy to tackle.

When we moved into this house, it had seemed almost too large for a single mom of three, but somehow, we'd managed to fill every bedroom—seven, to be exact—in this nearly 8,000-square-foot home. The second story was divided into two wings, with the master bedroom and a guest room—now nursery—in one wing, and four additional bedrooms in the other. A sweeping staircase was the focal point of the foyer, but a second, hidden staircase led directly to the living space on the ground floor.

Choosing the back staircase that spit me out into the living room, I encountered Natalie curled up on the chaise with a glass of pre-dinner wine.

A lot had happened in the three years since we'd left Belleston in the middle of the night. Unfortunately, the pregnancy that propelled us to leave so quickly had ended in a miscarriage, but the distance gave Natalie the strength to file for divorce.

Not long after officially breaking free of my brother's grasp, she was forced to move on with her life quickly due to an accidental pregnancy as the result of a one-night stand with the guy living next door—I swear that girl was the most fertile woman alive. There was never a dull moment when it came to keeping watch over Natalie.

Her new husband, Jaxon, was playing on the floor with their five-month-old daughter, Charlotte—or Charlie, as we so lovingly called her. The baby was not biologically related to me in any way, but had she stolen my heart the moment I laid eyes on her.

Slightly uncomfortable, I felt like I was intruding on a private family moment, but Natalie smiled when she saw me. "Thank you for bathing Beau."

Nodding my head in her direction, I replied, "Of course, but I'm afraid he left quite the mess."

Shrugging, she countered, "That's what kids do."

Priding my ability to be direct, I chose to lay out the situation. "Can you handle things here without me sometime next week? I've been asked to return home."

Frowning, Natalie's brows drew together. "Home? Did something happen? Is everyone all right?"

Her concern was valid. My grandfather—Belleston's monarch, King Victor—was in his late eighties, and though we never spoke of it, everyone knew he couldn't live forever. Pushing the unimaginable aside, I took comfort in knowing that my summons home would have been more immediate if it were something to do with Grandfather.

Shaking my head, I tried to dispel her worry. "No, but it was made clear that whatever they want to discuss must be done in person."

"But you haven't been home in . . ."

"Three years," I finished for her.

Unable to stop her involuntary shudder, she swallowed. "Uh-huh." Taking a large sip from her wine glass, she answered my original question. "It's still training camp. We can handle everything here if you need to go home. Besides, Amy is here. We'll be fine."

Jaxon was the star player of the local professional hockey team, the Connecticut Comets, and their season was about to begin. He and I got off to a rocky start, but eventually, I was forced to swallow my pride and accept that he was the right man for Natalie. Slowly, we were building a rapport, but it hadn't come easy.

Unlike my brother, I didn't like to control other people but felt the need to always be in control. Natalie's relationship with Jaxon sent my world reeling because so much about it had been beyond my control. I'd vowed to protect her and was forced to acknowledge that someone else would take on that role in her life.

As hard as it had been to recognize, I was convinced now that it was the right move. Natalie blossomed under Jaxon's care, regaining her confidence while finding a way to bury her past and move on with her life. Her independence was both exciting and alarming. I was beyond thrilled that she was free from the chains imposed upon her by Leo but uncertain of where I fit in her life. Having signed over the title to this house—I'd purchased it out of necessity during our escape—to the newly married couple this summer, I wondered how long it would remain appropriate to live here with them.

Maybe that was the matter my family wanted to discuss. I'd find out soon enough.

CHAPTER 2

Liam

BACK IN BELLESTON, INSIDE my childhood home, it all seemed so strange. Maybe they'd changed something, or maybe I'd changed, but it didn't feel the same. Perhaps I became accustomed to my life in America, where I was granted a more peaceful existence and freedom.

The differences were glaringly obvious the minute we touched down in the Bellestonian capital of Remhorn. No longer was I permitted to drive myself, relegated to the backseat of a black sedan while two members of palace security escorted me. My personal security guard, Jasper, who usually maintained a safe distance in the States—keeping to the shadows—was now required to stay close, reporting to his superiors of my whereabouts at any given moment.

I hadn't missed living in this fishbowl.

Upon arrival on palace grounds, I was informed that I would be granted an hour to freshen up, with the request that I don dinner attire before my audience with not only my parents but my grandfather as well. Having brought nothing formal, hoping for a quick turnaround, I was not surprised when I discovered a new dinner suit—what most considered as Black Tie—laid across my bed.

What in the world could this be about?

My time now up, I made my way to the formal sitting room that the family always occupied prior to dinner. While we'd been raised in a loving home, no one was above tradition in front of grandfather. He may have been our grandsire, but there was an ever-present reminder that he was also our monarch.

Walking through the hallways of Stonecrest Palace was like stepping back in time. Every item—ornate rugs, tapestries hung on the walls, pieces of furniture—was hundreds of years old, selected by our ancestors long gone. It was stifling, knowing the world was moving on, evolving, while we were holding on so tightly to the past.

The butler at the door announced my arrival, and I braced myself for what lay in wait once I crossed the threshold.

Dressed for a formal dinner inside sat my grandfather, along with his heir—Prince Adrian, my father—and my mother. They stood as I entered, and I made the requisite bow to those members of the family who out-ranked me. Formalities out of the way, my mother came close, and I leaned down so her kiss could land on my cheek as she'd intended.

"Hello, darling," she whispered.

"Mother." Then, I turned to the men in the room, addressing each in turn. "Grandfather. Father."

I hadn't seen my grandfather since I'd left for the States, and those three years saw him age more than I expected. He seemed almost frail. His gray hair had thinned, leaving him nearly bald on top, his shoulders hunched, making him seem shorter, and his blue eyes appeared sunken. It was clear that my grandmother's passing a few years ago had taken a toll on him. Despite his visible change in appearance, he still could command a room.

Gesturing to the two richly upholstered couches, Grandfather suggested, "Shall we sit?"

Although framed as a question, we all knew his word was law. Therefore, it was a direct order, and I was compelled to obey. Taking a seat last, I looked around the room, waiting for an explanation as to why I'd been recalled back to home base. My elders looked at one another, seemingly not knowing where to start, and an uneasiness settled over me.

Finally, my father took the lead. "Liam, we've asked you here to discuss your future."

Oh, boy. Here we go.

"And what future would that be?" I challenged.

Grandfather answered, "It's long past time that you marry, William."

Use of my legal name was never a good sign. He meant business. They all knew I had a compulsion to follow orders, but this was simply one I could not abide by.

"I have no intention to take a wife. I believe I've made that clear. There is no need." I would not budge on this point.

Father countered, "Circumstances have changed."

Assuming they meant my living situation, I acknowledged their concern. "Yes, they have. Natalie no longer needs my help now that she has remarried. I understand I must locate alternative accommodations, but I prefer to continue living abroad."

"While it may be deemed inappropriate to be living with a married couple, those aren't the circumstances to which I am referring."

Annoyed, wishing they'd spit it out already, I kept my tone calm. "May I inquire as to the circumstances? If they are so important as to require me to take a bride, I should think I have a right to know."

It was almost frightening how quickly I reverted to this way of speaking. While I waited for my father to explain, I pondered whether that was something I had learned growing up in a palace or if it was deeply ingrained in my royal DNA.

Eyes locked on mine, my father spoke. "Leo has been deemed unfit to rule."

Unable to contain myself, I muttered under my breath, "That's an understatement."

Father either hadn't heard or chose to ignore my words, continuing, "I am fully prepared to name you my heir."

Heir? Did he say heir?

My eyes snapped to the pair of blue ones that mirrored my own. Many said that I was a younger version of my father. His frame was large, often making my mother look tiny by comparison, and what was once a head full of jet-black hair was now threaded with silver. I might have been his physical replica, but that didn't mean I was meant to follow in his footsteps. That wasn't the role I was born for.

Taking a moment, I sorted through the implications of what he'd just said. That's when I remembered one significant detail. "While I tend to agree that Leo would make a terrible king, you forget one thing. Leo has three children, heirs of his own. You simply can't bypass the line of succession in this way. Leo is—"

"Illegitimate," my mother finished the sentence, effectively silencing me.

Stunned, it felt like we had entered a vacuum, the air being sucked out of the room. My collar suddenly became too tight, and I tore at it, hoping that if I loosened it, I'd be able to breathe—no such luck. My chest burned with the need to take in oxygen.

This couldn't be happening.

I had lived my whole life as the spare.

I didn't want this.

I wasn't raised for this.

"Liam?"

At the sound of my mother's voice, laced with concern, I could finally breathe, but there were still black spots in my vision. I bent over, head between my knees, trying not to pass out. Not exactly the perfect picture of a royal.

Allowing me the time to compose myself, they waited.

Finally able to calm my breathing, I glanced up. "Would someone care to explain?"

My parents shared a tense look. Mother nodded, signaling that Father should continue. Clearing his throat, my father looked extremely uncomfortable. Doing the math in my head, Leo was thirty-five, and my parents had been married for thirty-seven years. Clenching my fists, realizing he'd been conceived illegitimately during their marriage, I tried to hold back my rage.

My parents had a seemingly perfect marriage—a love match. How could he have done this to her? It was one thing to sneak around with a mistress, quite another to be so careless as to allow that relationship to result in a child. How had it been allowed for Leo to be raised alongside the rest of us as the heir when he was my father's bastard?

Finally, Father said, "A year into our marriage, your mother was, to put it delicately . . . attacked."

Attacked. Did that mean what I thought it meant?

My rage ratcheted up a notch, and I ground my teeth so hard that I swore I heard a molar crack. Through a clenched jaw, I responded, "Tell me that son of a bitch is six feet under."

Eyes downcast, my father whispered, "We never found the culprit."

"That is completely unacceptable!" I screamed back at him.

Blue eyes blazing, he looked directly at me. "Son, I would caution you to lower your voice. I'm the one who must live every single day with the knowledge that I could not protect the woman I love." Sufficiently chastised, I bowed my head in apology, allowing him to continue. "When your mother discovered she was pregnant weeks later, there was the possibility that Leo might be mine. We were married, after all. We had to wait until he was born to perform the paternity test, which ultimately revealed that he and I were not a genetic match. This is the first time we've spoken of it since we received those results."

It all made sense now.

Leo looked so different from the rest of us.

Leo's sadistic tendencies.

Nature had won over nurture.

While I felt some relief regarding my fears of becoming my brother and hurting those I was supposed to love, it was short-lived, given the circumstances. One thing still didn't add up. They'd kept this under wraps for over thirty-five years, so why were they willing to risk exposure now? This would cast doubt on the legitimacy of us all.

The irony was not lost on me that my brother questioned the paternity of his youngest son, when he was the one who'd been sired by someone other than the man we called Father.

Forming the words, I asked, "You would risk the scandal?"

My mother, who had remained silent during the explanation of Leo's existence, now spoke. "To protect the country we love? Absolutely. We've always known Leo was different. How could we not? It wasn't until Natalie became the proverbial canary in the coal mine, shining a spotlight on the depths of his depravity, that we realized he was mentally unstable. He cannot be allowed to rule."

Speaking of Natalie, I accused, "If you go public with this, you'll lead those wolves right back to her door. Doesn't she deserve peace after all she's been through?"

My mother softened. "You're forgetting something, Liam. Those children may not have royal blood, but they do have mine. I would never do anything to bring them harm. This a chance to set them all free."

Free. All I'd ever wanted for Natalie was to be free from my brother, and now I could free her children—children I loved. But at what cost? Removing the chains that bound them, only to don them myself?

Raising my chin, I debated, "And if I refuse?"

Not backing down, my father said, "Then it would fall to your sister."

Not Lucy.

Standing, I began to pace, needing an outlet for my frustration. My parents knew me well enough that I'd be unable to pass up the opportunity to protect both Natalie *and* Lucy. My baby sister, Lucy, was four years younger than me and was just now getting her fashion label up and running. She was living a hybrid royal life, having the freedom to pursue her passion while still contributing to the monarchy.

This wasn't fair.

They'd left me no choice.

I had one more question. "Why the need to marry? It's not in our laws that the monarch must have a spouse. I can rule without one."

My grandfather chose now to rejoin the conversation after initially declaring it was time to marry. "William, my boy. I do not doubt that you will make an excellent king. You have all the qualities one would want to see in an eventual successor. You are fiercely protective and loyal to a fault. You've proven that in the past and again today. Your sense of duty is unparalleled, having served our great country on the front lines. I know from experience that it is a heavy burden, even for those most prepared to serve as the head of state. Having a good woman by your side to share in the responsibility will greatly ease that strain."

With one last ditch effort, I asked, "Why now? God willing, it will be decades before I am called upon to serve my country as their ruler."

Mother stepped back in. "Liam, darling, we aren't asking you to get married tomorrow, or even this year. You are thirty-two years old. We want you to have the time and opportunity to find the right woman, who can withstand the rigors of this life by your side. It may take time. Begin thinking about it. That's all we ask."

"I'm being ordered to find a wife. Next, will I be ordered to procreate? If I make this one concession, will I be asked to make another?"

She twisted her hands. "Asking you to change the plans you had for your life is quite enough. If you choose not to bring forth children, that would be your decision. As you mentioned, it will be long before you are asked to rule, even longer before you must pass on the crown to your successor. Surely, by that time, Lucy will have a family who can continue our line."

A new question came to mind. "I've been ordered home for this meeting. Does that mean I am being permanently recalled back to Belleston?"

Mother's face shone with sympathy. "No, darling. We know you prefer to reside close to Natalie and the children in America. For now, you may remain abroad. In return, we would ask that you come home for specific functions. Even before we announce you as the new heir, we would like the people of Belleston to see you taking an active interest in the country over which you will one day rule. To start, we'd ask for six engagements your first year, possibly more once you move up the line behind your father as Crown Prince."

It was a good deal, the opportunity to remain near Natalie and the children while extending my freedom—even with a golden cage awaiting me at an unknown date. Six engagements a year was nothing compared to the rest of the family. Grandfather had pared back, but my parents sometimes attended an event per day, occasionally more than one. The more of us to share the load, the less each had to shoulder, so Leo and Lucy were instrumental in taking some engagements off my parents' plates. Guilt nagged at the back of my brain that remaining in the States, combined with Leo's change in status, would add to the already heavy burden on my family.

"Make it thirty a year to start. If traveling the distance for one, I can certainly do several during a single trip."

Sighing, Mother gave a small smile. "You always did have a hero complex, Liam."

Nodding at her words, I allowed them to sink in. I'd effectively thrown myself on the sword to protect my little sisters and, in the process, was releasing my niece and nephews from any chance of suffering the same fate. The only way I was going to be able to swallow this was to think of them. I was protecting them by sacrificing my life. The gravity of the conversation hit me in full force.

Someday, I would become the King of Belleston. God help us all.

CHAPTER 3

Amy

TODAY WAS THE DAY. Today I would find out if my years of hard work had paid off and I earned the promotion to Programs Director.

I'd worked at the Hartford Family Reunification Foundation for five years, joining them fresh out of grad school. During that time, I worked my way up from Case Worker to Case Supervisor to Manager of Special Projects, but it all led to this. If granted this job, I would head up all new programs and have my hand on each facet of our foundation to do the most good for our client base.

Social work was my passion. While I would miss the day-to-day interactions in bringing families back together, my ideas for continued outreach would support even more families. When the Foundation's director announced that the position would be coming available, I had leapt at the opportunity. With shaky hands, I'd compiled my vision for the Foundation in a program proposal for review by the board. There were other applicants, of course, but none matched my experience level internally. The wild card would be those currently applying from outside the Foundation.

Driving to work, I got in the zone, rocking out to songs about female empowerment. It was still difficult for women to work their way to the top, even if it was becoming "trendy" for companies to allow women to break through the glass ceiling. Everyone wanted to prove they were on board with equality, but we all knew there were still hidden roadblocks. Every day, women navigated the invisible corporate minefield. I was one of those women.

Unlike some women, I could focus entirely on my work—no outside distractions such as a man in my life or a family were holding me back. There never would be. Living with my best friend, Natalie, and helping to raise her kids was enough to fill that hole in my life.

Parking beneath the tall building in downtown Hartford, I rode the elevator up to the 20th floor, where my meeting with the board would be held. On the way up, I gave myself a positive pep talk.

You are qualified.

You provided excellent ideas.

You will *get this job.*

Too soon, the elevator dinged, signaling I had reached my destination. Moisture gathered at my armpits beneath my blazer but I pressed forward, meeting this challenge head-on. Walking to the reception desk, I gave my name, indicating that I had an appointment with the board. The receptionist acknowledged that I was expected, but it would be a few minutes more, offering a bottle of water while I waited. Declining her offer, I took a seat on a plush chair in the lobby of this floor. My eyes bore a hole into the large oak double doors that separated me from the boardroom where my fate would be decided.

Chewing the inside of one cheek, my nervous habit rose to the surface—the longer the wait dragged on, the more I began to doubt myself.

What could be taking so long?

Had they decided on another candidate already?

Just when I thought they'd forgotten about me, the doors opened, and the Foundation board's secretary appeared. Looking down at her clipboard, she called out, "Ms. Michaels?"

Standing, smoothing my pants, I stepped forward. This was it.

The secretary led the way inside the massive boardroom, indicating that I should take the seat opposite the rest of the board members across the table. From where I sat, I could see my program proposal in front of each member. This was the room where my body of work with the Foundation—and my plans for its future—would be judged.

Mr. Greiner, the Foundation's president, acknowledged my presence. "Welcome, Ms. Michaels."

You can do this.

Smiling—keeping my lips closed to avoid seeming too eager—I replied, "Thank you. I am excited for the opportunity to discuss my ideas for the future of our foundation."

Mirroring my subdued smile, he continued, "Wonderful. Before we discuss your proposal, we'd like to ask a few preliminary questions."

"Of course." I nodded.

"How long have you been here at the Hartford Family Reunification Foundation?"

The softball question soothed some of my anxiousness, and I replied effortlessly, "I reached my fifth anniversary with the Foundation this past June. Coming straight out of graduate school, I began as a case worker and have spent the last five years working my way up to the position of Manager of Special Projects that I hold now. I've been fortunate to have experience in the day-to-day operations and project coordination, giving me a broad scope of the functions of the Foundation."

Not touching on anything I'd said, he moved on to the next question. "What aspect of the Foundation do you find most compelling?"

I found myself smiling again. "Where do I begin? Coming from a privileged background, I was unaware of the hardships of families less fortunate than mine until I became a debutante. Our service project brought us to the Hartford Family Reunification Foundation, and my world instantly expanded. Working with the adults taking steps to regain custody of their children, as well as time spent with the children during Foundation-run programs, I saw both parties' faces light up when talking about their families. Parents were desperate to reunite with their children, and the children loved their parents—wanting to be with them, regardless of the circumstances of their legal separation. A foundation that spent its resources working to bring families back together spoke to me. My favorite part of working as a case worker was those days when families were finally reunited—there's nothing more powerful than parents' love for their children."

"You paint quite the picture, Ms. Michaels."

"I love my job, sir."

Tapping my proposal on the massive table, he added, "It's evident to see that when reviewing your program proposal. Your ideas for future programs are thoroughly captivating."

"Thank you, sir."

"That being said, this is merely a preliminary interview."

What now?

"Excuse me, sir?" I tried to keep my voice calm. This was news to me.

"We are narrowing down our applicants into a group of finalists, who will then be asked to take one of the programs from their proposal and create a pilot program with a generous stipend from the Foundation. The response from our client base regarding each finalist's pilot program will factor into our ultimate decision on appointing our new Programs Director."

Disappointment flooded my body, realizing that today definitely *wasn't* the day as I had previously been led to believe. Choosing to maintain the appearance of graciousness, I responded, "Understood."

Folding his hands on the table, Mr. Greiner declared, "Ms. Michaels, you have been selected as a finalist for the position."

Relief replaced disappointment—there was still a chance. I was confident that bringing even one of my many proposed programs into practice would knock their socks off.

Clearing his throat, Mr. Greiner continued, "However, there is concern regarding your relationship status."

Excuse me, what?

Trying to maintain that cool façade, I answered diplomatically, "I'm not sure I see how that is relevant, sir."

"We want to clarify that the Foundation's main focus is family," he explained.

Was he implying that it was required to have a significant other to obtain this job? A quick glance across the table confirmed that each board member visibly sported a ring on the fourth finger of their left hand. They were all married.

What a load of shit.

Not only was it illegal to discriminate based on marital status, it directly contradicted our work at the Foundation. Most of our clients were single parents—often, a divorce or unsafe domestic situation was the cause for child removal. The asset of having no familial ties distracting me from my job performance suddenly seemed like a detriment.

Frankly, my relationship status was none of their business. If I were to get married tomorrow, there was no law stating I had to disclose that to my employers.

Knowing I was risking my shot at the position, I asked for clarification, "Sir, are you saying the applicants must be romantically attached to be chosen for the position?"

Having the good sense to look mildly embarrassed, he protested, "Of course not, Ms. Michaels. We would never say that."

Message received. They could allude to the requirement and make their selection based on it, but they would never outright admit to marital status discrimination.

Great. There goes my chance of landing this job.

I thanked the board for their time and the opportunity to continue pursuing this position as a finalist. Standing, I exited the room. Walking silently to the elevator and then to my car, I turned the ignition before resting my forehead on the steering wheel.

What the hell was I going to do now?

———⊰❈⊱———

Taking the long way, it was past dinner when I finally made it home. When my childhood best friend, who incidentally had married a European prince, moved back to Hartford, I'd moved without question into the house her brother-in-law had purchased. Running from an emotionally abusive situation that affected her physical and mental health, she needed help caring for her three young children. More than happy to jump to the aid of my oldest friend, part of my decision to move into her home—along with her brother-in-law—was selfishly motivated.

Living at home, the only daughter of an oil tycoon, I was beyond ready to escape my overbearing parents. After what happened in college and my reluctance to discuss why I'd begged to change schools barely a year into my degree, they were hesitant to let me venture out on my own. I placated their insistence that I live at home after graduating with my master's in social work as it helped me save money—I refused to touch my trust fund. So, when Natalie called needing my help, I was grateful for the opportunity to move out.

Natalie—along with our other best friend, Hannah—was among the few people on this earth who knew why I'd taken a self-imposed vow of celibacy. I had no interest in any man, primarily based on my distrust of their ulterior motives and their need to use women. My best friend had found her happy ending, moving on with a new man—a good man. I knew they were out there, but she'd also been with a bad man. There was no way of knowing which one they were until it was too late.

I hadn't always been so jaded, but my innocence was lost during a single night inside the dimly lit room of a frat house. After that night, I promised myself I would never again be swayed by a man, as I could not ascertain their motives. Truth be told, I wasn't missing out on anything. Women had a reputation for drama, but men were just as bad. I didn't need that in my life. I was fulfilled enough.

Venturing forth from my car, I entered the house through the garage. The sounds of the happy family reached my ears as I walked through the mudroom and down the side hallway leading toward the kitchen. Rounding the corner, I found them seated at the kitchen table, enjoying dessert together.

They created the perfect picture of family. Natalie had three children from her previous marriage, and together with her new husband, Jaxon, they shared an infant daughter. Four beautiful children in total, whom I was fortunate to be able to know and love as my own—being Aunt Amy was perfect for me.

Passing through the kitchen, I went straight into the butler's pantry, honing in on the wine chiller. Grabbing a bottle before selecting a glass, I walked back into the kitchen, emptying my full hands onto the island.

Natalie approached while I silently filled the glass with a heavy pour. Eyeing my actions, she asked, "Did you eat?"

Shaking my head, I grabbed the full glass, leaving the bottle behind, and walked into the living room without a word. The two-story room was bathed in the golden hue of the setting sun through the floor-to-ceiling windows facing west. Sinking into the chaise, I took a long pull of wine before closing my eyes. I wanted to forget everything that happened today.

Natalie's plop onto the nearest couch was audible, and she sighed. "So, I take it the meeting didn't go well?"

I scoffed. "That's one way to say it."

"Did you not get the job?"

Opening my eyes, I looked at my best friend, whose kind brown eyes shone with sympathy. "The decision wasn't made today. I am a finalist, though."

"That's great!" she exclaimed with excitement written across her face.

"There's a catch."

Brows drawing together in confusion, she asked, "What kind of catch?"

Exhaling deeply, I replied, "It was made clear, in no uncertain terms, that they want someone married to fill the spot. The emphasis on being a 'family-focused' foundation."

Indignant, she cried, "That's illegal!"

Taking another sip of wine, I shrugged. "You think I don't know that?"

"You can't let them get away with this! You've worked so hard."

For how much I loved her, Natalie had never worked a day in her life. She spent time with various charities during her time as a royal but had never been on the back end like I was. She didn't understand the nuances involved.

Trying to explain, I countered, "Nat, if I go nuclear and blow the whistle on this, I will likely end up fired for some bogus reason and then blacklisted from working with other charities in the area."

Natalie was undeterred. "Fine. They don't deserve you. We will start a charity you can run—anything you want." Throwing over her shoulder, she called in the direction of the kitchen, "Jaxon? We can start a charity for Amy, right?"

Jaxon's voice called back from the kitchen. "Anything you want, baby!"

Smug, Natalie turned back to face me. "See? We've got your back. You've always had ours, so it's long past time to repay the favor."

They certainly had the resources and the connections to pull off the herculean task of creating a foundation from scratch. Jaxon had ties to the entire professional hockey community, but it wouldn't feel like I earned it.

Grabbing a pillow, I used it to muffle my frustrated scream.

I'd spent years taking the necessary steps to take control of my own life, but once again, I felt helpless. More than that, I felt hopeless. Having read the finalist packet, I knew there would be multiple events to attend, making it impossible to fabricate a fictional significant other. Even if my pilot program knocked the socks off the board, I wasn't confident it would be enough to overlook my lack of conformity to the "family-focused" standard they had set.

My dreams might go up in smoke, and I was powerless to stop it.

CHAPTER 4

Liam

UPON MY RETURN FROM Belleston, I took a few weeks to work out my frustrations over the situation—the only way I knew how. Day after day, I pushed myself to the point of physical exhaustion, hoping that the anger stemming from lack of control would dissipate at some point. It ebbed somewhat but remained present beneath the surface.

How could I not be angry? My future had been stolen from me.

I understood my parents' decision to conceal the circumstances surrounding Leo's birth, avoiding drawing into question the legitimacy of future heirs before they were even born. I shuddered to think what it would have done to my mother to have such a horrible event broadcast to the world for analysis. My father had protected his wife—at least, after the fact—and I could respect that. He claimed Leo as his heir, and no one had been any the wiser. I likely would have done the same if placed in his shoes.

Not in any mood for company, I holed up in my basement apartment for weeks. I had everything I needed down here—a bedroom with an ensuite, an office, a small den, and a kitchenette. Initially advertised as an in-law suite, it suited my needs perfectly. My work schedule demanded odd hours as I worked closely with those back in Europe, so I wasn't bothered during my daytime sleeping.

Not any closer to wrapping my mind around my new life circumstances completely, I knew I couldn't stay down here forever. I was beginning to miss the kids. Reminding myself that part of why I hadn't outright refused the role—one I was apparently born to assume—was to protect them. Knowing they would be released from the cage that had always held me captive, I made my way upstairs to spend time with them after dinner. What good was being the live-in uncle if you couldn't rile them up before bedtime?

Live-in uncle—those days were numbered.

At least, I was still biologically their uncle. Half-uncle, but who's counting? If there was anything I'd learned this past year from Natalie moving on with her life and creating a family with a new man, it was that blood didn't matter. Your chosen family was just as important as the one you happened to be born into.

Speaking of chosen family, I ascended the basement steps to find Jaxon standing at the kitchen island, baby Charlie on his hip. I quickly kissed the top of her head—her black hair matching that of her father's—as Jaxon gestured to the fridge. "I just put away the ice cream, but I can get it back out for you. You missed dinner. Again."

Remember how I said Jaxon and I had gotten off to a rocky start? Yeah, well, we worked it out, but we still threw subtle digs at each other now and again. Having two men fighting for dominance under the same roof was challenging, and that was an understatement. On today's episode of *Jaxon and Liam Throwing Shade*, we had Jaxon insinuating that Liam hadn't been around as much as he should be. I let it slide because he was right. I had been distant, but I had a good reason.

Holding my arms out, I declined. "I'd rather eat up our super sweet Charlie girl instead. Hand her over."

As he relinquished control of the baby in his arms, I pulled her into mine, raising her high to blow raspberries on her soft belly. The resulting giggles from her mouth soothed my frayed nerves. There was nothing quite like the feel of a baby in your arms. How they loved and trusted you unconditionally was overwhelming. Charlie had been a surprise for us all, but now that she was here, it was hard to imagine a world without her gummy smile.

Tucking Charlie into my side, I noticed Jaxon craning his head toward the voices coming from the living room. Instantly intrigued, I trained my ears on them as well. Natalie's soft, sweet voice was easily recognizable. The second voice sounded like it could be Amy's, but it wasn't her usual calm tone—an inflection and a hint of desperation set me on edge. Having spent some of my military service in interrogation, I was trained to pick up on subtle cues in how people talked. Amy was in distress. That much was clear, just from her voice.

Nudging Jaxon, I nodded toward the living room. "What's going on?"

Jaxon frowned. "Something happened to Amy at work."

Hackles raising, I assumed the worst, especially after discovering what had happened to my mother. "What kind of something? Did someone hurt her? Do we need to find a place to bury a body?"

Turning to face me, Jaxon crossed his arms. "Since when do you care so much about Amy?"

"So long as she lives under this roof, she falls under my protection. End of story. Now, answer the question." I wasn't in any mood to play games.

Loosening his defensive stance, Jaxon chucked. "Down, boy. It's nothing like that. Something to do with her promotion. Doesn't sound like it went well, especially when Natalie got all hyper asking if we could start a foundation for her to run."

Interesting. Amy and I were more like roommates who worked together these past three years to help care for Natalie and the children. If we were talking in terms Jaxon would understand, we were like a team—Team Natalie, to be exact.

Living with someone for so long, you came to understand what made them tick and what they valued. For Amy, it was her job. Her work was meaningful—helping those less fortunate bring their families back together, no matter the circumstances. She'd spent years working her way up and was more than qualified for the promotion she sought.

The talking abruptly stopped, and footsteps became audible, headed in our direction. Jaxon and I began bustling around the kitchen to appear as if we hadn't been trying to eavesdrop. Thankfully, Natalie entered the room alone, dropping onto a stool along the island with a sigh.

Jaxon walked over to her, throwing an arm around her shoulders in comfort. "How's she doing?"

Natalie's mouth twisted, unsure. "Emotionally exhausted. Went right up to bed. It's so wrong what they're doing to her."

My curiosity got the better of me. "What did they do?"

Her warm brown eyes met mine, but they were full of sadness for her best friend. "She's been chosen as a finalist for the promotion—"

"That's great! Then why—"

She cut me off. "But—"

"But, what?" My defenses rose—a "but" was never good.

Hesitating, noticing how I was tensed from head to toe and the way my jaw was clenched, she backtracked, "I really shouldn't be telling you this. This is her business, not ours."

"Spill, Natalie." My tone left no room for argument.

"Fine." She sighed. "There's one condition. They want someone who's married. Some bullshit about wanting to promote a strong stance on family values with those highest within the foundation."

"That's illegal!" I roared, furious.

"I know, and so does she."

My protection mode switched on, and I was ready for action. "What are we going to do about this? We can't let them get away with it."

A corner of Natalie's mouth quirked up as she tucked a strand of honey-blonde hair behind her ear. "There's the brother I know and love. Ready to burn down the world to save someone he loves."

"I don't *love* Amy." I protested.

Dismissing me with a hand, she clarified, "Fine. Someone you care about. Is that better? It's semantics, Liam. You want to protect her."

"Well, it's not fair to force that on someone."

I should know.

Natalie leaned into Jaxon. "Well, she doesn't want us to *do* anything. Amy's a big girl who wants to figure it out by herself. She's worried that if she makes a big stink about this, they'll make sure she never works in her field within the tri-state area again. So, we respect her wishes and let her deal with this in her own way—it's her life, her career."

I wasn't so convinced she didn't need help. Maybe I was upset about Amy's situation because it reminded me of my own. Like me, Amy had made it clear she had no intention of marrying. She was happy living her single life, focused on her career. There had to be *something* we could do to help her. That foundation was fooling itself if it thought that a piece of paper and a wedding ring made someone more qualified for a job or more "family-focused." We had an untraditional family here—of which Amy was a key member—and they'd see that if they spent even one day observing her at home.

Like a bolt of lightning, it hit me, and I jumped involuntarily, startling Charlie, whose bottom lip jutted out dramatically before she began to cry. Jaxon and Natalie glanced over in question, but I shook my head, bouncing the baby to soothe her. It was all so clear.

I needed a wife.

Amy needed a husband.

What if there was a way we could both cross that off the list while still maintaining our independence? My brain moved so fast that I barely felt Natalie lifting Charlie from my arms.

I had an idea to help us both. I just needed to flesh out the logistics before presenting it to Amy.

This might actually work. I was going to ask Amy to marry me.

———— ✦ ————

Halloween was right around the corner, and with the Comets planning to be on the road during the actual holiday, they were having their annual Halloween party the weekend before. Natalie was finding her place with the hockey wives and girlfriends, helping to further boost her confidence by having another group supporting her beyond the few of us at home. The party was adult-only, so Amy and I would have the kids for the night. Tonight was the night I planned to propose to her.

Charlie began eating solid foods recently, so I had her strapped into a highchair, feeding her mushy carrots when Natalie walked in to say goodnight to her baby. As she kissed the top of Charlie's head, I assessed her appearance. Dressed in her standard Comets jersey with Jaxon's last name and number on the back, paired with leggings, she looked like she was going to watch a hockey game instead of attending a costume party.

Voicing my confusion, I asked her, "Who are you supposed to be for Halloween? Jaxon?"

Looking down at her clothes before reaching up to her hair, she touched the top of her head, mussing her golden locks. "Oh!" she called out before racing back into the living room.

Spooning another bite of carrots into Charlie's open mouth, I whispered conspiratorially to the six-month-old, "I think your mommy might be losing her mind."

Natalie rushed back into the room, skidding to a stop before us, breathing heavily from running. As I raised an eyebrow at her, she only smiled before placing a pair of bunny ears on her head, declaring, "I'm Hannah."

Thank God I wasn't drinking anything when she said that because I would have spit it out all over Natalie and Charlie. The costume suddenly made sense—she was a puck bunny. That meant a woman who was only looking to score with a hockey player, and it was no secret that Hannah was trying to snag one. Especially since her father, the Comets' head coach, had forbidden any of his players from messing around with his daughters. Hannah was a girl on a mission.

Holding back a snort, I announced, "I think you just won Halloween."

Giving an exaggerated bow before straightening, she smirked. "Why, thank you. I did think it was quite clever."

"Hannah know?"

Natalie's face transformed into a mischievous grin. "Nope, but she'll see it tonight."

"My guess is that she'll get a kick out of it." I declared.

"Get a kick out of what?" Jaxon's voice preceded him into the kitchen. He was dressed up as some kind of jungle man, with his chest exposed and a leopard print skirt covering very little of his bottom half.

Natalie smiled at him like he hung the moon, and my heart clenched. I may have been the one to save her physical body, but Jaxon was the one who saved her soul.

No woman would ever look at me like that, but that was my choice. I couldn't lament that now, even if they did paint a perfect picture of domestic bliss. It worked for them, but it wasn't for me.

I grumbled under my breath, "You've got muscles. We get it."

"What was that?" Jaxon asked in my direction.

"Nothing."

"Liam, are you jealous that I'm comfortable in my own skin?" He teased with a smirk. "Do you feel threatened that maybe you're not the most ripped guy living in the house anymore?"

I knew he was messing with me—I had a good thirty pounds of muscle on the guy—but I ground my teeth, muttering, "Showoff."

Natalie looked between us and smiled. "Now, now, boys. Play nice. You both have very muscular bodies. One isn't better than the other. They're just different."

Jesus. What next? Would she be telling us that dick size didn't matter and that it was more about how you used it? Then, the thought occurred to me that maybe, just maybe, Jaxon wasn't blessed in that department.

Doubtful. The universe wasn't that kind.

Scowling at Jaxon was my default response, honed over many years. Yes, he may have only been in Natalie's life properly for a little over a year, but he'd been pining for her for close to a decade and was not skilled at hiding it. Natalie was the only person who hadn't ever noticed the puppy dog eyes he'd always had for her. He'd been receiving death glares from me for a long time and, unfortunately, hadn't been deterred.

"You have a party to attend, or what? Hang around much longer, and I might change my mind about watching your kids."

From the open archway into the living room came Amy's voice in response, "Don't listen to our resident grump. Go have fun. Happy Halloween."

Taking that as their cue to leave, Natalie and Jaxon disappeared toward the garage for some adult fun. Grudgingly, I admitted to myself that they did deserve some time out—they'd not been granted the advantage most couples enjoyed of time alone before having children. Natalie came to their marriage with three children already, and Charlie had been their surprise baby. Four kids were constantly underfoot before you added in Jaxon's rigorous hockey schedule.

Amy walked to where I sat feeding Charlie, eyeing up the mess we'd made, smiling, "You almost done here? Little Miss looks like she could use a bath."

Scraping the last of the carrots from the bowl, I spooned them into Charlie's mouth, announcing, "Finished."

Undoing the buckles, she scooped up the baby while I went to wash the bowl. Amy called over her shoulder, "I've got her. You think you can handle the older ones?"

Nodding, not looking back, I responded, "Yep."

I was nervous about tonight, although I didn't know why. It wasn't a *real* proposal, but I found that I desperately wanted her to say yes. It would solve both of our problems—on paper, at least. If she said no, I'd have to start from square one. I was sure there would be women lining up down the street if I put out an ad for a fake wife to become a real princess and, someday, queen.

Finding a woman to play pretend with wouldn't be the problem. Finding one I could trust was critical.

Several hours later, all the kids were tucked into bed, and I discovered Amy unwinding with a glass of wine in the kitchen. The massive gourmet kitchen was the heart of our home. Featuring a marble island larger than most families' dining tables, state-of-the-art stainless steel appliances, and a butler's pantry, it was every chef's dream, but it was more than that for us. Over the past three years, we spent countless hours in here, making meals and sharing them, but more importantly, creating memories.

On nights like tonight—with Natalie and Jaxon gone—Amy and I usually went to our separate spaces once the kids were settled, so she was surprised when I asked, "Care if I join you?"

After a brief pause, she gave a nod. "Sure. Would you like some wine?"

Eyeing her glass, I shrugged but accepted. The need for liquid courage was something I'd never needed before, but I found myself welcoming it now. The result of this conversation had the potential to change my life. Many conversations had been doing that lately, so I guess it was par for the course.

With a cool stemless glass of white wine in my hand, I took a sip before clearing my throat. "Amy?"

Green eyes, flecked with gold, peered back at me from where she sat cozied up to the island on a stool. "Yes, Liam?"

Just go for it. She either says yes, or she says no.

"I think we should get married." There. I'd said it. No taking it back now.

Those same green eyes widened at my words before Amy blurted out, "Excuse me? Can you repeat that? Because it sounded an awful lot like you said we should get married, and there's no way you meant to say that. So, try again." She shook her head, her red curls bouncing, almost as if to physically clear it.

Steeling my nerves, I repeated myself, "We should get married."

Confirmation that she'd heard me correctly the first time finally dawned, and her mouth dropped open. Then, she began to laugh. "Oh, I get it. It's a joke."

"When have you ever known me to joke, Amy?" I kept my voice even.

The laughter stopped, and she stared at me again. "Why in the world would you think we should get married? I don't want to get married. You have made it clear that you also don't have any desire to get married. So, I'll ask again. Why?"

"I heard about your work problem." There was no point in beating around the bush.

Blowing out a breath, she looked skyward, muttering, "Damn Natalie and her big mouth." Training her eyes back on me, she added, "I don't need rescuing."

Calmly, I responded, "Never said you did."

"What's in it for you?" It was fair for her to be skeptical.

"This would be a business arrangement, Amy," I explained.

"A business arrangement . . ." she repeated.

"Look. You need a husband—which I think is ridiculous, by the way—to advance in your career. My family insists that I find a wife—which, as you pointed out, I have no interest in but I find my back against a wall. So, I propose that we marry each other. Problem solved for both of us."

Amy's nose wrinkled, drawing attention to the smattering of freckles beneath her eyes. "I appreciate the offer, Liam, but I think I'm going to have to turn you down. I'll find some other way."

Undeterred, I pressed again, "How?"

Frustrated, she threw her arms wide. "I don't know. I'll think of something. One thing I do know is that I'm not 'princess material.'"

Using my fingers to count them off, I listed the many reasons she was incorrect in that assumption. "You come from a wealthy family. You've got an education from an elite university. You are well-seated in the world of philanthropy. Sounds exactly like 'princess material' to me."

Narrowing her eyes, she tried a different tactic. "Fine. I'm not thin enough to be a princess."

"Are we doing this again?" I was referring to Natalie's extreme weight-loss tactics, which had resulted from my brother's underhanded tactics with the press.

"Let's be real, Liam. Natalie was an average size—on that, we can agree. I am not Natalie. I'm a size eighteen, for crying out loud."

Taking a moment, I scanned her body. On days like today, when she didn't go into the office, she wore her auburn hair loose, falling past her shoulders. She was full-figured, sure, but in the way of a real woman. I had grown weary of those painfully thin women long ago. Even if she was drawing attention to her size now, she'd never felt the need to hide her body, wearing clothes that fit her well and projecting an air of confidence in her shape.

"I don't see anything wrong with the way you look," I stated simply after my perusal.

Scoffing, she muttered, "I may have made my peace with my size, but that doesn't mean everyone else is as accepting. Growing up, it was painfully clear that guys only ever got close to me to gain access for a shot at Natalie."

"I'm not interested in the opinions of *boys*. I am a full-blooded man, and I'm telling you that your body is perfectly acceptable for that of a princess. Royals are human. We come in all shapes and sizes."

A devilish gleam entered her green eyes, and I sensed the Hail Mary coming before she said, "What about sex?"

Schooling my features to remain calm when all I wanted to do was laugh, I deadpanned, "What about it?"

"I'm not interested. How will that work?"

If there was one thing I knew about this woman, it was that she was rational-minded. The best chance at getting her to agree to my proposal was to appeal to her logical nature. "Amy, the arrangement I'm suggesting is nothing different than our current relationship—we would essentially remain roommates. The marriage would be on paper only. A solution to you needing a husband and me needing a wife. That's it."

Realizing she was running out of reasons to say no, she challenged, "You're a public figure, Liam. I can't afford to have you photographed with other women when everyone knows we are married."

"What women? The shower has been my only sexual companion for years, and I don't feel the need to change that situation."

Eyes widening, understanding my meaning, a barely audible gasp escaped her lips. Softly she responded, "Without sex, there will be no children."

"Do you need children?" I challenged, already knowing the answer.

"No."

"Good, I have no desire for children. Natalie's children are plenty to fulfill my life in that capacity," I declared.

"Finally, something we can agree on." Chewing on her bottom lip indicated she had something else to say but was hesitant.

I prodded, "What is it, Amy?"

Releasing the lip in question, she sighed, "I need more than a piece of paper. My problem in needing a spouse extends deeper—there will be events I must attend for work. Anyone even posing as my husband will need to be present."

"That won't be a problem as I'd need the same from you. I've created a contract for you to review and amend to your specific needs, but it already contains mine."

"You had a contract made up . . ." Her words trailed off into stunned silence.

"Of course."

"So, what you're proposing is that I would be essentially playing pretend with a prince?"

Shrugging, I replied, "If that's how you'd prefer to look at it—yes. A fake, but legal marriage. We each play a role for the other, and both get what we need."

Once again, my military training came in handy as I used her body's physical cues to determine that she was at least considering my proposal. When she took the time to think about it, she'd realize it was the only way to solve her problem. I was counting on her consistently rational nature.

Taking another sip from her wine glass, she lowered it to the island with a soft clink. "Okay, so . . . Say I do agree to this outlandish idea. Who in their right mind would believe it? I find out that a caveat of my promotion is having a spouse, and suddenly, I show up with one? When I've been the spinster of the office?"

"Don't be dramatic, Amy." I fought the urge to roll my eyes. "You're not a spinster. You haven't even turned thirty."

"Answer the question, Liam." There was a fire in her eyes, turning them more gold than green.

"As you mentioned, I am a public figure. It's no secret that my past relationships have been well-documented by the press, who are hungry to find out what lucky girl will become the next princess of Belleston as my wife. Here, we have a classic story of a secret romance that budded while living under the same roof with my sister-in-law's best friend and not wanting to go public to protect our relationship. Simple."

Amy gawked at me. "How long have you been thinking about this? You seem to have every detail ironed out. Almost makes me afraid to look at your contract."

"It's been constructed as mutually beneficial." The rest of my life was on the line, and I needed to be thorough. The only facet left out was that I would assume the role of my father's heir. It was a gaping hole in my proposal, but I knew she'd never agree if she learned that now—we could cross the bridge down the road. I wasn't even sure when my parents planned to go public. I couldn't jump the gun in case they changed their minds.

Please, God, let them change their minds.

Bringing a hand to her forehead and sighing, she asked, "Can I at least tell Natalie? Or does that risk the whole charade?"

"Natalie would never believe that we had a real marriage." I conceded that point.

"Good. So, you haven't completely lost your mind," Amy mused.

"I only ask that you keep this quiet until the marriage is legal."

"Why?" I should have known she would pick apart every detail before making a decision.

"It'll look better when we elope that we have surprised even those closest to us. Gives credibility to our story of a rushed marriage."

Eyebrows raised, she shrieked, "Eloping?!"

Challenging her, I asked, "Would you prefer a state wedding? That's what will be required of us if we don't elope. That kind of affair would take six months to a year of planning. Do you have that kind of time?"

Amy's eyes closed as the reality of what I was asking began to sink in. "Fine. Send me the contract."

"There is one more thing."

Exasperated, her eyes reopened as she exclaimed, "What else could there be?"

What I said next might be the deal-breaker. "If you agree to this—and we get married—you will become a public figure. Coming out of nowhere, the press will be extremely interested in finding out as much about you as possible to fill in the gaps. I need to know about any skeletons in your closet to get ahead of them."

Stunned—as if the thought of her life on public display had just occurred—she nodded slowly. "Skeletons . . ."

Showing my hand that I'd already done my research, I asked, "Why did you transfer during your first year at university?"

Cheeks flushing pink, her eyes dropped to avoid my gaze, whispering, "How do you know about that?"

Not wanting to scare her but also needing her to know the necessity of handing over anything important before someone with less than honorable intentions could dig it up, I continued, "A surface-level dig shows you began at one university and finished at another. Someone determined will go deeper to discover why, so I'm asking you now. I can't protect you if I don't know the whole story."

"Um." She swallowed, then shuddered. "There was a bet."

Alarm bells rang inside my head, knowing how stupid teenage boys could be. That was an ominous statement combined with her physical reaction. Tension filled my body.

"What kind of bet?"

She sniffled, and the realization dawned that she was trying not to cry. *Jesus, what the hell happened to her?*

Another sniffle, and she forced out, "There was a guy. He was in a frat, and we got close—close enough that I let him take my virginity. When I tried to see him again after that, he told me it was all a bet. To see if he could find out if-if the carpets matched the drapes. What, with me being a redhead and all."

Red filled my field of vision, and my fist clenched so tightly around the wine glass in my hand that I barely heard the sound of it shattering, let alone the pain of glass shards cutting into my palm.

Amy's panicked voice cut through the haze of my rage. "Liam!"

I was still clenching the broken glass when Amy rounded the island, trying to pry my fist loose. While she fretted over the blood, the countless cuts, and whether any shards were embedded beneath my skin, I forced out through clenched teeth, my voice lethal, "What's his name?"

Startled out of her frenzy, she dropped my hand like it burned her and stepped back, searching my face, before declaring, "It doesn't matter anymore."

"The hell it doesn't!" I roared.

She flinched at the volume of my voice, and remorse washed over me for scaring her.

How was it that I continued to find myself surrounded by women who had been mistreated by men? Had I been blind in thinking that most men respected women when, more often than not, they were monsters lurking in the shadows, waiting for their next victim?

Amy returned to my bloodied hand, and I focused on taking calming breaths while she picked the glass out of the open wounds.

Finally convinced my voice had lost its edge of rage, I whispered, "I will never let anyone hurt you again."

Looking at me sadly, she shrugged. "Don't make promises you can't keep."

Once she was satisfied with the debridement of my hand, I took my leave and returned to my dungeon, as Natalie had once called my basement apartments.

I'd taken the leap and asked Amy to help me in a way that would also benefit her. My fate now rested in her hands.

CHAPTER 5

Amy

STUNNED, I WATCHED LIAM walk away after he practically proposed to me and then proceeded to ask about the absolute worst day of my life. Only Natalie and Hannah knew about that day. When he asked—implying that someone else would dig until they found out—that should have been enough to turn his offer down outright. Then I watched as he—blinded with anger for me—crushed a glass with his bare hand before asking me to reveal the name of the boy who hurt me so that he could hunt him down. In his current state, I did not doubt he would do just that.

Shaking off the demons of my past and Liam's subsequent reaction, I focused on the deal he outlined. I needed to think of my future and what it would mean if I accepted.

Natalie was the one who believed in that fairy tale crap, but even with my more cynical view of love, I never imagined my first marriage proposal would be presented as a business deal. The way Liam's striking blue eyes—the famous Remington Blue, an almost a bright cobalt—bore into mine as he declared that we should get married would be forever branded into my memory.

He was the textbook definition of tall, dark, and handsome, with his midnight black hair and broody attitude, but he might as well be my older brother as much as he was Natalie's. Our relationship to date was purely platonic. Hell, with his constant scowl and surly demeanor, there were many days when I didn't even like Liam.

Was I out of my mind for even considering this?

Liam was right that it would solve my problem of being fairly considered for the promotion. Without a serious romantic relationship, my pilot program was likely to be overlooked, even if it was the best of all those presented to the Foundation's board. Could it really be as simple as Liam said?

Why did his family suddenly require him to get married?

Liam was the second son, and Natalie's children were in the direct line of succession. If he never married, never had children, it wouldn't impact the survival of their family line. That also didn't take into account his little sister, Lucy, who would succeed him without an heir. None of that mattered. Liam was unlikely to ever be called upon to rule, which helped me consider his proposal.

Natalie might have been the perfect arm candy for a powerful man, but that was not where I saw myself—ever. I was a strong, independent woman, and fully intended to remain as such, regardless of my decision regarding a marriage to Liam.

My phone buzzed, the sound magnified by its resting place on the kitchen island marble. Glancing over revealed it was a text from Liam.

Liam: *Attached, you will find the contract as is. Please feel free to make any modifications you see fit.*

Ugh. Couldn't he even let me have a night to sleep on it before sending over the legal paperwork? My mind was still reeling. No way could I focus on the legal jargon enough to make an educated decision tonight. I needed time to make lists of my needs before I responded.

If I even accepted this deal.

Some small part of my brain told me I'd be an idiot to say no on principle. This was a loophole, ready to be exploited, allowing me to keep my single life but have a fair shot at letting my work speak for itself regarding this promotion. The decision wouldn't be clouded because I didn't conform to society's standards for women my age.

Liam and I would remain, as we always had been, roommates. Like two ships passing in the night, with my work schedule during the day and his nocturnal habits, being on video calls with various teams in Europe.

Could we really pull this off without anyone being the wiser?

* * *

Well, the count may have still been out on whether I was brilliant or the dumbest woman alive, because here I found myself on a private plane, Vegas-bound, with my "fiancé" seated across from me, fully engrossed in whatever was on his laptop. We boarded this plane hours after Jaxon, Natalie, and the kids left for Minnesota for a few days. The Comets were playing a game in Minneapolis, and they'd taken the opportunity to drag the whole family out there for the away game to spend time with Jaxon's parents, who lived nearby.

It'd been two weeks since Liam "proposed." When the shock finally wore off, I sat down and read the contract he'd sent line by line. It had outlined no requirement for consummating the marriage, a fidelity clause, and a specific number of engagements where my presence would be required annually as Liam's wife in his home country of Belleston. Our finances would remain separate, but Liam would fund our cost of living. When I questioned the need for this because we shared the house with Natalie and Jaxon's family, he explained that for our marriage to appear legitimate, we would need to acquire our own lodging.

So, not only had I been lying to my best friend for the last two weeks about marrying her brother, now I had to tell her we were moving out. She was going to hate me.

Liam's contract had no major issues, so all it required in amendments were my additions to fit my needs for our fake but very legal marriage. I had my own events that would need Liam's presence to validate our marriage to the higher-ups of the Foundation. Beyond that, I asked Liam to remove his responsibility to cover my living expenses, but he insisted. While I had no desire to depend on a man, I agreed to let him finance our new house, apartment, or whatever, because—as he pointed out—he'd paid for the house I lived in these past three years. There was already a precedent, damn him.

As we began our descent to the desert town where we could obtain our quickie wedding, Liam placed a velvet box on the table between our seats. He nudged it closer toward me when I merely stared at it in silent question.

Glancing back to the far end of the plane to ensure his security guard, Jasper, was out of earshot, he kept his voice low. "The moment we step off this plane, we must play the part. Open the box and put it on."

I wasn't an idiot. I knew what was in the box. Reaching out hesitantly, almost as if it might bite me, I held it in my grasp and slowly opened the lid.

An involuntary gasp escaped my lips when faced with the giant, brilliant marquise-cut diamond settled on a gold band inlaid with tiny emeralds.

Liam's face was impassive when I peered back at him, protesting, "No, Liam. This is too much."

His blue eyes were so intense, it felt like they could see into my soul as he stated matter-of-factly, "After today, legally, you will be a princess. This is a ring befitting your new station as my wife."

Fuck. He's right. Gotta play the part.

Grudgingly, I plucked the ring from its box and placed it on my left hand. It slid on easily, a perfect fit.

Well, if the ring fits . . .

Waving my hand, hoping to catch a beam of light on the stone to blind Liam, I made a show of compliance. I might have agreed to this ludicrous plan, but that didn't mean I was pleased about it. Liam was right—it was a necessity—but that didn't make me like him for it.

Satisfied, Liam held up a finger. "One more thing."

"What now?" I couldn't help my exaggerated eye roll. I'd reached my limit, and the day had barely begun.

"We will need proof. This wedding needs to look real."

Narrowing my eyes, I dared to ask, "Meaning what?"

"There must be a photo of us sealing the marriage with a kiss—no one would believe a wedding where I gave you a chaste peck on the cheek. Then, one more photo with proof of our marriage license signed that will be sent back home."

"You want to kiss?" So much for his vow that this relationship would remain entirely platonic.

Liam scowled back at me. "No, Amy, but it's necessary. We are putting on a show, and it must look real, or this is all for nothing."

I wanted nothing more than to tell him where he could shove his show, but I nodded. "Fine. One kiss. No tongue."

His expression didn't change. "Agreed. Once we land, we will head directly to the chapel, where we can change. Our biggest asset is the element of surprise. Even stopping at a hotel puts us at risk of alerting the media if someone happens to snap a pic and post it on social media. After the wedding, we will return directly to the plane to depart for our honeymoon."

Our honeymoon.

Liam had declared that even though we were eloping, it would aid in our marriage looking official if we spent a few days away afterward. I took a long weekend, letting my superiors know I'd work remotely. I was knee-deep in my pilot program already and couldn't afford to take too many days away, but I had conceded to Liam's point.

The plane landed, and a black SUV awaited us on the tarmac of the private airstrip. Grabbing only my purse, a makeup case, and the garment bag containing the outfit I'd chosen for the ceremony, I allowed Liam to help me down the short staircase onto the ground. Stowing our items in the massive trunk, we entered the backseat of the SUV, and within moments, were headed toward the chapel—the place we would say our vows and legally become man and wife.

Far from the Las Vegas Strip, we pulled up to the chapel Liam had preselected but took care not to make a reservation lest the information be leaked that we were coming. Behind the tinted window, I stared at the white building with a steeple.

Not too late to back out.

Shaking off my doubts, I steeled my nerves while Liam rounded the car to open my door. This would work. It had to.

Entering the chapel, there was thankfully no wait—no happy couples there as a reminder that this was a sacred bond people usually entered into because they were in love. The woman at reception asked for our identification and if we brought a witness or needed the add-on package containing a chapel witness. Liam identified Jasper as our witness and made the few other decisions that needed to be made while I took in our surroundings.

If we were looking for kitschy, we'd found it. The chapel featured a garish red carpet, an old-school rock-and-roll impersonator officiant, and fake flowers adorning the few pews—every little girl's dream.

Liam paid for the license and the ceremony, and then we were pointed toward his and hers dressing rooms. Before I could take off to prepare for what was supposed to be the most special day of my life that I had never wanted, Liam asked, "Are you okay? If you've changed your mind, we can go home right now, and I'll tear up the papers. I won't be upset."

Braving a glance into his piercing blue eyes, I remained steadfast. I'd made my decision. "I'm fine. Let's get this over with so I can sit on a beach for a few days."

Searching my face for signs that I was lying, he gave a curt nod. "Good. I'll see you at the end of the aisle."

Walking into the dressing room marked for the bride, I closed the door and leaned against it momentarily, taking a calming breath.

You are Amy Michaels, badass boss bitch. You can do this.

Hanging the garment bag on a hook near the door, I placed my purse and makeup bag on the vanity table. Taking a quick glance at my appearance in the mirror, I realized my tossing and turning last night had caught up to me—there were dark circles under my eyes. Normally, I didn't wear makeup, but if there was going to be proof sent around the world from this tacky little chapel, I needed to look at least semi-put together.

In less than half an hour, I would be a princess.

Unzipping the garment bag, I pulled out the cream pantsuit I purchased earlier in the week. Not something a princess normally would wear on their wedding day, I was determined to maintain some semblance of my own identity. The suit was cut to showcase my hourglass figure, and I paired it with a shimmery pink camisole and matching pink pumps. The finishing touches were pearl drop earrings and a pearl strand necklace gifted by my parents on the occasion of my high school graduation. A quick application of natural makeup, and I was ready.

My look portrayed femininity without being overly girly. Maybe I'd be more of a modern-day princess—a new role model for little girls, showcasing a strong, independent woman.

A knock at the door sounded, and the receptionist—who doubled as the wedding director—identified herself as the person on the other side. Calling out for her to enter, she cracked the door and slipped inside.

She smiled as she took in my appearance. "You look lovely."

Blushing, I smoothed hands down my suit. "Oh, I don't know. It's not very traditional."

Handing me a bouquet of fake white roses, she attempted to set me straight. "Honey, you should see half the people who come in here to get married. My bet is that most of them end up divorced within a few months. You are probably the classiest couple we've seen in years."

Her words made me feel slightly better. "Thank you."

"And your man. Whew. I sure hope the fire alarms don't trip because he is smoking hot." She fanned herself to emphasize her point.

To see a middle-aged woman swooning over Liam released some of the tension I'd been carrying for days, and I laughed. It could be worse. At least Liam was decent to look at.

Exiting the room, the doors separating the lobby from the chapel were closed. Standing before them, I took a deep breath. It would be over in fifteen minutes, and then I could drink myself into oblivion once we reached the Caribbean. Hell, I could probably get a head start on the plane.

The woman, who I now knew as Marcy, asked if I was ready, and I nodded. She spoke into her headset seconds before I heard the harsh notes of the classic wedding march playing so loud that I could hear them through the closed doors. Marcy counted down from five with her fingers before opening the doors, and I was revealed to my groom, who was standing at the front of the chapel with the costumed officiant.

Marcy gave a motion, and I began my march down the aisle. Less than fifteen steps later, I stood directly before Liam. He wore a custom-tailored black suit that molded to every hard plane of his body, his dark hair expertly slicked back. He looked almost like a stranger, so unlike the man I'd lived with for the past three years. Liam was a tall man, but at five-foot-nine, I was on the tall end for a woman, so my pumps put me almost at eye level with his intense blue stare.

As the ceremony commenced, Liam took my hand and gave it a gentle squeeze of reassurance. The ceremony was quick, with us repeating traditional wedding vows and exchanging wedding bands. Then, it was time for the kiss.

My heart began to pound, and I could feel the moisture of sweat gathering over various body parts—I hadn't kissed a man on the lips in over ten years. Liam leaned in, and I closed my eyes, allowing him to take the lead.

The softness of his lips brushed against mine, and I felt a zap, causing my eyes to pop open and my feet to take an involuntary step backward. Looking down at the plush red carpet, I wondered if I had created some static electricity with my nervous shuffling.

Looking at Liam, he had the back of his hand pressed to his mouth, so it was apparent he felt it too.

Liam looked at Marcy, holding the camera. "Did you get it?"

Marcy glanced at the display screen on her digital camera and nodded, confirming that our first kiss as a married couple was captured on film. Satisfied, Liam took my hand and led us back into the lobby, where our marriage license awaited signatures. Handing me the pen, he allowed me to sign first, then followed with his own quick flourish of ink. Once the officiant signed, Liam brought our left hands into view of his phone—the signed license as a background—before snapping a picture.

We were shoulder to shoulder as he typed out a text, so I glanced over, noticing he was sending the picture to his parents.

Liam: *Send security for my wife. We can be found honeymooning in St. Maarten. Jasper will have the details.*

After hitting send, he powered down the phone, clearly not willing to deal with the ramifications of eloping. I couldn't say I blamed him. Telling my parents wouldn't be a picnic, either.

Liam entrusted Jasper with the license, then we gathered our street clothes and any remaining bags before returning to the SUV. Within minutes of becoming a married couple, we were headed back to the airport to board the plane that would take us to the Caribbean, where we would spend the next four days. Alone.

What have I done?

CHAPTER 6

Amy

THE SOUND OF WAVES crashing in the distance was soothing, calming the tension flowing through my body as I rested under a cabana with my laptop. I'd been working on setting up the logistics for my pilot program and hit a snag. Nothing could be done about it until my return to Hartford, so I'd closed my laptop and was now lying back on the giant bed inside the cabana, just listening to the ocean, my wide-brimmed straw hat pulled over my eyes.

This moment of tranquility allowed me time to reflect upon the past few days since becoming Liam's wife. Our time zone hopping—going from the Eastern to the Pacific, then shooting back even further to the Atlantic in the Eastern Caribbean in a single day—took a toll on my body. At least, that's what I was telling myself. Once we reached the resort in St. Maarten, I passed out for a solid fifteen hours, waking up mid-afternoon the following day.

Liam secured the largest suite available—ensuring that we had separate rooms while still giving the appearance on paper of staying together—and I saw very little of him since our arrival. We were essentially having separate vacations. He was off doing God knows what while I spent the past few days working—a preview of our life together as a married couple.

I was lonely. I missed Natalie and the kids, but looming over my head was our return home tomorrow and having to tell her not only about the marriage but that we would be moving out. Not for the first time in the past few days, I wondered if I made the right decision. Was the chance at this promotion worth this isolated existence? Maybe I'd spend all my free time at Natalie's.

Who are you kidding? They're a happily married couple and have a real family now. They don't need you hanging around like a third wheel. Moving out was always on the horizon.

Even if I felt alone, I now had a physical shadow. My personal security guard arrived within twenty-four hours of our arrival in the Caribbean—the man known as Marcus was young enough to have served alongside Liam in the Bellestonian military. Liam was pleased to see a friendly, trustworthy face. I was briefed on what to expect regarding my security now that I was an official member of the Remington family. Marcus would always be nearby, even if out of sight. He'd share lodgings with Jasper on our travels and back in Hartford, and while I was still free to drive myself in the States, that required alerting Marcus of my comings and goings so he could follow and keep me safe.

I was overwhelmed, pure and simple.

No matter how strong I was, the implications of my actions hit me with full force, and tears threatened behind my eyes. Blinking furiously under my hat, I took a few deep breaths, trying to calm myself.

Something, or someone, grabbed my ankle, and I sat bolt upright, yelping, as my hat fell to my midsection. Sitting at the edge of the cabana bed was Liam, bare-chested, clad only in his swim trunks.

Sensing my panic, he released my ankle, muttering, "Sorry."

Heart racing, I reacted instinctually, grabbing the pillow behind me and throwing it at his head. "Jesus, Liam! What the hell?"

Catching the pillow easily, he set it next to where he sat. Raising his sunglasses to rest atop his dark hair, he fixed that harsh blue gaze on me. "I *said* I was sorry, Amy. I thought you were sleeping."

"That doesn't make it better." I reached up to quickly wipe away any moisture that pooled in the corner of my eyes from when I'd been about to cry.

Liam had been trained in reading people and assessed me before tensing. "What's wrong?"

Blowing out a breath, I laid back on the bed, staring up at the thatched ceiling. "I need to get back to work."

Matter-of-factly, he stated, "We're going home tomorrow." When I let out a frustrated scream, he added, "You seem stressed. Maybe you should get out in the sun and enjoy yourself on our last day."

Sitting back up, my frustration boiling over, I snapped at him, "Do I seem stressed? I wonder why?"

Not sensing my sarcasm, his demeanor remained calm, asking earnestly, "Why?"

"Look around you, Liam! We are on our 'honeymoon.' Don't you see how ludicrous this whole situation is? Throw in the security guard and the fact that I need to get back to work—otherwise, marrying you for a chance at this promotion was pointless—yeah, I'm stressed. Doesn't take a genius to figure out I'm reaching my limit. Something's gotta give."

Undeterred by my outburst, he shrugged. "I stand by my suggestion that you get some sun."

Narrowing my eyes at him, I gestured to myself. "I'm a redhead, Liam. Even if I love the sun, the sun does not love me."

Taking this into consideration, he finally conceded. "Fair point. Then tell me about what's wrong with work."

"Why do you want to know about work?"

"Amy, the whole reason we are here right now is to give you a fair shot at advancing your career, even if I think that's bullshit. You've outlined work events where I will be required to accompany you. Don't you think it would be prudent to share what you're working on? So that I can be enthusiastic about my wife's project?"

Snorting before I caught myself, I challenged, "Enthusiastic? You?"

Raising a single eyebrow, he countered, "I can be charming."

"Yeah, okay." I scoffed.

"You doubt me?" Those blue eyes were daring me to argue.

"Liam, husband of mine, the day you are charming is the day that pigs grow wings and fly."

"Are you done yet? Tell me about your project."

Glaring at the stubborn man, I finally agreed. "Fine. The Foundation's main goal is to reunite children with their biological parents. One of the largest roadblocks for parents attempting to regain custody of their kids is the lack of a proper place to live. Often, they don't have the funds to find large enough lodging for both themselves and their children—most have more than one child. So, my pilot program aims to provide low-cost or free housing for the families we are trying to help. It wouldn't be an instant fix for all our clients, but it would eliminate a huge hurdle for most of them."

"That sounds like an up-and-coming program." Liam's tone was sincere, impressed almost.

Huffing, I added, "Yeah, well, it would be if the building I was looking into hadn't just told me they didn't want to lease to us. Now I need to start all over again, and that was the only one in the price range of my stipend from the Foundation."

"You need an apartment building?"

Having known him for a long time, I could see what he was thinking, so I stopped him. "No, Liam. You can't just jump in and save me. I need to do this on my own."

Over the years, I learned that if there's one thing royalty doesn't like, it was someone telling them no. Liam tilted his head. "What's so wrong with buying and then donating a building so my wife can help those less fortunate reunite with their children? Some might even call it romantic. I'm sure your higher-ups would eat that right up."

Damn him. I hated that he was right. "You would really be willing to buy an apartment building to help me?"

Raising his left hand, he waved it, showcasing the gold band on his ring finger. "Would I be wearing this if I didn't want to help you?"

"It's too much. I can't ask you to do that," I protested.

His tone brooked no argument. "You're not asking. I'm offering. When we get back to Hartford, we can tour some buildings."

"Is this your attempt at being enthusiastic about my project?" Sarcasm seeped into my voice.

"If it's solved your roadblock, then yes. Now, take the rest of the day off. Work will be waiting for you when you get back."

Pushing off the bed, he walked away. To where? Who knew? If it were anything like the rest of our stay, I wouldn't see him again until we checked out tomorrow morning—such was life as Mrs. William Remington, not that I had any intention of changing my last name. There was nothing in our contract about that, so he'd just have to deal with it.

Back in Hartford, my palms were sweaty as we pulled through the gates of the private community I'd called home for the past three years. Natalie, Jaxon, and the kids had returned yesterday, and Natalie wasted no time in texting, asking where I was. I was certain that if Liam had turned his phone on at any point in our trip, he'd have had similar texts from her. I chose to ignore them, but the guilt gnawed at me, nonetheless.

Time had run out. It was time to tell my best friend what I—what *we*—had done.

Liam pulled his car into the garage and turned off the ignition. Exiting, emptying the trunk, he rounded to my still-closed door. Rapping gently on the window, I heard him ask, "You coming inside?"

Nodding, I closed my eyes and took a deep breath before letting it out slowly. Turning the diamond on my engagement ring to face my palm, I opened the car door. Barely able to clutch my purse in shaking hands, I allowed Liam to carry the rest of my bags.

It was Monday, late afternoon, so the kids would all be home from school. A full house to tell our news. Lucky me.

Having heard the mudroom door open, I heard Natalie call out, "Amy? Is that you?"

Walking down the hallway toward the kitchen, I called back, "Yeah. I'm home."

Rounding the corner from the kitchen, she spotted me, relief etched on her face. "Where have you been? You didn't answer any of my texts." Looking over my head, she spotted Liam, accusing, "You're in the doghouse too, mister."

Before she could see the bags Liam carried, I ushered her into the kitchen, deflecting, "How was Minnesota? Mama and Papa Slate doing well? Who won the game?"

Jaxon became visible once we entered the kitchen, working on mixing something with several bowls laid out. He might be a big, tough hockey player to most, but we all knew he was a softie who baked.

When he saw me, he nodded, acknowledging my presence, "Amy." Then looking behind me, another nod. "Liam."

Natalie shushed him before turning back to me. "Where were you?" Then narrowing her eyes at Liam, she asked, "And why are you so tan? It's November."

This was my best friend, so before Liam could answer, I took the lead. "First Vegas, then St. Maarten."

Eyes widening, her jaw dropped. "You were on vacation? Why didn't you tell me? We could have gone together during one of Jaxon's longer road trips."

"Not exactly a vacation," I muttered.

Natalie asked Liam, "And where were you?"

Behind me, Liam's answer was identical to mine, "First Vegas, then St. Maarten."

Eyes darting between the two of us, she couldn't comprehend that our answers matched, asking, "You were together?"

Now or never, Ames.

Flipping the giant rock on my hand to face outward, I lifted my hand. "We got married."

For a second, Natalie stood there in stunned silence. Then she managed, "Ma—married?" When I nodded, she continued, "Like, drunk-in-Vegas married? Need-a-quickie-divorce-or-even-an-annulment married? Because my best friend, Amy Michaels, has been adamant for years that she will *never* get married. And to Liam?! How did you two even end up in Vegas together? Something doesn't add up."

"We got married so I could have a shot at my promotion," I admitted. "We both know I don't have a shot in hell without a ring on my finger."

Shock turned to disbelief. "Are you *insane*? So, you're telling me that instead of telling them where they could shove their very illegal requirement, you played into it?"

Throwing my arms wide in frustration, I asked, "What was I supposed to do?"

"Not this!" Addressing Liam now, she asked, "How did you get roped into this?"

Liam crossed his arms. "It was my idea."

Jaxon snickered, and Natalie whipped around with a death glare aimed at him. "This is *not* funny!"

Jaxon continued mixing whatever concoction was within the bowl on the island, murmuring, "It's a little funny."

Natalie's nervous tendency was to ramble, and I knew we'd pushed her over her limit when she began to pace. "You both have lost your damn minds! Who is going to believe the two of you are married? Amy, he's a prince! Did you learn nothing from me? Your life, your every move, will now be on the front pages of the tabloids. Did you even think of that? Maybe it's not too late to undo this. That's it! If no one knows you're married, you can get an annulment, and it'll be like it never happened. But wait, did you two *sleep* together? Is this like a *real* marriage? Ohmigod, I need to sit down."

Winded from the rush of words without taking a single breath, she swayed slightly, causing Liam to step forward to usher her to the nearest kitchen stool.

Beau bounded into the kitchen, taking in the scene before him, with his mother leaning her head down on the island, breathing heavily. Glancing at the standing adults, he asked, "What's wrong with Mommy? Does she have a boo-boo?"

Jaxon, God bless him, was trying desperately not to smile but losing the fight. "Aunt Amy and Uncle Liam got married."

Confused, Beau's forehead wrinkled. "Weren't they already married?"

Natalie's head slowly lifted to look at her four-year-old son. "Why would you think that, Beau?"

His tiny shoulders shrugged. "They live in the same house and are an aunt and uncle. Aunts and uncles are married."

Jaxon's mouth quirked up. "Surprisingly, that four-year-old logic checks out. Well done, little man."

Pleased with himself, Beau skipped out of the room.

Taking pity on my oldest friend, I sat beside her, exhaling. "No, it's not a real marriage, and no, we are *not* sleeping together. I know exactly what I've gotten myself into. I already have a security detail."

Groaning, she put her head back on the island. "I'm never letting you out of my sight again."

"Would you like to be the pot or the kettle today? If I recall, the last time *you* disappeared with a man, he knocked you up."

Jaxon chuckled. "Yeah, that was a good day."

Natalie shot daggers from her eyes at her husband. "You are on thin ice."

"Baby, I'm always skating on thin ice." The reference to his ice hockey career in response to her veiled threat broke the tension in the room, and we all laughed—well, everyone except Liam. I could count on one hand the number of times I'd seen the patented scowl leave his face.

Lightening up a little after the laughter, Natalie sighed, grabbing my hand. "Do you think there's a chance this will work?"

Glancing at Liam before turning back to her, I squeezed her hand. "It has to."

My best friend, my ride-or-die since I was three years old, sized me up. "Answer me this. Vegas, I understand, but why head to the Caribbean? Why not just tie the knot and come home?"

"The people in this room are the *only* people who know this is a fake marriage. So, it has to look real. A few days in St. Maarten looks like a honeymoon."

"That makes sense." Natalie nodded in understanding.

"Nat, there is one more thing." After everything that had happened the past few days, this was going to be the hardest part.

"What? Did you adopt a secret kid?"

Laughing so I didn't start to cry, I shook my head. "No, no kids. But in the spirit of believability, we have to move out."

Natalie froze, then gave a single shake of her head. "No. I forbid it. We are a family."

Taking her hand in mine, I said, "Nat, we will always be family, but we can't stay here. The world will expect us to be head over heels in love, so we have to act like it. We will find somewhere nearby so we can still help with the kids, have family dinners, and game nights. It won't be that much of a change. I promise."

Jaxon cleared his throat, and we all turned our attention to him. Smirking, he offered, "I might know of a place. Can't beat the location."

Intrigued, I asked, "Where?"

"Take my house next door."

Liam chimed in, putting his foot down. "We're not living in your house."

The more I thought about it, the more it made sense. Jaxon's house was much smaller than Natalie's but had more than enough space for two people. Plus, we could walk next door any time we wanted.

Mind made up, I blurted, "We'll take it!"

Liam's icy glare met mine in challenge. "No, we won't."

"I believe the words you're looking for, *husband*, are 'Yes, dear.'"

Liam merely growled in response, knowing that I'd compromised enough, and he wouldn't win this battle.

Jaxon laughed at our exchange. "Damn, Liam. You messed up somewhere because your wife is bossing you around, and you don't even get the benefit of pussy to ease the pain."

My jaw dropped as Natalie yelled, "Jaxon!"

Unashamed, he shrugged. "Tell me I'm wrong." When no one did, he continued, "Look, man. You took care of my wife when she couldn't take care of herself. You bought this house, so she had a refuge and graciously signed it over to us. Let me now do the same for you. My house is now your house. We will make it legal, and then it will no longer be mine. Do with it what you will. Consider it a wedding gift."

Humbled that my best friend's husband was willing to help us, generously handing over the keys to his home, I looked to my own husband, determined. "Pack your bags, Liam. We're moving next door."

CHAPTER 7

Liam

JUST WHEN I THOUGHT Jaxon was no longer the bane of my existence, he offered Amy the chance to move into his house next door. The second the words left his mouth, I knew it was a done deal, no matter my protests. Amy could be as headstrong as me, and an opportunity to stay close to Natalie offered her a security blanket while she struggled to adjust to our new situation.

Yes, I said it. Our marriage was just that, a situation—something to be dealt with.

A week after that fateful kitchen encounter, I found myself unpacking in Jaxon's—no, *our* house. Trying to buy some time, my only stipulation was that we not move in until the deed transfer was complete. Leave it to Jaxon to have that done in less than a week. I had a hard time not hating the guy right now, even if he was good to my little sister.

That week gave us the time to tour the house and make logistical decisions. Amy took the master bedroom and bathroom while I claimed one of the guest rooms. All the furniture was being replaced. I didn't want to think about what had been done on any of the beds or couches in this former bachelor pad. The finished basement would become my office. It was far enough from the bedrooms so that my late-night video calls wouldn't disturb Amy's sleep. I had a feeling I'd be spending most of my time down there.

The house was half the size of Natalie's, featuring an open-concept first floor with a modest-sized kitchen having a full view of the living room. All four bedrooms were on the second floor, only the master containing an ensuite bathroom. Every single wall was white, but I suppose that made sense. Jaxon was on the road for half of the season. When he was home, a majority of his time was spent at the rink. This house was a place to crash, so why bother decorating? At least it had a pool. Despite being smaller than what we were used to, it was plenty big enough for two people.

Amy found me poking around the kitchen, having discovered Jaxon's secret stash of scotch and making a mental note to crack into that later. A good stiff drink was exactly what I needed.

Shifting on her feet, she sent silent signals that she was nervous. My patience was short these days, so I was direct. "What do you need, Amy?"

Her cheek pulled inward, indicating she was chewing on the soft inner flesh. Eyes shifting, looking anywhere but at me, she asked, "I have an appointment to look at some buildings for my project tomorrow and was wondering if you might want to come? You know, since you offered to help?" Pausing, taking a moment to look me in the eye, she backtracked, "But if you've changed your mind about the whole thing, I will totally understand. Don't think you owe me anything. You've done enough."

That's what she was nervous about? Fuck me. Amy was the most direct of Natalie's girlfriends and was afraid to talk to me?

Folding my arms over my chest, I challenged, "Amy, if I said I was going to do something, that means I'm going to do it. End of story. Tell me when and where to meet you."

Swallowing, she nodded. "That's not all."

Confident the second issue was on par with the first, I shrugged. "Whatever it is, yes."

Eyes widening, her mouth dropped open. "Just like that?"

"Would you rather I say no?"

"Of course not, but what if it was something completely ludicrous? You'd still do it?"

Narrowing my eyes, I responded, "Try me."

The gold in her eyes sparkled, indicating mischief was incoming. "All right, big guy. Can you run to the store and grab me a box of tampons?"

Completely unfazed, knowing she was testing me, I shot back, "Sure, let me know what brand and absorbency."

Amy flushed pink from head to toe, and satisfaction flowed through my body—I'd beaten her at her own game.

Unable to meet my eye, she shook her head. "No, that's okay."

Finding humor in the discomfort of having the tables turned on her, I pressed, "Amy, I can handle it. Your menstrual cycle is a natural process. What kind of man would that make me, being squeamish about your monthly visitor?"

Not thinking it was possible, her skin took on an even deeper pink hue as she called out, "Enough! I don't need tampons."

"Then tell me what you do need."

Letting out a breath, she declared, "I need you to come with me to the Foundation's annual Christmas fundraiser. I know you're not their biggest fan right now, but it would go a long way for the higher-ups to see us together."

"As I said earlier, yes." When was she going to realize that I intended to uphold my end of our bargain?

"It's in Manhattan, and we'd need to spend the night. I can arrange for us to have a two-bedroom suite similar to what we had in St. Maarten."

"Amy, it's fine. Part of our arrangement involves being present for each other at engagements. This falls under that category. We'll give them a show. Cover the required bases, so your work can speak for itself."

"Right. Thank you," she said softly.

"Just doing my job, Amy. Fake husband reporting for duty." I gave a mock salute gesture to emphasize my point.

As she walked away, I wondered if it was because our arrangement was so new or if she was accustomed to taking care of herself that she was so nervous to ask me for clearly outlined attendance at her functions. I would have no such qualms when it came time for her to accompany me home to Belleston.

For the first time, I wondered if we made a mistake. Perhaps I'd misjudged Amy, and this was too much for her. I needed her full co-operation to pull this off.

We were only a week into this marriage. It had to get better with time. Right?

———⟨⟨⟩⟩———

I'd agreed to look at apartment buildings with Amy, but I hadn't expected to lose my whole day touring properties. As we entered the sixth building, my vision began to blur. They all looked the same to me, but

Amy saw something different—her imagination would fire off, causing her to become animated, picturing how to use each space.

Even though I was tired and desperately hungry, I played the dutiful husband, following Amy around like a damned puppy through each building. Knowing this was child's play compared to what I would ask of her, I sucked it up but bordered on "hangry." Maybe I just needed a small snack to make this more bearable.

"Liam?" Amy's voice broke through my hunger-induced haze.

"What was that?"

"I was asking what you thought of this one?" Her tone indicated she had already asked me a question, but I'd missed it.

Looking around, I shrugged. "It doesn't matter what I think. This is your project. You don't need my approval if you think it'll work better than the others."

"Maybe you'd like to look at the paperwork first, *darling*?" Her voice took on a sickeningly sweet tone.

Right. I was financing this, and it would look odd if I didn't take a moment to consider the price tag. Giving the listing agent a curt nod, I held out my hand, pretending to survey the cost and specs of the building. The truth was that money was no object. Amy needed this, and I was willing to help her.

Handing the listing sheet back, wanting this to be over with, I said, "Let's do it."

Amy's face lit up as she bounced on her feet. "Really?"

"You're happy." It was a statement, not a question.

"Yes, I'm happy! This place is perfect!" She gushed. "The lobby even has enough space for a daycare! Do you know what that means?"

"Um, that people have somewhere to leave their kids when they go to work?"

"It means that we can reunite even more families! Housing is a *huge* hurdle, but having gainful employment is also necessary. Single parents don't often have someone watch their kids or the funds to send them to daycare so they can work, and it becomes a vicious cycle. No childcare means no work, so they can't get their kids back. If I can find a way to provide housing *and* childcare, there's no way I won't win this job."

Damn, she was passionate about her work. Suddenly, it made sense why she hadn't been able to walk away, even if I still felt like she should have. Amy was making an impact on these families, but it was clear that she was just as impacted by helping them. There was no doubt that she would make an excellent queen. My country had no idea how lucky it was.

I glanced at the agent, and was concise. "Shall we make this official?"

Knowing she'd scored a massive commission, she smiled. "Of course. We can convene at my office to sign and file the paperwork. I'll order some food brought in since we skipped lunch in our quest to find your wife the perfect property."

Thank God.

Amy—now a ball of energy, her eyes moving around as she made invisible plans for this space—dismissed the offer. "Oh, no. I couldn't possibly eat. There is so much to do!"

Watching my only chance at a meal for the next few hours while we dealt with the legalities of this acquisition slip away, I quickly interjected, "Amy, you need to keep your strength up." Turning conspiratorially to the agent, I added, "She gets like this when she's excited. Forgetting to eat, her blood sugar crashes, and she doesn't get any work done."

Eyes lighting up, the agent threw a hand to her chest. "Well, aren't you sweet, taking care of your wife?" Addressing Amy, she added, "You are a lucky girl."

If only she knew.

Having secured my meal ticket, it struck me as odd that the agent was practically swooning over me because I made sure Amy ate. Was the bar set that low by the men of this country?

Placing a hand on Amy's lower back, I guided her from the vacant building, settling her in the car.

Sagging against the seat in visible relief, she breathed out, "Thank God."

Seeing how mentally drained she was from the search, I cursed myself as the words flew past my lips before I could stop them. "I can handle the paperwork if you want me to drop you at home. It'll be donated to the Foundation anyway, so your name doesn't need to be on the deed."

Eyes wide, she gawked at me. "You would do that?"

"You don't need to sit there and watch me sign all the documents. Go home and work on your mock-ups. Or whatever you do."

A corner of her mouth turned up. "Mock-ups?"

"You know what I mean."

Chewing her lip, she nodded. "Okay, you can take me home. I have plans to go out with the girls tonight, and I might need a nap."

Tonight was girls' night? Good to know. Maybe I'd head next door to help out with the kids. Some time spent with my nieces and nephews was just the ticket to relaxing after the day I'd been put through.

Lost in thought, I felt warm, soft skin grasping my hand as it rested on the center console. Peeking over, Amy was staring at me.

Squeezing my hand, she was sincere. "Thank you, Liam. You don't know how much this means to me."

I did, but it didn't bear saying. Squeezing her hand back in response, we drove the rest of the way home in silence.

CHAPTER 8

Amy

THE DEEP BASS THUMPED through the speakers at the club, vibrating my body with every beat. Spades was the nightclub of choice for the Connecticut Comets, and Hannah was the head coach's daughter, so by default, it was her favorite.

Girls' night out with Natalie and Hannah became a monthly tradition after Natalie's permanent return from Europe. This past year, it had evolved into more of a girls' night in while Natalie was pregnant with Charlie, but we began to venture out again this fall. Last month, our outing had been to the Comet's home opener, so this was our first time hitting a club in a long time.

Couldn't say that I missed it.

Clubs were merely an excuse for guys to grind on girls—that's why Hannah loved them. Most of her sexual exploits resulted from clubbing. For me, it was stressful. I had zero interest in any man, even before I was "married." Trying to fend off drunken males seemed like a chore. You'd shake off one, and then another would magically appear to replace them. It was exhausting.

Jaxon hadn't been thrilled when his wife came downstairs in a mini dress with the intention of going dancing. He'd spent more than his fair share of time at Spades with his teammates and knew she would get hit on, his anxiety further heightened by the fact that he wouldn't be there to protect her from unwanted advances.

That's why currently, his best friends and teammates, Cal Berg and Benji Mills, were at the club and acting as guard dogs. I was grateful, but Hannah was pissed.

Hannah glared at Cal, yelling over the music. "You're scaring away all the hot single men! Go away!"

Smirking at a red-faced Hannah, he shook his head. "I'm under orders!"

"Fuck your orders! Go find some pussy for yourself and stop cock-blocking me!"

Cal's molten blue eyes flared. Hannah's dirty mouth was affecting him, but she was utterly oblivious in her rage. Hannah's mission was to land a hockey player—or at least sleep with one—but her father had forbidden any players from messing around with his daughters. That decree only spurred Hannah on, and she was even more determined, knowing it was against the rules. It would be game over if she could see how Cal looked at her. They were like a powder keg—someday, a single spark would set off an explosion. It was only a matter of time.

Hannah turned her back on Cal, continuing to dance, causing her short brown curls to bounce, but I caught how his eyes dropped to her backside as it swayed. Being removed from the situation allowed me to take a step back and see the whole picture regarding those two. They got on each other's nerves to no end, but they were perfect for each other—Hannah needed someone to put her in her place, and Cal needed a woman with spunk. Smiling to myself with that secret knowledge, I danced with my friends, thankful not to have a barrage of drunken men attempting to paw at us.

Lost to the rhythm of the music, I jumped when a hand grabbed my arm. Expecting to have to throw an elbow at some overly enthusiastic man, I realized it was Hannah before my reflexes kicked in.

Blue eyes wide in fear, she glanced over my shoulder, leaning close to scream in my ear over the music. "Don't panic, but there's a man who has been watching us all night."

My pulse kicked up. If Hannah was frightened, that meant whoever was watching us seemed menacing. Glancing over my shoulder, I groaned inwardly as the man she identified was merely Marcus. He was dressed down but doing his job—keeping watch over me.

Grabbing Hannah's and Natalie's hands, I nodded toward the stairs to the VIP section, indicating it was time for a break. Understanding, they came with me, with Cal and Benji following closely behind.

High above the dance floor, the music wasn't quite as loud, and we sat at a black velvet-lined booth in the corner. Hannah glared at the boys, pointing to a table in the opposite corner. Grinning, Cal obeyed her command as we placed our drink order with the waitress who stopped by our table. Hannah relaxed until she saw Marcus come up the stairs, taking a seat nearby.

Eyes bulging, she leaned into me. "Oh my God, he followed us up here!"

Natalie peeked at Marcus, then threw a pointed stare in my direction. Her message was clear—it was time to let Hannah know what I'd done.

When I hesitated, looking for the words, Natalie prodded, "Would you like to tell her, or should I?"

Hannah looked at Marcus as understanding dawned on her face. "Oh. Oh!" Whispering, she asked, "Are you with him?"

Feeling heat creeping up my neck, I shook my head. "No!"

Hannah frowned, her brow wrinkling. "Then what?" Natalie grinned, and when she noticed, Hannah's mouth dropped open before accusing, "I swear to God, Amy . . . If you are dating or knocked up by a hockey player after all your 'I don't need a man' schtick, I'm going to scream!"

"Oh God, no!" I blurted out.

Hannah relaxed into the plush cushions of the booth, breathing out, "Thank God."

Flipping the ring on my finger, I held it up. "But I am married."

If Hannah's brain was a computer, it would be short-circuiting and smoking right now. Her eyes moved wildly, trying to comprehend what I just said because it didn't make sense. Hell, I was living it, and it hardly made sense.

Natalie was amused. "Look, Ames. You finally did it. You've rendered Hannah speechless. Never thought we'd see the day." To add to Hannah's mental anguish, she offered, "She's married to Liam."

Hannah's brain was so overloaded that she didn't initially understand, asking, "Liam, who?"

Natalie bit her lip, trying not to laugh, but it was a losing battle. "Our very own Liam Remington. The man following us all night is her personal protection officer, Marcus."

"Liam?!" Hannah yelled. "What the hell, Amy?!"

Groaning, I closed my eyes. "It's not what you think."

Hannah's voice was laced with hurt. "What *I* think is that you've been hooking up with Liam on the side all these years and didn't trust me enough to come clean. Sounds like Natalie knows all about it."

Forcing my eyes open to see how devastated Hannah looked at the prospect of being excluded, remorse hit me that I hadn't told her sooner. It had barely been a week, but I could have found the time. Even though we were a trio and no relationships in our group were stronger than any of the others, Hannah often felt on the outside since I'd moved in with Natalie.

Glancing around the VIP section to ensure no one else was in earshot, I said low, "Hannah, it's not a real marriage."

Scoffing, she gestured to my hand. "That ring sure as hell looks real."

My hand twitched. "Yes, the ring is very real, but the marriage is on paper only."

"I don't understand. Why would you marry Liam?"

"Remember that promotion I was up for?"

Hannah narrowed her eyes at me. "Yeah . . ."

"It would seem they don't want a single woman in that position."

Outraged, she cried, "They can't do that!"

Natalie added her two cents. "That's what I said, but there's no talking to this one."

Toying with my ring, focusing on why it rested on my left hand, I sighed. "I love my job. I wish I could walk away, but I know I'd be miserable if I did."

Hannah scanned my face. "So, you married Liam."

"Yep."

"What does Liam get out of all this?" she asked.

I sighed. I was still trying to figure that out myself. "He said something about his parents requesting that he get married. So, it works out for both of us."

Natalie chimed in, "That's what I'm trying to understand. Why would Adrian and Adelaide make Liam get married? It doesn't add up."

A waitress dropped off the drinks we ordered, and I brought my vodka cranberry to my lips, savoring the burn of the alcohol as it slid down my throat. "I don't know. He didn't go into details. I thought about asking him today after we toured properties, but I put him through enough."

Hannah asked, "Touring properties? Are you moving out of Natalie's?"

Natalie leaned across the table. "Yeah, what properties?" Answering Hannah's second question, she added, "They already moved out. Jaxon gave them his house."

Turning on me again, Hannah's eyebrows raised almost to her hairline. "How long have you been married?!"

More alcohol would be required to continue this conversation, so I raised my hand, signaling to the waitress that I wanted another round. Draining what was left in my glass, I swallowed, answering, "Ten days."

Natalie repeated her question, "Why were you looking at properties?"

Where is that damn drink?

"I was having trouble finding an apartment building for my pilot program, and Liam offered to help by buying one that fit my needs and then donating it to the Foundation," I explained.

Both ladies stared at me wide-eyed.

Unable to bear the silence, I snapped, "What?"

A secret smile crossed Natalie's lips, and Hannah laughed, proclaiming, "Oh, Ames, you are so screwed."

Confused, I asked, "Why?"

"He bought you a building? There's no way this stays a 'fake' marriage. You'll be repaying him in sex before too long." She waggled her eyebrows.

"Stop it. It's Liam. Neither one of us is interested in sex."

"Come on, Amy. This is a classic story—pretending to be married, forced into close proximity, and then falling for each other. Before you know it, it'll be a real marriage." Pointing at Natalie, she added, "Just like this one protested that she would end up with Jaxon after he knocked her up. The writing was on the wall. All you have to do is read it like I am now."

Natalie pretended to be outraged. "Hey! How did I get dragged into this?"

Holding up my hands to cut them off, I said, "Listen, we have our separate spaces. I don't even like Liam most days. I'm not going to want to sleep with him. Ever."

Hannah's lips quirked up smugly. "Famous last words. Don't say I didn't warn you. The man may be a grouch, but he is one hell of a male specimen. And marriage to him makes you a princess."

Groaning, I downed my second vodka cranberry in half an hour. "Don't remind me."

Eyeing my collection of empty glasses, she smirked. "Better slow down, or you'll climb into his bed tonight."

"Can we be done with this conversation? We solved the issue of the mystery man following us. Let's go back to dancing, or else I may as well go home."

"Fine. Let's go dance. Maybe you should flash around that ice rink you're wearing on your finger. That'll keep the undesirables away."

Another hidden feature I hadn't even realized was a benefit due to my new marital status. Attempting to shut off my brain while dancing to the heavy beat was useless. Hannah's words bounced around in my mind, but she was wrong. There was zero chance that Liam and I would end up together. I'd never been more certain of anything in my life.

CHAPTER 9

Liam

AMY AND I FELL into a comfortable rhythm as married roommates in Jaxon's house. In other words, we were living completely separate lives, staying out of each other's way. While Amy slept, I stayed up most nights on video calls with the charitable foundations of which I was a patron. I went to bed shortly after she left for work and was often asleep when she returned home. There was a slight overlap—late evening when we were both awake—but we kept to ourselves.

That was about to change.

The holidays were coming up, and we both had events requiring our joint presence. Amy's holiday fundraiser was this evening, and shortly after Christmas, she would accompany me to Belleston for a New Year's Eve party. She would introduce me to her work colleagues, whereas I would present her to the world—the stakes were high.

Amy doubted whether I would be successful in playing the doting husband and "lover," but I had a few tricks up my sleeve. Yes, I might have buried any outward charm to differentiate myself from my brother, but that didn't mean I couldn't dig it up and resurrect it from the dead. I was royalty, after all. Fundraisers were our bread and butter. It was in our DNA to charm the pants off donors.

Amy wouldn't know what hit her.

It was Saturday, and she'd been bustling around all morning, getting ready for a night spent in the city. Bags were piling up by the front door as Amy expected us to be driving to Manhattan. That drive would take a little over two hours on a good day with zero traffic. Anyone who'd ever been to New York City knew there was no such thing as zero traffic.

I had a surprise in store to set the mood for Amy—preparation for Charming Liam to make his appearance.

"Liam?" Amy's voice called from the entryway.

Standing from my position on the couch, I turned to face her. Dressed down for the drive, in leggings and an oversized sweater with her hair pulled back, the relaxed look directly conflicted with her body language. From twenty feet away, I could see her muscles coiled with tension. Tonight was a big deal for her, and she was visibly stressed.

Striding toward her, I gestured to the pile of bags. "You ready to go?"

Nodding, she tucked a loose strand of red hair behind her ear. "If we leave now, it'll leave us a buffer in case we hit any traffic. When we arrive at the hotel, I'll need to shower and do my hair, so any extra time would be welcome."

Bending at the waist, I grabbed her items, heading toward the waiting car. Jasper would be driving my SUV, with Marcus riding shotgun. They were on high alert for tonight. Not only were we heading into one of the world's largest metropolitan cities, but we were also attending a large event and spending the night in a hotel. They were slightly miffed at me for not giving them enough lead time to bring in backup for the weekend, but I wasn't concerned. Some days, if I closed my eyes, I could pretend that my every move in public wasn't being watched by someone trained to take a bullet for me.

There would be time for an overabundance of security later in my life. Tonight, I was determined to be just Liam—not Prince William Frederick Edmund Remington, as the world knew me. Regardless of my bloodlines, I was simply a man. And this man had plans to accompany his wife to her fundraising event this evening. End of story.

I didn't *want* my life to be a big deal, but—as I was constantly reminded—that wasn't up to me. That had been determined long before I even developed conscious awareness. Everyone thought I was lucky, but they had no idea what it was like. I'd trade any of them in a heartbeat.

Adding Amy's bags to my own already in the trunk, I slammed it shut before rounding to open the back door for her. Allowing her to slide inside, I closed the door before joining her from the other side. She was fidgety—her leg bouncing uncontrollably as she scrolled on her phone, chewing the inside of her cheek.

I'd never seen Amy this nervous, and it was unsettling. Amy's confidence was her signature, and I always admired that she felt free to be herself, not caring much about what others thought. Anger gripped my body, my fists tightening with the realization that her beloved job had done this to her. They'd told her she wasn't good enough as she was, and she believed them. Now, she was nervous, rattled almost, because she feared our ruse wouldn't be enough to convince them.

I hated them for it.

Amy peered up from her phone long enough to notice the route we were taking. Her brow furrowing, she pulled up the navigation app on her phone, eyes widening in panic. "We're going the wrong way! We're heading north toward Hartford instead of south toward I-95."

Despising myself for causing her even more stress, I kept my tone even. "It's fine, Amy."

Green eyes wild, she huffed, "It is *not* fine, Liam! I can't be late, and I need time to get ready! You know how important tonight is for me." Fortunately, we had just pulled into the private airstrip, and Amy recognized our location from when we'd chartered our flight to Vegas. Calming slightly, she asked, confused, "What are we doing here?"

Grateful her panic appeared to be subsiding, I smirked. "Thought it would be fitting to arrive with my wife in style."

Stunned, she blinked. "Style?"

Ignoring her request for clarification, I exited the car, allowing Marcus to help Amy by opening her door and lending a hand as she stepped out. Grabbing our luggage, I led her toward the waiting passenger helicopter I secured for our flight into Manhattan.

Amy's voice softened from a few steps behind me when she realized my plan. "Liam. This is too much."

Reaching the chopper, I looked back at her. "Amy Michaels," I started, emphasizing the fact that she elected to keep her maiden name. "You are my princess. The sooner you become accustomed to the extravagance befitting your station, the sooner you can convince the world that what we have is real. Own it like you own every other aspect of your life."

Mouth dropping slightly open, she whispered, "You did this for me?"

Tilting my head, I surveyed her. Amy was hands down the most confident woman I'd ever met, but it struck me how her one bad experience with a man had changed her. She didn't trust that a man would care for her without ulterior motives. That perception had to change, but it would seem I had my work cut out.

She might not show it the same way, but she'd allowed a man to break her, the same as Natalie had.

Handing our bags to the pilot, I reached out to my wife. "I'm all in, Amy. Are you?"

Swallowing, she took my hand, confirming, "I'm all in."

"Good. If that's settled, we should be on our way. Can't have the princess being late to the ball, now, can we?"

That earned me a small smile, and she allowed me to lead her up the steps inside the chopper. Relieved that the tension seemed to have left her body, I could focus on the task ahead. I'd done my research on Amy's program and made the deed donation to her foundation. That alone would likely be a topic of conversation amongst her superiors this evening.

The pilots did their pre-flight checks, and within minutes, we were in the air, flying high above Hartford before turning south toward Manhattan. Early winter in New England meant an early sunset; pinks and purples tinted the clouds as we made our way over the Long Island Sound.

Amy gasped softly when the city came into view. New York City was breathtaking from this angle. The lights in the skyscrapers' windows began to stand out as the sky gradually darkened around us.

Landing at the East 34th Street Heliport, we disembarked, making our way to an oversized black SUV waiting to take us to the hotel where the fundraiser would take place. Amy was quiet but no longer jittery, for which I was grateful. Arriving at the hotel, we entered the ornate lobby, stopping at the check-in desk, bellhop in tow. Amy grabbed our keys, and we headed to our room on the 25th floor.

As she opened the door, I noticed an instant shift in Amy's demeanor as she whispered, "No, no, no."

Quickly tipping the bellhop, I grabbed our bags, ushering her into the room before she had a meltdown in the hallway. The door slammed heavily behind us, causing Amy to jump. Panicked, she rushed around the room, poking her head through doorways and into closets.

Her constant motion was making me nauseous, so I dropped the bags, demanding, "What's wrong?"

Gesturing wildly, she yelled, "There's only one bedroom! I specifically requested a two-room suite."

Walking around myself, I quickly discovered the miscommunication. Leaning against the bathroom doorframe, I stated, "Amy, this is a two-room suite. It's just not a two-*bedroom* suite."

"Well, a two-room suite doesn't help us! We need two bedrooms! I can't very well go down there and make a big deal about this—it would draw attention. What are we going to do?"

"You're right. We are married, so it would look odd to ask for another room. Take the bed. I'll sleep on the couch in the sitting room." The solution was simple enough in my mind.

Shaking her head, Amy protested, "You can't do that. You're not exactly a small man, Liam. You take the bed."

No way in hell.

Crossing my arms, I countered, "You're not exactly a small woman, Amy. I'm—"

"Watch it," she cut me off, her tone bordering on murderous.

I had the feeling I would need to guard my royal jewels if she were any closer. Yes, it had been a poor choice of words, but she'd taken it the wrong way.

"You're tall, Amy." I sighed. "That's all I meant. You're taking the bed, and that's final."

Narrowing her eyes, she lifted her chin. "That's final?"

"You heard me. If you want to play a game, then let's play. Try to sleep on the couch, and you'll find me on the floor. I *refuse* to take your spot on the bed." She wasn't going to win this round.

"You're a stubborn ass. You know that?"

I shrugged. "It has been mentioned in the past, yes. Now, get ready."

Rising on her tiptoes, she attempted to peek behind me into the bathroom, timid, as she said, "I need to shower."

"Then shower." I stepped aside to allow her entry.

Amy's nervous trait of chewing on the inside of her cheek was back, and realization dawned. If she was showering, that meant she'd be naked, needing to dress for the evening, and she didn't want me around while exposed.

"While you're in the shower, I'll dress and head down to the bar for a drink or two. You can join me down there once you're ready," I offered to set her mind at ease.

That plan seemed to satisfy her, and she began organizing the items she needed in the bathroom. As soon as she closed and locked the bathroom door, the sounds of running water reached my ears, I began to dress for the evening.

I had a new tuxedo custom-made for the event, which fit like a glove. Classic black always made a statement and would pair nicely with whatever color Amy chose for the evening. Fastening my cufflinks, I quickly styled my hair, then took my leave of the room before Amy finished her shower.

Nursing my second bourbon at the hotel bar while waiting for Amy's arrival, I turned on my phone. It had been off since the day Amy and I got married three weeks ago. I knew our Vegas wedding was not what my family had been hoping for when they'd practically demanded I find a wife, but if I had to play by their rules, I would do it on my terms.

The high-pitched dings indicating incoming messages went off immediately and in quick succession. Switching the toggle to place notifications on silent, I watched as my screen lit up with what was easily hundreds of messages and missed calls. Most were from my father, but I didn't read a single one. My decision had been made, and my marriage was legal. Nothing anyone said now could change that.

I was forced into this situation, so they were forced to deal with how I handled it.

As I angrily cleared my phone, a feminine voice purred close to my ear. "Is this seat taken?"

Not in the mood, I reached onto the barstool on my left, making sure to flash my wedding band, which still felt foreign and heavy on my hand. Gruffly, I responded, "Yes, my wife should be down soon."

The last thing I needed was someone recognizing me and pictures plastered on the front page of the tabloids with some random woman who wasn't my wife.

Undeterred, the voice held a trace of amusement when responding, "She must be a lucky girl."

There was something familiar about that voice, so I turned slightly, causing me to stare into the stunning green eyes of none other than the wife in question. Those eyes sparkled as a corner of her lips rose, and I drank in her look for the night. A sleek, floor-length black dress skimmed over her generous curves. Her hair was almost auburn in the bar's dim light, pinned behind her ear on one side while the other fell in loose waves. Drop diamond earrings graced her earlobes, matching the necklace against the column of her throat.

Our conversation indicated she was in character for the evening, so it was time to turn on the charm and play along. Standing at my full height, I was near eye level with her now that she was wearing heels.

A slow smile spread across my face, my voice sincere. "I'm the lucky one."

A rush of air flew past Amy's lips, which was satisfying. She might have had doubts, but my charm stunned her into silence.

Stepping back, I offered her my elbow. "Shall we?"

Slipping her hand into the crook of my arm, we made our way toward the ballroom reserved for her foundation's fundraiser, joining the line of partygoers queued to grab their table placements.

These events were always the same—open bar to loosen wallets, a video pitch to garner sympathy for the cause, and small groups targeting the biggest donors with promises of naming rights if they hit a certain donation level. It was monotonous but predictable.

Reaching the table holding place cards, we found ours, which read: Table Five, Ms. Amy Michaels and HRH Prince William Remington of Belleston. That's who I was in this world—*Prince* William.

Showtime.

The massive ballroom featured an upper-level balcony along three of the four walls. A stage with a giant screen hanging from the ceiling indicated the front of the room, while a dancefloor was situated at the center, surrounded by tables accented in black and silver.

As we moved toward Table Five, Amy whispered, "They've seated us with all the other finalists."

Whispering back, I was confident. "Perfect. Gives us a chance to evaluate our competition."

"They most likely won't want to talk about their pilot programs. Everyone is keeping that fairly close to the vest."

Dropping my hand to the bare skin of her lower back, revealed by the extremely low cut of her gown—delighting in her resulting shiver—my voice dropped an octave. "Sweetheart, I mean our competition when it comes to the most compelling couple."

Amy's eyes flashed to mine. To an outside observer, it would look like an intense stare between lovers, especially with how I had a possessive hand on her body. We had this in the bag.

Table Five was packed when we arrived. Four other couples were seated at the massive round table, leaving two empty chairs for Amy and me.

Pulling back a chair, I allowed Amy to sit before sliding her chair beneath the table. Leaning down, I kissed the side of her neck before coming next to her ear, saying loud enough for the others to hear, "Shall I fetch us some drinks, sweetheart? Or perhaps you'd like to go? You know how much I love to watch you walk away."

Her alabaster throat bobbed as she audibly swallowed, and I suddenly envisioned my hand on that throat as I pounded into her soft body.

Whoa.

Fighting the urge to pull back suddenly and ruin our ruse, I closed my eyes and breathed deeply to calm myself—bad idea. That deep breath only served to fill my nostrils with Amy's perfume—something floral but not overpowering enough to be nauseating. Blood began to pool in my groin.

What the hell is wrong with me?

I hadn't been with a woman in years, which had never been a problem. Why was being close to one suddenly putting erotic images in my brain and turning me on? This was *Amy* we were talking about. None of the random women I'd been near in recent years had elicited a response like this, so why now? Why her?

None of those other women were your wife.

Straightening, my voice sounded like it'd been dragged over gravel as I said, "I'll be back with those drinks."

Turning on my heel, I headed toward the bar. Without looking, I could feel Amy's gaze on my back. Her body's response betrayed her as well. She'd been similarly affected—or at least shocked—by my actions.

We were in dangerous territory.

I couldn't muck up our arrangement by being attracted to my wife. Giving in to my baser instincts and fucking Amy would ruin everything. Besides, she wasn't even interested—she'd made that crystal clear. Making a move would likely cause her to push me away, creating an unbearable cohabitation situation, and I needed her in the long run.

Nope, couldn't go there.

Telling my dick to calm down, I decided on a new plan. We would have to interact at events like this and in Belleston, but outside of that, I would keep my distance. Staying far, far away from my wife had to work, and eventually, whatever my body was reacting to would fade.

I gave myself a mental pep talk—get through tonight and steer clear of Amy until the next event. Simple.

CHAPTER 10

Amy

WHAT THE HELL JUST happened?

I stared at Liam's back as he walked away. I didn't know who that man was. He certainly wasn't my Liam—not that I thought of Liam as *mine*, but you knew what I meant.

It started with the flirting at the bar, and granted, I'd initiated that. Then, he put his hand on my exposed lower back—precariously close to discovering that I wasn't wearing underwear under this silky creation sent from his sister, Lucy, when she found out we were married. Those actions were child's play compared to the intimate kiss he dropped on my neck in front of an audience, causing goosebumps to rise along my flesh and heat to pool between my thighs.

My hand unconsciously went to the side of my neck—still damp from his lips—and my cheeks flamed.

A feminine sigh sounded from my right before someone said, "Damn, where do I get one of those?"

Reminded of the full table, I turned to find all eyes on me. Dropping my gaze to the tablecloth, I muttered, "Sorry about that."

The woman fanning herself beside me was visible from the corner of my eye. "Don't be sorry. That was *hot*."

My co-worker, and fellow finalist, Daniel, chastised the woman, who was clearly his wife. "Daphne!"

Daphne smacked Daniel playfully on the arm. "Take some notes, Danny. You could learn something."

The table chuckled, and to my left, another finalist, Grace, asked, "Amy! Where have you been hiding that hunk of a man?" When I waved my hand before responding, Grace's eyes widened, falling on my massive engagement ring. Grabbing my hand to inspect it, she screeched, "You're engaged! Shut up!"

Blushing, I couldn't meet her eye as I admitted, "Actually, we're married."

Grace shrieked. "Oh. My. God! Shut up again!"

Suddenly, I was reminded why I had a tiny circle of female friends. This over-the-top reaction was more than I could handle. It grated on my nerves and was beginning to give me a headache.

Undeterred, Grace continued, "Tell me everything! Where did you meet?"

Glancing back to the bar, praying Liam was on his way back to save me, I was disappointed to find him still in a long line. Turning around, bracing to sell the story on my own, I smiled slightly. "He's my best friend's brother-in-law. We've had a casual thing for years, but it became more serious recently." It wasn't exactly a lie.

"That is *so* romantic," Grace crooned. "I just love a good friends-to-lovers story! My Oliver and I were high school sweethearts, so I'm partial."

Nodding, I didn't know what to say. Liam and I weren't exactly "friends," but we'd tolerated each other over the years. Living together for years, we hadn't killed each other, so that had to count for something, right? Our common bond was caring for Natalie and her children.

Grace continued, "What's his name?" Before I could stop her, she reached over and plucked our place card from its resting spot in front of my plate, frowning as she read it. "What does HRH mean? I've never seen that before."

Oh, boy. Here we go. Put on your big girl panties, Amy, because shit is about to get real.

"Wait, he's a prince?!" Grace had clearly moved past the HRH and read that it said *Prince William Remington of Belleston.*

Wincing, I offered, "He's just Liam to me."

"Amy. You married a prince!" she exclaimed, bouncing in her seat. "How did none of us know about this? What are you doing still hanging around at the Foundation? Shouldn't you be off somewhere, wearing a tiara?" Gasping, she asked, "Does that mean you'll be a queen someday? This is so exciting!"

God, she was obnoxious. Where the hell was Liam? He'd opened this can of worms and needed to help clean up the mess. I needed that drink more than ever.

My smile was tight as I replied, "He's a second son, so he won't become King. We much prefer our quiet, simple life."

Taking the hint, Grace calmed down, and thankfully, Liam returned carrying a champagne flute and a lowball glass with some form of brown liquor. Downing the champagne as soon as the glass touched my fingertips, I grabbed his drink and let the liquor burn my throat as I tossed that back as well—I didn't even taste it to know what I ingested.

Liam draped an arm over the back of my chair, leaning over to whisper, "Are you okay?"

I shot him a look that screamed *what do you think?*

Taking the hint, he turned to the rest of the table and began to make small talk. I was good at my job, but functions like this were not my favorite. Everyone was so phony, and I preferred to be authentic.

Said the girl with the fake marriage. Who's the phony now?

After dinner came the big fundraising pitch, which involved a video presentation showcasing some of our more extensive programs, capped off with a montage of families hugging, happy to be reunited, and parent testimonials about how much the Foundation's work had changed their lives. It was a tear-jerker for sure, and there was a hushed overtone of sniffles in the crowd.

Instead of becoming emotional like most of the crowd, I became more determined. My program had the potential to change the lives of so many families, and I would do everything in my power to ensure the Foundation board chose my program. It didn't matter that I had no idea what the others were planning. I knew mine would be better.

The harsh notes of the band warming up their instruments filled the air inside the ballroom, indicating the more relaxed portion of the evening would begin momentarily. Slowly, people left their seats, congregating in smaller groups around the room as the music formally began.

I excused myself to use the restroom and freshen up my makeup quickly. I needed a breather more than anything else. No matter how hard I tried to change the subject during dinner, the conversation always found its way back to Liam and me, and our new marriage and royal status. It was mentally taxing, and the night was only half over.

Perhaps most exhausting of all was trying to figure out what had possessed Liam tonight—he was charm personified when all I'd ever known was the cranky version of the prince I married. Everyone *loved* him.

Returning from the powder room, I visually searched the vast ballroom to find Liam. Frowning, I scanned the room, trying to locate him, when someone on the edge of the ballroom—standing with Mr. Greiner and a few other members of the Foundation's board—lifted a champagne flute in my direction. The gesture seemed odd, so I honed in on the man who appeared to be signaling me from across the room.

Holy shit, is that Liam?

My chest tightened, and I found it difficult to draw air into my lungs. I hadn't recognized him because he was *smiling*. Don't get me wrong, Liam was a handsome man even with his permanent scowl, but with a natural smile gracing his lips, his face transformed, and one could even call him devastatingly gorgeous.

I'm in big trouble.

Liam watched as I stared at him, raising an eyebrow in silent question. Finding my footing, I walked toward the group standing in a semi-circle. Liam handed me the drink in his hand while sliding the now free hand behind my back.

Smiling when he noticed I'd joined them, Mr. Greiner exclaimed, "Hello, Ms. Michaels! We were talking with His Royal Highness about his generous donation to the Foundation to aid your pilot program."

Liam chided, "Jacob, it's Liam, please." Pulling me closer, he added, "It was my pleasure to help such a worthy cause. Amy is so passionate about her work."

Mr. Greiner gave a slight bow of his head. "Liam, of course. Your wife has been instrumental in our work at the Foundation. I hope you're not planning on whisking her off to Europe permanently."

The hairs on the back of my neck stood on end. This asshole made it clear that if I remained unmarried, I'd have no shot in hell at my promotion, and now he was implying that because I *was* married, I would consider giving up my job? He was clearly living in the wrong decade.

Where the hell did he get off? Perhaps Liam had been right from the start—maybe this wasn't worth it. I'd reached the bar they had set, but how long before they raised it again without warning?

Feeling myself tense slightly, Liam rubbed soothing circles along my lower back before responding, "I wouldn't dream of it. I find Amy's drive intoxicating. We may have minor obligations back home, but we plan to remain in Hartford for the foreseeable future." Determined to have the last word, he added, "Now, if you'll excuse me, I promised my wife a dance."

Draining my glass of champagne as he led me toward the dance floor, I placed it on the tray of a passing waiter.

Liam was in my ear. "Are you ready to give them a show?"

Under my breath, I muttered, "Who *are* you?"

I hadn't meant for him to hear me, but must've been unsuccessful, as evidenced by his response. "Sweetheart, so far as all these people are concerned, I'm the man of your dreams."

Maybe I *was* dreaming. This whole night had been so surreal that I half expected to wake up and find that it had all been a figment of my subconscious.

And what was with him calling me sweetheart? No one could hear him most of the time, so what was the point?

Already disoriented from the strangeness of the evening, when Liam spun me onto the dance floor, I flailed slightly before clinging to him, trying to anchor myself. Good thing he was a wall of solid muscle.

He chuckled. "Easy there, tiger. It's just a dance."

Unable to look away from his eyes—suddenly burning like twin blue flames—I huffed, "Easier said than done." Awareness prickled at the back of my mind of being watched. "Why does it feel like everyone is staring at us?"

Keeping his head steady, he shifted his eyes to the side, smirking. "Probably because they are."

"Oh God," I breathed. I did *not* do well with being the center of attention.

Panicked, I began turning my head to look, but Liam's commanding tone stopped me. "Eyes on me, Amy."

Obeying, I kept my gaze on Liam's face as he took my right hand in his left, clasping it before giving a little squeeze of reassurance. His right hand dropped to that familiar patch of bare skin directly above my ass. Following his lead, I slid my left hand up his chest to rest at the back of his collar.

Fully in position, Liam moved me carefully around the dance floor. Determined to divert my attention from our spectators, that smile touched his lips again before he asked, "Do you remember the first time we danced together?"

Relaxing slightly in his arms, I scoffed. "First? There's only been one other time."

Pressing, he accused, "So you *do* remember."

"Of course, I remember. Hard to forget when your best friend marries a prince."

A smirk crept onto his full lips. "Ames, you married a prince."

Did he just call me Ames? Where did that come from?

"Technicality, but you know what I mean. They had that fairy tale wedding, even if Leo became the villain instead of the hero in their marriage."

A shadow passed over Liam's striking blue eyes. I learned long ago that he held himself personally responsible for not finding out sooner how awful Leo had been treating Natalie.

Shaking his head so slightly that no one watching would notice, the shadow retreated, and the charming stranger version of Liam was back. "We've changed a lot since then—we've both grown up."

"Would be hard not to. I was barely eighteen when they got married, and you were what? Almost twenty-one? We knew nothing about life." My fingers brushed against the silky strands of black hair curling at the nape of his neck, and I noted, "Your hair was different then."

Back then, he'd had a buzz cut instead of this perfectly styled mop of hair that, until tonight, I hadn't known was swoon-worthy.

Shrugging, he commented, "My hair was an unfortunate casualty of my military service."

Liam's diversion was working, and I kept our conversation going, forgetting about the show we were putting on for the crowd. "Do you miss it?"

"Sometimes, but not in the way you'd think."

"How so?" I asked, tilting my head.

"I miss the camaraderie, but I don't miss the actual service—what I was asked to do."

There was a darkness in his tone, and it wasn't hard to surmise that he'd been in on some deep-level secret operations. I'd seen the movies, which were likely dramatized, but those visions caused a shiver to run down my spine. Maybe if this were a real marriage, he would confide in me about what he'd seen and done, but perhaps not—those missions were likely classified.

One thing was clear. Even if I'd lived with Liam for a long time, I barely knew the man beneath the hard exterior. But he was my husband, nonetheless. Would I ever really know him?

Lost in thought, our conversation ended, but Liam kept leading me around, dancing like it was the most natural thing in the world—maybe it was for him. He'd grown up a royal. Didn't they force their kids to take ballroom dance lessons? I had learned quickly while preparing for my cotillion that I had two left feet, but in Liam's arms, I moved effortlessly.

Melting into his casual embrace, my hand slid back down to the center of his chest, where I could feel his heart hammering against his ribcage. Liam made a sound in the back of his throat, and I looked into his eyes. If I didn't know any better, it almost appeared as if he was in pain. Glimpsing down, I checked to confirm I hadn't stomped on his feet with the stiletto heels I wore.

Peeking back up at Liam, his stare was so intense that I began to squirm. Unable to bear it a moment longer, I stepped closer into his embrace—my cheek to his—as we continued to dance. At almost six feet in my heels, I knew I was a tall woman, but I never felt as small, as surrounded, as I did in Liam's arms. He was a protector, and I felt the weight of that protection descending over me like a blanket. It was strangely comforting.

I didn't just feel it—I *knew* I was safe with Liam.

Something was changing. I could sense it, but I couldn't quite put my finger on what.

Buzz buzz. Buzz buzz.

Groaning, I rolled over in bed, grabbing my head—it was pounding. I'd had too much to drink last night.

Last night. Oh, God. It all came flooding back.

Liam's smile.

Liam charming the Foundation board.

His lips on my neck, his hand on my exposed lower back.

Dancing.

Everyone watching us like we were in an enclosure at the zoo.

Reaching blindly to stop the endless buzzing from my phone, my hand connected with the nightstand. Finally, grasping the phone, I blinked against the bright screen in the darkness. Liam must have pulled the black-out curtains because it was pitch black, but my phone revealed it was 10 AM.

The caller ID read: *Mom*.

Crap.

Initially intending to blow off whoever was trying to reach me while I was hungover, I knew there was no possibility of putting off this call.

There would never be enough mental bracing to take a call from my mother. We'd never seen eye to eye on my life choices.

Jacqui Michaels was a socialite. Her sole purpose was to "support" my father, who was the CEO of the family oil empire. She'd tried so hard to steer me toward the life she enjoyed, so it was quite a disappointment that I threw myself into my career, even if it was a career that focused on helping others. She would prefer that I be more like Natalie—an ornament for a wealthy man, with my charity work focused more on throwing parties than boots on the ground making a real difference.

Hitting the button to accept the call, I moved the phone to my ear. "Hi, Mom."

"Amy Anne Michaels, you got married?!" Her voice was too high-pitched for my hungover brain, and I winced.

"Maybe?" I replied, pinching the bridge of my nose.

"Maybe?! You don't so much as bring a boy home—ever—and this morning, we had to see you on the front page of the Society Section in the Sunday newspaper!"

Oh, shit. This is bad.

"The newspaper?" I asked cautiously.

"Yes, Amy." Her annoyance with me seeped through the speaker. "The newspaper. The headline read: *Michaels Oil Empire Princess Marries Belleston's Last Bachelor Prince.* My phone has been ringing non-stop, and I don't know what to tell people! How could you do this to me?"

There it was. She wasn't so upset that I got married—eloped, really—but that she didn't know what to tell her friends. Classic Jacqui.

Blowing out a breath, I tried to reason with the most unreasonable woman alive. "Mom, look . . . We just wanted to enjoy a little bit of quiet before everyone found out. Is that so wrong?"

"Yes. It is wrong. Don't even get me started on how he didn't ask your father. What kind of well-bred man marries a girl of high social standing and doesn't ask for permission? He should know better!" Under her breath, she added, "Well, maybe he wasn't raised properly, considering what his brother did to poor Natalie."

I was *so* over this conversation. "Jesus, Mom! You know damn well he's nothing like his brother. He was the one who helped Natalie get out of there."

"And for what? To drag you back in her stead?"

Before I could respond—telling her how ridiculous she was being—light filtered into the room as the adjoining door to the sitting room opened. There stood the man in question, a pair of jeans slung low over his hips, his chest bare. The words died on my lips, and I sat there, stunned, as he moved toward where I lay in bed.

I'd seen Liam countless times without a shirt—we shared a house with a pool—but there was something different this time. The slow swagger as he approached was almost sensual, like an animal stalking its prey. If nothing else, the shadows from the dim light highlighted the sheer number of defined muscles covering his chest and abdomen. He appeared to be carved from marble, and I licked my lips as my eyes trailed lower to the V-shape between his hips that disappeared beneath his jeans.

If he's this gorgeous above the belt, what's he packing beneath those jeans?

My eyes widened at the thought. I hadn't thought about a man like that in over a decade, but then again, I'd never encountered a man as massive and ripped as Liam.

Wait a minute, was I objectifying Liam?

I was intrigued by the thought that maybe the tables had turned and—as a woman—perhaps it was within my rights to use a man's body. My mouth dropped open as a sigh escaped.

Quirking an eyebrow, he gestured to my phone.

Snapping out of my thoughts, I shifted to holding it to my ear with my shoulder while waving him off with both hands. I had enough to deal with without my mother hearing his voice.

"Amy? Amy, are you listening to me?" My mother's voice was getting louder.

Liam held out a single hand, but I shook my head. He climbed onto the bed, and I froze, my heart beating loudly enough to hear it in my ears as he crawled over me, pinning me to the bed with his large frame. My breathing became erratic as his head lowered, kissing the inside of my wrist. Shocked, my grip loosened on my phone, and it dropped silently onto the pillow.

Pulling back, Liam snatched the phone, placing it to his ear. "Hello?"

Finally able to draw a deep breath, I realized what he'd done. Anger washed over me, knowing he'd purposely used my body's reaction to get what he wanted.

This. This was the reason I stayed away from men. Liam was no better than the rest.

Sitting bolt upright in bed, I clutched the blankets to my chest, almost like a shield, while watching in horror as Liam began to speak to my mother. I could only hear Liam's half of the conversation, which added fuel to the fire.

"Of course, Mrs. Michaels, I understand why you'd be upset."

Pause.

"You're right. I should have asked for permission. Please forgive my error in judgment."

Halt.

"No, we have no immediate plans to leave Hartford."

Lull.

"You've been young and in love yourself. I simply couldn't wait to make Amy my wife."

Hold the phone. Did he just say *love?*

He's playing a part. Did you notice how he didn't say he loves you?

Right. It's all an act—just like last night.

None of this was real.

Maybe if I repeated that enough, I would start to believe it. This marriage was fucking with my head.

CHAPTER 11

Amy

FOLLOWING THE FOUNDATION FUNDRAISER, Liam and I returned to leading our separate lives. Burying myself in my work as we sprinted toward the holidays, I barely saw him. I needed that space to clear my head. The picture of us dancing went viral, and I was fielding, or more accurately, dodging calls from various media outlets asking for a comment. Being best friends with Natalie and having married royal brothers had upped the ante, at least in the press' eyes.

When recounting the night of the fundraiser with Natalie and Hannah, they hadn't believed my description of Liam. It was entirely out of character for him. I started to think I'd imagined it. I'd certainly had enough alcohol to impair my memory of the night's events.

No. I hadn't even had a single drop when he kissed my neck and called me sweetheart. Was he that good of an actor? He'd made it all feel so real.

Whatever it was, I needed to put it in the rear-view mirror. It was in the past, and we had a lot coming up in our future. There were only a few months left before the finalists' pilot programs would be evaluated at the Foundation. My eyes had to be on the prize—it was the only reason I married Liam in the first place.

Speaking of marriage to Liam, as soon as Christmas was over, we would be flying to Belleston for our first official appearance as a royal couple. It was a big deal, even if Liam wasn't the heir. Natalie's wedding to Leo had been over a decade ago, and the country was seemingly eager to meet their new princess—the last of this generation.

Yep, that's me. A freaking princess. How did I get here?

Focus, Amy.

That's just what I did. I went to work, came home, and spent evenings at Natalie's helping with the kids. Some nights were more fun than others as I helped as an extra set of hands at Jaxon's hockey games. Watching how excited the kids were to see him play warmed my heart. They loved Jaxon, and he loved them. Every single one of them deserved the happiness they now enjoyed.

Christmas was fast approaching, so my spare time was spent planning what presents to buy the kids. This year would be Charlie's first Christmas, and it already promised to be extra magical. These kids were so loved, and I was proud to be considered a part of their extended family.

Quickly, I learned that shopping in person was no longer an option. People were curious about the local girl-turned-princess, and I suddenly understood why my best friend had often hidden inside her own home. It was overwhelming to go out in public and have perfect strangers whip out their phones to take pictures or videos as you roamed the grocery store aisles. Then, the next day, the internet would debate which type of apple reigned supreme based on which one I chose.

Forget shopping for clothing—I didn't need anyone commenting on what size or style I selected in that arena. That had nearly wrecked Natalie, even if Leo had been the driving force in the feeding frenzy. As I'd told

Liam, I was happy with how I looked, and others' opinions wouldn't change that. But it didn't need to be a topic for open discussion—people needed to mind their own damn business.

This wasn't some cartoon fairy tale where an instant transformation happened to the girl who married a prince.

If only people knew how non-glamourous being Liam's princess actually was.

With the current circus surrounding my life, I resorted to buying all my Christmas gifts online this year. It hurt my soul because it stole some of the magic from the season. Every year, I made a point of going to the Christmas market in downtown Hartford, where I found unique gifts for family and friends while admiring the handiwork of locals sharing their craft with the community. Clicking a button on a website seemed cold and clinical by comparison.

Perhaps that foreshadowed what the rest of my life would be like.

Christmas was over in a blur of making cookies, watching movies, and excited, screaming children. I tried desperately to savor these moments, knowing how quickly the children were growing up. Amelia was already ten and starting to realize that Santa might be fictitious—another reminder their innocence was fleeting. I needed to soak up every minute of their youth before it became a distant memory.

Days later, Liam and I boarded a private plane that would take us to Belleston for our debut as a couple. Our names were trending on all social media platforms as they anticipated our arrival. This New Year's Eve party became the country's most sought-after ticket—everyone wanted to be there to see us together.

Not only did the country want to see us madly in love as a couple, but the same would also be expected of us from Liam's family. From my brief text interactions with his younger sister, Lucy, no one had any inkling that our marriage wasn't real. That was good news but stressful in its own right—our act would have to be believable on a grand scale to convince not only Liam's parents, the Crown Prince and Princess, but also his grandfather, the King.

No pressure.

Our plane departed at 6 AM, so with the six-hour time difference and an almost nine-hour flight, we would land in Belleston in the late evening. I'd declined the option for a red-eye last night to spend the time on our flight working, hopeful that I could sleep through the night upon our arrival and avoid jet lag.

The joke was on me as I stared blankly at my computer screen, unable to make my eyes focus. Frustrated that I was losing half a week of work on our trip, I shut my laptop. Digging into my travel tote, I searched for my earbuds so I could listen to music and unwind. Right on top was a book with a cartoonish cover and a sticky note with a message.

> *It's a long flight. Figured you'd need something to pass the time.*
> *Keep an open mind.* —*Nat*

Removing the note, it became clear the book was a romance novel—one of Natalie's weaknesses was that she was a hopeless romantic and devoured sappy stories guaranteeing a happy ending. I'd never believed in that crap, and she knew it.

Sighing, I was still bent over my bag, staring down the offending book, when Liam asked, "Something wrong?"

Glancing up, I saw his scowl was back, which comforted me—I didn't know why. Maybe because that was normal, and I was spinning out.

Tucking a loose strand of hair behind my ear, I asked, "Was Natalie at the house?"

"Yeah, she dropped by last night. Said something about leaving something behind."

Typical. "Yeah, I bet she did."

"Is there a problem?" he asked, eying me closely.

"No, just a meddling best friend. Nothing to worry about." I sighed.

"All right." Not pressing further, he returned to working on whatever occupied his time on his own computer.

Snatching out the book and the earbuds I was searching for, I mentally rolled my eyes but read the back book blurb—something to do with two friends becoming lovers, then falling in love.

Really, Natalie? Could you be any more obvious?

If she thought that would happen to Liam and me, she had another thing coming. Yes, I found myself speechless more than once during the fundraiser. And again the following morning, but that didn't mean anything. We had an agreement—business with no pleasure. Sex was off the table.

Is that what the contract said? No sex? Or that sex wasn't a requirement?

Willing my brain to stop asking questions I didn't want the answers to, I opened Natalie's "gift" to Page 1.

An hour later, I was sucked into the story, where the main characters' attraction crept up on them before they finally gave in and slept together.

It was so mushy and would never happen in real life—that was not how things worked. People were either attracted to each other, or they weren't. You didn't one day realize you were hot for a friend.

Practically throwing the book on the table before me, I muttered, "So unrealistic."

"Excuse me?" Liam asked, eyeing the offending book.

"Nothing," I huffed.

"Doesn't look like nothing," he countered.

"Freaking Natalie and her fairy tale bullshit." I let out a breath so heavy a lock of hair blew away from my face.

The tiniest smirk curled on Liam's lips. "Now we're getting some-where."

"Don't get me wrong, I'm thrilled she got the happy ending she was searching for, but that's not for everyone. These books she reads—there's no way ninety-nine percent of these scenarios would ever happen. It's false advertising for how life and love actually unfold, creating unrealistic expectations for men and women alike."

"How so?"

Narrowing my eyes across the table at him, I challenged, "Have you ever read one of these romance novels?"

"Can't say that I have," he admitted.

"Well, let me enlighten you. They're all variations of the same story—the girl usually has some kind of a hang-up, and this perfect man comes along and makes her believe in love. Blah, blah, blah. Then something happens, a conflict, and they break up—every damn time. Then someone realizes they're an idiot and apologizes—sometimes there's a grand gesture—but they always end up back together. Life doesn't work like that. Not all women are broken, and not all men are perfect. And don't even get me started on how all the men are gods in bed with huge dicks."

Liam snorted. "Are they not, then?"

"Don't." I was not in the mood and threw him a death glare.

Throwing his hands up in defense, he asked, "What? I can only speak for myself, so I don't know what all the other men are up to."

"Not funny, Liam."

Those piercing blue eyes found mine. "Who said I was joking, Amy?"

The male hubris was strong. Was Liam sitting across from me, implying he was a sex god? Maybe the women he'd been with had been exceptional fakers—he had no way of knowing. The "huge dick" part of the equation gave me pause, and I couldn't help myself from discreetly trying to peek over at his lap, but my lack of X-ray vision left that question unanswered.

"All you have to do is ask, Amy."

Gasping, I looked up, cheeks flaming at having been caught staring at his crotch.

As if I wasn't humiliated enough, he added, "There is a bedroom in the back. We are married, after all."

Was he serious right now? I couldn't tell. There was no inflection in his voice that would hint at whether he was messing with me, or if he was willing to take me into the bedroom and not only confirm the size of his dick but show me that he knew how to use it.

My only experience in bed with a man had been bumpy, awkward, and painful as hell. The only bright spot was that it hadn't lasted very long. I wasn't naïve. I knew it got better, that some men were more skilled, but there was no way they were handing out female orgasms at will—no matter what Natalie said about Jaxon's skills. It simply defied common sense. There wouldn't be thousands of sex toy options designed for women to take control of their own sexual pleasure if they could get that easily from a man.

Shaking the notion of Liam's offer—genuine or not—from my head, I changed the subject. "Can we talk about the New Year's Eve party?"

Liam crossed his legs, bringing an ankle to rest atop the opposite knee. "Sure. What do you want to know?"

"I'm just curious as to which Liam plans to show up, so I can be prepared."

His dark brows drew downward. "Which Liam? I'm not sure I follow. There is only one of me, the last time I checked."

"Cut the crap, Liam," I snapped. "I want to know if I'm going to get the normal, surly Liam or if that freaky, smiling, charming Liam from the night of the fundraiser will reappear."

"You don't like it when I'm charming?" A hint of that smile tugged at the corner of his lips.

Crossing my arms, I glared at him. "It's unsettling, to say the least, especially when I had no warning that was going to happen. I only want to know what to expect in front of your family, so I can get my head straight. Is that too much to ask?"

Pressing further, he crossed his arms, mirroring my actions. "What are you really asking, Amy?"

Was he going to make me say it? Fine. "I want to know if I should expect any kisses on random body parts without warning. Or unauthorized terms of endearment."

"Unauthorized?" Leaning back in his seat, he carefully surveyed me from across the table.

Rolling my eyes, I scoffed. "It's not like we discussed it beforehand—I was caught completely off guard. Just tell me what the night will look like regarding our interactions. That's all I ask."

"All right. No, this will not be quite like your event. This will be slightly more formal."

"Black Tie wasn't formal enough?" I challenged.

"If you thought that party was an act, you have no idea. All eyes will be on us as royals the night of the New Year's Eve party. When we land, there will be a day dedicated to protocol, as you did not get that benefit prior to our hasty marriage—there is an image we are expected to portray to the public. No, there will not be any public displays of affection from me beyond perhaps a kiss on the cheek or a hand around your waist. Dancing will be for others, not for us. We will be expected to make the rounds, work the crowd, and entertain as hosts."

That was a relief, but I couldn't help but ask, "And before that? In front of your parents, the rest of your family?"

One of his eyebrows raised in response. "Are you asking if we are expected to be pawing each other in front of my parents? If so, the answer is hell no."

"Okay, just checking how deep our level of commitment is."

"'Til death do us part." Liam shot me a smug look.

"Smartass," I retorted.

Done with the conversation, I shoved in my earbuds and cranked up the music. It was time to turn off my brain before I had to put on the show of a lifetime.

CHAPTER 12

Liam

IT WAS LATE EVENING when we touched down in Remhorn, and even with the long day of travel, I was wired. Amy went straight to bed in her designated bedroom in our apartment inside Stonecrest Palace, but I was wide awake. My brain simply would not shut off.

Sitting across from Amy for nine hours was torture, especially once the word dick had left her mouth, followed by her eyes dropping to the vicinity of my fly. I could see the curiosity in their green depths after I teased her over her book. My offer to take her into the bedroom of the private plane had been genuine. If she'd said yes, I would have taken her back and shown her exactly how a real man fucked. Then, she could decide whether the explicit scenes in her book were fictitious.

I was losing my damn mind. There was no other explanation.

I'd convinced myself that my reaction the night of the fundraiser had been a fluke. In the following weeks, my mind was clear as I steered clear of my wife. Over Christmas, seeing how vibrant and happy she was around our nieces and nephews showcased how beautiful I found her—not only her face and body, but her spirit. She cared so much for others. It was a part of who she was, and I could picture how incredible she'd be by my side as my queen.

I was in big trouble.

I only managed to fall asleep by downing a generous amount of bourbon. It was an alcohol-induced slumber, but I was restless even then. Tossing and turning as images of Amy invaded my dreams—above me, below me, on her knees, against a wall—my subconscious knew no bounds. The echo of her moans haunted me as I woke.

None of it was real, and I needed to get a grip. Fast.

That idea went up in smoke as I made my way into the breakfast room of our apartment to find her standing, staring out the floor-length window. Stopping in my tracks, I drank in the sight of her. Amy wore a silk robe, her bare calves and feet peeking out. Hair pulled atop her head haphazardly; the sun streaming through the window cast it in an orangey glow. Her fingers were delicately curled around a china teacup as steam rose toward her face.

Inextricably drawn to her, my feet moved automatically until I stood behind her. Amy hadn't noticed my presence, even though I was close enough that her scent invaded my nostrils. The view framed in the window was that of the snow-capped Alps.

"Beautiful," I breathed barely above a whisper. I wasn't talking about the mountains.

Amy stiffened slightly, the sound of my voice startling her. Turning her head, those gorgeous green eyes met mine, and my heart squeezed.

Looking back out the window, she agreed, "It is. I've never visited in winter before. The view is breathtaking."

Glancing at the majestic mountains I'd taken for granted—much like the woman standing before me—I began to see them through her eyes.

"Maybe next time, we can make some time for recreation. Have you been skiing?"

The smile in her voice was audible. "Yes, but it's been a while. Not sure we need to add a broken leg to our narrative."

"You think I will ever let anything hurt you?"

Turning her to face me, there were barely six inches of space between us. My body was hyper-aware of how close we were, tingling in response.

Searching my face, Amy sighed. "Liam, even you can't protect me from myself."

The words were at the tip of my tongue that I would spend the rest of my life trying, when the door to the room burst open. The sudden intrusion shocked us both, and we spun to see who had entered without knocking—the staff knew better than that.

My baby sister, Lucy, rushed into the room, and I instantly forgave the interruption. Her coloring matched mine—with her long raven-colored hair and Remington Blue eyes—but she was petite, a stark contrast to my bulky frame. Following Lucy were several women pushing in racks of clothing. My sister's fashion label had taken off, and I may have been slightly biased, but she deserved the accolades she received.

Spotting me, Lucy crossed her arms. "Get out."

"Why? Last time I checked, this was my apartment," I challenged. The pair of us were stubborn to a fault.

"Because I'm mad at you," she declared.

"What sin have I committed now?" With Lucy, any minor transgression could be blown out of proportion.

"You got married and didn't tell me! Then, you ignored all my calls and messages. Some big brother you are." She was full-out pouting by this point.

Stalking toward her, I grinned before grabbing her in a bear hug and teasing her, "Aw, LuLu, are you mad that I got married before you?"

Wiggling in my arms, she kicked her legs wildly. "Put me down!" Obeying her request, I allowed her feet to touch the ground before releasing my grasp. Glaring at me, she added, "And don't call me LuLu. I'm not a baby anymore."

"You'll always be my baby sister," I teased.

"I'm twenty-eight years old," she huffed.

Amy approached, coming to Lucy's defense. "And a badass boss bitch."

Lucy squealed. "Amy!" Throwing her arms around my wife, she pulled her close before continuing to lecture me. "At least one of you knows how to pick up the phone."

Filled with a mixture of annoyance at my little sister and joy at seeing Amy lighting up, I shrugged. "I didn't answer anyone's calls, Lucy. I turned off my phone."

Narrowing her eyes, she scoffed. "Likely story."

"I just wanted some time. Is that so much to ask?"

"Well, your time is up. The Big Wigs are waiting for you in the gold drawing room."

Big Wigs was our code name for Grandfather, Father, and Mother. Cringing, I dared to ask, "How bad is it?"

"You eloped, Liam. What do you think?" She popped her hip, giving me attitude.

Yeah, I'd known that was going to ruffle some feathers, but I was exercising my right to rebellion at having my life suddenly altered. It was subtle, but there was gratification to be found in knowing they were upset. I only hoped they wouldn't take it out on Amy. I wouldn't allow it.

Dropping into a mock bow, I straightened before taking my leave. "Ladies, I'll leave you to it."

Exiting the breakfast room, I turned down the hallway that would take me out of our apartment before spitting me out into the main corridor of the palace. I was assigned this apartment on my twenty-fifth birthday—a silent implication that I was old enough to begin thinking about settling down. The term "apartment" was used loosely. The two-leveled lodging contained as many rooms as the average house. The first floor featured the breakfast room, living room, dining room, and a basic kitchen. The second floor housed a master suite containing dual master bedrooms—each featuring its own ensuite bathroom—separated by a small sitting area. Across the hall was what was meant to become a nursery suite eventually. Three years ago, when I left, I never imagined bringing home a wife to this apartment, but I knew for sure that the nursery suite would never be occupied.

I was walking into the lion's den once I entered the gold drawing room—I knew that. I followed their rules but with a twist. My irritation with the current situation was further heightened by the fact that I suddenly found my wife irresistible. Unless I spent all day jacking off, I would be in a constant state of sexual frustration, which was bound to affect all other aspects of my life.

The door was slightly ajar, so I waltzed in unannounced, hoping the element of surprise would lessen whatever reprimand I was about to receive.

I was wrong.

Immediately, Grandfather spotted me and accused, "Another American, Liam?"

Dripping my head out of respect, I countered, "What's wrong with Americans?"

"Didn't we learn anything from the last one? They aren't cut out for this life."

Clenching my fists, I struggled to keep my tone respectful. "Are we basing Natalie's shortcomings on her nationality and pretending it had nothing to do with Leo's mind games?"

Conceding my point, he responded, "Be that as it may, they don't understand the rigors of royalty, having no point of reference in their own country."

Father jumped in. "What was the rush, Liam? You've never been one to be impulsive."

Shrugging, I was unapologetic. "You stripped me of control of my own life, so I decided to hang onto one of the few things I could still command. My life will become a circus, and I didn't want my wedding to be."

Grandfather spoke again. "Is this a joke to you, William?"

"Feels more like a bad dream," I muttered.

"What was that?" His voice rose, sensing my defiance.

"Nothing, sir." I held his gaze, not backing down.

"Does she know?" He was referring to my change in circumstance.

"No, sir."

"Good. Keep it that way. We can't afford a leak. This is a delicate matter."

Delicate matter—that was putting it mildly. There was no way Amy would have agreed to marry me if she knew. There was going to be hell to pay when she found out.

Thankfully, we had been discussing the matter vaguely because that was when Leo decided to appear.

Spotting me, he was smug. "Well, well, well. The spare returns. And it seems he brought a little extra baggage." Pausing, he wrinkled his nose in disgust. "Well, maybe not that little. Didn't anyone tell you don't mix business with pleasure, little brother?"

Itching to punch him in the face—not just for the slight against my wife but for all he'd done to Natalie—somehow, I held myself in check. "Shut up, Leo."

Undeterred, he continued, "If you were going to follow my lead and pick an American, you could have chosen better. That one's got too much self-confidence. You need a weak-minded woman you can lead blindly and that won't talk back."

"Marriage is a partnership, not a dictatorship." I forced the words out through clenched teeth—the leash I held on my anger was beginning to fray.

A sinister smile lit up Leo's face. "It suddenly makes sense."

I knew better but took the bait. "What?"

"You're not man enough to dominate a woman, so you require a strong one to lead you by the nose. You'd have made a terrible king if you were the firstborn."

Lunging for my brother—the shocked look on his face was satisfying—I stopped dead when my grandfather's voice boomed, "Enough!"

Facing the man whose current command identified him more as our sovereign than our grandfather, my eyes shifted toward the floor as I apologized. "Sorry, sir. I was out of line."

Leo, however, was as arrogant as ever. "See? Proving my point that you don't have what it takes." He couldn't help himself and added, "At least he knows how to grovel. That'll be a useful skill, especially in the bedroom, it seems."

Father stepped in. "Get out, Leo."

Entitlement was never more evident as Leo protested, "What did I do? He's the caveman who attempted to attack me!"

Using the same tone as our king, Father brooked no argument. "You were not invited to this meeting. See yourself out."

Huffing with indignation that there might be any meeting he would not be privy to, Leo threw one last parting shot as he left the room. "Be grateful I'm not already on the throne because I would have you thrown into the dungeon and left you to rot."

Having the good sense to know I was already in trouble for my unapproved marriage, combined with losing my temper, I remained silent, glaring at my older brother. Karma was coming for him.

Once he was gone, Grandfather chastised, "You need to keep a level head, William."

"Yes, sir."

"While nothing can be done about your marriage as the headlines have already made their way around the world, it will fall upon you to ensure she fits the role. Don't disappoint me."

The implication was that if our photograph hadn't landed in the newspaper and gone viral, he would have forced a dissolution of our union. The idea of losing Amy—even the small part of her that I had—hit me like a punch to the gut. No, that wasn't an option. I'd turn my back on my country if I had to choose. Damn the consequences.

Grandfather took his leave, and I bowed to my king as he retreated.

Father also headed out with a few parting words. "I hope you know what you're doing, son."

That makes two of us.

With both men gone, Mother approached where I stood, a slight smile on her lips. She'd been through enough, and I felt remorse for complicating this situation.

"I'm sorry, Mother." I dipped my head.

Reaching up, she cupped my cheek. "Nothing to apologize for, darling. Don't let them bully you. I think Amy was a wonderful choice."

Stunned after the verbal discontent by the male members of our family, my voice was barely a whisper. "Truly?"

Mother's smile widened to reach her walnut-colored eyes, which sparkled. "You're well-suited. She shares your sense of loyalty and is fiercely passionate about helping others. Amy will be the perfect complement at your side as your queen."

"Thank you, Mother."

"Everything will sort itself out. You'll be fine." With that, she left the room, leaving me alone.

Mother's confidence was a stark contrast to the confusion I felt when it came to Amy. She didn't believe in love, and I feared hurting any woman who got too close. It was better for us to keep our distance and treat our marriage like the business arrangement I'd promised, but I couldn't get her out of my head.

The sex would be incredible, of that I was sure, but was it worth the risk? Nights filled with pleasure versus a lifetime of partnership? It didn't feel possible to obtain both.

The fashion and makeup team for Amy arrived in our apartment on New Year's Eve to help prepare her for the evening, several hours before our presence was expected. Trying to distract myself, I absconded to the palace library. This room, with its floor-to-ceiling stacks of books, had been my childhood refuge. I'd curl up in a chair and lose myself in worlds created with words. The fact that Leo never set foot in there had been an added bonus.

Scanning the shelves containing first-edition classics among newer prints of thrillers, historical fiction, science fiction, action-adventure, and even romance, I made a choice, plucking a book from the masses. Sitting in my favorite chair, I cracked open the book in my hands, taking a deep whiff of the pages within. There was nothing like it.

As hard as I tried, I couldn't get my eyes to focus on the words as they blurred on the page. My mind was elsewhere and wouldn't settle. Eyes straying back to the shelves, I spotted the colorful section of romance novels and smiled.

Mother shared Natalie's addiction to a guaranteed happy ending. Natalie was supposed to be Belleston's future queen—instead of her best friend—but life had other plans. Could I make Amy as happy as Natalie now was with Jaxon?

What did I know about relationships?

My grandparents had been in an arranged marriage, but they'd been happy together, at least on the surface—you never really knew what happened in any marriage behind closed doors. They had produced only a single child, after all. My father was their only heir.

My parents were a love match. Mother was the daughter of an earl, but their relationship hadn't been forced. The home I was raised in had been full of warmth and love. More times than I could count, we'd caught them kissing, their eyes shining with silent promises. They were living the fairy tale—well, mostly. Leo's origin story was a black mark on that perfection, again proving that nothing was as it seemed.

While I'd been single since before following Natalie across the ocean, finding female companionship had never been an issue. Women were intrigued by my royal status, but I had to be discerning. Being careful in my screening process not to have nude photos of myself sold to the tabloids led me to date women within my social class—heiresses or nobility, with the occasional model or two thrown in the mix. Every one of those relationships had been superficial. I never let them get close enough to do more than scratch the surface of my steely exterior.

Amy fit that mold in that she was an heiress, but she was so different from all those who had come before her in my life. She wasn't a bored, spoiled brat living off her daddy's money—Amy made a difference in the world. Her emotions and style weren't carefully crafted to garner the perfect reaction from those around her. Amy was authentic and unfiltered, and I admired that about her.

This world had the power to destroy her. *I* had the power to destroy her.

The only way to keep her safe was to keep my distance. Those words kept finding their way into my mind, but I couldn't seem to listen. Like a virus, the need for Amy had taken root inside my body, and I felt powerless to stop the inevitable.

At some point, being near Amy would push me past the breaking point, and I'd be unable to control making her mine in every sense of the word.

CHAPTER 13

Liam

THIS EVENING REQUIRED WHITE Tie, and I was quickly reminded how much I hated a tailcoat whenever I attempted to shove my hands into its nonexistent pockets. Pacing outside Amy's bedroom—awaiting her appearance so I could escort her to our formal staging area for the ball—my annoyance was escalating.

I'd already downed my fair share of pre-party alcohol, knowing the press would report on how much we drank in front of our guests. The familiar warmth of bourbon in my blood only fueled my impatience.

Checking my pocket watch for probably the fifteenth time in as many minutes, I finally dared to rap my knuckles on her door, trying to keep my tone level as I announced, "We have five minutes, Amy. Are you almost ready?"

Amy's soft voice was laced with anxiety in her response through the door. "I'm going to need every one of those five minutes. Can I meet you down there?"

Dropping my forehead to the wood of her door, my shoulders rose and fell with my silent sigh. "Sure. Do you know where to go?"

"A footman can point me in the right direction if I get lost. They've been helping me all week."

"All right. I'll see you down there in five."

Pushing off the door, I walked toward the antechamber to the ballroom, where we were expected to wait before being announced to the ball already in progress. It was all very pretentious. Were you even a royal if you didn't make a grand entrance?

Our entrances would be staggered. Junior royals, which included me and my siblings, would go first, followed by senior royals, such as my parents, culminating with the entrance of the King.

I hated this part of our life.

Anyone who wanted to trade places with us wouldn't last long. No one would sign on for their life being made available for public scrutiny with nonexistent privacy. You weren't allowed to be upset that others were constantly watching you like you were in a display case for their amusement. You didn't get to be selfish. Your life was about service to others.

No amount of money was enough to make this gilded cage bearable.

And now, I'd brought Amy into this life. My pace quickened, thinking about her voice betraying how uncertain she must be feeling about this evening. If she crumbled under the pressure, I would never forgive myself. It would be my fault.

Pushing through the double doors and down the stairs of the antechamber above the ballroom, I was grateful to be the first to arrive. Already on edge, I didn't need to deal with Leo until I absolutely had to. He had never been my favorite person growing up, but I hadn't grown to hate him until I watched him destroy Natalie's life. If Leo tested the limits of my restraint—thinking that his position as heir was enough to protect him—he'd be surprised to find that I would gladly strangle him with my bare hands.

You didn't fuck with the ones I loved and be allowed to live to tell the tale.

Like all rooms within Stonecrest Palace, this one was richly appointed with centuries-old rugs on the floor and priceless works of art along the walls. Gold crown molding accented the hand-chosen décor—painstakingly curated by a team of royal decorators and changed each time a new monarch took the throne.

The doors at the top of the staircase opened, and the woman who appeared stole the breath from my lungs. Green satin hugged her upper body—the swell of her breasts peeking above the bodice—before flaring out to full skirts that swirled around her hips. Her perfect hourglass figure was on full display. As she walked down the steps, the creamy white skin of one leg peeked out through a thigh-high slit. The color of the dress accented that of her eyes, causing them to shine like emeralds.

I swallowed involuntarily. My clothes, tailored to perfection, suddenly felt too tight.

Amy's red hair was pulled up, drawing attention to the long column of her throat. A sparkling diamond tiara graced the top of her head, announcing her royal status to the world. The icing didn't stop there as the jewels gracing her earlobes, neck, and wrist caught the lights of the room. Most important of all was the diamond on her left hand, silently communicating to anyone who saw it that she belonged to me.

That gorgeous creature is my wife.

Possession—primal and overwhelming—hit me in full force. My Amy was professionally made up, but the makeup merely highlighted her incredible facial features. I was mesmerized as she descended the stairs, seemingly in slow motion.

"She looks incredible, doesn't she?" I nearly jumped out of my skin at Lucy's voice in my ear. Where had she come from? Barely sparing her a

glance, my gaze returned to my wife as she approached. Lucy continued, "I knew that color would be perfect on her." She sighed apprecia-
tively. "And her curves deserve to be celebrated."

Afraid to even blink in case the vision before me disappeared, I asked
my sister, "One of yours?" Lucy's creativity in fashion knew no bounds.

"Custom-made. Seemed only fitting, considering I did Natalie's
wedding dress." Nudging me with her elbow, she teased, "Like waiting
a couple of months would have killed you."

"Might have." My throat was tight. Waiting hadn't been an option
for Amy, and for that, I was grateful. Had we waited, she might have
changed her mind, and we wouldn't be here now. This moment was
too precious to have let slip through my fingers.

"Consider it a wedding gift."

Wedding gift indeed.

Amy reached the bottom of the stairs but avoided my gaze as she
gracefully glided to where I stood with Lucy. When she moved within
an arm's reach, I snaked my hand around her waist, pulling her close
enough to kiss her cheek, whispering low in her ear, "You're stunning."

Taking a half step back, I got a front-row seat to the blush that crept
up her neck. But I found myself frowning as her eyes remained glued
to the floor. Grasping her chin, I tilted her face upward, forcing her
to meet my eye. Those emeralds shone back at me, uncertain. She was
nervous, which was understandable, but she needed to know I meant
what I said.

My hand at her waist tightened, and Amy's eyes widened slightly.

Sheepishly, she asked, "Are you sure I'm not showing too much leg?"

Seizing an opportunity to lighten the mood, I smirked. "Honestly?"
Amy stared, waiting for me to answer my own question. "I think Lucy
may be losing her touch. I need at least six more inches showing."

Her laugh vibrated through her chest, and the aftershocks reached my fingertips, still holding her close. Seeing Amy loosen up, a smile gracing her lips, warmed me from head to toe.

Blushing again, she countered, "Not sure we need to cause an international incident involving indecent exposure."

The question of whether she wore panties under those skirts had my cock hardening.

Biting back a groan, I forced out, "Ames, you look gorgeous. They're going to love you." Her eyes searched mine, and I knew what she was thinking, so I added, "I've never lied to you, have I?"

Good thinking. Dig the hole deeper for when she discovers your lie of omission regarding your new place in the line of succession.

Amy's eyes sparkled, her confidence returning as she shook her head carefully, mindful of the tiara gracing her head. "No."

Every cell in my body screamed for me to kiss her, but I promised her tonight wouldn't be a repeat of my actions at her fundraiser. I knew what would be expected of us once we entered the ballroom, but damn if I didn't want to have a private moment with her first.

Seconds away from mentally saying "fuck it" and kissing my wife, my blood ran cold when a voice behind me drawled, "Hello, little sister."

Amy stiffened beneath my grasp, and her voice was low, forced out between clenched teeth as she glared past me to where Leo must have been standing. "I am *not* your little sister."

Turning to face Leo, I kept my arm around Amy's waist in a silent show of solidarity.

Leo was his usual, polished self, ready to fool the world once more into believing he was the charming, perfect prince. Only those closest to him knew the truth.

Leo ignored Amy's statement, continuing, "Can't say I'm surprised you got your claws into my brother. It was awfully *convenient*."

There was no chance that Leo had uncovered the truth behind my marriage to Amy, but he was pushing invisible buttons to provoke a reaction from either of us. That's what he did.

"Leave them alone, Leo. You're not exactly the poster boy for the perfect marriage. Remind me, where is your wife again? Oh, that's right. She's moved on with a younger, hotter man."

I'd almost forgotten Lucy was there until she spoke, as Leo tended to suck all the air out of a room. To her credit, Lucy could be feisty when she wanted, a testament to her being the baby sister and having to fend off two older brothers.

Leo only sneered at Lucy before stalking closer to where Amy and I stood. My grip on Amy tightened, and I heard her breathing quicken—textbook fear response. I'd seen it in Natalie countless times, and my rage simmered beneath the surface that he was scaring my wife. Leo didn't deserve to breathe the same air as Amy. She was innately good, the antithesis of Leo's inherent evil.

We stood our ground, and Amy kept her head held high. From my peripheral vision, I could tell she was fighting a war within herself, not to show a single sign of weakness. We both knew what would happen if she did.

Leo sized her up from head to toe as he moved toward us, stopping mere inches from where we stood before smirking and remarking, "Do yourself a favor, *little sis*. The next time you wear something tight, consider wearing shapewear. Something to suck you in. No one wants to see all of *that* on display."

I didn't remember having a conscious thought before I had Leo pinned against a wall, my forearm pressing against his throat, cutting off his air supply. Letting him squirm, trying to gasp for breath, I knew I could crush his trachea if I wanted to. I was taller and more muscular than my "big" brother, and his eyes widened when he realized he couldn't escape—he was wholly at my mercy.

Leaning in close, my vision hazed with red, I gritted out, "You don't look at my wife. You don't talk to my wife. Hell, you don't even think about my wife, or I will crush you with my bare hands. Do you understand me?"

Leo's chin dipped, barely able to move with how I had him immobilized, but I took satisfaction in watching his face turn red as he struggled beneath my arm. Putting him in his place had been long overdue.

Deaf to the commotion in response to my assault, my mother's voice finally broke through as she tugged my arm. "Liam! Let him go!"

As I removed my arm suddenly at her command, Leo crumpled to the floor, gasping, trying to fill his lungs with the air he'd been deprived of while in my grasp. Standing over his cowering form, my own breathing was heavy as I tried to control the rage flowing through my veins.

Leo clearly hadn't learned his lesson. As soon as his breathing calmed, he looked up at me with a snarl on his lips. "Someday, you will both bow to me as your sovereign."

That's what you think.

Resisting the urge to kick him while he was down—he'd get what was coming to him—I turned my back on him, returning to my wife. The sight before me only fueled my anger.

Amy was pale and shaky. Her eyes no longer sparkled. It didn't matter how strong a person was—my brother was a master manipulator whose strengths lay in exploiting the hidden insecurities of others. Watching the light dim in Amy's eyes, I realized Leo would have broken any woman that fell under his grasp.

Suddenly, I understood why my parents were willing to risk everything to keep him from tainting their legacy. Some of the anger I felt toward them began to melt away.

My focus narrowed on protecting my wife. That took priority over all else.

When I reached out for Amy, she flinched, driving home the fact he'd hurt her mentally.

Dropping my hand, my voice was soft, "Sweetheart, look at me."

The shock of using that name got her attention, and her eyes flashed to mine, but the hurt I saw there broke my heart. Trying desperately to bring back the woman who'd met me at the bottom of the stairs, I joked, "It's not too late for me to finish the job. Want me to kill him?"

Amy's voice was flat, emotionless in her response. "I'm not worth it."

Pain sliced through me at her words. Even if it took the rest of my life, I would make sure she knew she was worth everything to me—no one else mattered.

Leo would not ruin our lives, even if he had ruined this night for us both. Instantly, I decided that we would depart tomorrow. The sooner we got away from his toxicity, the better.

Space and time would help heal this hurt. It had to.

Taking her hand in mine, I tugged her toward the doors, which would open and present us to the party already in progress.

Squeezing her hand, I whispered, "Stay close to me."

Glancing over when she didn't respond, I found Amy's body rigid and tense, her eyes staring straight ahead. I squeezed her hand again, praying she'd squeeze back, showing me she was still in there somewhere. My hopes were dashed as she remained stone-still.

Lucy took her place ahead of us in front of the doors a moment before they opened. Music floated to where we stood as the ballroom glittered before us, full of smartly dressed partygoers consisting of politicians, nobility, and others of high social standing or wealth. It would be beautiful, exciting even, if this event wasn't just an opportunity for the country to have us royals put on display.

Nights like tonight were why I didn't want a permanent place in this world.

The band finished their song when it became known the junior royals were ready to be announced, as our butler, Maxwell, hit a staff against the marble flooring. All eyes turned to the ballroom balcony, where we stood at the top of a sweeping staircase.

Lucy would go first as the youngest sibling, and as Maxwell announced her, she turned back, giving a wink to Amy before descending, whispering, "You've got this. I'll be waiting for you at the bottom. Us Remington girls have got to stick together."

Once Lucy reached the bottom of the staircase, she moved just off to the right, standing and waiting as promised. Amy let out a shaky breath, untangling her fingers from mine before sliding them up my arm and grasping my elbow. Almost as if on autopilot, I propped that elbow out to escort her as our names were called. Amy's hand tightened on my arm as the party below us gave a raucous round of applause as the newest royal couple.

My main objective was getting Amy through tonight in one piece, which may have already become impossible thanks to the asshole I called brother.

How much longer until midnight?

The night droned on endlessly. Amy pasted a small smile on her face as we made the rounds—the perfect princess on my arm—but I knew she wasn't herself. Her green eyes were flat, expressionless. Only I could tell that her spark had been extinguished. She was suffering in silence while upholding her end of our bargain at great personal cost.

Lucy held true to her promise of staying close, and we moved as a pack around the room. Amy's fingers curled around the same glass of champagne she'd been nursing all night, lifting it to her lips but rarely taking a sip. That was a testament to her strength. A weaker person would be throwing back alcohol to numb their mind in hopes of forgetting the source of their pain.

Thankfully, we'd made it past the older generations of guests and were making it toward those closer to our own age. While conversations became less formal, these interactions brought new challenges—their questions surrounded how Amy and I fell so helplessly in love that we couldn't wait to get married. Our elopement brought out excitement and curiosity.

Amy fielded the questions effortlessly and gracefully. I was in awe that she could push past her struggles of the evening and put on a show. While it was impressive, deep down in my bones, I hated it.

I didn't want the perfect, polished Amy. I feared that too long in this world would turn her into a robot, and she'd lose herself. Everyone tonight seemingly loved her like this, but if they truly knew her as I did? They'd adore her.

"That can't be Liam Remington! He's been gone so long that I thought they'd revoked his citizenship!" A voice came from behind me, but I knew without looking precisely who the owner was.

Turning, I exclaimed, "Preston!" Pulling him into a hug, I added, "Man, it's been too long!"

Releasing my friend, I turned to my wife. "Amy, this is Preston Scott. We grew up together, only a year apart, in prep school. Preston, this is—"

"The woman of the hour," Preston finished for me, reaching out to take Amy's hand and placing a kiss upon her knuckles.

"Pleasure to meet you, Preston." Amy's lips quirked up slightly, and I could have sworn I saw a tiny flash of life re-enter her eyes. Maybe, just maybe, she was coming back to me.

Preston was charming. It came so naturally to him. "Tell me, Amy, how did you get this sourpuss to settle down? Between you and me, I think we had a silent game of chicken going to see who would get married first. You have my gratitude for allowing me to emerge victorious."

Amy laughed, the sound a balm for my battered soul. "It was challenging, but I can truthfully say it was all his idea."

They continued to have an easy banter. I held Preston in high esteem before, but tonight, he had my utmost appreciation for drawing Amy out. Busy watching Amy come back to life, a slight movement caught my eye, and I shifted my gaze to Lucy beside her. Her posture had become stiff, arms crossed, a scowl on her face as she glowered at Preston.

Raising an eyebrow in question at my little sister, she gave a slight shake of her head. Lucy stalked off, not even bothering to excuse herself, practically stomping in her heels.

What was that about?

Preston had teased Lucy when we were children, but she couldn't still be holding a grudge about that, right? They were adults now. Certainly, that was water under the bridge, but Lucy was known to be dramatic, so it could be anything.

Knowing how these events worked, Preston moved on after a time to allow others access to us, but I promised him we'd have to get together the next time I was in the country. A few more groups of young people gushed over us, and I reached my limit, especially when Amy withdrew again once Preston took his leave.

Checking my pocket watch, we were closing in on midnight, but I was done for the evening.

Leaning over to Amy, I whispered, "Would you like to leave?"

Sighing, she replied, "Please."

Grasping her hand, I led her to where my parents held court after Grandfather had left. He was too old for the late-night events and had only presided over the ball for an hour, leaving my father the most senior-ranking royal in the room, to which people flocked.

Pulling Mother to the side privately, I explained, "We are going to call it a night if that's acceptable?"

My mother nodded. "Of course. These events can be quite taxing, and you're newlyweds, after all." Reaching for Amy's hand, she beamed. "You did wonderful, darling."

Amy gave a slight curtsy. "Thank you, Ma'am."

There was a twinkle in Mother's eyes when she looked up at me. "You did good, Liam."

Giving a slight bow of my head to my mother and father, I pulled Amy from the ballroom through a side door. She was silent as we walked through the maze of hallways until we reached the private wing housing our apartment. Amy didn't allow me to open our entry door as she pushed past me, turning the knob before rushing down the interior hallway as fast as her legs could carry her in heels.

Slamming the door closed behind me, I stalked after her, calling out, "Amy!"

Ignoring me, she turned to head up the stairs. Taking them two at a time behind her, I caught up just as she burst into the sitting room between our dual master bedrooms.

Overheated from chasing Amy through the house, I shrugged out of my tailcoat and began to unbutton my waistcoat when I heard her blurt out, "This was a mistake."

My hands froze on the buttons over my abdomen as she moved about the room frantically, reaching down to remove her heels.

"What was a mistake?"

Distraught, Amy worked on removing her earrings next. "Coming here. This marriage. It was too much to think we could pull this off. I'm not good enough for this life—not good enough for you. You don't want me here. I'll ruin everything."

Her back was to me as she spoke, so she couldn't see when the dam finally broke. Ripping the waistcoat open, buttons scattered silently across the floor before I reached up to unknot my bowtie. Unable to stand hearing her doubt herself a moment longer, I crossed the room in three strides, turning her to face me.

Using the element of surprise, I ignored Amy's gasp as I walked her backward, only stopping once she was pinned between myself and the wall.

Eyes wide, she searched my face. "What are you doing, Liam?"

Placing one hand on the wall beside her head, I was losing control. My chest heaved, each breath causing it to brush against the swell of her breasts tightly contained in her dress. Aroused and angry was a dangerous combination—I was ready to explode in more ways than one.

Every ounce of my energy was being poured into holding back, so when I didn't respond, it prompted her to ask again, "Liam?"

Without her heels, I had a slightly larger height advantage, and her head craned to look up at me.

I forced out through clenched teeth, "You think I don't want you?" Leaning forward, I pressed my erection against her soft waist, groaning even though countless layers of fabric separated us. "Does that feel like I don't want you?"

Amy's mouth dropped open, and her body shifted beneath mine, rubbing against my hardness in silent invitation.

That's all it took, and the floodgates opened. Dipping my head, I tugged a bare earlobe between my teeth until I heard a moan slipping from her mouth. Moving down her jaw, I trailed hungry kisses until I reached her collarbone.

Her erratic breathing pushed the tops of her creamy breasts higher as they begged to be set free. Barely able to fit more than a finger inside the tight bodice hugging her curves, I reached inside, giving a gentle tug until a single breast popped free of its binding. The pretty pink nipple hardened into a tight little bud when encountering the cooler air before I palmed it, the heavy mound overflowing my large hands.

A thud from above signaled Amy's head dropping back against the wall. I knew I was on borrowed time. At some point, she would realize what we were doing and ask me to stop—it was inevitable. Amy had a past, and I respected how that would come into play. Locking eyes with her now had the power to break whatever trance of pleasure she was in, and I needed to show her how irresistible I found her just as she was.

Leaning down, I took that enticing peak into my mouth and sucked hard, eliciting a throaty gasp from Amy's mouth as she arched into my ministrations. Using my teeth, I rolled the hardened nub between them, nibbling as she writhed against me, searching for more. Giving one last pull, I released her before dropping to my knees.

Gripping her full hips hard with both hands, my voice was strangled. "Your curves are gorgeous."

Amy whimpered above me, a single word giving me pause.

"No."

"No, what?"

"No, they're not."

Growling, I dug my fingers in harder. "Dammit, don't you get it? These hips are what men dream about. Lush, full, and perfect for grabbing ahold of."

My right hand dropped to the slit of her skirt, circling her ankle before traveling further north, reaching her knee. Amy's leg shook, and I could have sworn a hint of her arousal entered my nostrils. My cock was throbbing, insistent against my fly, but I had no intention of releasing it—not tonight. This was all for Amy.

Teasing the sensitive flesh at the back of her knee, Amy's legs almost buckled, but I pressed her harder against the wall, holding her up. Spreading my fingers, I continued their journey up her thigh until I reached the top of the slit on her dress. The only thing keeping me from ripping it open the remaining six inches was respect for the time and effort that had gone into creating this green masterpiece.

Shoving both hands under the skirt, I lifted the fabric, bunching it until I had a full view of those luscious hips. Groaning, I damn near swallowed my tongue when I discovered that not only was she not wearing panties, but that her pussy was completely bare.

Playing with fire, I looked up at her, asking reverently, "Did you do this for me?"

Thankfully her head was still tilted back against the wall. Her eyes remained closed as she shook her head. "Never again."

Understanding dawned that the last man to see her this vulnerable had used it against her, and she'd taken drastic steps to prevent that ever being a factor again. This mouthwateringly bare pussy was Amy's protection.

Intent on worshiping the woman quivering in my arms, I nudged her legs apart, exposing the glistening pink folds that awaited my attention. Dropping my forehead to her stomach, I took a few deep breaths to calm myself before continuing, but all that served to do was heighten my arousal with the scent of her overwhelming my senses.

"Liam." My name was almost a plea on her lips as Amy's hips shifted, searching for contact.

Giving in to her silent demands, I lowered my head, tongue darting out for that first sweet taste. Making contact through her slit, I groaned as her juices coated my tongue—sweeter than honey—and I was instantly addicted.

Spreading her wider, pinning her hips to the wall, I dove in like a man dying of thirst in the desert, her sweet nectar the only cure for my parched throat.

When I flicked that swollen pearl hidden within, Amy grasped my hair as her hips bucked against my face, a cry on her lips. "Liam!"

Spurred on by her raspy voice, I threw one leg over my shoulder, going deeper, my tongue penetrating her. I was a man on a mission—not only did I want to make her come, but I was also determined to leave an invisible brand, staking my claim on this woman, my wife. This was my sanctuary between her thighs. *Mine.*

Amy's grip on my hair grew tighter, neither pushing me closer nor pulling me away, just holding on for the ride. Her nails bit into my scalp, giving a bite of pain to aid in my pleasure as I ate her delicious pussy.

Taking my time, I savored her with my lips and tongue, but my girl was impatient—moans echoed from above as her hips urged me to pick up the pace. Grazing her clit with my teeth, I felt her legs begin to shake. She was teetering on the edge, but I wasn't done with her yet.

Moving to her inner thighs, I teased the soft skin there, eliciting frustrated whimpers from Amy that I'd pulled back my attention from where she needed it most. Licking a path up her thigh, I came close to where she wanted my tongue before changing course and moving back down toward her knee.

"Please." The words were barely a whisper from above.

The limits on my restraint broke as Amy begged, needing release—a release only I could give her.

Growling, I plunged back into her dripping honeypot, feasting on her like it was my last meal on Earth. Amy's moans grew in volume as her thighs tightened around my ears, muffling the sound. Circling her clit, I used a single digit to penetrate her warmth, groaning at how tight she was as she thrust against the intrusion. She was slick, coating my finger completely, so I added a second finger, causing Amy to scream my name.

She was so close, and I was finally satisfied enough to allow her to climax. Curling my fingers deep inside her, I sucked on her clit hard, unrelenting, even as I felt her come apart in my arms. Amy's whole body tensed, and if possible, I grew even harder in my pants at the sound of her frantic cries. Amy always tried to remain in control of her emotions and reactions, so watching her come undone was a rare treat.

I lapped at her slowly as she came down from the intense high, and she jerked against my mouth wildly, squeals escaping with each pass over her overly sensitized flesh. Carefully removing my fingers, I set her leg back on solid ground before rising to my full height before her. Skin flushed, her breasts heaved as she panted, trying to settle her breathing—she'd never looked more beautiful.

Amy's eyes were closed so tight that a wrinkle formed between her eyebrows.

I had a primal need to drive my point home, so I commanded, "Open your eyes." The only response was her shaking her head against the wall, so I dropped my voice an octave. "That wasn't a request."

Compelled to obey, her eyes opened wide in shock for a split second before drooping in her satisfied state, darkened to almost a forest green. When they locked on mine, she dropped them to the floor, but I gripped her chin to force her to look at my face. Slowly, I raised my other hand to my mouth, sucking clean the fingers that had been inside her.

Amy couldn't control the gasp that slipped past her lips.

Every instinct told me to be gentle, but I couldn't curb the harsh tone that colored my words as I ordered, "Don't ever doubt that I want you again. Understood?"

Not giving her a chance to answer—the question was rhetorical—I turned on my heel and left the room.

CHAPTER 14

Amy

"DON'T EVER DOUBT THAT I want you again. Understood?"

I couldn't breathe as Liam's words echoed in my brain. Lungs burning, I attempted to draw air through giant gasps to no avail. Clawing at the fabric constricting my chest, I finally found the zipper under my armpit. Pinching the cool metal cylinder between my thumb and forefinger, I yanked hard, causing the material to fall away in a rush, leaving me standing naked in the empty room.

At last, I could take a deep breath, but it did nothing to ease the tightness in my chest or my persistent lightheadedness. My pulse pounded in time with the throbbing between my legs, and my knees almost buckled at the memory of Liam's head there, his tongue drawing me higher and higher until I exploded.

I saw the fire in his eyes when I descended the stairs this evening—and maybe my heart had fluttered seeing him dressed so formally—but the bucket of ice water known as Leo had extinguished any heat from that moment. The rest of the night was torture, smiling and playing a part when I only wanted to hide in my room. I knew my worth, not needing it to be defined by a man, but Leo made me feel insignificant with only a few words.

Natalie deserved a medal for being married to that man for as long as she had. As a result, she carried battle scars, but it was no small miracle that she hadn't walked away completely shattered.

I was ready to leave it all behind—job be damned—once we returned to our apartment, but something changed in Liam. The raw, animal hunger burning in his eyes when he pinned me to the wall had been frightening and thrilling at the same time. Then he'd consumed me, coaxing an orgasm from my body better than anything I had ever experienced from my collection of battery-operated handy helpers.

Perhaps even more shocking than Liam dropping to his knees and putting his mouth *there* was that he'd walked away, taking nothing for himself.

Where had he gone, anyway?

He seemed almost angry afterward, which didn't make sense. Was he frustrated that I hadn't immediately offered to return the favor?

Stepping over the puddle of green silk at my feet, I tiptoed toward the door to his master bedroom, which he'd left wide open. Peeking inside, I saw it was dark, but a sliver of light filtered from the ensuite bathroom door partially shut, and the telltale sounds of running water reached my ears. Liam was in the shower.

My eyes widened, and my pulse kicked up, remembering what he'd once told me.

"The shower has been my only sexual companion for years."

No. He couldn't be, could he?

Stalking closer to the cracked bathroom door, I pushed it open a bit more to glean just enough to know what he was up to. The shower glass door was fogged up, but I could see Liam inside, his back to me. It seemed innocent enough, and I was ready to walk away when I heard him groan.

Oh my God.

Transfixed, my feet were glued to the spot as I watched Liam in the shower. His groans began to rise in volume, and I shifted on my feet as slickness coated the inside of my thighs once more. Liam's head dropped seconds before I heard the sharp crack of a hand slamming against the tiled wall, and a guttural groan echoed through the room. His posture relaxed as the water flowed over his body. Liam had seen the most intimate parts of me tonight, but all I got was fogged glass blurring his massive frame into vague shapes.

The water turned off—jolting me back to reality—and I was suddenly very aware I was naked, peeping on Liam. Running from the room as fast as my legs could carry me, I didn't stop to grab my dress off the ground as I dove into my own bedroom, bolting the door behind me. My breathing was ragged from my mad dash across the room, combined with my renewed arousal at watching Liam in the shower.

The heavy ache between my thighs was insistent, and I knew I wouldn't be able to think straight about tonight's events until I took matters into my own hands—literally.

Grabbing an oversized sleep T-shirt from the dresser, I threw it over my head before climbing into bed. Silently cursing myself for not bringing a single toy on our trip—afraid one of the maid staff might find it—I ran a hand between my legs. I'd have to ease this incessant need the old-fashioned way.

My hips bucked as fingers barely grazed my clit—still hyper-sensitive from Liam's earlier performance. Chest heaving, I gritted my teeth as my hand slid lower, rubbing the slickness all over. Quick, tight circles down below as I pinched a nipple with my free hand sent shockwaves of pleasure straight to my core. My stomach hollowed out as the tingles began, and my back arched off the bed before the orgasm hit me hard, causing a silent gasp as tears sprang to my eyes.

Removing my hands from my body, I lay there, spent, breathing heavily, my heart pounding in my ears. Not as good as Liam's, but it eased the ache. For now.

I'd been picturing Liam between my legs and in the shower, which helped throw me over the edge into my second climax of the night. As my heart rate slowed to its normal rhythm, I wondered if he thought of me when he came.

Unequipped to handle this confusing situation alone, I grabbed my phone off the nightstand and checked the time. It was almost 1 AM in Belleston, which meant it was only 7 PM back home in Connecticut—not even the new year there yet.

I knew what I was about to do would cause a frenzy, but what else was a girl to do when she had boy trouble? That was the whole reason for having girlfriends—to help work through your problems with a fresh perspective.

Screw it.

Amy: SOS.

Natalie: What are you doing awake? It's the middle of the night over there.

Amy: Something happened.

Hannah: It better be good if you're invoking an SOS.

Amy: In all our conversations, neither of you prepared me to have a man drop to his knees before me.

Hannah: *Gasps* Holy shit. Did Liam kiss your kitty? More details!

Amy: *Covers face* Oh my God. I'm already embarrassed enough.

Natalie: *Shrugs* To be fair, I had no experience in that department before Jaxon.

Hannah: Was he sloppy or skilled? Inquiring minds need to know. *Eyes emoji*

Natalie: No. Hannah's mind wants to know. Did everyone forget we are talking about my big brother?

Hannah: Don't listen to her. Spill, Amy.

Amy: *Biting lip emoji* My knees almost gave out. It should be illegal how good that was.

Hannah: What happened next? Did you drop down on your knees for him? Did he carry you to bed and finish the job?

Natalie: *Hands covering ears* I don't want to hear any of this.

Amy: You can rest easy, Natalie. Nothing else happened. It was strange. He seemed almost angry afterward and stalked off.

Hannah: *You're saying he rocked your world then walked away? Where did he go?*

Amy: *That's the strange part. I followed and found him in the shower, jerking off.*

Natalie: *Ew! I am seriously considering leaving this group chat.*

Hannah: *Don't listen to her, Amy. She lives in a fantasy world, where only girls are allowed to get their rocks off. Spoiler alert—I'm sure even Jaxon yanks his crank on long road trips.*

Natalie: *That's it. I'm getting new best friends.*

Hannah: *Empty threats.*

Amy: *Can we focus?*

Natalie: *It's bad enough that you married my brother, but that was fine because you insisted it wasn't real. It doesn't seem so fake anymore.*

Hannah: *I want it noted that I called this.*

Amy: *Called what? That he'd rather get off on his own than with me? Maybe I did something wrong. I don't exactly have much experience.*

Hannah: *Oh, no, we're not doing that. Maybe we need to back it up. How did he end up kneeling with his head buried between your legs?*

Natalie: I hate you both so much right now.

Amy: I was upset and doubting this whole thing and myself. I said something about him not wanting me, and the next thing I knew, he had me pinned against the wall, his eyes burning into mine as he pressed his erection against me, asking if it felt like he didn't want me.

Hannah: *Fans self* Oh my. Why did you doubt yourself? That doesn't seem like the Amy Michaels I know.

Amy: Leo happened.

Natalie: Oh God. I'm so sorry, Amy.

Amy: It's not your fault.

Hannah: What did the douche canoe do now?

Amy: Liam and I were having a moment before being announced into the party, and Leo came out of nowhere, telling me I needed to wear shapewear if I was going to wear a tight dress.

Hannah: Fuck him. Oh, wait. Natalie already did that.

Natalie: Yeah, don't remind me. Sounds like Liam is the better brother in more aspects than one.

Amy: I don't know how he does it. A few words, and I doubted everything.

Natalie: Years of practice.

Hannah: Don't listen to that pile of human garbage. Lucy sent us a photo. You looked fucking fire tonight! Green is definitely your color.

Amy: That's the thing. I felt amazing. Liam was practically eye-fucking me when I walked down the stairs, and then Leo came in and deflated me. I couldn't shake the doubt after that and ended up spiraling.

Natalie: Knowing Liam, he felt the need to protect you from your own thoughts by showing you how sexy he finds you.

Amy: Then why did he walk away? If he found me sexy, why not try to take things further?

Hannah: Oooh! I know! Pick me!

Natalie: If she gets it wrong, I've got it.

Amy: Will someone spit it out?

Hannah: He's trying to protect you from himself. Do I win?

Natalie: Sounds about right.

Amy: That doesn't make sense! Why would he walk away to protect me if he was also protecting me by putting my handy helpers to shame?

Natalie: He prides himself on always being in control. That's something you two have in common. The only thing I can think of is that he feels out of control around you, which scares him, so he forced himself to pull back, afraid that his loss of control might hurt you.

Amy: It was intense. He seems different here. I don't know what it is.

Natalie: It's a different world over there—different expectations. I'd be lying if I didn't say I couldn't breathe over there.

Hannah: But was that because of the role you were expected to play or Leo's closed-door dealings?

Natalie: Maybe a little of both? Amy, maybe it's because he never wanted that world. It does seem odd that he stayed away for three years and now, all of a sudden, has been home twice in a matter of months.

Amy: That's what I'm saying!

Hannah: Don't you worry, Ames. We will figure this out.

Amy: What am I supposed to do in the meantime? How do I face him after what happened?

Hannah: Do you regret what happened?

Amy: No, but . . .

Natalie: But what?

Amy: I'm just confused. What does it all mean? Are we a couple now?

Natalie: Is that what you want?

Amy: I don't know!

Natalie: Then, I think the two of you need to talk to each other about what it means and how you move forward.

Amy: Ugh. I was afraid you were going to say that.

Hannah: It's all fun and games until your own relationship advice comes back to bite you. *Evil cackle*

Amy: That's funny coming from the only one not in a relationship.

Hannah: Not for lack of trying. And for the record, are you confirming that you and Liam are in a relationship?

Amy: We're married. Even if it's not romantic, it still qualifies as a relationship.

Natalie: Sleep on it, Amy. See how you feel in the morning. But I stand by my advice that you two should talk.

Amy: Fine. Love you guys.

Natalie: Love you too. Happy New Year, Amy.

Hannah: *Happy New Year. Girls' night when you get back!*

Amy: *It's a date.*

Placing my phone back onto its charging base on my nightstand, the crash from the adrenaline rush hit me, and I was suddenly exhausted. Tomorrow was a new day, and Liam and I would have to be adults and figure out if what happened tonight changed anything.

How could it not?

My slumber had initially been deep but turned fitful sometime during the night. Images of Liam on his knees before me—the words he said, how he made me feel—had me tossing and turning. Annoyed that I couldn't shake those thoughts—couldn't shake him—I flung back the covers, deciding that trying to fall back asleep was pointless.

Still dressed in the oversized T-shirt with nothing underneath, I threw on a classic pajama set and silently exited my room. One step into our adjoined sitting room, and I froze. Liam was sitting there, drinking coffee, with a newspaper in his hands. A quick glance at the window showed the sun was not yet up, but that didn't mean much as winter in the Alps saw sunrises as late as 8 AM.

Liam glanced up from his paper with no expression other than the usual scowl gracing his face. "You should eat something. We are leaving today."

That was news to me. "Today? I thought we were here for another three days."

"I've canceled my last engagement of the trip. Lucy said she'd cover for me. I thought you'd be happy to get home and back to work."

He wasn't wrong, but something about how fast he wanted to get out of here felt like he was running from something. "Are you sure? I don't mind staying."

"We're leaving." His tone brooked no argument.

"Yes, sir." There was sarcasm in my voice, and that caught his attention.

Blue eyes flared, turning an almost sapphire color before he brought the paper back up, obscuring his face. From behind the newspaper, he added, "We leave in three hours."

Knowing he couldn't see me, I rolled my eyes and stuck out my tongue. Usually, I was more mature, but it felt almost as if he'd toyed with me last night. That silver-tongued deity was gone, replaced by the gruff man I'd knowingly married. I berated myself for being a fool to think that something had changed between us.

Grabbing a scone off the platter on the coffee table, I retreated to my room without another word. Closing the door, I dressed for the day in dress slacks and a sweater—casual enough to be comfortable on the plane trip home but professional enough to roam the palace hallways. I needed to get out of this apartment and get some air if I had to spend nine hours trapped on a plane with Liam before we arrived home.

Keeping an eye on the time, knowing the palace staff would repack my bags, I walked to the open areas of the palace. I got a brief tour during our first few days, but today, I wanted to get as physically lost in this cavernous dwelling as I felt inside my mind.

I was so confused.

"Don't ever doubt that I want you again. Understood?"

How could he say those words after he'd performed that intimate act and then pretend as if nothing had happened? My mind reeled, recalling that morning-after in college when I was told it was all a ruse, a joke. Just hearing that story, Liam had crushed a wine glass in his bare hands, so it didn't make any sense.

Reflecting on my text conversation with the girls, Natalie's words rolled around in my brain. She thought Liam was afraid of hurting me and that we needed to talk. Even if that's the last thing I wanted, I knew she was right, but he made it damn near impossible when he closed himself off like this.

I would give anything to go back to last night right after I came down the stairs. That moment had been perfect—Liam had been perfect.

My aimless wandering through the maze of hallways led me to a portrait gallery. So many painted portraits lined this hall of monarchs from times past, plaques below each with their name and years of reign. It was like a fun little history lesson as I slowly made my way from one end to the other, giving my mind a much-needed distraction.

The one at the end of the hallway stopped me dead in my tracks. It was a portrait of Prince Adrian and Princess Adelaide with their three children—Leo, Liam, and Lucy.

It must have been done decades ago because my husband and his siblings were depicted as children. A glance at the plaque below stating the year gave me an idea of their ages. Lucy was barely two years old, making Liam six and Leo nine.

Wow, Liam was a dead ringer for his father. Staring at the depiction of Prince Adrian in what had to be his late thirties or perhaps early forties, it was almost like looking at Liam now. Liam and Lucy favored their father's dark coloring, whereas Leo stuck out like a sore thumb with his blond hair. Studying Liam's boyish face made me smile as I realized he had that scowl even then—what could make a little boy that serious?

"He was such a stoic little boy. I always prayed he'd grow out of it, but until last night, I thought those prayers had been in vain."

I jumped at the voice interrupting my thoughts with its own musings. Turning, I found it belonged to my new mother-in-law, and I gave a quick curtsey of acknowledgment. "Ma'am."

Waving her hand, she dismissed me. "It's just us girls here. Please, call me Addy behind closed doors."

Relaxing, I gave her a small smile. "I'm sorry if I'm somewhere I'm not supposed to be, Addy. I needed a moment to think."

Glancing at the portrait, her lips turned up. "This is your home as much as it is any of ours. Takes a brave woman to marry into this family."

"Oh, I don't know that I'm very brave." I dropped my gaze to the rug beneath my feet.

"Of course you are, dear, or you wouldn't be married to our Liam. He needs a strong woman to push his boundaries. I can already see that you do that."

Peering up at her, my brows drew down. "I'm not sure I know what you mean."

Addy eyed me carefully. "Certainly, you've noticed his need to be in control."

That was putting it mildly. An unladylike scoff flew past my lips. "That's what makes him Liam."

"That's true, but life isn't always something you can control." There was something about the way she said that. Like she wasn't talking so much about Liam anymore, but I didn't want to pry, so kept my mouth shut. "Liam wouldn't do well if he didn't have a woman to challenge him daily.

He carries the weight of the world and needed to find an equal to share that burden, to take the reins when necessary, allowing him to live freely without controlling every situation."

"He hates being out of control."

Addy nodded. "I've never seen him lose control like he did last night."

If only she knew how truly out of control things had gotten last night, but I kept that to myself, referring only to what she witnessed. "I'm not sure that's a good thing."

"I think it is," she countered. "He's been bottling up his emotions for so long—going through the motions in his own life—that it was refreshing to see."

"Even if it meant practically strangling his own brother?" I arched an eyebrow skeptically.

She shrugged. "That was a long time coming, but it took the right person to push him over the edge. He never laid hands on Leo over anything that happened with Natalie, but it took very little for him to defend you physically. That's how I know you're the one."

That didn't mean anything. "Liam's always been a protector."

"He has, but you're the first one he's ever protected on instinct rather than thinking through the consequences first. You're special to him."

There was something more to this. I felt it in my gut. "What advice would you offer us as newlyweds, especially to a couple of control freaks?"

Smiling, Addy grasped my hand. "Keep pushing back. Break him if you must. He needs to see that marriage is a partnership, where you share control instead of one person taking the lead."

"You want me to break your son?" I said the words carefully, almost unable to believe what she was saying.

"I think he needs it more than any of us realize." She squeezed my hand and winked. "You might even enjoy it."

With that, she walked away, leaving me speechless, wondering if perhaps the walls had spoken to her about what went down last night. Liam might want to pretend as if last night hadn't happened, but what did he know about relationships?

Addy had been happily married for decades and knew her son better than anyone. Should I let the stubborn man I married take the lead on how our life would go, or should I follow his mother's advice and push him past the breaking point?

If last night had been a taste of life approaching the breaking point, it wasn't much of a choice in my mind. We were going home today, and I had a singular mission: Breaking Liam.

CHAPTER 15

Amy

LIAM BARELY SPOKE TO me during our long flight back to the States. Once we reached the house, he disappeared, keeping his schedule the opposite of mine. Frustrated that he was shutting me out after the intimacy we shared, I returned to work. Not that I got much work done as I sat at my desk, trying to figure out ways to "break" Liam.

Accepting that I didn't have the knowledge or experience to create an effective plan myself, I knew there were two women who did. Calling an emergency girls' night, we decided to meet at Natalie's house to watch the Comets game on TV. They were on the West Coast—meaning a late puck drop—and the kids would be in bed, so we didn't need to worry about someone watching them.

Liam was nowhere to be seen when I left, even though I knew he was awake, as evidenced by the dishes in the sink from whatever he'd cooked for himself. It had been a week since our return home, and I hadn't seen him once, so I didn't feel guilty for leaving the house late at night without alerting him. Going next door also didn't require informing Marcus, so I slipped out, relishing that small freedom.

I still had a key to Natalie's house but knew better than to use it without knocking when Jaxon was home. Since he was gone for the next week, I let myself in, finding Natalie in a set of Comets pajamas, moving around the kitchen putting together snacks. Having snagged a bottle of the "good" wine on my way home from work, I placed it on the countertop.

Natalie recognized the label and immediately asked, "Are we celebrating or complaining?"

Sighing, I shrugged. "I need my girls."

Her brow wrinkled, concern evident. "You okay?"

"Yeah, just need some help."

"Then it's a good thing I'm here!" Hannah's voice was loud and bright as she entered the kitchen. Seeing the bottle of wine, she scoffed. "That's not strong enough for whatever is so important that it couldn't wait another week." Eyes widening, she asked, "Wait. Did something else happen between you and Liam?"

Of course, that was where her mind would go. Hannah always had sex on the brain, but that's exactly what I needed her for tonight.

Groaning, I replied, "No, but that's why I'm here."

Natalie grabbed the bottle, uncorking it before handing us each a glass and ushering us into the living room, where the game had already started. Keeping one eye on the game, she accused, "I take it you didn't have that talk."

Throwing my arms wide, careful not to spill any wine, I replied, "I woke up the next morning, and Liam acted as if nothing had happened. Like it meant nothing to him."

Hannah muttered, "He's an idiot."

Natalie prompted, "So instead of forcing him to talk about it . . ."

"He's thrown up his walls. There's no talking to him when he gets like this. You should know that," I challenged back.

"What do you want, Ames?" I could always count on Natalie to push me, as I'd always done for her.

"I'm not sure," I grumbled, sinking further into the couch. "I felt desirable when he pinned me against that wall, telling me how much he loved my curves. He promised on the plane that this trip wouldn't be like the fundraiser and would be more formal, but then it was even more heated. I'm so confused."

Hannah smirked. "I like hot and bothered Amy."

Natalie rolled her eyes. "If you don't want to talk to him, what do you want to do?"

Exhaling deeply, I replied, "That's where I need help. After he pretended like nothing had happened, I went for a walk, and Addy found me. She said Liam and I were perfect for each other and that I was exactly what he needed to challenge him to lose control."

Natalie's jaw dropped. "*Addy* said that?"

"Yeah, she told me to break him, and that I might have fun doing it."

"Go, Addy." Hannah raised her wine glass in silent cheers before drinking.

"But she thinks your marriage is real," Natalie mused.

"Exactly, but I can't take the hot and cold anymore." Tipping up my glass, I wanted nothing more than to drown in the wine I found there. Maybe then I could forget how Liam had made me feel.

Natalie raised an eyebrow. "So, you want to break Liam?"

I bit my lip. "Maybe?"

Hannah fist-pumped the air. "I'm so down for this. Liam deserves to have his world shaken up a bit. He's way too uptight."

"I want it on the record how hard it is for me to talk about my big brother in this capacity. But with that being said . . ." Natalie searched my eyes before asking, "Do you want something more with Liam? A real marriage?"

Protesting, I rushed out quickly, "No, I'm not saying that. . ."

"Ames . . ." Natalie probed.

Covering my eyes, I spoke the words out loud. "It felt so damn good. I want more but don't know how to get more."

Hannah whopped, "It's about time! Amy, you've somehow managed to snag a smoldering hunk of a man. You might as well use him to get back on that horse. If you know what I mean." She waggled her eyebrows suggestively.

They both knew how I'd shut myself off from any possibility of letting anyone get close to me again after what Chet had done. Yeah, I know. The stereotypical frat boy name should have been a red flag, but I was young and dumb.

I was fine before this marriage to Liam. I was happy, secure, and what I thought was sexually satisfied, but boy had I been wrong. But one part of what she said stopped me in my tracks.

Holding up a hand, I asked, "Wait, you think Liam's hot?"

"Oh, yeah," both said in unison.

Natalie assumed my role as the voice of reason since I'd clearly lost my damn mind. "Amy, I'm not sure this is a good idea," she cautioned.

"Says the woman who thought a relationship with Jaxon was a bad idea," countered Hannah.

"Are you two going to help me break him or not?" I asked, frustrated.

Natalie's brown eyes widened. "Help? How are we supposed to help you?"

"I don't know! You two have more experience. One of you has got to have something up their sleeve I can use."

Hannah poured herself another glass of wine before offering me the bottle. "Maybe we get you drunk and send you back home to maul him."

Natalie scoffed. "That won't work. He's too chivalrous to take advantage of a drunk woman, let alone Amy."

"Well, then, what do you think?" I challenged, putting it back on her.

"Are you sure you're not developing feelings for Liam? This doesn't seem like something you'd do otherwise."

"It's just sex, Nat," I huffed, annoyance getting the better of me. "Adults are allowed to have casual sex, the last time I checked."

"Sure. Casual sex with your husband. What could go wrong?" I didn't miss the hint of sarcasm in her tone.

"I don't care anymore! If it's not real anyway, who cares about the consequences?"

Hannah stared at me. "Who are you, and what have you done with our friend?"

Natalie added, "This isn't 'some guy,' Amy. It's Liam. I have a responsibility to look out for both of you. If you go through with this and it ends badly, what then? How are you going to continue to live together? Travel together? Attend events together?"

"You think I haven't spent the last week thinking about this?" I yelled. "It's driving me insane! At this point, I'm the one who's going to break!"

Natalie put her hands up. "Okay, calm down, Ames. I'm not judging you. I only want to make sure you've thought this through. Once you sleep with him, there's no going back."

"We've already crossed a line—or rather, he did. Why should I have to sit on the sidelines and be caught unawares if or when it happens again?"

"Right on, girlfriend! Take some control and get some!" Hannah's voice rose in volume with every word. She tended to drink a little too much when we stayed in for girls' night.

"It's just a physical attraction," I tried to ease Natalie's concerns. "Chemistry, nothing more."

Hannah sat bolt upright. "Chemistry! That's it!"

Natalie sized her up. "Hannah, you're not making any sense."

"No! I've figured it out!" She put her wine glass down on the coffee table. "We use chemistry. I'll give you my pheromone oil. Put some of that on, and voilà! He won't be able to resist you."

Natalie gawked at Hannah. "Why in the world do you have pheromone oil?"

"I wear it to the club." She shrugged.

"Oh my God. Is that why the men won't leave us alone when we go?" I was stunned, but everything suddenly made sense.

"See? Proof that it works." Hannah grinned mischievously.

Mulling it over, I mused, "Can't hurt to try it."

Natalie interjected, "All right, if you're going to do this, you should do it right. Might be time to make a little call to your new sister-in-law."

Hannah giggled. "See? You came to the right place. Between the two of us, we'll have Liam begging at your feet in no time."

I was confused. "I don't understand how Lucy plays into this."

They shared a look, and I felt like I was on the outside of an inside joke. Not a great feeling when you have two best friends, and they knew something you didn't.

Natalie clued me in, "Have you heard about the lingerie line Arabella Reign?"

"Sure." I nodded. "It's trending right now."

"Well . . . One of Lucy's middle names happens to be Arabella . . ." She trailed off, hoping I would catch her drift.

I knew Lucy was a creative fashion genius, but she'd never given me any reason to think she was designing lingerie on the side. It made sense that something so sensitive would be kept secret due to her high-profile public status.

"You both knew?" I accused. "Why didn't you tell me?"

Hannah snorted. "Not like you had much use for it before now."

Fair point. "So, we ask Lucy to send some lingerie and use Hannah's pheromone oil. You two think that'll work?"

Hannah threw both arms into the air in triumph. "Yes! Operation Seduce Liam is on!"

Natalie bit her lip not to say anything else, but I knew what she was thinking as she turned her attention back to the hockey game on TV. Hannah was a horndog, but Natalie believed in love. Natalie's single reckless sexual encounter had led to Charlie's existence, so of course, she was skittish, even if she got her happy ending as a result. She worried about both Liam and me and the emotional consequences of consummating our marriage.

Emotionally, I was already a wreck riding shotgun on this rollercoaster with Liam.

I'd signed a contract that stipulated that Liam was the only man I could sleep with during our marriage. Maybe it was time for me to retake the driver's seat in my own life. Liam could ride shotgun with me and experience how it felt not to know which way was up.

CHAPTER 16

Liam

I WAS A COWARD. I ran from Amy because she'd tested the limits of my restraint, resulting in me taking things too far. We had been hurtling towards that moment for weeks, and while it had been incredible, it couldn't happen again.

Fuck. I couldn't get her out of my head.

Her skin had been so soft, and the taste of her on my tongue still haunted my dreams. It had crossed my mind more than once that maybe I needed to get her completely out of my system, so we could move on with our lives.

No, that would never work. Amy deserved more.

Long-term companionship was the goal, and that plan could go up in flames if I gave in to the sexual attraction I felt for her and finished what I'd started against that wall. Amy would develop feelings I was certain I couldn't reciprocate, and then she'd resent me. I was already running the risk in not telling her why I needed a wife.

We were currently speeding toward disaster. I didn't need to hit the accelerator.

My focus needed to be on acclimating Amy to her royal role, getting her to love it so that it would be impossible for her to walk away once she learned the truth. She loved helping people and would have so many opportunities to do so in Belleston. Allowing her to choose causes that spoke to her and getting her involved early would be the hook that I needed.

The promise of mind-blowing sex with my wife took a backseat to my loyalty to my country.

Putting on that mask of indifference the morning after had nearly killed me when I'd heard the hurt in her voice. I told her I wanted her and then pretended nothing had happened. When in reality, my body begged me to bend her over the arm of the couch and finish the job.

The flight home had been pure torture. Just looking at Amy—studying her every curve, each feature of her face—filled me with regret. Regret over crossing the line, and regret over not taking things further.

Not to mention my constant state of arousal when she was near. Have you ever had to sit for an entire Trans-Atlantic flight with a hard-on, afraid to stand up for fear of your female companion noticing? Yeah, I did not recommend it.

The second we landed, I knew exactly what I needed—space. I had to stay far away from Amy. Being near her clouded my judgment, and that terrified me.

Physically, I hadn't seen Amy in over a week, but there were subtle reminders of her everywhere in the house. Seeing her shoes by the door, I could almost feel her delicate ankle in my hand. She left her laundry in the dryer too long, and I'd had to move it to a basket, tempted to steal a pair of her panties. The book Natalie had given her lay on the coffee table, and I skimmed some of the passages, agreeing with Amy's assessment that it seemed improbable at best.

But damn, if my eyes didn't bulge out of my head when I stumbled upon one of the racier scenes. I spent half an hour trying to picture if the position described was even logistically possible. No wonder women flocked to these books with cutesy cartoon covers—this shit was hot, and they could read it in public, with men being none the wiser.

Amy thought she was sly in sneaking over to Natalie's house without a word earlier tonight, but I had security cameras set up around the exterior of our house as soon as we'd moved in.

In truth, I didn't mind. The only time I could breathe was when Amy was out of the house. There were a few hours in the evening when our offset schedules overlapped, but even when she was sleeping, I was tense, on alert in case she woke up and wandered downstairs, our paths crossing when I took a break from working.

My phone alerted me when Amy returned close to 1 AM, and I was getting on my first video calls of the day. Today, I had a lighter-than-average workload and was done by 5 AM, so I crept upstairs to change before working off some of my pent-up sexual frustration in the home gym.

Reaching the landing on the second floor, I noticed light filtering out of a crack in the door to Amy's bedroom. I was a large man, but had spent years honing my stealth skills, so I silently padded toward where I knew Amy was behind the door. I knew it was a bad idea, but I just wanted a glimpse of her.

Pausing outside her room, I listened for any signs of movement—the only sound I heard was deep breathing, indicating that Amy was asleep with the lights on. Pushing it open silently, I leaned against the doorframe, afraid to move, afraid to breathe.

Amy was sound asleep, sprawled on the massive king-sized bed centered in her room. I bit back a groan staring at her, clad only in an oversized T-shirt. She must have moved during her slumber because it had ridden up, the curves of her hips on full display, causing my hands to curl into tight fists, wanting to grip her there hard, take control, and make her scream in pleasure.

I wasn't one of those guys who bragged about their sexual prowess when, in reality, the women they took to bed were faking every orgasm. No, there was no faking when I was with a woman. I knew I could make Amy's pussy clench tightly around my cock as I brought her to climax, the same way she had around my fingers when I'd held her trembling against my mouth.

In case you were wondering, yes, the little general was at full salute watching my wife sleep. It didn't matter that her red hair was tangled and falling over her face or that I could see a light sheen of drool escaping her lips—she was somehow always gorgeous to me.

Her laptop was open on the bed, precariously close to the edge. Amy worked hard, and I had no clue if her work was backed up on another device. Compelled to ensure nothing happened if she rolled over and knocked it to the floor, I moved into the room slowly, having no idea if any floorboards creaked. If I hit one and she woke up, I knew I would never hear the end of how I was creeping on her in her sleep, even under the guise of trying to help.

Treating Amy like an unexploded hand grenade, I eased the computer off the bed, holding my breath. When she didn't move, I exhaled silently, ready to close the laptop and place it on her nightstand, when an image caught my eye. Pictures of the construction at the apartment building I'd purchased for her were on the screen, and I could see her vision taking shape. What had once been a cold and clinical space—all walls painted white—was becoming a home for whichever families were afforded the opportunity to live there.

Amy did this. Her job was her life, her passion, and she loved it. She loved helping families reconnect and get a fresh start.

I wanted Amy more than I'd wanted anything in my life, but I couldn't ruin this for her. Hell, her job was the only reason I offered to marry her in the first place.

I would rather live in this sexual purgatory than see her dreams crushed. She meant that much to me.

Closing the laptop, I placed it gently down where she'd find it in the morning, before dimming the lights in her room and retreating to mine. It had never been more evident that I needed to steer clear of my wife for her own protection. I could not fail her.

As a former military man, I knew how to follow orders, so I gave myself one—under no circumstances was I to fuck my wife.

Another week down, avoiding my wife. Only a lifetime to go.

Staying away physically kept her safe, but I grew more agitated the longer our separation dragged on. I'd snapped at my personal assistant on the phone and had needed to apologize more than once this week.

This wasn't me. I was known for being firm and tough but never unkind.

I'd end this whole thing if Amy didn't need us to remain married. I wouldn't survive another week, let alone years of this.

The shower wasn't cutting it anymore.

I'd signed a contract stating I wouldn't seek outside female companionship, but the joke was on me. Amy was the only woman I was allowed to have—the only one I wanted—but she also happened to be the only one I forbade myself from touching again.

It was enough to drive a man insane.

Sleep was eluding me, further adding to my aggravation. When I finally managed to fall into a state of restless unconsciousness, the doorbell rang, rudely awakening me before someone pounded on the front door. Checking my phone's security app, I saw it was a delivery driver with a box.

Pushing the button accessing the microphone to the doorbell camera, I gruffly called out, "Just leave it!"

My irritation reached new heights when the driver said, "No can do, buddy. This one needs a signature."

I was *not* his buddy. Throwing the covers off in anger, I stomped down the stairs. Wrenching the door open, I grabbed the signature tablet out of his hands without a word before thrusting it back at his chest and taking the box. Slamming the door in his face, I looked at the package, groaning when I saw it was for Amy. Even when she wasn't here, she was driving me mad.

The box felt light, and I wondered what the hell she'd ordered from a European company called Arabella Reign. Placing the package on the kitchen counter where Amy would easily find it, I went back upstairs, all hope of getting any sleep today vanishing.

Lying in bed, staring at the ceiling, I heard when Amy returned home from work. Patiently, I waited as I listened to the sounds of her making dinner before she went upstairs to her room. The second I heard the master bedroom door latch, I bolted for my basement office.

Unable to focus on answering emails from "overnight" in Belleston, I pulled up a monotonous computer game. I needed something, anything, to distract me from the thoughts of Amy.

My phone buzzed, and I glanced away from the computer screen.

Speak of the devil.

Amy: Are you home? I can't get the satellite to work on the TV in the bedroom. Can you help me?

Fuck.

Taking a few calming breaths, I reminded myself that she needed me for tech support and nothing more, before pushing off my desk chair and practically stomping up the stairs.

As I reached the second-floor landing, I grumbled to myself, "Fucking Jaxon. Doesn't he know the trees are too tall here for a satellite dish? Why couldn't he get cable like a normal—"

The words died on my lips as I pushed open the door into Amy's bedroom. There she stood, leaning against the mahogany dresser, wearing only an emerald green silk camisole and shorts set, the edges lined with lace. It was January—there was snow on the ground—but suddenly, the temperature of the room was stifling.

Swallowing, trying to bring moisture back to my dry mouth, I squeaked out, "What are you wearing?"

Amy's brow furrowed, and she looked down at herself before shining emerald eyes met mine. "Um, pajamas?"

My head moved side to side of its own volition. "No, I've seen you in your pajamas."

"They're new." I could have sworn there was a tone of a pout in her voice as she asked, "You don't like them?"

I could see where her nipples stood proud against the thin fabric, and her long, smooth legs were on full display—of course, I liked them. Why did she care if I liked them?

Why was I up here again? Oh, right. The TV.

"You needed help with the satellite signal?"

"Yes!" she exclaimed.

Reaching behind her to the dresser, she grabbed for the remote but, in her haste, smacked it onto the floor. She stepped toward where my feet were glued to the floor and did a quick about-face before bending over at the waist, putting her rounded ass on full display.

I felt the groan rise in my throat, and in my piss-poor attempt to tamp it down, a strangled noise escaped my lips. With Amy bent like that—the shorts barely containing her luscious ass, with the bottom curve of her creamy cheeks visible—I could have sworn I caught a hint of pink when the skimpy fabric shifted between her thighs. Was she not wearing panties again?

I had to get out of here before I did something stupid. A man could only take so much.

She began to straighten, and desperate for any excuse to escape, I asked, "Do you really need the TV tonight, Amy?"

Spinning to face me, she held out the remote. "Please?"

Oh God, her begging was going to be the death of me.

Get it together, man. She just needs help with her television.

Willing my feet to move—feeling as if they were weighed down by concrete blocks—I trudged closer to where she stood. Just as my hand closed in around the remote, something happened.

Unable to explain it, an overwhelming urge rolled over me, almost like a tidal wave. My feet moved involuntarily, and Amy was cradled in my arms before I could realize what I was doing. She was as soft as I remembered as her curves molded perfectly against me. I wanted to devour her.

Eyes bright, she looked up at me, breathing, "Liam." It almost sounded like a plea.

Her arms snaked around my waist, pulling me closer. My brain told me no, but my body was screaming yes. I'd always had enough self-control to tell my body to shut the hell up—my brain always won—but something was different about this moment, and I couldn't put my finger on it.

Peeking down at Amy, the swells of her breasts pushed tightly against my chest as they rose quickly with her rapid breathing. Her pulse pounded at the soft hollow of her throat. Daring to look at her face, her lips were parted slightly, her pupils dilated. There was no doubt this woman was as turned on as I was.

Dropping my forehead to hers, I teased her nose with mine. "This is a bad idea."

Nuzzling against my jaw in response, she whispered, "I'm cashing in on your offer from the plane."

There was zero blood left in my brain. Her words didn't make sense. "What?"

A soft hand trailed a path up my back, over my shoulder, leaving a trail of fire in its wake. The only thing I knew was that I needed to have fewer clothes on. Maybe if I stopped overheating, I could get my brain to work again.

As if she could read my mind, Amy's other hand gripped the hem of my T-shirt, pulling it up over my abs. I instinctively raised my arms so she could remove the offending garment. Cool air rushed over my torso, but the inferno within raged on. Amy's hands smoothed over my bare skin, tracing the lines of my muscles before reaching the waistband of my jeans, mere inches away from my barely contained erection.

Peering up at me, there was a determination in the shining green depths of her eyes. "You offered to take me back to the bedroom on our flight." Her gaze shifted to the king-size bed occupying the room, and she tilted her head in that direction. "We're in a bedroom now, and as you pointed out, we are married."

"Married," I repeated, still unable to comprehend what she wanted.

Looping fingers into the empty belt loops, she pulled my hips closer to her softness, and this time, I couldn't contain the groan that tore up my throat as my throbbing cock pressed against where I knew heaven was waiting between her thighs.

Practically batting her eyelashes at me, Amy smirked. "You've seen mine. It's only fair I get to see yours."

"Fuck me," I breathed out.

"I thought you'd never ask."

Arms resting loosely behind Amy's back, I reached one hand over and lightly pinched the opposite forearm. I'd dreamt of her for so long—I needed to make sure this was real. The sharp bite of pain told me I was very much awake.

All this time, I'd kept my distance to protect her from my primal need to claim her, and here she was, telling me that was exactly what she wanted. God, I wanted her so badly, but what would happen in the morning? Did fucking her mean we were a couple?

Who the fuck cares? She's here, begging you to fuck her. Give her what she wants!

Just like that, my brain agreed with my body, and all hope was lost. There was no question—tonight was the night I would fuck my wife.

CHAPTER 17

Amy

NEVER IN MY ENTIRE life had I felt more powerful as a woman than when Liam stopped dead in his tracks at discovering me in the sexy silk pajama set. I came home from work this evening to find the package from Lucy sitting on the kitchen counter. Immediately, I rushed to my room and opened the box overflowing with various types of lingerie in an assortment of colors and fabrics.

My eyes had been immediately drawn to the green set I now wore. Not only was the color perfect, but it wasn't flashy enough to immediately clue in Liam to my plans. I got a small thrill playing coy when he asked what I wore. The strangled noise he made told me his control was hanging by a thread. I knew I could make it snap if I pushed a little bit.

Granted, I had some help. The pheromone oil from Hannah worked like a charm, and once Liam got close enough, I saw how it affected him—his eyes darkened, and he looked like a man possessed as he pulled me into his arms.

The light smattering of dark hair on his chest tickled the exposed tops of my breasts, and I arched into him, desperately trying to get closer. His hard length, restrained behind the zipper of his jeans, pressed right above the juncture of my thighs. Biting my lip, I shifted my hips against the insistent ache where I needed him.

Liam's control was slipping. His eyes turned a midnight blue right before his mouth dropped to the delicate skin of my neck, teasing with his lips and teeth, using his tongue to lick that pulse point at the base of my throat. Moaning as he hit a particularly sensitive spot, I heard him growl before his hands gripped my hips almost painfully, pulling me flush against his body as his mouth hungrily trailed lower toward my breasts.

He had no idea how badly I wanted this—needed this—and if he thought being rough would scare me into changing my mind, he had another thing coming. Two could play at this game, and to show him I wasn't afraid, I threaded fingers into the silky black tresses of his hair and tugged. The hiss that slipped from his lips as his fingers dug deeper had arousal dripping down my thighs.

Having only a moment to relish that small victory, Liam's head dipped lower, sucking a pebbled nipple through the silk of my camisole. My head dropped back as my chest pushed closer, gasping at the friction of the wet silk against my sensitized flesh. My counterattack to this move was to slide a hand from his hair between our bodies, cupping the bulge in his pants. Liam groaned with my nipple still deep in his mouth, the vibrations eliciting a moan from deep within my chest.

The two of us were fighting for dominance and driving each other insane.

If insanity feels this good, sign me up for a padded cell.

Going for broke, my shaky fingers managed to undo the button at the top of his jeans, but when I reached the zipper, Liam's hands locked down on my wrists in an iron grip. Feeling him rise to its full height, I sheepishly glanced up at him, expecting him to finally put a stop to this. He'd been honing his control for so long that I knew breaking him wouldn't be an easy task and might require more than one attempt.

Meeting his eyes, I stumbled a few steps backward at the intense stare I found there, his pupils blown wide with lust. Liam released his hold on me easily. Seeing his dark, menacing look, I had to remind myself that I wanted this.

My voice shook when I asked, "Liam?"

Liam's voice was pained as he begged, "Tell me to stop, sweetheart. Please."

I had him exactly where I wanted him. Liam was at a breaking point and wouldn't be able to stop unless I told him to. He *needed* to hear me say those words, but I couldn't. I wanted him—no, I needed him—too badly. His one mistake had been giving me a taste of that raw animal hunger he harbored. Now, I craved more.

Barely above a whisper, I uttered, "Never."

There wasn't time to think, to react, as his hands moved with lightning-quick precision, snapping the thin straps of my camisole, the material sliding down, catching on my hips, baring my chest to his greedy gaze. Stalking closer, rough hands reached out, massaging the aching swells. I was transfixed, watching him mold them as they overflowed his large palms, thumbs catching on my distended, sensitive nipples.

Liam's head dropped once more, taking one pebbled peak into his mouth as he tweaked its partner with his skilled fingers. Jolts of pleasure shot straight down my body, pooling in my core, as I arched into his touch, needing something—anything—more. Liam dropped to his knees before me, almost causing my own knees to buckle with the memory of the last time we were in this position.

Sliding hands over the curves of my waist to my hips, his fingers skimmed my flesh, leaving goosebumps in their wake. The anticipation of what came next had me close to the edge. It wouldn't take much to send me careening over. Hooking his thumbs into the waistband of my silk shorts, Liam eased them down over my hips so that they dropped easily to the floor. Green silk pooled at my feet, and a growl was torn from Liam's throat when he discovered I wore nothing beneath.

The now strapless camisole still hung on my full-figured hips, but Liam made quick work of it, giving a gentle tug, the sounds of seams ripping filling the thick air in the room. Aroused out of my mind, my hips shifted, trying to ease the ache growing there with each passing minute.

Liam nudged my thighs apart with his hands, grazing the slickness that coated them before inching upward, closer to the throbbing nub screaming for his attention. Feeling his breath so close to my core, my hips jutted forward, begging for more.

"Do you want my mouth on you, sweetheart?" Liam's voice barely broke through my lust-filled haze. When my only response was a moan, he used his thumbs to spread my dripping center, baring me completely to his view, commanding, "Answer me, Amy."

My brain was misfiring, focused only on the promise of release, but I managed to choke out, "Please."

Apparently, that was acceptable enough because Liam nearly growled a breath away from my pussy, "I fucking knew you'd be sweeter than sin right here." Without hesitation, he delved between my thighs with his tongue.

"Oh, God." I was on sensory overload. We'd been racing toward this moment for weeks, so the buildup had me ready to explode within minutes of Liam feasting on my pulsating core.

Liam's oral assault was relentless, his tongue teasing, flicking, and sucking on my clit until my thighs began to tremble. My hand reached down to anchor in his hair, holding on for dear life as I strained against his mouth, edging closer and closer until every nerve ending in my body fired off at once, creating a release so powerful that I forgot to breathe. My eyes clenched shut, rocking against his mouth to prolong the intense sensations flowing over me, never wanting this feeling to end.

Eventually, my body couldn't take any more, and I sagged against Liam. Strong arms gently lowered me to the ground and onto his lap, stroking my hair and peppering soft kisses against my shoulders. Lying limp in his arms, I'd never felt more protected. He knew when to use strength but also when to be gentle. That, in and of itself, was intoxicating.

After a while, my eyes began to drift closed. Being held by Liam was so comfortable, but I jolted back to awareness as I felt his arms shift, feeling nothing but air beneath me as he carried me across the room.

"Let's get you to bed."

Instantly reinvigorated, I was ready to please him. Allowing him to place me upon the plush comforter, I reached for him, but he pulled back enough that my hands caught nothing but air. Frowning, I sat up, asking, "Where are you going?"

The conflict in his eyes was clear. He wanted to stay but needed to go.

Fuck that.

He'd left me once after shattering my world, and I wasn't about to let that happen again.

My feet met the cool hardwood, and I stepped toward him but was stopped by his words.

"Amy, please," he begged.

Anger colored my words. "Please what, Liam?" He was struggling, but I no longer cared.

"We shouldn't have done that. I need to leave. Let me leave."

"Are you saying you don't want me?" I tried desperately not to let him see how much that idea hurt me.

Running a hand through his thick black hair, he shifted on his feet. "You think I don't want you? Amy, I want you so fucking badly I can't sleep. You're all I can think about."

"Then why are you running away from me? Again."

"Because it's my job to protect you!" he blurted.

The words hit me square in the chest, even though I knew that was his hangup. Not backing down, I challenged, "I'm not scared of you."

"You don't understand," Liam pleaded with me.

"Then help me understand because I'm confused as hell right now."

Exasperated, he flung his arms wide. "I need you, Amy!"

Raising my voice right back, knowing he was right on the brink, I shouted, "And I need you to take off your fucking pants!"

Liam's chest rose and fell rapidly, the war within himself raging. His eyes darkened to that sapphire color that had my blood heating in response. Clenching and unclenching his fists at his side, his jaw was locked tight as he asked, "Is that really what you want?"

"I'm standing before you naked, Liam. What do you think?" I couldn't stop the scoff that rushed past my lips. I was fed up with his hero routine.

"I need you to say the words."

"Liam, I haven't wanted a man to touch me in over a decade, and I am asking you, my *husband*, to take off your goddamn clothes and fuck me. Is that good enough?"

Liam's jaw twitched, and without another word, his hands went to the fly of his jeans which was still resting unbuttoned. Slowly, he moved the zipper down, the sound deafening in the silence hanging between us. Blood rushed in my ears as I watched him hook his thumbs into the waistband and shove his jeans to the ground before stepping out of them. Tight black briefs contained the considerable bulge I'd only had the pleasure of feeling against me through several layers of fabric.

Wondering if he was as skilled with his cock as he was with his mouth made my legs weak, and I sank onto the edge of the bed. He was stripping for me—and me alone—so I was going to enjoy the big reveal.

Big was an understatement.

A gasp left my mouth as soon as Liam shed his briefs, his raging erection jutting in my direction, taunting me. Liam was a large man, and it would seem he was proportionate *everywhere*. I hadn't thought it possible for him to put some of my larger toy replicas to shame, but I was wrong.

Holy shit, he's going to put that monster inside of me. How am I going to be able to walk tomorrow?

Having read my thoughts—my face likely giving them away—Liam was confident, declaring, "It'll fit. Just prepare to be sore tomorrow, and remember you asked for this." Throat tightening, I swallowed as he asked, "Do you still want this?"

My mouth was dry, and words escaped me as I stared at his massive dick, but I managed to nod. As Liam stalked toward me, my heart hammered inside my chest. Yes, I wanted this more than anything, but that didn't mean I wasn't nervous. It had been a long time, and the last time hadn't been exactly fun.

Once he stood before me, my hand extended to wrap around his shaft. I'd never held a man's dick in my hands before, and while it was stiff, it was also velvety smooth. Trusting my instincts, I moved my hand to stroke up and down his length, causing Liam to drop his head back as a groan ripped from the back of his throat.

Feeling powerful having this control over him, I leaned forward and licked the underside of his swollen flesh. In a flash of motion, he had me on the bed, both wrists pinned above my head with one of his large hands. The fire in Liam's eyes told me he was unwilling to allow that small power exchange.

Desperate to touch him anywhere, I strained against his restraint, arching my back. "Please, Liam," I begged.

"Tell me what you want, Amy," he demanded, voice husky and low.

"I already did," I whimpered, struggling against his hold.

"You need to be more specific than 'fuck me.' How would you like me to fuck you, sweetheart?" He nipped at the sensitive spot on my neck, and I moaned.

"I don't know," I whined, thrashing my head from side to side.

Liam pulled back enough to stare at me with those twin blue flames. "Would you like me to tell you how I've dreamt of fucking you?"

"Yes," I breathed out, feeling moisture gather between my thighs.

"Oh, sweetheart, I've dreamed of you in a hundred different ways. Above me, below me, taking you from behind, against a wall, in the shower, bent over the couch—the possibilities are endless."

My breathing hitched at his words. I didn't care how he took me so long as he put me out of my misery. "Take me however you want. Just let me touch you."

"With pleasure." Releasing my hands, I immediately anchored them on his strong shoulders, loving the feel of them bunching as he held himself above me. Slowly, he trailed his tongue along the column of my neck, paying homage to each of my breasts, before dipping toward my navel as my stomach hollowed out. Liam's mouth drew a path over my hips before returning to the apex of my thighs.

Even though I was certain my body couldn't handle a second round of his mouth pleasing me there, my hips thrust up involuntarily in need. Instead of his tongue, his fingers grazed my pussy this time, causing Liam to groan as I bucked against his hand.

"Jesus, Amy, you're soaked." Slipping those digits into my tight passage, Liam asked, "Do you want my cock here, sweetheart?"

Delirious with desire, all I could do was whimper in response. Taking that as confirmation, Liam moved back up my body, and all I wanted was his lips on mine, consuming me. Spearing my fingers into his dark tresses, I tried pulling his mouth to mine, but he shifted at the last second, trailing hot, open-mouthed kisses along my jaw.

Liam's knee spread my thighs apart, settling his hips into the cradle created by mine. Feeling the tip of his cock probing my entrance, every muscle tensed, recalling how painful it had been the last time a man had been there. Chet wasn't half the size of Liam, so I was bracing, knowing it would be uncomfortable.

I hadn't realized my eyes were tightly shut until Liam's husky voice reached my ears.

"Look at me." Compelled to obey, I forced them open to find Liam's blue eyes blazing at me. "I need you to relax, Ames."

My chest heaved as I desperately tried to breathe, warding off the panic. I gritted out, "I'm trying."

Smoothing the hair away from my damp face with one hand, his eyes searched mine. "Do you trust me?" As I nodded, he continued, "Promise you'll tell me if anything I do hurts you."

Biting my lip, I shifted my hips in response, feeling the pressure as he slipped in that first inch. Liam moved his head to nibble my earlobe, and my hips lifted again, taking more of him as he held firm, allowing my movements to control the level of penetration. So far, nothing was painful, but I felt my inner walls stretching, accommodating his size.

Liam dropped his head to my breast, taking one of the pebbled pink peaks between his teeth and tugging gently before sucking it firmly inside his hot mouth. My pelvis jolted in reply, and Liam took advantage, surging his hips forward until he was fully seated inside me.

At least, I prayed he was. Shifting to see if more was coming, Liam groaned against my breast before releasing it, his head falling to the crook of my neck. "Fuck, Amy. Don't move a muscle."

At the pained tone of his voice, I grew concerned. "Did I do something wrong?"

Liam grunted out, "I need a minute. You're so fucking tight that if you move, I can't promise this will last more than a minute."

Oh. "Tight is a good thing, right?"

A strangled noise slipped past Liam's lips as I lightly gyrated my hips against his. "Take a moment to adjust because once I'm ready, I can't guarantee I will be gentle."

Taking his advice, I took inventory of the sensations coursing through my body. My clit pulsed almost painfully as my pussy was stretched to the limit by Liam's enormous dick. It was a tight fit, as he said, but not uncomfortable like I was expecting. It was a feeling of fullness, and I became desperate to move—there was an overwhelming urge to ease the ache.

After what felt like an eternity, Liam pushed up onto his elbows, testing with a gentle rocking of his hips, and on impulse, I pushed back, gaining some of that delicious friction I was craving. His forehead fell to mine, and I could hear his hoarse breathing as he pulled out a few inches and surged forward, coaxing a moan from the back of my throat at the intense sensations the action caused.

"So hot, so tight. You feel like heaven, sweetheart." Liam exhaled as he thrust in and out, the angle of his pelvis causing it to graze against my clit with each pass.

Writhing beneath his relentless rhythm as he pounded into me over and over, I felt the first tremors of an impending release as my body strained against his. I was close, so close. A few more pumps, with my hips' movements matching his, and I'd be there. The guttural sounds ripped from my throat were so foreign that I hadn't realized they were coming from me until I heard Liam's grunts hot in my ear.

Just as the tingles started climbing up from my toes, my body tensing in preparation, I felt the abrupt loss of Liam as he pulled out, flipping me onto my stomach. Gripping my hips, he propped me onto my knees as he drilled into me from behind. The smacking sound of our flesh colliding filled the air.

This new angle had him pressing against that sweet spot inside me, driving even deeper than before. Pushing up on shaky arms, I got onto all fours, rocking my hips back to meet his punishing pace. Each time our hips collided, it sent an intense wave of pleasure crashing over me, and I couldn't contain the near screams falling past my lips.

Behind me, Liam pulled my hips to meet his, uttering, "God, you should see how well you take all of me."

Moaning at the mental picture his words painted, I could feel my climax creeping up on me. Liam's movements became less measured and more erratic, signaling that he was close as well. Releasing one hand, he reached around, lightly pinching my clit as he continued battering into me from behind.

That was all it took. Blinding pleasure ripped through my body, stealing my breath as it rolled over me in intense waves as Liam's grunts grew in volume, pulling my hips to meet his with increasing force. Shaking from head to toe, I could feel my pussy clamping down on his dick, and suddenly, I went from overly full to empty in an instant.

Glancing over my shoulder, I saw his eyes screwed shut as he gripped his heavy cock, slick with my arousal, stroking it quickly before roaring as thick ropes of cum shot onto my back. In my lust-induced delirium, I hadn't even considered the need for a condom. Having no interest in sex before Liam got under my skin, I'd never needed birth control.

We had been playing with fire, but thankfully Liam had the conscious thought to pull out. It was overwhelming to know that he was always protecting me, even when we were at our most vulnerable.

Having fully emptied himself, Liam patted the side of my thigh, his voice soft. "Stay here."

Not moving a muscle, I waited as he crawled off the bed, walking into my ensuite bathroom. When he returned, his hands held a damp washcloth, which he used to clean up the mess on my back before folding it in half and pressing the clean side between my thighs. The heat felt amazing, soothing after the punishment my nether regions had endured.

Once satisfied with my aftercare, he removed the cloth, allowing me to collapse onto the bed as I still felt the aftershocks of the earth-shattering orgasm he'd rung from my body. I was so satisfied, my breathing evening for the first time in what felt like hours. Instead of joining me, Liam stood, pulling his briefs and jeans back on.

Rolling onto my side, I dared to ask, "Are you leaving?"

I didn't like this feeling. I wanted to be held, cradled in his strong arms, where I knew I'd always be safe.

Crouching to grab his shirt, he tossed it over his head, forcing his arms through the holes. "Our days and nights are mixed up. I have to work."

He was right, but it didn't hurt any less.

Seeing the crestfallen look on my face, he took three strides forward, dropping a chaste kiss on my forehead. "Rest, Amy."

I had been moments away from passing out when he began redressing, but now had too many thoughts running through my head as I watched his retreat, the sound of the door latching behind him crushing my soul.

This was just sex. I couldn't get emotional, but my job here wasn't done. Liam had been in control tonight, even if I'd pushed him to give in to whatever physical attraction we felt toward each other.

Dragging myself out of bed, I threw on my favorite oversized T-shirt before grabbing my phone and crawling under the covers. The smell of sex hung in the air—a reminder that we had crossed an invisible line tonight.

I needed my girls. They'd know what to do.

Amy: Phase 1 complete. Unfortunately, some of Lucy's work didn't survive.

Hannah: Holy shit. That's hot.

Natalie: Please tell me there's not a need for Phase 2.

Amy: He was in complete control the entire time. When I tried pleasuring him, he wouldn't let me.

Natalie: Maybe there's a reason.

Amy: He was so gentle afterward, cleaning me up, but then he just left.

Hannah: Typical man.

Natalie: If I know Liam, he's punishing himself right now for allowing things to go too far. For not protecting you in the way that he had built up in his mind.

Amy: *Nat, I didn't force him. You should have heard how tortured he was when he told me he wanted me so badly that he couldn't sleep.*

Hannah: *Damn, girl. At least tell me it lived up to the hype. It's always the broody ones that are intense in bed.*

Amy: *Oh my God. There aren't words.*

Natalie: *I don't want to hear any of this. *Covers ears**

Hannah: *Stop acting like a prude, Nat. You have four kids. It's not like you've never had sex.*

Natalie: *That's different.*

Amy: *Remind me how we were graced with Charlie in our lives. Was it because you jumped Jaxon's bones or the other way around?*

Natalie: **Sighs**You've made your point. Can you get on with breaking the poor man, so we can all go back to our lives?*

Hannah: *All right, now we're talking. Ames, I think Phase 2 needs to focus on you taking control in bed. Catch him off guard and then go for a little ride, if you know what I mean. *Winking emoji**

Amy: *I think you're right. He will probably go into hiding again, so I'll have to figure out how to draw him out.*

Hannah: *You've got this, Ames. Keep us updated.*

Natalie: *Or don't. That's fine too.*

Amy: *Rolls eyes* Night, ladies!

CHAPTER 18

Liam

WHAT THE HELL DID I just do?

I'd tried to walk away—giving Amy pleasure without taking any in return—but the hurt in her eyes when she asked if I didn't want her was the final nail in my coffin. I couldn't bear the notion of hurting her emotionally or physically, which was almost an oxymoron, knowing that giving her what she begged for could be more than a little uncomfortable.

I knew she was inexperienced, so had hoped that seeing my size would have been enough for her to back down. Nope. Not Amy. When she set her mind to something, it didn't matter if she was slightly frightened. She always saw it through. Her spirit was almost as sexy as her body.

My dreams of Amy had been child's play compared to the real thing. Her luscious curves had taunted me for months. But seeing them fully laid bare was intoxicating. She'd taunted me with her body and words until I snapped.

Amy had me so out of my mind that I hadn't realized I wasn't wearing protection until it was almost too late. No wonder it had felt so incredible that I'd nearly blown my load once she'd taken me fully inside her depths.

Her walls had gripped me like a velvet vise, soft, warm, and wet. I was instantly addicted, already craving another hit.

I had never had a woman drive me to the point of such primal desire that I claimed her without thinking of the consequences. I always wore a condom. It was automatic. Running a mental inventory in my head, I wasn't even sure there were any in the house. There hadn't been a need before now.

Terror pierced my heart, thinking about what could have happened if I hadn't had the wherewithal to pull out. Amy had been abstinent even longer than me, so the odds of her being on any form of birth control were slim to none. I could have gotten her pregnant, and then what? Sure, I was out of my mind aroused just thinking about her, but that didn't translate to a relationship. Amy had made it crystal clear that she wasn't interested in children.

She also said she had zero interest in sex.

Lines were blurred now, setting my world off-kilter. My need for control demanded that I live my life in black and white, but after one night with Amy, there were colors everywhere, each offering a different path or possibility.

Stumbling my way into the kitchen, I recalled Jaxon's secret stash of scotch, grabbing the bottle of brown liquor from its perch high in the cabinet next to the fridge. Pouring a generous amount into a lowball glass before adding a few ice cubes, I retreated to my basement office.

Reclining in the leather office chair, I took a large pull from the glass, relishing the burn as the liquor moved down my throat. Swirling the glass in my hand, I thought of Jaxon and how our lives and families had become intertwined. Natalie was always adamant that she'd gone next door to his house—this house—and, on a whim, propositioned him. How many nights had he sat here alone, a glass of scotch in his hands, mentally torn apart over my little sister?

Suddenly, I felt a kinship with the man I'd put through hell. My firm belief had been that, as a man, he should have had enough control to turn her away. He should have been strong enough not to have his judgment clouded by his long-standing attraction to Natalie.

That bastard would be laughing if he could see me now.

If Jaxon had felt even a fraction of what I felt toward Amy tonight, the poor bastard never stood a chance. The only difference was that they hadn't been married, and he had gotten her pregnant. Everything worked out for them, so why couldn't that be true for us?

Because your life is no longer your own, and you've lied to your wife.

The shadow cast by my lie of omission hung over my head, darkening any chance at happiness we could have had if it weren't for an accident of birth. All my life, people said I'd won the genetic lottery, but they had no idea how much I sacrificed because of that "win."

When Amy found out, there was a real risk that I'd lose her forever. The pain caused by my deception would only hurt more if we continued down this route of a sexual relationship. The physical intimacy could easily be misconstrued as emotional intimacy, and she'd be crushed that I lied. I would be no better than that asshole frat boy in her eyes.

Reminding myself that I was human, and we all made mistakes, I chalked tonight up to just that—I'd deviated from the plan but could get back on track.

One day at a time, right?

———⊰❈⊱———

Hi. My name is Liam, and it's been eight days since my last sexual encounter with my wife.

Each passing day required every ounce of mental resolve I possessed as my body yearned to get close to Amy again. It was physical agony knowing she was in the house—accessible and willing—when I was determined to keep my distance.

I can do this. I can do this.

If this week had been torturous, how would I survive the rest of our lives? Dreams of Amy had only become more vivid now that the physical sensation was burned into my memory to accompany the visions.

Restless, I checked my phone, praying it was time to wake for the day—or night, in my case. The tricky part was timing my escape from my room. I knew one glimpse of Amy, and my resolve would crumble, so I waited until she was in bed before venturing out.

The screen was bright, piercing the darkness of my bedroom. 10:30 PM.

Amy often worked in her room late at night, so I knew she didn't linger too long in our shared spaces past 9 PM. It was safe to emerge, eat something, and then begin catching up on emails before getting dressed in preparation for today's video calls.

Opening my bedroom door to all the lights on should have been my first warning signal. The next was the starchy smell of carbs floating up the stairs, combined with the scent of frying meat. There was no denying that Amy was still awake.

My brain was screaming to hunker down in my room and wait her out, but my stomach betrayed me, grumbling at the promise of food. This situation exposed flaws in my current setup. What I really needed was a mini-fridge and snack drawer up here in case of emergency.

That's it! An avoid-your-wife emergency stash!

What the hell was Amy still doing in the kitchen at this hour anyway?

My curiosity won out, and I ventured down the stairs, clad only in a pair of flannel pajama pants, even as the nagging voice at the back of my head told me to throw on a T-shirt. The shirt wouldn't matter in the end. Dressed like this, it wouldn't take much imagination on Amy's part to see that just the sight of her aroused me.

Reaching the last step, I froze. The open-concept house was both a blessing and a curse. From where I stood, I had a clear view of Amy in the kitchen, her back to me as she concentrated on whatever she was cooking on the stove. If—no, *when*—she turned around, she would know I had been watching. There was nowhere to hide.

Accepting inevitable discovery, I leaned against the banister, watching her. Amy's silky red locks were thrown atop her head in a messy knot, several curled strands escaping as she moved. The exposed column of her neck taunted me, begging to be kissed, sucked, and licked. My fists clenched at the memory of how soft that delicate skin was to the touch.

Raking my gaze down her body, I noticed Amy was wearing a loose button-down shirt. The blue pinstriping seemed familiar. Too familiar.

Is she wearing my shirt?

Craning my neck for a better view without daring to step forward to reveal my presence, I searched for any telltale signs that it was, in fact, my button-down she donned. As if on cue, she raised her arm, a hand slipping through the open slit created by the French cuffs not being secured. There was no doubt that it was a shirt from my personal collection.

Why the hell was she wearing one of my dress shirts? Did I miss the conversation where I gave her carte blanche to help herself to my closet?

Don't get me wrong. It was so fucking hot that my pajama pants were now tented with my straining erection. It pointed directly at my wife, indicating where it wanted to go.

I'd spent years honing my control. Sure, as a teenager, we all had those awkward moments where you had to cover your crotch with a textbook, but as an adult, I could command my dick to obey. I took pride that it only rose when the occasion called for it.

That all went out the window when I married Amy. Apparently, *she* was in control.

Fucking fantastic.

Spinning around with a plate in each hand, Amy spotted me, and her smile hit me square in the chest. I was still rubbing the tightness gathered there when she called out, "Hey, honey. How did you sleep?"

I'm honey now? Am I still asleep?

Rubbing a hand over the stubble on my jaw that would need to be shaved before getting to work, this sure felt real. Besides, my dreams of Amy didn't involve much talking.

Amy's eyes dropped to my pants, where I was blatantly aroused from watching her, and I could have sworn hunger flashed in those intoxicating green depths.

As much as I was enjoying the show, Amy yearned for a more active participant, commanding, "Come and sit. Have something to eat."

Don't tempt me.

Approaching the kitchen cautiously, I opted to sit on a stool, needing the buffer that the island provided. Space between our bodies was the only way I would to be able to keep my hands to myself. Amy turned back around to man the several pans she had on the stovetop, and that's when I noticed she was wearing my shirt and nothing else.

I'm not going to make it out of here alive.

"What are you doing?" I croaked out.

Her back still to me, Amy shrugged. "Cooking my husband breakfast before he goes to work. Isn't that what good wives do?"

Sure, maybe in a real marriage, but ours wasn't the last time I checked. "Are you wearing my shirt?" I knew the answer but wanted an explanation.

Looking over her shoulder, she smirked. "What's yours is mine, right, baby?"

Honey, and now baby? What the fuck is happening?

Speechless, I sat there while she plated eggs, pancakes, and bacon before spinning around and placing the bounty on the island. Sliding an empty plate to where I sat, along with a fork, she added, "I really like this pocket. So convenient."

Maybe I was having a stroke? Nothing she was saying made any sense, so that was the only logical explanation. Something was wrong with my brain.

Forking a stack of pancakes along with some bacon onto my plate, I asked, "Why do you need a pocket?"

A mischievous look crossed Amy's face, and she winked. "You'll see." Quickly changing the subject, she questioned, "Syrup?"

I barely managed a nod, causing her to walk toward the pantry, reaching for a high shelf where she must have stored the syrup. Mesmerized by her long legs, I couldn't help but stare as my shirt rode up her milky thighs, enough to glimpse the generous curve of the bottom of her bare ass.

Jesus, no panties again?

A groan escaped my mouth, knowing how completely accessible her pussy was at this moment.

Hearing the sound, Amy asked, "What was that?"

"Nothing," I mumbled as she returned with the syrup bottle, placing it on the island.

Drizzling some of the sticky brown liquid atop my pancakes, I could sense her watching me, so I looked up. "You going to eat?"

Licking her lips, her voice was sultry in her response. "Maybe later."

Needing the distraction, I cut into the food on my plate and took a bite. Amy had done a large share of the cooking when we'd lived with Natalie, so it wasn't surprising that my taste buds exploded in appreciation of her skill. While keeping my distance, I often cooked for myself, and this meal reminded me how much I had missed Amy's cooking.

I must have made an unconscious noise of ecstasy because I heard Amy giggle. "Enjoying yourself?"

"Mm-hmm," I practically moaned around the food in my mouth. Glancing up to thank her, I nearly choked on the bite I was about to swallow.

Amy was perched on the kitchen counter opposite the island. Her legs had fallen open, and her enticing pussy was taunting me on full display.

Sputtering at the sight, I grabbed the glass of water by my plate, downing it, trying to clear my throat. Amy swung her legs back and forth, watching me as I struggled to find my voice. "Wh-what are you doing?"

Biting her lower lip, she undid a button at the top of her shirt. Correction—*my* shirt. Peering at me from beneath her lashes darkened with mascara, her voice was low but playful. "I thought maybe once you were done, you'd be open to dessert."

Who is this woman, and what has she done with Amy?

The Amy I knew didn't use sexual innuendos while indecently exposing herself in our kitchen. The Amy I knew had zero interest in sex, and her experience level was near virginal.

Do you really want that old Amy back?

The answer was a resounding no, but I still didn't understand how we'd gotten here. Had I done this? Had I unknowingly turned Amy into this siren who was finding new ways to lure me into fucking her senseless?

Eight days was a good run. Tonight, the count would reset at zero because there was no chance of me walking away from the gift of Amy laid before me.

Praying I'd consumed enough carbs to ensure my stamina for everything I wanted to do to this woman, I shoved off the stool, stalking toward her. Amy was a sure thing, but I felt compelled to tease her as I stepped between her open thighs.

"I don't think you can handle me, sweetheart."

Amy's emerald eyes glinted with determination. "Wanna bet?"

Leaning forward to nip at her earlobe, I whispered, "What do I get if I win?"

Arching her back, my barely contained dick brushed up against her wetness, causing me to hiss as she clutched at my shoulders, breathing, "Me."

"Hmm." I moved down her neck, licking and sucking the soft flesh causing her to moan. "And if you win?"

Amy's chest was heaving against mine, her breathing already ragged. "You."

Growling, I pulled back enough to slowly undo the shirt's remaining buttons, eliminating the only barrier between me and a fully naked Amy. "I like those odds." Freeing the last button and pushing the sides wide, I ran my hands up her luscious curves, enjoying the flush creeping up her alabaster skin. "Where to, sweetheart?"

Her gasp was music to my ears when the pad of my thumb brushed over one of her erect nipples.

Panting, she forced out, "The couch."

That sounded perfect. I couldn't wait to see her full breasts bouncing in my face as I fucked her hard from below. "Your wish is my command."

Slipping my hands lower, I gripped her bare ass, loving how full and round it was. There was nothing better than a full-figured woman. Pulling Amy away from the counter, I felt the bite of her bare heels as they dug into my lower back with her legs locked around my hips.

Even though she clung to me like a spider monkey, she squealed, "Liam! Put me down! I'm too heavy!"

Pinching her ass, Amy jumped in my arms as I held steadfast, threatening, "If I hear you say one more unflattering word about your size, I'll be forced to punish you."

Her breathing hitched, and when I glanced up at her gorgeous face, the fire was back in her eyes as she taunted, "Promise?"

"You're going to be the death of me," I groaned.

Reaching the edge of the couch, I sat, settling Amy onto my lap. This location had seemed like a good idea, but as she began to grind over my throbbing cock, her arousal soaking through the thin flannel of my pants, I wasn't sure if I'd survive.

Gripping her hips, I lifted her easily, breaking the contact of our hips and causing Amy to whimper, "Please."

Trying to control my breathing, I rasped, "Let me take care of you, sweetheart. I'm not going to last long like this."

Her red hair created a curtain around us, and she tilted my chin up. "I want you inside me. Now."

God, how could I refuse her? My Adam's apple bobbed as I swallowed, and my hands allowed her to sink back down. Reaching into the shirt's pocket, Amy pulled out a foil packet, waving it victoriously. She came prepared, the clever girl. I had been in so much denial that the thought of purchasing a box of condoms hadn't crossed my mind.

If she's got a box stashed somewhere, this won't be the last time.

Shimmying off my lap, Amy knelt before me, grasping the waistband of my pants. I raised my hips to allow her to pull them down my legs. My dick was ready for action, bobbing against my stomach once it sprang free.

Eyeing my thick length, I watched Amy lick her lips, causing me to practically yell, "No!"

Those green eyes met mine, and her bottom lip stuck out in a hint of a pout, but she nodded. Reaching out, her slender fingers wrapped around my girth, and my hips bucked involuntarily. Amy's hand was soft as it stroked me gently, but I knew she was softer elsewhere.

Amy was smart enough not to push me too far, ripping open the foil packet and rolling the condom over my cock. Rising, placing a knee on either side of my thighs, she lined up our hips and sank down, taking all of me at an agonizingly slow pace.

Fuck. I'd talked myself into thinking I had imagined how incredible she felt that first time, but it was replicated now. Her tight walls were practically strangling my dick, and I dropped my head to her chest, the sensations threatening to overwhelm me.

Not caring that I was barely hanging on, Amy rocked her hips, moaning as she took pleasure from my cock. Never one to sit on the sidelines, I dug my fingers into the hot skin of her hips, sliding her body up before slamming it back down on my length, ripping a near scream from her throat. Before I could repeat my actions, Amy lifted far enough that we were no longer connected.

Missing her warmth, I looked up at her in question, to which she replied, "No."

"No?"

"Grab the couch cushions. If you touch me again, I'll be forced to tie you up."

Was she serious? I'd never allowed a woman total control in bed. None of them had ever complained about my take-charge attitude. My body craved contact with hers so badly that I considered what she proposed. Amy knew I was bigger and stronger, so she'd need my compliance to follow through on her threat to restrain me. Yet, she was brave enough to demand it anyway.

How could I deny this sexy, spirited woman?

Gripping the cushions as she'd ordered, a smirk crossed her lips, and I decided it was worth it to see that look of triumph on her face.

Satisfied, Amy sank down once more, offering, "You can use your mouth."

She didn't need to tell me twice. Her plump breasts were right in my face, so I shifted until I could nip one of the pink peaks with my teeth, latching on. My eyes rolled into the back of my head as Amy rode me at a maddeningly slow pace. Up and down, up and down, adding the occasional swirl of her hips as she reached the base of my cock.

My fingers itched to grip her hips and fuck her hard, but I willingly relinquished control for the first time in my life. Instead, I took my frustration out on the soft flesh I could reach with my mouth—biting, nipping, licking, and sucking every inch that became accessible.

Feeling her thighs shake and her motions become jerky and unmeasured, I knew she was close. Releasing a nipple from my mouth with a pop, I looked up at the goddess riding me as if her life depended on it, racing towards release. Amy's head was thrown back as her fingers dug into my shoulders so hard I knew she'd leave marks. Uninhibited like this, she was stunning, and the sight of her so free was enough to have my balls tightening, nearing the edge myself.

Keeping true to my promise of no hands, I thrust my hips upward, meeting her downward thrusts, giving her what she needed to shatter around me.

Moaning at the change, her voice was thick with lust. "Oh God, Liam."

"Take what you need, sweetheart."

Amy's moans rose in volume as I felt her walls clench around my dick before she strained against my body, her head dropping to my shoulder as the waves of pleasure overtook her. Convinced I'd given her what she needed in terms of control, I released my death grip on the couch cushions, anchoring my hands on her hips as I pumped into her warmth from be-low— prolonging her orgasm as I took my own, grunting into her shoulder as my toes curled into the plush carpet at my feet.

Holding her against my chest as our breathing steadied, she finally pulled back to look at me, her eyelids heavy and a sated smile gracing her lips. "You know what I like about this house?"

I barely knew my own name right now as I lazily stroked her back beneath the open shirt she still wore. "What's that?"

"No kids."

Amy started to laugh, and it was infectious. My chest began to rumble as my own laughter joined hers. She was right. We were free to fuck in every room of this house, any time we wanted.

Stroking her cheek with my thumb, I remarked, "Always glass half full, aren't you?"

"One of us has to be."

God, she was perfect. So full of light and optimism, and I had the power to crush that. Shaking away those dark thoughts, I carried her to bed, tucking her in with the promise of cleaning the mess in the kitchen.

Hi. My name is Liam, and it's been zero days since my last sexual en-counter with my wife.

CHAPTER 19

Amy

LIAM WAS DRIVING ME insane. I'd tempted him twice now to sleep with me, but beyond that, he was a ghost. It was exceedingly clear that he was avoiding me, and it hadn't escaped my notice that he had never kissed me on the lips. What was that about?

He may have underestimated my determination because I had no plans to give up on my mission. It went beyond the mental aspect of sparring for control and was now purely driven by the physical need to chase the high created when our bodies were connected. There wasn't a manufactured orgasm that came close. Liam's words and caresses only heightened the pleasure I couldn't replicate alone. Trust me, I'd tried.

It had been over a week since I'd enticed him half-naked in the kitchen. The drought ended tonight.

This evening, we were going out for a belated thirtieth birthday dinner for Natalie. The actual date was last week, but the Comets had been on the road. I was mildly surprised that Jaxon didn't want to do something bigger, but Natalie wasn't a fan of being in the spotlight. Couldn't say that

I blamed her now that I'd had a taste of what she had endured married to a prince.

Maintaining separate bedrooms would allow me the element of surprise. Liam made it no secret that he loved my curves, so I planned to show them off tonight. Another call to Lucy, and I dressed for the intimate dinner in a tight purple halter mini dress. It was rare that I sported a hemline above the knee, so I knew it would catch Liam's immediate attention.

Adding to Liam's shock at my appearance would be that I'd cut my hair, which now hung in loose curls that barely brushed my shoulders. I felt like a new woman, and this change reflected that. Smokey eye makeup—a departure from my signature natural look—was accented with a bold splash of red across my lips. He wouldn't know what hit him when I met him downstairs.

Checking my appearance in the full-length bathroom mirror, a shiver raced down my spine in anticipation. If Liam reacted the way I expected, I would get a little appetizer before we left for the restaurant.

Showtime.

My heels clicked on the hardwood as I walked the length of the second-floor hallway and down the stairs to where my husband waited. Each click matched the beating of my heart. The build-up was exhilarating.

Reaching the bottom, Liam waited on the couch but didn't look away from whatever occupied his attention on his phone. His suit jacket lay folded over the seat next to him, and his open collar revealing a smattering of dark chest hair had my mouth watering and my thighs clenching.

Damn, my husband is hot.

Sweetening my voice, projecting an air of innocence, I beckoned, "Liam, are you ready to go?"

"Uh-huh." Still not glancing up, he stood, shoving the phone into his pocket and grabbing his jacket.

Liam made it two steps toward where I stood when he looked up and stopped dead in his tracks. Watching the transition in his demeanor might have been my favorite part of the game we were playing. Immediately, his free fist clenched by his side, his hungry blue eyes scanning me from head to toe as his breathing became shallow.

Tapping my foot in mock annoyance, I questioned, "Are you okay?"

Liam's head nodded absently while he rubbed the center of his chest, an almost pained expression creeping onto his face. "Yeah. Uh. You're going out like that?"

Peering down, I assessed my look before peeking back at him, batting my eyelashes. "You don't like it? It's new."

"You've been doing a lot of shopping," Liam remarked, his eyes never leaving mine. Reaching up, I twirled a curl with a single finger, prompting his focus to shift enough to ask, "New haircut?"

"Felt like a change." I lifted one shoulder before letting it fall.

He was still rooted to the spot, so I approached slowly, knowing his restraint was barely leashed. Bringing my body flush with his, I ran a hand up his chest, purring, "You look good enough to eat."

A shudder moved through him, and I couldn't stop the corner of my mouth from quirking up with the knowledge that I had him exactly where I wanted him. There was a rustle of fabric as Liam dropped his suit jacket before anchoring his hands on my ass, pulling me tighter, close enough that I could feel the growing bulge in his pants pressing insistently against my pelvis.

"Ten fucking days," he muttered.

"What was that?"

"Doesn't matter." Dropping to his knees, he ran both hands up my thighs and beneath the hem of my dress.

Playfully shimmying away, I protested, "Liam, we'll be late."

Rising to his full height, the aroused look on his face made him devastatingly handsome. Voice rough, he skimmed the skin of my upper thigh. "I can make this quick."

Nearly panting at the thought of a rough coupling with this virile man, I bit my lip, trying desperately not to show how much his words were affecting me.

It was useless. He saw right through me, whispering in my ear, "That's what you want, isn't it, you naughty girl? You want it quick and dirty?"

A moan escaped from deep in my throat as I shamelessly ground my hips against his, my voice quivering. "Yes."

Liam's fingers stopped teasing my flesh, moving higher with purpose, grazing the edge of my lace thong. He looped fingers around the waistband, easing them down my legs and over my heels. "I was beginning to believe you didn't own underwear."

"Skirt. Short." Jeez, that didn't even make sense; the words were all jumbled. I could barely manage a coherent thought when he touched me—talked to me—like this.

Bringing the black lace to his nose, he breathed in deeply, and a rush of heat pooled between my thighs. Damn, why was that so provocative? Stuffing the tiny scrap into his pants pockets, he chided, "That's a shame. They're mine now."

Gasping at his boldness and the idea of being bare at dinner, I began to throb, needing him between my legs more than I needed to breathe.

Liam might be beating me at my own game. Control was an illusion and, frankly, overrated if you asked me. If he wanted to be a caveman, who was I to stop him?

Slipping a hand between my thighs, finding me wet for him, Liam groaned. "Fuck, Amy."

"Yes, please," I taunted. Slipping the loop of my wristlet over my hand, I took a step back, unzipping it and removing a condom.

Liam's eyes flared, an arm snaking out to pull me back into his embrace, his voice smooth. "All you have to do is ask, sweetheart. Why must we play these little games?"

"Half the fun is in the chase," I taunted.

Growling, he plucked the condom from my hand trapped against his chest, his husky voice sending shivers down my spine as he retorted, "Then I think it's long past time I fuck that smirk off your face."

Gripping the hem of my skirt, he yanked it up so I could feel the room's cool air rush across my ass right before he took two handfuls, lifting me and backing me toward the wall. Once he had me braced, sandwiched between the drywall and the solid brick wall of his chest, Liam urged my thighs around his hips before unbuckling his belt.

Using one forearm beneath my ass, he held me steady as he shifted, undoing his zipper before rolling on the condom I'd provided. Without warning, he slammed home, stealing the breath from my lungs. Pinned as I was against the wall, I was at Liam's mercy as he began his punishing pace. Head dropping to my shoulder, he held me steady, changing angles and noting which elicited either a verbal or physical response from me, then honing in on those until I was panting, desperate for release.

Liam's breath was hot against my neck as he ground out, "Come for me, sweetheart."

Shifting slightly, he hit right where I needed him, and the world faded away as pleasure blasted through me so forcefully that I saw stars behind my tightly clenched eyes. Liam's repeated chanting about how wet and tight I was only served to spur me on as the sensations were as unrelenting as his continued thrusts into the very core of me.

Just when I thought I might die from the unending waves of pleasure, his grip on my ass grew painful, and he stilled, grunting his release so loudly I was afraid our bodyguards waiting in the car would hear him. Our harsh breathing filled the air as I sagged in his arms, grateful for the support of his rock-hard body.

Mind hazy, my hands toyed with the sweaty strands of hair at the nape of Liam's neck, wondering if this kind of explosive connection was typical. My body had become Liam's to command. The mind-blowing pleasure was never a question—it was a guarantee. Don't get me wrong, I wasn't complaining, but had I just hit the orgasm jackpot with Liam as a partner, or was something deeper involved?

Good thing we had all the time in the world to find out.

Liam nuzzled my neck, dropping a few light kisses along my collarbone before drawing back to look at me. He was a sweaty mess, but he was my sweaty mess. A lock of his jet-black hair had fallen over one eye, so I smoothed it back, laughing when it immediately fell again.

His chest vibrated against mine as his chuckles reverberated through the room. "You think this is funny?"

"I love seeing you like this—human."

Squeezing my ass, he teased, "I thought you liked the animal side of me."

"Animal is good too. Just so long as the stick is removed from your ass."

Liam's eyes flared. "Oh, sweetheart, don't get me started on all the things I'd like to do to your ass."

My face flooded with heat at what he implied. We'd only fucked three times, and I was *not* ready to explore beyond the traditional avenues of sex yet. Averting my gaze, I croaked out, "We have to go."

"We could stay." He was serious.

Ugh. I finally had him ready and willing, but there was no way I could take him up on his offer. If it were anyone other than Natalie, I'd stay here with him all night, but we couldn't, and deep down, he knew that too.

Tapping his shoulder in a silent signal to set me down, it pained me to shut him down. "It's for Natalie."

Nodding, he acknowledged the meaning behind that simple statement, pulling back enough to end the connection between our two bodies and easing me down until my bare feet met the floor. I couldn't even remember losing my purple pumps somewhere along the way. I'd been that lost in Liam.

I shimmied my hips while pulling my tight skirt back down as Liam headed to the powder room to clean himself up. A quick glance in the entryway mirror confirmed that my hair was a mess, but my makeup was untouched. Yet another reminder that Liam continued to steer clear of my lips. Running my fingers through my curls to loosen them, trying to hide the tangles in the back from where I'd thrashed my head against the wall, I began searching for my shoes and wristlet.

Finally put back together, I grabbed a shawl as Liam returned, and we made our way out to the waiting SUV. Already a half hour behind schedule, I could only imagine our absence had placed us at the center of the conversation, with speculations running wild.

The hostess led us back toward the private dining section at Nomad, bought out for Natalie's milestone birthday celebration. The intimate setting was dimmed, softly lit by candles, with red roses adorning every table's centerpiece. If the evening had a theme, it would be romance. Perfect for our resident hopeless romantic.

Two seats were held for us at the head table, reserved for the guest of honor's closest friends and family. As we approached, Natalie and Jaxon stood, smiles gracing their faces. Pure happiness and love radiated off them in waves, and I couldn't help but feel a bit jealous. The Slates made marital bliss look effortless.

My rational mind knew it wasn't a competition, but it was human nature to compare yourself to others.

Reaching the standing couple, Natalie pulled me into a tight hug while Jaxon and Liam did some kind of awkward handshake.

Switching partners, Jaxon leaned in, kissing my cheek and whispering, "You look incredible, Amy."

It was humbling to have this man that women had once fawned over as the league's most eligible bachelor complimenting my appearance. Most women would have dissolved into a puddle with a simple word of admiration from him. I could appreciate that Jaxon was a good-looking man in his own right, but he had nothing on my Liam.

Whoa. When did he become my *Liam?*

Technically, he was mine in a legal sense, so that was my story, and I was sticking to it.

Jaxon had barely pulled away when Liam's firm grip, possessive around my waist, pulled me into his side. Looking over at him in surprise, he was staring daggers at Jaxon. Had I somehow ended up in the middle of their pissing contest?

"Let's sit down." Liam's words were edged with steel.

Was he jealous? Of Jaxon? The man had barely grazed my cheek with his lips. It had been chaste, almost brotherly.

Rounding to the other side of the table, where two empty seats sat waiting for us, I noted who else had been granted the honor of sitting at the head table. There was Hannah, of course, two of Jaxon's closest teammates, Cal and Benji, and then Jaxon's much younger brother, Braxton, rounded out our eight-top.

Liam pulled out my chair, allowing me to sit, before guiding it under the table. I was not expecting him to bring his chair closer to mine, sitting to my right with his thigh flush against mine.

It was painfully obvious he was staking his claim, so I nudged his side, leaning close to whisper, "Are you going to pee on me next?"

His only response was a grunt, having reset to his caveman factory settings. I wasn't going to complain if that meant we would be maintaining body contact during dinner. His touch was oddly comforting, even in a non-sexual capacity.

Hannah, seated to my left, tugged my wrist to get my attention. Turning to her, she almost fell out of her seat trying to get close enough to say under her breath, "I've never known you to be late. Must have been hot as hell. You'll have to share later."

A blush crept up my neck as my eyes darted around the table. If Hannah knew exactly what had prompted our tardiness, there was a good likelihood that they all did. Our newlywed status didn't do us any favors in that department. Adding to my remorse was Jaxon signaling the wait staff to begin the six-course feast he'd had prepared for the occasion. They'd been holding dinner for us. This was Natalie's night, and we'd provided a distraction.

Hors d'oeuvres were offered tableside, and champagne was poured. Once everyone was settled, Jaxon stood, clinking the side of a knife against his champagne flute, signaling he wanted the attention of the room. The din of conversation slowly softened to hushed whispers before the room descended into silence.

Jaxon was easily the face of the Comets franchise, and public speaking came with the job. He was relaxed, with an easy smile, as he addressed the room.

"I want to thank everyone for coming out tonight to help us celebrate Natalie." He turned that brilliant smile on my best friend, addressing her like they were the only two people in the room. "Baby, you are my dream come true."

He continued his toast, but I focused on the couple, the words fading away. Natalie beamed up at Jaxon from her seat, her eyes glassy with unshed tears, while Jaxon had to clear his throat more than once as emotions threatened to overcome him.

Feeling Liam's fingers tracing lazy circles along the bare skin of my shoulder, I realized I'd unconsciously leaned into him while blinded by the love on display between my best friend and her husband. My hands had been clenched together tightly in my lap, but as I surrendered to the comfort of Liam's touch, one hand dropped to his thigh pressed tightly to mine as my head dropped onto his shoulder. When his free hand, warm and soft, covered mine, a contented sigh fell past my lips.

Enveloped in the safety of Liam's arms, I focused back on the pair opposite us. What Liam and I had was new and, at this point, purely physical. I wondered if he'd ever look at me how Jaxon looked at Natalie—like she was his whole world.

That begged the question—did I want Liam to look at me like that? Did I want more? What would that even look like in our situation? Could we turn this initially platonic, mutually beneficial transaction into something real?

Lost in thought, I barely heard the chorus of "cheers" as Jaxon finished his speech, and everyone toasted the birthday girl. The warmth of Liam's hand left mine as he gripped my chin, turning my face to his. His thumb stroked my cheek, and only when I felt wetness spread beneath his touch did I realize I was crying.

What the hell was wrong with me? I was not that weepy type of girl. I didn't cry over babies or sappy movies. Maybe I was getting my period. That would explain everything—an uncontrollable hormonal imbalance. That had to be it. The alternative was simply too terrifying to put into words.

Liam's blue eyes shone with concern as he whispered low, "Are you all right, sweetheart?"

Nodding, my voice was thick as I forced out, "I'm fine." I was lying, and he knew it—as evidenced by the way his lips turned down, deepening his signature scowl.

Hannah grabbed my hand before he could press the issue, declaring, "We need to freshen up. Come on, Ames."

Hannah practically ripped me from Liam's arms, and I felt the loss of our body contact immediately, shivering in response. Liam's jaw clenched, the stormy look on his face signifying that he wasn't pleased with the interruption of the intimate moment we were sharing in front of a room full of people.

Stumbling slightly, I struggled to keep up with Hannah's pace as she dragged me toward the bathroom, signaling for Natalie to join us with a tilt of her head. Bursting through the bathroom door, she dropped my hand, quickly checking under the stalls to confirm we were alone. As soon as Natalie entered behind us, Hannah locked the main door.

Hannah turned back to me, hands on her hips, demanding, "Spill, Amy."

Emotionally rung out, I leaned against the wall of sinks as I groaned, "Spill what?"

"Oh, I don't know. Maybe about how you showed up almost an hour late to our best friend's birthday party, or perhaps, let's discuss why you started crying during Jaxon's toast. Unless there's something else you'd like to add to the list?"

Always the mother of the group, Natalie chimed in softly, "I think what Hannah is trying to ask is if you're okay. Acting out of character is understandable. You're dealing with a lot right now. Let us know how we can help."

Eyes trained on the floor, I whispered, "I'm so confused."

Natalie moved to my side. "About what?"

"Everything."

"Liam?"

"Of course, Liam!" Frustration flowed through me, and I began pacing the tiny space as it poured out of me. "I can't figure him out! He ignores me unless I'm blatantly offering up my body. But God, when I do offer it, he brings me to my knees, saying things and doing things that shock and excite me. The man has my panties in his pocket right now, for crying out loud! And then there's the fact that he won't kiss me on the lips. Like, at all. Ever. Then there are the moments like tonight. When he acts possessive, staking his claim when Jaxon complimented me, making sure the entire room knows I'm his. I don't even know why I started crying tonight. Maybe I've reached my limit. Tell me what to do because I'm so lost. I'm in way over my head."

That stream of consciousness had seemingly come out in a single breath, and my chest heaved with the effort to breathe again.

Natalie's eyes were wide as she uttered, "That's a lot to unpack."

Hannah smirked. "I'd like to circle back to the comment about panties." Tilting her head, she assessed me. "Does that mean you've been sitting next to me commando this entire time?"

Natalie sighed. "Oh, Hannah."

"What? I don't have a date tonight, and I'm seated next to Baby Braxton, who isn't even legal to drink. I'm not getting laid tonight, so sue me if I want to hear about the hot sex Amy is having." Natalie threw her a pointed look, and Hannah threw her hands up in surrender. "Fine. I get it. Amy's struggling, but damn, girl."

Natalie turned her attention back to me. "What do *you* want, Amy?"

"I don't know what I want!" I yelled back. "I barely know who I am anymore! Liam has twisted my life inside out. He's never turned me down when I've tempted him with sex, but he's not all there. Why won't he kiss me? Am I just a warm body?"

Hannah blurted out, "Fuck that. I'll go out there right now and beat some sense into that man if he can't see the prize he has in front of him."

She was halfway to the door when Natalie stopped her. "Hannah, the last thing Amy needs is us getting involved." Then she trained her always-kind eyes on me. "Ames, you need to decide if this is the relationship you want—where you keep everything to yourself—or if you want a true partnership with Liam."

I scoffed. "He's not the easiest person to talk to."

"No, he's not," Natalie agreed with a chuckle. "But I saw the tortured look on his face when he wiped the tears from your face. He can't bear to see you like this, so do yourselves a favor and lay all the cards on the table. Define what you want so that you're both on the same page."

My eyes dropped to the floor. "I'm sorry I ruined your birthday."

"It's not ruined. You've saved my ass more than once over the years, and maybe now it's time for us to save yours. Let us know when you figure it out, and we will have your back like you've always had ours."

"Preach," Hannah agreed.

The promise of unconditional love from my best friends had fresh tears threatening to spill. I was the rational one of our crew, so I knew figuring out what I wanted out of a life with Liam would require listing the pros and cons and hypothetical scenarios. The idea made my head spin, so I pushed it aside. I'd deal with it later. Not tonight. Tonight was for Natalie. I'd already stolen enough focus from her celebration.

We shared a group hug before unlocking the door and returning to the party. The rest of the night passed in a blur, and I welcomed the distraction of mingling with the guests and sharing small talk. As Liam led me to the car at the end of the evening, the thought of figuring out what I wanted for our future weighed heavily on my mind.

Maybe breaking Liam was breaking me.

CHAPTER 20

Liam

HI. MY NAME IS Liam, and it's been six days since my last sexual encounter with my wife.

Yes, I was still counting.

I found myself paranoid most days, looking around every corner, wondering when the minx of a woman I'd married would appear, tempting me with her body to the point of insanity. Walking away from her was damn near impossible, and she knew it. The need for Amy was rooted so deeply inside my brain that I knew it was only a matter of time before I stopped the charade of waiting for her and initiated our next sexual encounter.

Hell, I was the perv with her dirty panties in my nightstand drawer.

Even with thoughts of Amy always in my mind, I was on a mission today. Time was not on my side, and I needed to warn Natalie and Jaxon of the potential media shitstorm they would end up entangled in if, or rather, *when* news broke that Leo was no longer my father's heir.

Coward. Telling them before you tell your wife.

More than once, I contemplated throwing it all away—letting Lucy become Father's sole remaining heir—to eliminate all risk of Amy bolting once she found out. There was no winning. I couldn't protect both Amy and Lucy. I convinced myself that since Amy and I had no plans for children, my standing in as heir only prolonged the inevitable. At some point, Lucy would be called upon to rule, which might only be a difference of mere years. Yet somehow, I couldn't force myself to make that call and end this elaborate ruse. Deep down, I knew I couldn't do that to my baby sister.

A man was expected to choose his wife over his family, but I didn't have that luxury. My marriage to Amy wasn't typical, and neither was my family. Somehow, that made me just as bad as Leo, and I hated myself for it.

I decided to walk next door, even though a foot of snow was on the ground. The brisk winter air was exactly what I needed to clear my head. Knocking lightly on the front door, everything else faded away, replaced with pure joy as Natalie opened the door, Charlie in her arms. That baby girl had become a beacon of light in all our lives, and I was incredibly grateful when she reached her chubby arms out to me, loving and trusting me without question.

Snatching her from her mother's arms, I kissed Natalie's cheek in greeting before walking inside and slipping off my shoes.

Natalie laughed lightly as she closed the door behind me. "Good to see you too, Liam."

Tickling Charlie's soft belly, she laughed, and the soft sound soothed me. In avoiding Amy, I'd spent too much time away from the kids, and that reality twisted in my gut. Something had to give. I couldn't keep living like this.

Looking around, I asked Natalie, "Jaxon home?"

Folding arms over her chest, she eyed me warily. "Yeah, he got home from practice about an hour ago."

"Good. There's something I need to talk about with both of you."

"All right . . ." She could tell something was up but went to grab Jaxon as I took Charlie into the living room, sitting with her on the floor surrounded by her mountain of toys. I was playing her a classic nursery rhyme on the piano play mat when Natalie returned, Jaxon in tow.

Leaving the security blanket of Charlie, I pushed off the ground, sitting on the couch, and inviting Natalie to join me. Jaxon was stiff, tension radiating off him in waves as he elected to stand.

Clearing my throat, I made the snap decision to go off-script. Surprising even myself, I blurted out, "I want to throw Amy a surprise birthday party."

Their bodies visibly relaxed, and a smile stretched across Natalie's face. "Oh, Liam, that's a *wonderful* idea! We can throw it here! She'll never be expecting it."

Jaxon chimed in, "Amy deserves to be celebrated. She's done so much for all of us."

"I couldn't agree more." I was playing it cool, but internally, alarms were sounding off. That had come out of left field. The idea hadn't so much as crossed my mind before it flew out of my mouth.

Natalie sagged against the couch in relief. "Thank God. I was worried it was something to do with Leo."

Time to lower the boom. "Actually . . . I do have news about Leo."

Sitting up, her back was ramrod straight, and I could see the beginnings of tears shining in her eyes. "Oh God," she whispered.

Considering her fear surrounding Leo stemmed from his sudden reappearance about a year ago threatening to take the kids, maybe my news wouldn't seem so bad. Grabbing her hand as Jaxon placed a reassuring one on her shoulder, I quickly dispelled her worst fear. "Nat, no. It's not what you think."

"Nothing good comes from anything involving Leo."

She wasn't wrong.

"There's no delicate way to say this. It has recently been revealed that Leo does not share the same father as Lucy and me. He is the product of an assault on my mother."

Natalie gaped at me, hands flying to her mouth. "Oh, God. Poor Addy."

"Father claimed Leo, but they've decided he can't be allowed to rule," I explained.

The full ramifications of what I said hadn't sunk in yet, so she shook her head, her brown eyes wide with panic. "No, not Jameson."

"It won't be Jameson. Leo and, by extension, your children, do not have a drop of royal blood." I paused before admitting, "It'll be me."

"You." The word was barely above a whisper. I nodded, fully accepting my sacrificial role. "Does—does Amy know?"

The guilt of keeping this secret became a constant dull ache in my chest, and I knew that Amy should have been the first to know. Even Natalie knew that. "No, she doesn't. I can't bear to tell her. She'll leave me."

Natalie threw her arms around me. "Oh, Liam. I'm sorry." I was sorry too. For so many things. When she pulled away, her voice was shaky. "Does this mean . . . Oh my God. Can Jaxon . . .?"

Tears slipped down her cheeks, and Jaxon moved lightning quick, rounding the couch, kneeling before her, and cupping her face. "Baby, I don't need a piece of paper to tell me those are my kids. I am their father in every way that matters."

"But—but," she stammered. Natalie turned to me, "I never thought it was possible." Her voice broke, "Thank you, Liam."

Jaxon's eyes never left her face, but he echoed her sentiment. "Yes, thank you, Liam."

Even though I knew it would rip my heart out when Amy discovered the truth, this moment reminded me that I was protecting my family by assuming this role. They were freed from the chains that now bound me.

Children shouldn't have to live with this burden. I was strong. I could carry the weight for the people I loved.

"Right now, nobody knows. My parents have kept it hidden my entire life, never intending anyone to find out. I don't know when they plan to make this announcement, but it'll bring the media circus back to your door when they do. The royal children not being royal will be quite the story."

Natalie nodded. "But it'll be the last story. Their lives will no longer be public domain. I'll never be able to repay you for everything you've done for us."

"Just be happy," I replied. "That's all I ever wanted for you, for the children."

Pulling me into her embrace, Natalie whispered, "You are the best big brother I could have ever asked for." My heart twisted inside my chest. I'd done right by at least one of the women in my life. That had to count for something, right?

Charlie began to whine where she sat on the floor, and Natalie excused herself to put her down for a nap. I was preparing to leave when Jaxon stopped me.

"You look like you could use a drink."

"God, yes," I breathed.

Clapping me on the back, he led me into the kitchen, grabbing a bottle of scotch. The label indicated it was the same brand as the one left behind next door. I took a sip from the offered glass, the taste reminding me of Amy. I'd savored this same drink the night we first slept together.

"Come on." Jaxon headed for the basement stairs toward my former living quarters. My apartment of rooms was untouched, and we settled in my office. The oversized leather couch beckoned, and we sat on opposite ends. Getting right to the point, he remarked, "You're falling for our Amy, aren't you?"

"*My* Amy," I growled.

Jaxon laughed, giving mock cheers with his glass of scotch. "That answers that question."

"Is this funny to you?"

"No, but it's fresh in my memory how agonizing it is to pine after the woman you love before she loves you back."

Despair filled me. "She'll never forgive me."

"A word of advice? Tell her the truth." He was genuinely sympathetic. "If she loves you back, she'll be upset, but her feelings for you will outweigh any hurt or anger. It's understandable why you've kept this close to the vest."

"I can't lose her."

"Is there someone waiting in the wings to take your place? Realistically, how long can you keep this secret? Take it from me. The truth always comes out."

Jaxon was referring to his secret tattoo that inadvertently announced to the world that he had a daughter. Natalie had been furious and kicked him out of the house. It had been hell for them both. I'd never seen two people so absolutely wrecked in all my life, and for what? Love? It was more trouble than it was worth.

"I'm trying to protect her." It was the same story I'd been telling myself for months.

"Maybe that's the problem."

I threw back the rest of my drink and glared at him. "Come again?"

"Look, Liam. You're a stand-up guy. You took care of my family when I couldn't be there, and for that, I'm forever indebted to you. But your idea of protection is slightly misguided at times. You go overboard. It pushed Natalie away, and if you're not careful, it'll do the same to Amy. She's a big girl. Doesn't she deserve a say in whether she needs protection?"

He was right. I just couldn't bring myself to do it. I was on a path of self-destruction and seemingly powerless to stop it.

Hammering his point home, Jaxon continued, "Amy is such a special person to me, to Natalie. I want to see her happy, and it seems you're the one who brings her that happiness. Seeing you two together at Nat's party? She was glowing. You're good for each other, so I'll offer you the same advice she once offered me regarding my relationship with Natalie. Don't fuck it up."

"What if I already have?"

"Then you grovel. The longer you keep this hidden, the worse it will be when it comes out, especially if you're not the one to tell her. Just think about it."

That's all I was doing—thinking about it. Picturing her face when the truth was revealed that I'd deceived her, luring her unknowingly into a life she never wanted. I knew Amy well enough to know she'd feel as though I had betrayed her. The fear of that moment twisted in my gut, but it was inevitable. I'd be alone, and Amy would hate me.

Thanking Jaxon for the drink and the chat, I returned home to sleep before I chanced a run-in with Amy. Pressing the button on the blackout curtains in my room, I welcomed the sweet oblivion of unconsciousness for a few hours.

I should have known better. Amy owned my dreams, and there was no escaping her. The image of her naked body was glorious—she was the most stunning woman I'd ever seen—and at least in my dreams, I allowed myself to kiss her. My tongue slid against hers, and in my imagination, she tasted incredible as I swallowed her moans.

The memory of her touch only added to the reality of the dream. It had never felt more real as she rode me, a goddess taking her pleasure. The perception of release was so strong and powerful that I awoke suddenly, gasping for air. Holy shit, I'd never had a dream feel that intense.

Reaching down to ensure I hadn't made a mess of my sheets, my fingers tangled in a handful of soft, silky hair.

What the hell?

Giving a light tug on that fistful of hair, I heard a moan resulting in vibrations surrounding my entire dick. Fuck. I knew that moan. Rising on an elbow, I tugged again and felt a wet warmth as it moved up and off my length with a telltale pop.

No. She couldn't have.

Feather-soft kisses moved up my abs and chest until they reached my neck, confirming that the overwhelming feeling of release in my dream had been real. Amy had climbed into my bed and had sucked me off in my sleep. My emotions were torn between feeling used and disappointed that I missed that incredible sight.

This vixen was getting bolder by the day.

Still catching my breath from the orgasm she'd stolen from me, I gasped, "I thought I was dreaming."

"Weren't you?" she purred.

Gripping her hips, I steeled my voice. "Is this a game to you, Amy?"

Defiance colored her words. "Sure as hell seems like it to you, Liam. Hot and cold all day long. Maybe you needed a taste of your own medicine."

Without warning, I dragged her up my body until hers was vertical, with her hips hovering over my face. I could smell her arousal. She'd come to my bed naked, knowing she was poking the bear.

Above me, she flailed, trying to balance in this position, so I commanded, "Grab the headboard."

Obeying, she was indignant, squeaking out, "What do you think you're doing?"

Pulling her down enough that my nose nudged her clit, I relished the sound of that moan I'd come to know so well. "Oh, sweetheart. You stole from me."

Amy's hips instinctively rocked, trying to get closer to my face. "Stole?"

"Yes, you naughty little thief. You robbed me of the vision of you taking my cock in your mouth, watching you swallow every last drop as I exploded inside that tight, hot mouth of yours. Didn't you?" There were no words from above, only soft moans and gasps as I teased the sensitive flesh accessible to my mouth. "So now, I'm going to punish this pussy. I'm going to bring you to the edge of release so many times before easing back, over and over, until you're begging me to let you come as you ride my face."

"Fuck." She shuddered at my words. I loved how unfiltered her reactions were. There was no pretending with Amy—she was raw and real, and I would never get enough.

That was the last thing either of us said before I made good on my promise of punishment. I didn't let her come until she was sweaty and shaking in my arms, her words incoherent. Sliding her down my body, I held her naked form close to mine. We were on borrowed time, and I decided that I was done putting distance between us. If we only got this small window, we might as well enjoy the explosive pleasure we wrung from each other's bodies. Maybe that would be enough to convince her to stay when she discovered the depths of my deception, but I wasn't overly hopeful.

Amy was mine for the time being, and I would cherish our time together before the real world came knocking at our door. I knew one thing for certain—it would never be long enough.

CHAPTER 21

Amy

THERE'S A FINE LINE between begging your husband for sex and unleashing the sexual beast from his cage to the point where you're so sore you can barely sit down. Who knew all it took to cross that line would be surprising Liam naked in bed?

Our sexual relationship had changed significantly. Liam was no longer hiding, and I was getting to know the man behind the scowl. Having access to Liam's playful, thoughtful, passionate side made me feel special. No one saw him like this but me.

Falling into an easy rhythm, we ate a late dinner each evening once he rose from bed before cuddling on the couch, taking turns choosing a show. Without fail, our caresses would turn heated, and we'd end up in bed—it didn't matter whose. The fire between us was blazing hotter than ever. Liam would work throughout the night but always had breakfast waiting when I woke.

I dared to say it was marital bliss.

But.

God, how I hated the but. Correction—I loathed the but.

He was still holding back.

I'd tried so many times to steal a kiss. Just one. But each time, he found a way to move his head or direct my mouth elsewhere. I didn't get it. His lips had touched every inch of my skin, but he avoided my lips like the plague. Maybe I was overthinking it. Perhaps he was avoiding kissing because of where else our mouths had been, and he had a closet phobia.

I knew I was reaching, but I couldn't help obsessing over the fact that my husband, the man who had fucked me in ways I hadn't known possible, flat-out refused to grant me that most basic act of intimacy.

Shaking away the doubts and fears over where things were headed with Liam, I let the girls take me out for my birthday. Mine fell exactly one month after Natalie's, leaving me one day shy of being a Leap Day baby. We all turned thirty this year, but it was striking how different our lives were as we reached this landmark birthday.

Natalie had been married twice already and had four kids. She was happy and settled, living the life she'd always dreamed of.

I was married, but it was complicated. I had a promising career that I loved, where I got to help families come back together. I was fulfilled.

Hannah was the wild child of our group. Nothing tied her down, and she liked it that way.

We were three unique puzzle pieces that fit together perfectly inside our friendship, so it stood to reason that we'd each celebrate our birthdays differently. Nat had gotten her romantic candlelit dinner, with her husband fawning over her. Hannah had already booked Spades for her blowout party in May.

Then, there was me.

I had no plans, and it suited me. I wasn't flashy. I liked to keep things low-key.

Even attempting to fly under the radar on this milestone birthday, I couldn't deny a day out with my girls. The celebration had started with a boozy brunch at a fancy restaurant downtown that we saved for special occasions before we headed to the spa. As we relaxed, getting massages after getting our nails done and having facials, I made a mental note to add regular spa days to our monthly rotation of outings. This was heaven, having my sore muscles stretched and soothed. The motion of the masseur's hands on my body, combined with the warm oil, was almost enough to lull me to sleep.

Hannah waited until I was blissed out of my mind before asking, "So, how's your sex life with Liam?"

Natalie groaned. "Can we not, Hannah?"

"Don't worry. I'll ask about you and Jaxon next."

"Great. Can't wait." Her sarcastic tone had me smiling, my eyes still closed, enjoying the massage.

"I'm waiting, Ames," Hannah prompted.

"Things are good." I kept it vague, knowing it would drive her crazy.

"What does good mean? And what are things? Details, woman!"

"What details would you like, Hannah? That we're fucking like bunnies, christening every surface in the house?"

"I hate you guys." Natalie's voice sounded tortured. "You just had to marry my brother, didn't you?"

"Sorry, Nat." I could appreciate how awkward this was for her. Never in my wildest dreams could I have imagined the direction my life would take.

Sighing, accepting there was no avoiding talking about my relationship with Liam, she asked, "What about everything else?"

"He's not hiding anymore if that's what you're asking. We spend time together like a real couple. Eat dinner, watch TV—old married people things."

"Did you talk?"

"No. I don't want to rock the boat. I'm comfortable with the situation as is."

"Are you?" Natalie sounded skeptical.

This role reversal was unsettling. Last year, I was in her position, trying to get her to open up to Jaxon, and now the tables had turned. I never claimed to be a relationship guru, but you'd have had to be blind not to see that those two were meant to be together. I was doing a public service by pushing her to have an open mind.

Was I happy with my current relationship with Liam? The sex was mind-blowing, and our domestic routine was relaxed and easy. The best part was that I didn't have to think too hard. We could simply exist together, enjoy each other. There was no need to be one of those clingy girls asking where things were headed. I knew where they were headed. We were married, bound together for life. So yes, I was content maintaining the status quo.

Liar.

Hannah saved me from Natalie's serious line of questioning, commenting, "I bet the shower is glad to be getting a break. Your plumbing probably wouldn't have survived."

"Gross." Natalie fake gagged.

I knew I was opening a can of worms, but offered, "The shower's still seeing its fair share of action. It's just not of the solo variety any longer."

"Now we're talking!" Hannah's voice was full of laughter. "Is he into anything kinky? Please tell me that brooding hulk of a man is pierced."

"That's it. I'll see you two in the sauna. I can't listen to this anymore." I heard shuffling and turned my head in time to see a towel-clad Natalie leaving the room.

Feeling slightly guilty watching her flee, I turned toward the bed containing Hannah's prone form. "You did that on purpose."

Her shoulders lifted slightly. "Maybe. It's fun to get a rise out of her."

"She's been through enough," I chastised.

"We've reached the statute of limitations on the wounded-bird excuse now that she's happily married to the city's hottest hockey player."

She had a point. "Fine. Just give it a rest today as a birthday gift to me."

"Does that mean I don't have to buy you anything?" A smile graced Hannah's lips.

"You paid for brunch, and Nat paid for the spa. That's plenty."

"Day's not over yet, girlfriend." There was a devilish gleam in her eye.

Having known Hannah for half my life, I'd have been a fool not to be suspicious. "What aren't you telling me?"

Her voice was alarmingly sweet. "Oh, dear, sweet Amy. Do you think we are such terrible friends that we'd let you walk after a measly brunch and spa day? Oh, no. We are going shopping next. Dinner and drinks tonight before we catch a movie. I know you and Nat are thirty now and basically pushing retirement age, but I think we can top it all off with a night at the club. You are over the hill, after all."

I rolled my eyes. "That's forty, not thirty."

"Next, you'll be telling me that thirty is the new twenty, right before you regale me with stories about how you used to walk uphill to school both ways, candy used to cost a penny, and gasp, the internet used to not exist! Oooh, that story really gives me the chills. Can you imagine? No internet? How did people survive?"

"It truly is a wonder."

"The mind boggles. Did the dinosaurs let you get close enough to pet them?"

Hannah was too much, but that's why we loved her. "All right. I'll agree to shopping, drinks, dinner, and the movie. I draw the line at the club."

"Party pooper," she accused.

"My birthday, my rules."

"I thank God every day that I'm the young, hip one of this group." There was no point in arguing that she was younger than me by exactly eighty-four days. She'd only retort that she would always be the youngest.

It would seem the day was out of my hands, but my best friends had never steered me wrong, so I buckled up and prepared for the ride.

Returning home with a dozen shopping bags—courtesy of Natalie and Hannah's mandatory birthday shopping spree—I had an hour before I was expected to meet them next door so we could head back out for the after-dark portion of the day. Calling out to see if Liam was home, I was met with silence.

It was Saturday, meaning he hadn't worked through the night. In fact, he'd spent all night in bed with me, still asleep when I left for brunch. Probably because we'd kept each other awake during the darkest parts of the night.

A quick peek into the garage revealed his car was gone, confirming that he wasn't home. I hadn't mentioned that my birthday was coming up, but there was no chance Natalie hadn't reminded him. Liam knew I had plans with the girls today, and even though I barely had an hour to get ready and head back out, there was a sting of disappointment that I wouldn't see him on my birthday.

Our relationship was unique. It would be unfair to hold him to the same standards as a typical husband, where I could get mad that he forgot my birthday. Great sex didn't equate to a real marriage. The two were not mutually exclusive.

Truth be told, I wasn't mad, but I couldn't pinpoint the emotion I *was* feeling. Shaking off whatever it was, I rushed upstairs to prepare for the evening. You only turned thirty once, and I planned to enjoy it.

Hannah had insisted on new lingerie, so I clipped the tags on a new black lace bra and panty set before stripping and changing into them. Next came a new one-shouldered black jumpsuit from Natalie. The final touch was a pair of silver heels from Hannah. This outfit was only one of many they'd insisted on gifting me, but it seemed the most appropriate for tonight's festivities.

There was only enough time to quickly curl my hair and throw on some mascara and lipstick before grabbing a clutch that matched my new shoes and trekking to Natalie's. February was cold in New England, but I didn't feel like carrying a bulky coat all night, so I hustled my butt next door, praying Nat would open the door before I froze to death.

Knocking on the side door, I whispered to myself, "Come on, Nat, before I turn into a popsicle."

Thankfully, the door flew open, and Natalie ushered me inside. "Come in! Hannah's on her way over."

Rubbing my bare arms, I followed her further into the house, stopping in the kitchen. A bottle of champagne was on ice, three flutes beside it. Eyeing it, I asked, "I thought we were going out for drinks?"

Natalie poured the three glasses, remarking, "This was a little send-off from Jaxon. He took the kids out but wanted to tell you happy birthday."

"That was nice of him." Jaxon was in the running for the sweetest man alive. It didn't matter if he'd known you his whole life or just met you—he made everyone feel special.

"Come, let's sit down for a bit while we wait for Hannah."

Expecting her to sit at the kitchen island, she headed for the darkened living room. Trailing behind her, I turned the corner as she flicked the light switch on the wall.

When the lights came on, it revealed a room full of people who saw me and yelled, "Surprise!"

It took me a full minute to comprehend what had just occurred. Eventually, my brain registered the black and gold balloons, two giant ones in the shape of a three and a zero forming a thirty. Scanning the crowd, it contained everyone I knew, including Hannah, Jaxon, and at the center of it all, my Liam.

He hadn't forgotten my birthday.

My hand flew to my mouth, the shock of what was clearly a surprise thirtieth birthday party for me finally sinking in as my legs began to shake.

Liam stepped forward, his own glass of champagne held in his hand. The smile on his face stole the breath from my lungs. "Happy birthday, sweetheart."

Breathless, I asked, "This is for me?"

Turning to address the room, I could hear the smile in his voice. "Did anyone else here turn thirty today?" Smirking, he looked back at me. "Looks like it."

"But I'm going out with the girls," I protested weakly.

He gestured to Natalie and Hannah. "They're here. You tell me to send all these people home, and I'll do it. This is your day. You should get to spend it how you want."

Suddenly shy as the center of attention, I hid behind his massive frame. "Liam, this is too much. I don't need a big celebration."

Tipping my chin up, those blue eyes softened. "Our wedding wasn't what it should have been, and that's my fault. So, let me make it up to you and spoil you on your birthday."

Blinking furiously to keep the tears at bay, I nodded in acceptance of his gesture. Peeking past him to survey the small gathering in my honor, I asked, "You have food?"

The sound of his chuckle did things to my insides, and I couldn't wait to celebrate privately with him when we got home. "Yeah, we've got food." Pulling me close, he grabbed a fistful of my ass. "Can't have you wasting away. This ass is too delicious."

"Liam!" I whisper-yelled. "We have company."

"Let them stare."

"Later," I promised.

Confident, he responded, "Oh, sweetheart, you say that like you have a choice."

Hannah's voice broke into our intimate moment. "You two know you're not an exhibit in the zoo, right? People didn't come here hoping to view a mating ritual." Pausing, she added, "Well, some people."

Liam pulled back enough to glare at her. "What would we do without you, Hannah?"

"Love you too, Liam." She smirked up at him, not the least bit intimidated.

Slipping his hand around my waist, he tugged my body to his side as he addressed the small crowd, lifting his champagne flute. "My stunning wife has touched the lives of everyone in this room, none more so than mine. She radiates compassion, helping others in any way she can. We spent so many years just passing by, and I never stopped long enough to discover the treasure hidden in plain sight. It's funny how life works sometimes. You think you're headed in one direction, and suddenly, everything changes in an instant. We found our way together, and I've never been happier in my entire life."

Oh no, here come the tears again.

Liam squeezed my waist, and I turned to stare at him to find he was looking at me exactly as Jaxon had looked at Natalie. There was no doubt that he meant every word he'd shared, and my heart twisted in my chest.

Liam continued, "There aren't many who can put up with my some-times-moodiness or the craziness that is the life I've been born into, but Amy has never been one to shy away from a challenge. I know how lucky I am to have a strong, confident woman like her by my side as we navigate our complex lives together."

"Not to mention she's way out of your league!" Hannah interrupted, eliciting a laugh from the crowd.

Expecting Liam to snap at her as he normally would, he surprised the hell out of me when his smile widened, tilting his glass toward where she stood. "For once, Hannah, we can agree." Addressing me like there was no one else in the room, his piercing blue eyes bore into my soul. "There's no one in the world better suited for me than you."

My chest tightened, and I found it harder to breathe. He practically declared his love for me before everyone gathered here tonight. Did he genuinely feel that way about me? Or was I reading too much into it?

Punctuating his speech, Liam declared, "To discovering what's been waiting for you all along. To Amy!"

Everyone called out a chorus of "To Amy!" before sipping from their glasses. I was too shell-shocked to lift my glass to my lips. Liam turned me in his arms so that we were facing each other, and as his head dipped slightly toward mine, my breathing hitched.

This is it. He's finally going to do it.

Coming closer, our lips were close enough that I could feel his breath, warm and smelling sweet like champagne. My brain screamed that I should take charge, close the distance, and take what I'd wanted for so long, but I was frozen to the spot. I'd spent so much time trying to break him, to get him to give up control, but what I truly wanted was for him to take that leap and claim me in front of this room full of people.

My chest burned as I held my breath, waiting for him to make his move. Just when I thought he was about to put me out of my misery, he moved a fraction of an inch closer before veering to the side and brushing his lips against my cheek.

It was like he'd dumped ice water over my body. Every muscle tensed, and embarrassment flooded my veins. What kind of married couple didn't kiss on the lips in front of an audience? He couldn't even do it for show? What the hell was wrong with him? Maybe something was wrong with me?

I was the fool who thought this could turn into something more. That was my biggest mistake. We'd signed a contract, and I needed to remember that.

Happy fucking birthday to me.

CHAPTER 22

Liam

THAT HAD BEEN CLOSE. Too close.

The emotions of the evening, combined with how fucking incredible she looked when she arrived and the feel of her in my arms, had me a breath away from kissing her—the one thing I'd avoided since the day we got married. If I kissed her, I knew there was no going back. My heart would be hers.

There was nothing I wanted more than to claim her mouth with my own, the last unexplored frontier on her body. A body I owned night after night. Giving her my heart meant she'd rip it right from my chest when she left.

I'd felt her tense against me when I realized almost too late what I was about to do and quickly changed course, kissing her cheek instead. She wanted it. Amy had tried so many times to kiss me, but I told myself I was holding this piece of myself back for her own protection. I was falling for her hard, and if I allowed her to fall too, we'd both be broken beyond repair when the walls came tumbling down.

Regret instantly flooded me when she pulled back, hurt evident on her face. Pain pierced my heart, seeing her upset, knowing I was the one to blame. I would throw down my life to protect her, but I was torn. Protecting her from future hurt was hurting her now. This beguiling woman had backed me into a corner.

Twisting the knife in my heart, she whispered, "I should mingle." Leaving my side, she walked toward her guests.

"That was . . . awkward." Jaxon pointing out the obvious had me itching to punch him in the face.

"Fuck off." I wasn't in the mood.

"The speech was halfway decent, and the emotion was there, but . . ."

"Are you still here?" My only hope was that he'd leave me alone if I was hostile enough.

"You have this incredible woman—that it's pretty clear you're in love with—and on her *birthday,* you give her a chaste kiss on the cheek in front of all these people?"

"If you have a point, I suggest you get there faster." My free fist clenched by my side.

"I'm not in your relationship, and even my head is swimming from the mixed signals you're sending."

"Who made you head of the marriage police? Not everyone feels comfortable sucking face in public. Did you ever think of that?"

He wasn't buying it. "Sure. That's why Amy looked like she wanted to cry."

"Fuck." Jaxon knew how to push my buttons.

"I take it you didn't have that chat." Leveling him a glare, I clenched my jaw to avoid giving myself away. It was pointless. He saw right through me. "You're not doing yourself any favors putting it off."

Shrugging him off, mainly because it hurt to think about the level of my deception, I walked away. Tonight was about Amy, and I already messed up, so I'd be working overtime to get the evening back on track.

"Make a wish, baby." My mouth was right next to Amy's ear as she leaned toward the candles on her cake.

She closed her eyes, pausing for a second before pursing her supple lips and blowing a puff of air, extinguishing the candles. A cheer reverberated from those gathered as I pulled Amy tight against my chest.

After my initial blunder with the cheek kiss, I became overly affectionate. Thankfully, Amy hadn't balked at the physical contact. Surprisingly, she'd leaned into it, soaking it up, and I prayed she could feel how much I cared for her pouring out through every touch. When I got her alone, I had plans to worship her body so that she had no doubts about my feelings for her.

Amy looked irresistible in that curve-hugging jumpsuit, and I couldn't wait to get her home.

Guests were filtering out torturously slowly. Internally, I was screaming for them to get the hell out so I could be alone with my wife.

When all that remained was our core group and Jaxon's closest teammates, I grabbed Amy's hand, dragging her toward the door, calling behind us, "Goodnight, everyone!"

Hannah retorted, "You're welcome, for keeping your wife occupied all day so you could set up!"

Opening the hallway coat closet, I flipped through the rack, asking Amy, "What does your coat look like?"

"I didn't bring one," came her reply from beside me.

It was like she knew exactly how to give me anxiety. "Why not?" I snapped. "It's below freezing, and your arms are exposed."

Hands on her hips, she gave me some attitude, letting me know I wasn't entirely out of the doghouse. "You know, that's the funny thing about surprise parties. The person you're throwing it for doesn't know it's happening. Hannah mentioned clubbing after the movie, and I didn't want to deal with a coat."

"Fine." Ripping the sports coat I was wearing down my arms, I handed it to her. "Take this." Eyes shooting daggers at me, she snatched it from me, and I'd be lying if I said the sight of her being swallowed by my jacket didn't turn me on. "Let's go home."

Cursing her need to wear heels in winter, I allowed her to grip my hand so painfully I was convinced I heard a pop as she balanced and skidded on the icier patches of the walkway between our house and Natalie's. Sagging with relief she'd made it home without a broken ankle, I unlocked the door and ushered her inside while turning on the lights.

Calmly, Amy removed my sports coat and unstrapped her heels before heading toward the stairs.

Desperation filled me that our night was over, so I blurted out, "I have a gift for you!"

Slowly, she turned around, eyeing me warily. "Okay. . ."

"It's upstairs."

Narrowing her eyes, her tone was deadly. "I swear to God, Liam. If it's some bullshit with you naked, wrapped up in a bow, I will punch you in the dick."

Yep, she's still pissed.

Holding my hands up in surrender, I moved closer. "I swear it's not." Stepping past her, I climbed the stairs, feeling her presence behind me. Her anger was palpable. Grabbing the tiny velvet box off my dresser, I walked without permission into her bedroom.

"Don't be getting any ideas." Amy's voice was edged with steel.

Turning around, I handed her the box, knowing she wasn't superficial enough to let something shiny distract her from her feelings. I'd have to use my words if I had any hope of fixing what I did tonight. Unfortunately, that wasn't my strong suit.

Running a thumb over the velvet, her green eyes met mine, and the sadness in them broke my heart.

"Open it. Please," I begged.

Cracking open the box, her soft gasp filled the air. "Oh, wow." Nestled inside was a pair of teardrop emerald earrings encrusted in diamonds.

Pleased at her reaction, I prompted, "Try them on?"

Swallowing, she nodded. "They're stunning." Plucking them from the box, she stepped toward the vanity mirror attached to her dresser and affixed them to her ears.

Stepping behind her, I locked eyes with her in the mirror, running my hand up her neck, teasing the soft flesh behind her ear with my thumb. "Do you know why there are emeralds in your engagement ring?" When Amy shook her head in response, I continued, "Because they reminded me of your eyes." Her breath caught, and I added for good measure, "Amy, you are the most beautiful woman I've ever seen." Eyes fluttering closed, I went for broke, whispering, "I'm sorry about tonight."

Amy's eyes—a perfect match to the emeralds dangling from her ears—flashed open, a fire burning in them as she asked, "Do you know what I wished for?"

Knowing she was setting me up, I willingly took the bait. "What, sweet-heart?"

Holding my gaze in the mirror, her voice was clear. "A kiss."

Dipping my head to the side of her neck where I knew she was sensitive, I dropped a feather-light kiss there, hoping to distract her. "I am happy to worship your body with my mouth, sweetheart. Where would you like me?" Trailing my hands to her breasts, I asked, "Here?" Reaching further down, I cupped between her legs, nearly groaning at the heat I felt there. "Or maybe here?"

Amy dropped her head back onto my shoulder, moaning softly as she thrust her pelvis into my touch. I was so close to getting her to lose herself in the pleasure I offered when she whispered, "My lips."

Fuck. I knew that's what she meant the first time. Dropping my hands, I stepped away, putting space between us. "Please, don't ask me for that."

When she whipped around to face me, any trace of the aroused woman I'd devoured with my eyes in the mirror was gone. Amy was furious, poking her finger into my chest as she followed my retreat. "Oh, no, you don't. Don't you dare push me away. Not again."

I wanted nothing more than to give her the world, but I couldn't. "I just can't. Please, Amy. You don't understand."

Sneering at me, her words dripped with ice. "Right. I got it. You can fuck me, but you can't kiss me. Makes perfect sense. Except that it doesn't. Kissing comes before sex. So why won't you kiss me, Liam? Just fucking tell me!"

Pulling on my hair with both hands, I yelled in frustration, "Because I'm afraid if I start, I'll never be able to stop! Are you happy now?"

Amy's mouth dropped open as she blinked at me. "What?"

Oh, God. "Do you remember when we kissed on our wedding day?"

Brows drawing down, she nodded. "Yeah."

"Did you feel that zap when our lips touched?"

She stared at me like I had three heads. "Sure. It was some static electricity. I was nervous. My feet were shuffling on the carpet. Are you afraid that's going to happen again?"

"No, it wasn't. It was a spark, Amy."

"A spark. . ."

Here goes nothing.

"If I kiss you again, that spark will ignite, and the flames have the power to consume us both."

As she took a moment to process what I was trying to tell her, I watched her demeanor change. Anger and hurt slipped away, replaced by desire, lust, and determination. Stalking toward where I stood, tortured after laying all my cards—at least, the emotional ones—on the table, Amy stopped once her body was flush with mine.

Running her hand up my chest, she never broke my gaze as she declared, "Let us burn."

Those three little words were all it took for my resolve to weaken, and I knew I was fucked. At long last, I snaked a hand into her hair before descending on her mouth like I had a thousand times in my dreams.

Moaning at the contact, Amy opened for me, and electricity flowed from my head to my toes as my tongue swept inside.

Amy's tongue tangled with mine, meeting it stroke for stroke, and I was lost. Forgotten were all the reasons why I'd put this off as my heart swelled, beating only for her. She was mine. Only mine.

Fingers clawed at my shirt, tugging it from where it was tucked into the waistband of my jeans. Tearing my mouth from hers, I undid a few buttons, enough to be able to rip it over my head. Chest heaving, I dropped my forehead to hers as she ran her hands up the muscles of my torso before cupping my cheeks.

Breathless, she said, "I feel it, too."

Lifting on her toes, she claimed my mouth, and I sank into it, letting her take the lead before stealing it back. It was a perfect balance, and for the first time in my life, I didn't have the overwhelming urge to control the situation.

My hands roamed her body, searching for an entry point, growing frustrated when I couldn't find a way to remove the jumpsuit.

Amy broke away with a chuckle. "Need some help?"

Growling, my need to get her naked had me seconds away from tearing the fabric. "How the fuck did you get into this thing?"

She stepped backward and presented me with her side, raising an arm and revealing a zipper up the side seam, beginning at her armpit. Amused, Amy couldn't help but taunt, "Who would have thought? Liam Remington, bested by a jumpsuit."

Yanking the zipper down with force, I retorted, "I must have overslept the day they taught that in Fucking 101." Even though I was driven by a primal need to sink myself deep inside her, the banter made me love her even more.

"Are you saying the boys get a class? No fair." Amy pouted, and I saw that as an opportunity to chew on that extended lower lip before sucking it inside my mouth as I claimed hers again.

Amy shimmied her hips, and the black one-piece fell to the floor, revealing a black lace strapless bra and matching panties that covered only half of her lush ass, exposing the bottom curve. Backing her toward the bed, keeping my lips locked with hers, I kicked off my shoes. Once the back of her knees hit the edge of her mattress, I pushed her onto her back before climbing atop her.

Instinctively, she spread her thighs to welcome me between them, and I pressed the bulge straining against my fly against her core, grinding against her as I sucked her nipple through the lace of her bra. Thrashing beneath me, Amy moaned as I used friction to my advantage in driving her wild. Her unfiltered reactions during foreplay were almost as good as burying my dick inside her and making her scream.

Almost.

Pressing her deeply into the mattress with my hips, I allowed her to arch and twist against my thickness, taking her pleasure as I kissed a path up her collarbone, to her neck, before drinking in the sweetness of her mouth. Deprived for so long, I'd never get enough.

My voice was rough as I asked against her lips, "How do you want me, sweetheart?"

Her lips turned upward beneath mine. "Do I have to choose just one?"

"Careful what you wish for." I groaned as I claimed her mouth again, freeing her breasts from their lace prison with a flick of my fingers. Amy arched into my touch as I thumbed her puckered nipples, silently begging for more.

My mouth trailed down to her stomach, loving her softness. Her body was perfect, almost as if it was custom-made for mine. Dragging the panties down her thick thighs, I was ready to love on her with my mouth when she lifted on her elbows, her sultry voice commanding, "Not so fast."

Pausing, I pleaded with the goddess in our bed. "Baby, I need you too badly."

"New rule. If I'm naked, you're naked."

Relieved, I turned on my side, undoing the button at the fly of my jeans, pulling down the zipper, and shoving the thick material down my legs. Amy didn't waste any time, shoving me onto my back and removing my underwear before grabbing a condom and rolling it over my length. Climbing up my body, she straddled my hips as my erection nestled against the curve of her ass.

Timid above me, Amy asked, "Is this okay?"

Gripping her hands splayed against my abs, I pulled her torso down, running my hands through her hair as I took her mouth hungrily until I felt her arousal spreading against my lower abdomen as she rocked against me.

Breaking the kiss, I stroked her cheeks with my thumbs. "Take me any way you want, Amy. I'm yours."

A slow smile spread across her face, and I prayed she understood the meaning behind those words. Dropping her lips to mine once more, I felt her hips raise as she positioned herself over my now throbbing cock, impaling herself easily with how slick she was. A strangled noise escaped from the back of my throat. Every time was like the first time with how hot and tight she was.

Pushing off my chest, Amy rose above me, a vision as she began to ride me, breathy moans falling past her lips as her hands rose to touch her full breasts. She kept her eyes on mine, silently daring me to take control away from her as I'd always done in the past.

Not this time.

My toes curled with the effort to hold off my threatening climax as she rode me harder and faster, her moans increasing with volume along with her pace. Making a snap decision that it wasn't taking control to help her along, I reached between our bodies, barely grazing her clit with my thumb, and that telltale flush crept over her skin moments before her body stiffened. Her pussy choked my dick as it clamped down, and her orgasm tore through her. Head thrown back, mouth open in a silent scream, she'd never been more beautiful.

Satisfied I'd allowed her enough control, I gripped her hips, moving her up and down over my cock, extending the waves of pleasure coursing over her as I allowed myself to fall over the edge. My hips rose to meet where I pulled hers down, and a release ripped through me so violently that I couldn't breathe. The edges of my vision darkened, and just when I thought I would pass out, I drew a breath into my burning lungs as Amy collapsed atop my chest.

Her ragged breathing matched mine, but she managed to ask, "You all right, big guy?"

Stroking her soft hair with one hand, I pressed a kiss to her forehead nestled against my shoulder. "Never better."

That was the truth. There would never be a moment more perfect than this. I held the woman I loved in my arms, and my life would never be the same. If only this feeling could last forever.

CHAPTER 23

Amy

BEST. BIRTHDAY. EVER.

My wish came true, and I finally understood why Liam had been hesitant to kiss me. He was right. Once we added that component, our shared physical connection soared to a new level—a deeply emotional one. The combination had been explosive, electric even, as we'd explored each other's bodies like it was the first time—rediscovering our partner through new eyes.

There was no denying that Liam had now claimed me, body and soul. This was a turning point for us. I could feel it. Would it really be so crazy to get fake-married, fall for each other, and have a real marriage? Natalie would get a kick out of it, that was for sure.

We had time to define our relationship later, and from what I'd seen, marriages tended to evolve over time, so there was no need to dwell on that today. Right now, I was naked, curled up in my husband's arms after he'd brought me to orgasm at least four times by my last count. If I knew Liam, we were far from done for the night.

Liam's hand traced a lazy path up my back, lulling me closer to sleep. But as relaxed as I was, I could recognize that he'd been vulnerable with me tonight, so felt obligated to do the same.

Working up the courage, I ran a hand up his chest. "Can I ask you a question?"

"Sure, sweetheart." The vibrations moving through his chest at the words were soothing.

"Promise to answer honestly?"

His body tensed beneath mine, and he lifted his head, concern filling the depths of his striking blue eyes, but he swallowed, nodding. "Of course."

That was an odd reaction. I would circle back to that later. There was no way he knew what I was about to ask. I hated harboring this minor insecurity, considering the intimacy we'd shared these past couple of months, especially tonight.

"Did you ever have feelings for Natalie?"

Liam seemed to relax, returning to drawing those hypnotizing circles with his fingers. "Honestly?"

"Please." I needed to know. I'd always played second fiddle to Natalie, and it was something I'd learned to accept over the years. I loved her and never held it against her. It wasn't her fault. She was pretty and thin and proper, whereas I had freckles, was curvy, and too often spoke my mind. I was far from the picture-perfect society daughter Natalie had portrayed so effortlessly.

Liam had put his life on hold to help her when she needed to escape her ex-husband—his brother. Who did that if they didn't have feelings? It was well past the scope of being a good brother-in-law.

"When Leo first brought her home, I'll admit I had a crush on her, but it was short-lived. She only had eyes for him—only God knows why—and the attraction faded well before they were married. My feelings for her now are purely that of a little sister, nothing more."

"Thank you for being honest." If I hadn't been draped across his body, I wouldn't have noticed the minor tremor that ran through him.

Was there something he was hiding from me? Maybe I was too jaded from what happened with Chet. Liam was different and could have easily lied about feelings for Natalie over a decade ago, but he hadn't, so I let it go.

"Do you know why I love the weekend?" Liam's baritone voice rolled over me.

I welcomed the change of subject. "Why's that?"

"I get to spend two full days with you. No work, no offsetting schedules. Just us. I plan to spend all day tomorrow in this bed with you."

"Mmm. A lazy Sunday sounds amazing." I nestled further into his embrace.

"And next week, we head back to Belleston, where we will be on the same sleep schedule."

"Sounds terrible," I joked. "Seeing too much of you might cure me of my obsession with you."

"Obsessed, you say?"

"Don't get too excited. The honeymoon phase will end, and then you'll be the old ball and chain."

Liam's hand trailed further down my back until his large palm gripped my ass. "Do you think I'll ever get tired of this ass? Don't get too complacent expecting a sexual reprieve anytime soon, my princess."

Oh, fuck. That was hot. I didn't care about the title. But hearing him claim me like that had me slinking down his body to show my appreciation with my mouth.

"There you are. You should be sleeping or participating in more entertaining activities in bed." Liam's voice was scratchy from sleep, and I looked up from where I was seated on the floor of the private jet.

He might have been half asleep, but he looked incredible with hair sticking up in all directions, chest and feet bare, clad in only a pair of pajama bottoms. He was sexiest when he was imperfect, undone.

"I couldn't sleep. Too much to do." I gestured to the file folders littering the floor around me.

Dropping to the floor to join me, he looked around. "All right. What are we up to?"

I sighed. "The impossible. These files contain the applications of the parents serviced by the Foundation who want a placement in my program. I need to narrow it down to twenty who will get to live there and increase their chances of getting their kids back. Who am I to play God and decide who gets to win this lottery?"

Pulling me into his arms, Liam centered me. "Then you're in luck. I'm an impartial party and can help sort some of these for you. Take the emotions out of it."

Melting into his embrace, my voice was thick. "You would do that for me?"

"Sweetheart, don't you know by now? I would do *anything* for you." Before I had time to ponder the deeper meaning behind those words, he got on his knees, flipping through the folders and making neat stacks.

Liam was methodical, almost clinical, as if the fate of families reconnecting wasn't hanging in the balance. Sitting back on his heels, he seemed satisfied with his work, declaring, "Let's start here."

Surveying the stacks of folders on the ground, none of what he'd done made any sense. "What am I looking at?"

"This stack contains applications with one child, this one with two, three, and so on. What we know about the building is that it only has two-bedroom apartments. Three kids in a room is a squeeze, but if we get creative, we can make it work."

Stunned, I was impressed with how logical he was when emotion had clouded my judgment. "Damn, my husband is smart."

For once, I found the smug look on his face sexy as hell. "You lucked out there. I'm not a charity virgin."

Laughter filled the cabin, and the task suddenly didn't seem so monumental. Liam was here, wanting to help shoulder the load, and knew what he was doing. He'd mentioned three kids being the max for the limitations of the apartments, but there were five stacks. Any sense of relief quickly vanished. "What about those with more than three kids?"

"You save them for the next building when you have bigger apartments."

Disappointment threatened to overwhelm me at the idea of cutting down the applicants, knowing I was crushing the hope of someone who desperately needed my help. Sensing my distress, Liam turned his body to pull my back against his chest while we sat on the floor.

Bear-hugging me from behind so I felt surrounded, he exhaled, "Ames, you can't help them all. Maybe someday, but not right now."

That wasn't acceptable. "But—"

"Honey, your compassion is what I love most about you. Understanding your limitations doesn't diminish that."

Relaxing further into his embrace, I let that word wash over me.

Love.

Liam hadn't exactly said he loved me, but that he loved something about me. Regardless, since my birthday, he'd made me feel cherished and, dare I say, loved. He didn't need to say it. I could feel it surrounding me every time he was near. All that remained was settling my brain enough to sort out my feelings for him.

Misunderstanding my physical reaction, Liam suggested, "You're tired, sweetheart. Let's go back to bed."

Sitting up, I grabbed the fourth and fifth stacks and set them aside. "I won't be able to sleep until I get this done. I want to send acceptance letters before we get home next week."

Without a word of complaint, he helped me sort the remaining applications in different ways until we had only twenty-four remaining. Four more needed to be removed before we were done.

Flipping through one I'd put into a maybe pile, he asked, "Why is this one a maybe?"

Plucking it from his hands, I read over the file until I discovered the red flag. "She's a recovering addict."

"Why does that matter?"

Pinching the bridge of my nose to ward off a sleep deprivation headache, I blew out a breath. "Historically, we see those suffering from addiction issues relapse and lose their kids again. It's heartbreaking, but I don't see how I can give her a spot over someone who doesn't have the same background. They need more support than we can provide. Housing won't change that."

I hated that certain families in need were told no repeatedly because of a less-than-spotless past. We were in the business of offering second chances, but there were still roadblocks for some. They needed the yes more than anyone, but I had limited resources to make that happen, even if I desperately wanted to help.

"But what if it could?" Liam's eyes shifted, and I could tell the gears were turning in his brain.

Reaching over, I rubbed my thumb over his temple. "What's going on up here?"

"What if—and hear me out—you offered meetings in your lobby? It wouldn't cost anything but would be priceless to those who need it."

My eyes were blurry from pouring over these files for hours, to the point where I couldn't see straight, forget about thinking straight. Chalking Liam's mental clarity at this time of night to the fact that he often remained awake at this ungodly hour, I leaned over and kissed him quickly before exclaiming, "You're a genius!"

Pleased with himself, he asked, "Can we move her to the yes pile then?"

"You really are something." I couldn't help but stare at him in awe.

"And you are everything." His counterstatement filled my body with warmth, beginning in my heart and spreading outward to my extremities. "They're going to love you."

"Who?"

"The people of Belleston." He said it so casually, like it was the obvious answer.

I stifled a scoff. "I don't know about that. I'm not your typical princess. Driven career woman doesn't exactly fit the mold."

"Don't you see it, Ames? That's precisely *why* they are going to love you. You're a breath of fresh air. You are inherently good. You want to help people not because it's the right thing but because it's a part of your soul."

My heart hammered against my ribcage. "Is that how you see me?"

Leaning forward, he cupped my cheeks. "When I look at you, I see the woman I love."

"Love?" I breathed out.

Pressing his lips to mine for a short, sweet kiss, he reaffirmed his words, "Yes, love."

I had spent weeks struggling to figure out where I wanted our relationship to go as he'd played me hot and cold, but in true Liam fashion, he took control, putting his feelings into words when I couldn't.

Sensing my need for more time before I could vocalize my feelings, he tucked a strand of hair behind my ear, and I saw the love shining in his beautiful blue eyes. "You snuck up on me, Amy, in the best possible way. I'd talked myself out of ever finding love, that I didn't need it. Hell, that I didn't even want it. Having someone I care this deeply about scares the living hell out of me. I'm paralyzed with fear, knowing that I don't deserve you, and that somehow, some way, I'll end up hurting you, and then I'll lose you."

Liam was baring his soul—beneath his brusque exterior, he'd been afraid this whole time. He might not be able to see it, but he kept everyone at arm's length to protect himself. His vulnerability tugged at my heartstrings.

"You would never hurt me, Liam," I whispered. "I'm not going anywhere."

A flash of pain flickered in his eyes, and he broke my gaze. "You don't know that."

Was he really torturing himself over the possibility of hurting me at some point in our lives? Life was way too short to worry over what-ifs. I wasn't naïve. I knew our marriage would have ups and downs. There would be times when I'd want to wring his neck and vice versa. We were both stubborn, so it was inevitable. We would have disagreements, but we'd work through them. I had confidence in that.

We were two sides of the same coin. Liam was held back by fear of something going wrong, while I had unwavering faith that he would never go out of his way to hurt me. Time would pass, and I was optimistic that he'd also see that truth.

For now, I allowed his love to roll over me, relishing how incredible the admission made me feel. Every day, he made an effort to show me that I was worthy of his adoration. I'd written off love long ago, but Liam made me believe in it again.

Better yet, I believed in us.

Chapter 24

Liam

AMY WAS A NATURAL. Whether it was outside on walkabouts interfacing with the screaming crowds or in smaller settings, she handled it all with ease. I'd been right—the people loved her. We would be on opposite sides of the street, and the citizens of Remhorn would beg to see her instead. How could I deny anyone who shared my infatuation with my wife the opportunity to be touched by her natural kindness? Beckoning Amy to my side, she would greet those screaming her name graciously, doing her best to make personal connections in the fleeting moments of each interaction.

The week was jam-packed with events. We went to libraries and schools, where Amy read to children, then to hospitals to spend time with patients, and finally, to the central location of my closest charity—a community center for veterans. Belleston required military service from all their young men. Having enlisted past my obligated term, I felt a kinship with those who were sometimes negatively impacted by their time in the service.

If Amy hadn't already stolen my heart, having her by my side at the veteran center would have sealed the deal. I fell in love with her all over again, watching her sit by their side, showing compassion like I'd never seen for my brothers-in-arms, both physically and mentally disabled from service alike.

Watching her shine in this capacity as a public figure, I felt hopeful that maybe her finding out this was my future—and possibly hers—wouldn't be a dealbreaker. Amy seemed fulfilled by our engagements. Maybe we could make this work. I couldn't imagine a future without her by my side.

On our final night before returning home, I arranged for dinner to be brought to our apartment instead of dining with the family. We needed a moment alone to decompress.

Crossing the threshold, I heard the faintest gasp from Amy's mouth as she removed her shoes. Glancing down, I winced, seeing the red marks where her heels had dug into the soft flesh of her feet. Without a second thought, I scooped her into my arms, carrying her up the stairs to our private sitting room. Normally, she would protest my display of masculinity, but she melted into my embrace—a testament to how exhausted she was after our busy week.

Setting her down gently onto the loveseat, I sat beside her and pulled her bare feet into my lap. Touching gently, afraid to cause her further pain in sore spots, I kneaded one foot with my hands.

Amy practically purred. "Oooh, that feels good."

The redness began to fade, but underneath were bruises. She'd been standing and walking in heels for days on end, and it became clear she'd been suffering this whole time without complaint. My brain screamed that I'd failed her. I should have noticed sooner and done something to prevent the pain she must have been in with every step.

"Baby, why didn't you say anything?"

Waving a dismissive hand, her voice was soft as if almost in a trance. "It's really not that bad."

Switching to her other foot, every muscle in my body tensed. "Don't do that."

"Do what?"

"Minimize this. I can't help you if you don't tell me when you need help."

"It's just sore feet, Liam." She brushed me off. "It's not life-threatening."

Grunting in response, not wanting to fight, I pressed my thumb into the arch of her foot, and she moaned softly. Working my way up to her tight calves, Amy sighed in pleasure.

"Have I told you how incredible you were this week?"

Eyes closed, a soft smile graced her lips. "Yes, at least once per hour."

"It wasn't that much," I protested.

"I didn't mind it." Arching in a full body stretch, she sighed. "It'll be good to get home. I'm so glad this isn't our life full-time."

With those words, the hope I'd clung to since we landed in Belleston shattered, causing my hands to pause on her feet. Amy didn't want this life. When I glanced in her direction, her eyes were now open, and I prayed she couldn't see how devastated I was that we didn't have a future together—a future I had foolishly begun to believe was possible.

Misinterpreting my shift in demeanor, Amy sat up, taking my hand in hers. "My cup is full, but it's exhausting, you know?"

I knew all too well. "Of course."

"Now I understand why Natalie struggled to keep up. It seems impossible to balance life as a full-time royal and having a family. The glam team two hours before dawn to make sure I look flawless, the briefings before each engagement . . . There has barely been time for us. I don't want to be so tired by the end of every day that I don't have time to enjoy you and what we have together."

Taking her hand and holding it in mine, I knew I was losing her, and I couldn't bear the thought of letting go. "You're right." She was, I couldn't deny it.

Not sensing my distress at the path this conversation had taken, she continued, "It seems so forced. Every event was a carefully orchestrated photo op. I'd rather do the same work without the cameras. I don't want to live in a world where if there isn't proof, it may as well never have happened. I prefer to help others out of the goodness of my heart privately. Those I'm helping deserve that privacy as well."

Each word was a dagger in my heart. Amy deserved the life she described, and I couldn't be the one to give it to her. All I could do was pray for a miracle, but I knew that was in vain. Amy's performance this week had likely cemented our fate. She was perfect in the role, but she'd never agree to stay. Their perfect princess and future queen had the freedom to turn down the job.

My lack of the same freedom would leave me a hollow shell when she left.

—⚬⚬⚬—

If I thought our week in Belleston was stressful and busy, it had nothing on the buildup to Amy's pilot program reveal. Every waking moment had been spent at the apartment building. She was there, so I was there—simple as that. Hours were spent painting each unit's designated kids' bedroom, assembling furniture, and decorating the daycare space.

Amy's vision was coming to life before our eyes, and she was blossoming along with it. Watching her meet with the lucky few applicants chosen—touring the space and handing them their keys to move in after the opening ceremony—was mesmerizing. Their hope was contagious, and I watched Amy glow, sharing their sentiment.

Today was the ribbon-cutting ceremony and move-in day. Amy was a bundle of nerves, running around the house getting ready. Dressed in a suit, prepared to stand by her side, I sat on the edge of the bed as she bustled about. Her constant pacing was making me nauseous.

Gone was the confident woman who had stood by my side a few weeks ago. The difference was that back then, she'd been playing a part, acting as an accessory. She'd poured her heart and soul into this project because it *mattered* to her.

As she stripped down for the fourth time, deciding that another outfit wasn't perfect enough, I intervened. Wrapping my arms around her from behind, pulling her against my chest, I could feel the nervous energy vibrating through her.

"Liam, I don't have time for this," Amy protested, struggling to free herself from my hold.

Refusing to budge, I shushed her. "You and I both know what you're wearing today doesn't matter." Feeling some tension leaving her body, I continued, "My wife has the coolest job. She makes dreams come true."

Amy went slack in my arms. My attempt at calming her seemed to have worked, so I turned her in my arms. Those big green eyes were swimming with tears, and I dropped my forehead to hers. "Baby, please don't cry. I'm so damn proud of you."

"I want everything to be perfect," she whispered.

"It will be," I promised. "You've poured your heart into this project, and it's going to change lives. You did that."

"Thank you."

Pulling back, I searched her eyes. "For what?"

Amy reached up a hand to toy with an errant piece of hair that I couldn't get to stay put. "For supporting me. For loving me."

My chest squeezed. "You make it easy." Grazing the bare skin of her shoulder with my fingertips, I offered, "Want me to take the edge off?"

She laughed. "Tempting, but not enough time."

"Fine. Tonight, we'll celebrate your success."

"Deal." Her eyes sparkled, and I loved her so much it hurt. "Now, help me pick out an outfit."

Eyeing the pile of discarded clothing on the floor, I shrugged. "Nothing was wrong with any of the ones you tried before."

Amy narrowed her eyes in annoyance, but the twinkle was back. "Men. You have it so easy. Throw on a suit—black, blue, or gray. The hardest part is choosing a tie." Fingering my tie, she smirked. "Although I do particularly like this one."

"My wife has impeccable taste." I was wearing the tie she'd gotten me for Christmas. It felt like a lifetime ago, long before our relationship had evolved beyond signatures on a piece of paper.

"That I do." Seemingly struck by inspiration, she put up a finger and disappeared inside her massive walk-in closet. When she returned, she carried a cream pantsuit on the hanger, laying it on the bed.

I was helpless to stop the smile that crept onto my face. "That looks familiar." It was the suit Amy had worn on our wedding day. That had been the best day of my life, and I hadn't even realized it then.

So much had changed in the five months since we'd said our vows.

Grabbing the same shimmery pink camisole she'd paired it with that day from a drawer, she admired the outfit assembled on the bed. "It holds a certain significance, don't you think? The last time I wore it, my life changed. Now, I'll wear it as I help change the lives of others."

Crossing the room, I pulled her back into my arms. "You're brilliant."

Raising on her toes, Amy rewarded me with a kiss. It was meant to be quick, but I sank my hand into her soft red curls and deepened it, conveying all the love I felt for her through our locked lips.

Reluctantly, she pulled away, her tongue darting out to run over her kiss-swollen lower lip. "I have to get ready."

"They don't really *need* you there today, do they?"

A smile lit up her beautiful face at my teasing. "Get out. I'll be down in fifteen minutes."

Giving her ass a little squeeze, I left her to dress. I could get used to the easy cadence we'd found, reciprocating support for each other in our professional lives. Eventually, mine would eclipse hers, and she'd resent me. Even if she didn't run when she discovered the magnitude of her role as my wife, it would extinguish her natural fire and passion. I'd watched it happen once already with Natalie. I couldn't bear to watch it happen again—this time, to the woman I loved.

———— ✖ ————

"The Hartford Family Reunification Foundation is pleased to announce the opening of the Remington Family Center." Jacob Greiner, the Foundation board president, began his speech to the crowd gathered outside the apartment building.

Surprised at the name, I glanced at Amy by my side on the front steps facing the crowd. A corner of her lips barely turned upward as she maintained her composure in this professional setting.

Greiner continued, "The Center will be a home for newly reunited families and parents in the process of regaining custody of their children, but it is so much more. The Center contains a childcare facility operating free of charge to its residents while also offering job counseling services and addiction recovery meetings for those who need them. We are confident that the families at the Center will thrive with the support provided."

There was a pause and a round of applause from those assembled.

I grasped Amy's hand, squeezing gently to show her how proud I was that her vision had become a reality. She squeezed back but kept her eyes straight ahead. I could see the emotion on her face as she struggled to keep it in check.

"None of this would have been possible without a generous donation from Prince Liam Remington and the hard work and vision of Ms. Amy Michaels. Ms. Michaels, please join me to do the honors."

As he beckoned for Amy, her fingers slipped from mine as she went to the front doors of the building, where a wide red ribbon was suspended. A pair of giant gold scissors was handed to her, and she took one handle while Greiner held the other. Turning slightly so the photographers present could get a good angle, they brought their handles together, effectively cutting the ribbon and marking the official opening of The Remington Family Center.

The crowd erupted in a collective cheer, and Amy blinked furiously as the reality sank in that she'd done it. She'd reached the finish line after months of hard work, and now, deserving families would have a place to live and reconnect.

The double doors propped open, and those assembled were invited inside. Entering the building, the excitement was contagious. Several of Amy's co-workers were in attendance in a social worker capacity, supervising as eager parents showed their children where they'd stay once they were reunited. Amy was in her element, the smile on her face genuine as she spoke with enthusiastic families exploring the Center.

Since the building had been furnished, the move-in process was seamless. One by one, the residents settled into their new homes, and the crowd thinned. I had to bribe Amy to leave with the promise of food once the last straggler disappeared.

Amy's work was done, and all that was left to do was wait for it to be judged. I hadn't been privy to the other finalists' programs, but I couldn't imagine how any of them could top what my wife had done—bias aside. I'd spent most of my adult life dealing with charities, overseeing their programs aimed at helping others, and very few had the life-altering impact of Amy's housing project.

CHAPTER 25

Amy

I HATED THE WAITING game. I felt helpless as the weeks dragged on between the opening of the Center and my scheduled meeting with the Foundation board to learn my fate. The questions I couldn't answer often kept me awake at night.

Had I done enough?

Had someone implemented a program with a more significant impact?

Did they see Liam's donation as a way of buying my promotion?

There wasn't much longer to wait. By the end of the week, I'd know. Thankfully, preparations for the celebration surrounding Charlie's first birthday were in full swing, providing a much-needed distraction.

Our favorite baby girl's actual birthday had been a week ago, but hockey playoffs had begun, and the Comets' schedule was unpredictable. There was a massive chart of possible game scenarios, which hinged on how many games they won and in which order, combined with the results of other series in the division. Charlie had been born on the first day of the playoffs last year, so this birthday party limbo would be the norm until Jaxon chose to retire.

When the Comets won their first series in five games, with their potential second-round opponents needing more games to decide a winner, Natalie pulled the trigger on a party date, giving us only three days to pull it together. It was the Easter season, so Natalie decided on a theme of Some Bunny is One.

Party day arrived, and the Slate house was covered in pale pink and gold. Liam and I arrived early to help with setup as the birthday girl's honorary aunt and uncle. Charlie wasn't a Remington, so she wasn't technically our niece by blood, but it didn't matter. We adored her just the same.

While our Charlie girl napped in preparation for her big day, the adults got to work setting up food, arranging party favors, and hanging last-minute decorations.

Liam snickered beside me when Jaxon came down wearing a T-shirt featuring a cartoon bunny that read: Dad of the Birthday Bunny. Throwing an elbow into his ribs, I couldn't stop the smile that crept onto my face at the sight of him in that shirt. Jaxon did look ridiculous, but it was arguably the sweetest thing I'd ever seen. He loved his baby girl. Hell, he loved all the kids with his whole heart.

Just before party time, Natalie brought down Charlie, wearing the cutest personalized onesie featuring a bunny next to a large number one with her name underneath. The outfit was capped off with a pink and gold tutu. Natalie sported a shirt to match Jaxon's, declaring that she was the mom of the birthday bunny.

Seeing them as a cheery, happy family unit, it was strange to think about how difficult the road had been for Natalie and Jaxon. They had been thrown together unexpectedly, weathered the storm, and were now the picture of married bliss.

They weren't the only ones who found their way to love in a roundabout way. The lesson I'd learned over the past couple of years—first with Natalie and Jaxon, and now with me and Liam—was that when life threw you a curve, you leaned into it, trusting in the journey and that the road would take you where you needed to go.

The house was packed. Thankfully, the spring weather had cooperated, allowing the children invited to play outside and giving those inside some breathing room.

Growing up in the upper echelon of society, I'd been to my fair share of first-birthday blowouts, but this one was different. Those parties had been events for adults, the parents using their children as an excuse to network and socialize. The birthday child was often an afterthought, and no other children were usually on the guest list.

This party was full of love and centered around the birthday girl. Charlie was passed from person to person, being fawned over as there wasn't a single person immune to her babyish charm.

She was a different kind of royalty than her siblings. Charlie was hockey royalty, the daughter of one of the league's superstars.

Like a true hockey princess, Miss Charlie brought all her hockey uncles to their knees. These big, strong men, who often fought to the raucous cheers of thousands, were making silly faces and saying nonsense words to get a laugh from her. It was entertaining but not necessarily shocking. I'd caught Liam doing the same thing more times than I could count.

The chorus singing to the birthday girl as she sat in her highchair was nearly deafening in volume with the number of guests assembled. Thankfully, Charlie had sat through her fair share of noisy hockey games and remained utterly unfazed. She was more interested in getting her hands on the bunny cake Natalie held before her. Beau helped his little sister blow out the lone candle, and then Charlie was allowed to tear apart her cake.

Everyone laughed, watching her grab fistfuls of cake in her chubby hands before trying to shove them both deep into her mouth. Natalie attempted to slow her down, but Charlie looked at her and shrieked. You had to respect a girl who knew what she wanted. Once she'd made enough of a mess—covered in frosting—Jaxon stepped in to remove the tray of her highchair.

Respecting that they had a houseful of guests, I stepped forward to grab Charlie. "Come here, messy girl. Let's get you cleaned up."

Taking her upstairs to the kids' bathroom, I stripped her down while the warm water filled the bathtub. Suddenly, I was hit with a wave of nostalgia. I had so many memories in this house—many in this very bathroom—helping to raise Natalie's children.

Reflecting on my time living here, Liam had been right by my side every step of the way. He'd been there through the skinned knees, midnight snacks, and playing Santa. He was the one who'd taken charge when Beau had croup as a baby, spending hours in the middle of the night running the shower to create steam in hopes of soothing him.

How had I never noticed the incredibly steadfast family man who had helped me co-parent Natalie's children when he'd been there the entire time? His gruff exterior disguised the kind man beneath, but the signs had always been there.

It was terrifying to think we might have never found each other. We had lived in the same house for years and never developed more than a platonic relationship. Neither of us had been looking for a counterpart.

Liam was such a huge part of my world, and I had only opened my eyes to the amazing man he was because we'd been forced together.

Placing Charlie into the filled tub, I soaped her tiny body, scrubbing away all traces of frosting until she was clean. She wanted to play but had guests waiting for her, so I rinsed her off before pulling her out and patting her dry with a towel. Dressing her in an adorable outfit featuring a bunny on the bum of her pants, we returned to the party.

When no one immediately stole Charlie from my arms, I sat on the couch, cuddling her. She was content to sit in my lap, watching those around her, while I inhaled the sweet scent of baby shampoo from the top of her head.

Awareness tickled the back of my brain, alerting me to Liam's comforting presence before I felt him lower his head to mine from behind, whispering in my ear, "You look fucking incredible with a baby in your arms."

I felt the gasp working its way up my throat but was powerless to stop it, and my mind began to race. Liam and I had been on the same page regarding children when we married. Then again, we'd also been on the same page regarding sex, and look at us now. Did he want kids now? Did my opinion on the matter change now that our relationship had evolved?

Speechless, my cheeks grew warm. Glancing up, I caught Natalie eyeing us from across the room as she conversed with one of her fellow hockey wives. If I didn't know any better, I would think that she could see right through me.

The truth was, I didn't know what I wanted. My whole life had changed and been flipped upside down mere months ago. The only thing I knew for sure was that I was enjoying my time with my husband, exploring our new relationship. I was content to continue doing that for now.

Liam had shifted toward the arm of the couch, crouching next to where I sat with Charlie. "Baby, I have to go."

He'd ripped the rug from beneath my feet, and now he was leaving. Liam had postponed his trip to Belleston to celebrate Charlie's birthday—a testament to his commitment to putting family first. As much as I wanted to go with him, this time I couldn't. My meeting with the board was scheduled before Liam was expected to return.

He wouldn't hear of it when I felt guilty about not accompanying him home; he respected and supported the importance of my career. I knew there would be times when we'd have to divide and conquer, but the idea of being in the house alone without him was almost more than I could bear. I might have to beg for a sleepover with Natalie once the Comets hit the road for the second round, but nothing could replace Liam's arms holding me close as I fell asleep at night.

Nodding, I accepted the inevitable that had been barreling toward us for days. "I know." I desperately tried to keep the quiver from my voice but failed miserably.

Reaching over to stroke my cheek, his brilliant blue eyes were full of tenderness. "It's killing me to leave you behind. You know that?" Biting my trembling lip, I nodded as he continued, "But my wife is a badass boss bitch, and she's needed here."

Tears leaked from my eyes despite my efforts to stave them off, but I laughed. Taking the leap, I finally said the words I knew in my heart but my brain hadn't allowed me to vocalize until now. "I love you."

Liam's eyes widened slightly, and those blue depths sparkled, shining with all his love for me. The hand on my face traveled to the back of my neck, and he pulled me into a deep kiss, not caring that we were in a crowded room at a kid's party—a kid who was currently sitting in my lap.

Breaking away once we were both breathless, he pressed his forehead to mine and whispered, "God, Amy. I love you so much."

Charlie squirmed in my arms, and I let out a shaky breath. "Well, you can't leave without giving our niece a proper goodbye."

He knew I was stalling, but his smile stole my heart. Turning Charlie to face me, I let her stand on my lap. She bounced excitedly and squealed when she saw her Uncle Liam.

Same girl, same.

Rising up, Liam leaned over, blowing a raspberry into the crook of her neck, causing her sweet giggles to fill the room. Pulling back, he dropped a kiss on the top of her head. "Happy birthday, Charlie girl. Be good for Aunt Amy while I'm gone."

Gone. Just hearing that word had tears burning behind my eyes again.

My brain and my heart were at war. My heart screamed that nothing mattered but Liam and that I should go with him. My brain told me I'd worked hard to create an incredible pilot program and would be a fool to throw it all away over a man. But he wasn't just any man. He was my husband, the man I loved.

It was only a week, right?

Moving to stand to see him out, Liam stopped me with a hand on my shoulder. "Stay. Enjoy the baby snuggles. We both know they're gone too soon." Placing a soft kiss on my lips, he tucked my hair behind my ear. "Call me after your meeting. They'd be fools not to choose you."

Swallowing hard, I let out a shaky breath. "You're biased."

Liam flashed his perfect white teeth at me. "Don't think I won't tell you if you put together something terrible. I can and will save you from yourself if I deem it necessary."

I was torn. Part of me wanted to drag this goodbye out for as long as possible to delay the pain I knew I'd feel with his departure. The other part knew that I couldn't put it off forever and that the sooner he left, the sooner he'd return. That rational side won out. "Text me when you land."

"I promise." Standing to his full height, Liam caressed Charlie's head once more before walking away.

One week. I could do this.

"To Natalie!" Hannah yelled over the bubbling water of the hot tub on the upper deck of Natalie and Jaxon's house. "No one gives the mom enough credit for making it through that first year. Even though Nat makes it look easy, we know there have been countless sleepless nights, tons of dirty diapers, and spit up in her hair."

"Hear, hear!" I seconded Hannah's praise of Natalie, whose face wasn't red just from the heat of the water surrounding us.

Natalie countered, "I had a lot of help. It truly takes a village, and I have the best one."

We all took a sip from our insulated wine tumblers. The party had been a success, and with the kids—and Jaxon—tucked in for the night, it was time for an impromptu girls' night in. The hot tub felt amazing, and I allowed my eyes to drift close, surrendering to the sensation of the jets and warm water easing away some of the tension from Liam's departure earlier this evening.

Almost as if on cue, Natalie remarked, "You and Liam looked pretty cozy this afternoon. Did you two finally talk?"

Forcing my eyes open to glare at my best friend, I reminded myself that she had our best interests at heart. These two women were my people. We had an unspoken agreement to push each other when we felt it was warranted. Clearly, Natalie deemed this one of those times.

Sighing, I responded, "He loves me."

Hannah squealed. "I knew it! You've tamed the beast, Amy. I didn't think it could be done, but you've always been an overachiever."

Natalie ignored her, asking, "And how do you feel about him?"

Draining the remaining wine in my tumbler in a single gulp, I wiped my mouth with my wet hand. "Today, before he left, I told him I loved him back. Moments after he told me I looked good holding a baby."

There was a splashing sound, and I turned my head to find Hannah fishing her tumbler out of the water. "Damn. That dude is practically celibate for years, then he gets a taste of our Amy, and he's thinking babies? Do you have some kind of magical coochie? Inquiring minds need to know."

Concern flashed in Natalie's eyes. "Have you changed your mind about having a family?"

I'd been asking myself the same question over and over since he'd left. "Maybe someday I'll want kids, but not right now. If I get this promotion, I have to show I'm committed. For such a *family-focused* foundation, you should have heard Mr. Greiner implying that now that I am married, I would defer to Liam's career over my own."

"Asshole," Hannah muttered.

"I can only imagine how he'd feel about maternity leave. I'm sure they'd have someone take my place in a heartbeat while spewing some bullshit about needing to spend time at home and focus on my family. Women can be so much more than wives and mothers." Realizing my mistake too late, I added, "Sorry, Nat. No offense."

Natalie brushed off my apology. "None taken. Our paths are different, but that doesn't make one better than the other. I'm in awe of what you've accomplished. Now, if only we could get Hannah to accomplish something, we'd be set."

Laughter filled the night air. Hannah was still figuring out her life. Even at almost thirty.

Feigning outrage, Hannah protested, "Hey! I have goals. "

"Besides hooking up with a hockey player?" Natalie challenged.

"Well, that's certainly the most pressing one. It's practically a full-time job."

Enjoying the slight reprieve from talking about my love life, I decided to stir the pot. "You know who I saw checking you out a while back?"

Hannah's eyes lit up. "Who?"

"Cal."

"Gag me." Her face transformed from one of delight to one of pure disgust.

"Why not?" I asked. "You can cross it off your bucket list. The way he was staring at your ass at the club, he's interested."

Hannah scoffed. "I don't know what you think you saw, but Cal hates me and always has. He's the single most annoying person I've ever met, acting like he knows more about hockey than I do."

Natalie chimed in, "He does play the sport."

"That doesn't make him an expert!" Hannah protested. "Cal plays it, but I've spent my entire life sitting beside Dad in film review. I can analyze it in a way he can't. Cross him off the list. That is *never* going to happen."

"You're running out of options unless you're reconsidering the rookies." I was enjoying riling her up.

"Ew, no. One night sitting next to Baby Braxton was enough to remind me why I steer clear of the young ones. They have an advantage in terms of stamina, but their experience is sorely lacking. I need one I don't need to draw a damn road map for. Maybe I'll put a bug in Daddy's ear in the off-season. Free agency could be like my own personal sex toy catalog."

Natalie groaned. "Gross."

"What? You want Amy to be happy with Liam. Why can't I find happiness?"

"Sex isn't love, Hannah," Natalie explained.

"Maybe not, but it sure seems like a gateway drug. Look at you and Jaxon, and now Amy and Liam. Sex first, love later."

"Be careful what you wish for," Natalie warned. "It wasn't easy for either of us."

Hannah didn't back down. "But you're both happy now. All I want is a chance at that. Even if it's hard work. Is that too much to ask?"

Natalie sighed. "All I'm trying to say is that you shouldn't have to try so hard. Let it find you."

Throwing her arms wide above the bubbling water, Hannah yelled, "I'm right here!"

I felt for Hannah. She'd sat on the sidelines while Natalie and I found love when we weren't looking for it. It had to be hard for her to watch her best friends move on with their lives and feel left behind.

She was feisty. Whoever had the courage to tame her had their work cut out for them. It would be fun to watch.

Looking across the water at my two best friends, we'd come a long way from those three teenage girls giggling over boys. Life had changed us, molding us into the women we became, but our bond remained the same. Our unspoken agreement was—that right or wrong—we'd always have each other's backs, and that hadn't changed with the passing of time.

How had I gotten so lucky? I had these two incredible ladies in my corner, no matter what, and an adoring husband I never knew I needed or wanted. Life was good.

Now, if I could only manage to shake the feeling that Liam was hiding something from me.

CHAPTER 26

Liam

THE FLIGHT WAS PURE torture. It had taken every ounce of my willpower to walk out the door after Amy told me she loved me. While everyone had been focused on the birthday girl, I'd spent the entire day watching Amy. She'd looked incredible—her ass looked as if it had been poured into her tight blue jeans, but her smile as she worked the room had me itching to drag her next door for a more physical goodbye.

Our apartment at Stonecrest Palace was cold and lifeless without Amy's presence. It was unsettling—ominous almost—causing those demons to resurface in my mind. This was what it would be like when she learned the truth and left me.

Exhaustion pulled at my body after the long flight, and I shoved those dark thoughts aside, making my way to our bedroom and collapsing on the bed. The pillows still smelled like her, which I knew was ludicrous. There was no possibility they hadn't been washed since our last stay, but I'd know that scent anywhere. It was comforting to the point where I grabbed a pillow, hugging it to my chest before falling asleep.

Far too soon, I was pulled from the depths of my slumber by my alarm blaring. Rubbing my eyes with my palms, I didn't wake feeling rested—a cruel reminder that jet lag was a bitch. I wanted nothing more than to close my eyes and succumb to the softness of my bed, but I came here for a reason. Postponing my arrival meant there was no wiggle room, and I had to drag my ass out of bed for a state dinner beginning in a matter of hours.

A cold shower helped jolt my unwilling body to shake off any lingering desire to return to bed. Toweling off, I checked the time, eager to call Amy. Staying connected with the time difference would be difficult—especially during the week when she had work—so with today being Sunday, I wanted to take advantage of her day off.

Early evening in Belleston meant late morning back home, so I hit the video call option next to Amy's number in my phone and sat on my bed against the headboard as it rang. On the third ring, my screen lit up with the gorgeous redhead I was lucky enough to call mine filling the frame. Her fiery tresses were fanned across the pillow as she stretched, yawning.

"Hey, there, sleepyhead." God, she was stunning even when she was barely awake.

"Morning," she mumbled, still fighting to open her eyes.

"Late night?" Knowing Amy, she'd stayed behind to help with the cleanup at Charlie's party.

Eyes fluttering open, she smiled. "Yeah, we had some girl time in the hot tub once we got all the kids in bed."

"Mm. Sorry I missed that." The mental image of water gliding over her soft curves had the towel covering my lower half tenting as blood pooled in my groin.

"Maybe we can sneak over when they go to Minnesota this summer," she suggested.

"It's a date."

"A date sounds nice." Her voice was still groggy from sleep.

"I wish you were here." Fuck me. I sounded like a needy asshole.

"I do, too. Our bed is so lonely without you."

"Confession—I curled up with a pillow that smelled like you and fell asleep when I got in."

For being half-asleep, I could have sworn I saw a sparkle in her eyes. "I have a confession, too." Amy bit her lip, and I nearly groaned. "On New Year's Eve, I watched you in the shower."

The hand not holding my phone dropped to my lap, flinging the towel aside to stroke my dick. "Naughty girl."

"That's not all. It turned me on, so I went into my bedroom and touched myself 'til I came."

"Fuck. Amy, you're killing me."

Her lust-filled gaze met mine through the screen. "I could touch myself right now thinking about it, but I have a feeling you already are."

"God, yes." I gripped my dick a little harder. "Take off your panties, sweetheart. I want to watch you make yourself come."

That smirk of hers almost threw me over the edge, and I had to ease off so I didn't blow my load before I enjoyed the show.

"What panties?" Amy bit her lip, playing coy.

I didn't bother to hold back the groan that rumbled from my chest. "Goddamn. You know it fucking drives me wild when your pussy is ready and waiting for me. I'm going to burn every pair of panties you own when I get home."

"Mm-hmm." I watched as her eyes fluttered closed, her breathing coming in short pants.

"Did I tell you to touch yourself?" my stern voice demanded.

Eyes popping open, they were full of defiance. "I don't take orders from you."

Growling at the show of insubordination, I promised, "You'll pay for that when I get home."

Her head dropped back, and I could picture trailing my mouth up the delicate slope of her neck as she gave herself pleasure. "Oh, Liam." Amy's moans had my cock throbbing against my palm.

"You are so beautiful like this. I could watch you pleasure yourself for hours." Giving my dick the attention it demanded, I went back to stroking myself as Amy's breathing hitched, her lower lip pulled between her teeth. She was close, and so was I. "Come for me, baby." My voice was strained with my impending release.

Amy's mouth fell open as her body shuddered and seized, a high-pitched moan punctuating her climax. Watching my wife lose herself so freely was my undoing. A few more pumps, and I gritted my teeth as pleasure tore through me. It didn't come close to the real thing but eased the ache.

Grabbing my discarded towel, I used it to wipe up the mess I'd made. Through the screen, Amy's eyes were still closed tight, but her breathing began returning to normal.

"Wow," she breathed. "What a way to wake up."

Laughing, I marveled at the woman I married. She exuded light and optimism. I felt lighter when she was near. "I'm going to be playing that on repeat all night."

Those emerald eyes opened, and a smile crept across her face. "That could get you in trouble in a room full of dignitaries. I won't be responsible for causing an international incident."

"You think you're funny, don't you, sweetheart?"

The smug look that crossed her face had my dick twitching again. "Oh, honey, I know I am."

"You get the last laugh. I would happily trade your lazy Sunday for my stuffy state dinner."

Snuggling deeper into the softness of the bedding around her, she sighed. "Hmm. Maybe I'll just stay here all day."

"You deserve it. Take the day off. Watch trashy TV all day and order in for every meal."

"Only thing missing is you." Amy sighed.

"If I can survive these next six days without you, next weekend will be our laziest yet."

A devilish gleam entered her eye. "Not too lazy, I hope."

"Let me try again. I intend to use and abuse your body until you can't walk, so you'll be forced to stay in bed."

"That's better."

"I wish I could stay on the phone with you all day, but I have to get ready to go."

"Oh, yes," she mocked. "My husband is a very important person."

"With any luck, everyone will leave me alone when they find out my brilliant wife won't be on my arm. You're far more popular than me."

The compliment made her blush, and I enjoyed watching the color move up her cheeks—it brought attention to her adorable freckles.

"All right. Enough of that. Give your parents my love, and don't get into too much trouble." Amy gave me a pointed look, and I knew she was referring to Leo.

"I promise." Blowing her a kiss through the screen, I added, "I love you, Amy."

I would never tire of how her face lit up at those words. Shyly, and for only the second time ever, she repeated those words, making my heart soar. "I love you too, Liam."

"Stay out of trouble, and I'll talk to you soon."

"I will. Goodnight." Amy sensed my reluctance to end the call—I could have stared at her face forever—so she clicked the button on her end of the line, and my screen went black.

It was going to be a long six days.

———❦———

Tonight's state dinner was in honor of the Crown Prince and Princess of Uthropia visiting Belleston. Every person with money or influence was in attendance, and it was suffocating.

I hadn't been to one of these dinners in over four years and was quickly reminded why I always hated them. I was not cut out for the politics involved. I knew how to play the game but loathed it. Everywhere I looked, people were making deals—personal and political.

Leo had always been far more suited to this life than me.

Drowning my discomfort in a second pre-dinner glass of bourbon, I heard a familiar feminine voice call my name.

"Is that you, Liam?"

Turning my head, I saw who so casually addressed me in this formal setting. Walking toward me was my ex-girlfriend, Penelope Ward. She looked stunning tonight in a floor-length blue silk gown, her long blonde hair piled atop her head to look regal. As the daughter of an earl, she looked the part—she was flawless. We had dated on and off for a few years, but I'd broken things off when I discovered how much Natalie needed me.

I hadn't thought about her in years. Everything beyond taking care of Natalie had fallen away. Ironically, that was probably why I hadn't ever taken the time to notice how incredible Amy was in all our years living together. Natalie had forced us together but also eclipsed our ability to recognize our counterparts in each other.

"It's been a long time, Pen." I pulled her close to drop an obligatory greeting kiss on her cheek.

Pulling back, her practiced smile made me wonder what I ever saw in her. Amy was her complete opposite, genuinely exuding grace without having to try.

"I've been here. You were the one who disappeared." There was no malice in her words. She was simply stating facts.

"I had some business to attend to, but now duty calls."

"You've been busy," she mused. "It would seem congratulations are in order. She must be an incredible lady to get you to settle down."

Any time Amy came to mind, my smile was automatic. "She is." I'd give anything to have her by my side right now.

"You look happy, Liam."

"I am happy," I admitted.

"I am only sorry I'm unable to congratulate her in person." Penelope and Amy's paths had crossed over the years, but they hadn't been overly friendly—hell, *I* hadn't been overly friendly to Amy.

"Amy had a work obligation she couldn't miss," I explained.

A look of surprise crossed Penelope's face. Being the wife of a senior royal was expected to be a full-time job, so it shocked many that Amy hadn't given up her career. Only I knew the truth that her commitment to her job was the only reason she'd agreed to marry me.

"How is Natalie? Did I hear she remarried?" Penelope was skilled in the art of conversation and quickly steered ours toward calmer waters.

I nodded. "She did. Nat's got a new husband who treats her well and a baby girl who is the light of our lives."

Penelope's smile was genuine this time. "I'm so glad. I always thought it a shame that sweet girl had fallen into Leo's clutches." She was one of the few who got a peek behind the curtain of Leo's not-so-charming personality by virtue of her relationship with me.

Pensive momentarily, she added, "I'm actually surprised she didn't end up with you."

That comment hit me like a slap across the face. It wouldn't have bothered me so much if Amy hadn't asked about my feelings for Natalie a few weeks ago. The tabloids had always suggested it, but they always went with the most shocking headlines, and I'd brushed it off. What kind of signals had I been giving off that those closest to me assumed I was hot for my brother's wife? It couldn't have been further from the truth.

Awkwardly, I pulled on the back of my neck. "No, Nat and I were never meant to be. I love her like a sister, nothing more."

Realizing she'd overstepped, Penelope backtracked. "Oh, I'm sorry. I didn't mean to imply . . . Well, it doesn't matter anyway. You're both happily married, right?'

"Right. Next door neighbors, in fact."

A fake laugh easily slipped past her lips. "Oh, well, isn't that the sweetest thing."

That. That right here was why I hated these dinners. The condescension dripping from her words had my fists clenching and my body screaming to abandon the whole thing. I was brought up to be polite, so I gave her a tight smile before taking another pull from my glass of bourbon.

The chime signaling that it was time to take our seats for dinner rang, and guests began filing toward the dining hall.

Batting her false eyelashes at me, Penelope's voice was sickeningly sweet. "Will you escort me to dinner? For old time's sake?"

I'd never missed Amy more, but I offered Penelope my arm as the gentleman I was raised to be. My skin crawled under my clothes when she draped her hand over my elbow as I led her into dinner.

Was it time to go home yet?

As if the state dinner hadn't been uncomfortable enough, Mother had cornered me in a hallway partway through my stay to let me know that Grandfather and Father planned to take advantage of Amy's absence to break the news to Leo that he would no longer be in the line of succession.

My blood ran cold at her words. There would be no turning back once Leo knew, and my time with Amy was running out. Leo wouldn't take kindly to losing the birthright he felt a sense of entitlement toward. He'd been raised to believe it, so he wouldn't let go without a fight. And if there was one thing I knew about my older brother, he never fought fair.

Two days later, there I sat in an armchair, waiting for the explosion that was about to happen. My presence was meant to be a prop as the Big Wigs laid out Leo's options. While I was happy to sit on the sidelines, I had a feeling Leo wouldn't allow it. I'd be dragged into this mess as he began to claw at anything he could to maintain the status quo.

Leo sauntered into our "meeting" half an hour late, having no respect for others' time and acting as if he owned the place. In his mind, he was untouchable.

Throwing a sneer in my direction, he addressed our elders with impatience. "What was so important it couldn't wait until after *he* left?"

I would have relished watching the smug look wiped from his face when he learned the truth if it hadn't also signaled the demise of my marriage. We would both be losers today.

Grandfather commanded the room. "Sit down, Leopold."

Leo rolled his eyes at the use of his legal name but obeyed. "Fine. I've got things to do. Can we get this over with?"

Not taking the time to sugarcoat it, Grandfather announced, "You will no longer be your father's heir."

Expecting outrage from my brother, it was almost jarring to hear his laugh. "This is a joke, right?"

"I'm afraid not. Liam will be named heir publicly when the time is right."

I watched the transformation of Leo's face—going from arrogance to outrage—as he turned on me. "You. How long have you been planning to overthrow me?"

The anger at my helplessness in this situation had never fully cleared, and I snapped back at him, throwing my arms wide. "You think I want this?"

"I do. You've always been jealous of me."

"Get over yourself," I spat.

"No, it all makes sense now. This is some twisted, self-righteous attempt to punish me for your precious Natalie's inability to hack it. So, you marry her best friend and try to take what's mine. Well, think again. Your precious Amy will *never* be Belleston's queen."

"You keep her name out of your mouth!" I roared, standing to challenge him.

Turning to our parents, he gestured to where I stood. "You want this brute to take my place? Look at him. He doesn't have the finesse or diplomacy required."

"Enough!" Grandfather yelled. "The decision is final, Leopold."

"Final." He scoffed. "Even if you skip me, what of my son?"

"*Sons*," I corrected.

"Debatable," Leo countered. "You would just cancel out my entire line? Good luck convincing Parliament to back that decision."

Father stood, commanding the attention of the room. "We don't need to convince anyone, Leo. The fact of the matter is that you're not biologically my son."

That finally seemed to get through to him, and I watched as the color slowly drained from my brother's face. The room remained silent while he took a moment to sort through his new reality. I'd have felt bad for him if he wasn't a narcissistic prick.

Within an instant, his ashen face turned almost purple as he screamed at our mother, "You whore!"

"Shut your fucking mouth!" I must have blacked out because I was standing over Leo's prone body the next thing I knew, my right fist throbbing as I shouted, "Stay down!"

Witnessing Leo cower in fear after I hit him should have been satisfying—it had been a long time coming—but I felt empty. Nothing would be the same after today. At a light touch on my arm, I flinched; the adrenaline coursing through my veins had me ready for another fight. Turning to find my mother's sorrowful face close to mine, guilt washed over me for causing her more pain. She'd been through enough, and the last thing she needed was for me to lose control.

Leo felt safe enough to sit up as I backed away, clutching his rapidly bruising jaw.

Grandfather retained his composure, addressing him on the ground. "There are two options regarding this situation. The first is that you voluntarily remove yourself and your children from the line of succession, stepping down publicly. For your cooperation, we will never reveal the circumstances surrounding your decision, and you will remain a member of this family with a generous stipend. The second is you do not cooperate, and we are forced to show Parliament the proof that you are not a Remington by blood, and the whole world learns why you will never be King. The choice is yours."

Public perception was everything to Leo. He *had* to choose option one, right? Saving himself and our family the shame of having a heinous crime committed against our mother from being exposed and dissected by the press seemed like the sane option. Unfortunately, that hinged on Leo's mental state, which was anything but stable on a regular day, let alone one where his future was seemingly stolen from him in an instant.

There was a murderous gleam in his eyes as he stared at me. He was out for blood—mine more than anyone else's. I couldn't control the fact that I was legitimate and he was not any more than he could. But he blamed me. I was the threat to his power.

Readying myself for yet another fight—verbal or physical—I was shocked when he rose to his feet and left the room without another word. A shudder ran through my body. I knew this wasn't over. Not by a long shot. Leo was a wild card. There was no telling what he'd do now that he was backed into a corner.

Wanting nothing more than to go home to be with Amy before the fallout began, I excused myself.

I barely made it halfway down the hallway when I heard Mother's voice softly say, "Liam, wait."

Emotionally wrung out, I sighed but halted my steps to allow her to reach where I stood. Taking a deep breath, I turned to face my mother. Expecting a mess after Leo's verbal assault and my resulting physical one, her head was held high. What took me aback was the concern in her eyes as she looked up at me. Guilt hit me like a tidal wave.

I hung my head. "I'm sorry, Mother."

"Don't apologize, darling. We've placed you in an impossible position."

Flexing my aching fist, I didn't want absolution. "You deserve better. From both of us."

Her small, soft hand covered my restless one. "I'm proud of the man you've become, and I have especially enjoyed the changes I've seen in you over these past few months."

"How can you say that? I've never felt more out of control in my entire life!" I cried. "I hate it."

Instead of commiserating with me, a soft smile graced her lips. "You have something to fight for. Possibly for the first time in your life."

"I don't want to fight for the crown."

She smiled up at me. "I wasn't talking about your birthright. You have a marriage to fight for and a woman you love."

Fuck. Like I needed any reminders of how my life was about to implode. "What if it's not enough?"

"What isn't enough, darling?"

"Love. Amy has this incredible career. How can I ask her to give that up for me? I don't know if I want her to. It's part of who she is, and I love her exactly as she is."

"Who says she has to? God willing, you two have decades to enjoy your lives together before the responsibility of this position comes knocking at your door." My mind was at war between my obligations to my family—and my country by extension—and my love for my wife. Seeing my hesitation, Mother added, "Liam, you were lucky enough to find your equal. Amy is a woman who compliments you and challenges you. She makes *you* a better person. We'd be fools to ask you to choose between a life of love and a life of duty. No one should be asked to make that choice. Go home and tell your wife. I can see how much she loves you, and if she's half the girl I know she is, you two will find a compromise. That's what you do for the people you love."

"Compromise." That word had never held a place in my vocabulary, but it gave me hope.

"It's your nature to give your all to everyone, but that's impossible. There's a give and take to be found in your marriage, the same as in this life you've been born into. We offered you a minor role, and you decided to take on a larger one. Your sense of duty can be a detriment at times. Focus on your new marriage. We would never ask you to put this job above your happiness, and happiness looks good on you."

Could I really have it all? Keep the woman I love and fulfill my duty to my country? Mother had made a compelling case, firmly believing that Amy would stand by my side. I was terrified to tell her, having kept this secret from her for so long, but I finally began to have hope. If she didn't have to give up her job in the immediate future, she might be willing to make this work. Maybe love could conquer all.

There was only one way to find out. One more event required my presence, and then I could return home—hopefully to a celebration of Amy's promotion. Perhaps I could use that new job high to my advantage. If all else failed, Jaxon's suggestion of groveling might come in handy.

CHAPTER 27

Amy

TODAY WAS THE DAY—FOR real this time. For better or worse, today, I would discover if I had convinced the Foundation board to grant me the position of Programs Director.

Liam would be home this evening, and he was on my mind as I dressed for the day. Choosing a simple black pantsuit, I paired it with an emerald green top for a pop of color—Liam's favorite color on me. Adding the earrings he got me for my birthday, it was as if a piece of him would be with me when I entered the room where judgment would be passed on my body of work over the past several months.

Sitting in the small lobby outside the boardroom, I was calm. A direct contrast to the last time I sat here when anxiety and stress had nearly crippled me. So much had changed since that day. No matter what the board's decision, my life had altered course. A chain reaction was set in motion when I applied for this job that had led me to Liam, and even if I didn't obtain the position, my future was bright.

The last time I was here, I thought my world—my career—was ending. Now, I knew it was only beginning. I'd gained a new perspective on my life. My profession no longer defined me.

The sense of déjà vu was strong when the boardroom's double doors opened, and the Foundation board's secretary appeared. Looking down at her clipboard, she called, "Ms. Michaels?"

Rising from where I sat, I followed her inside, taking the same open seat facing the entire board as I had over six months ago.

Just like that day, Mr. Greiner took the lead. "Thank you for joining us today, Ms. Michaels."

Folding both hands in my lap, knowing this would be a meeting where they talked and I listened, I politely answered, "Thank you for having me."

He got right down to business. "The Remington Family Center has been an incredible addition to our portfolio of programs here at the Foundation. You've found a way to eliminate multiple barriers to reunification in one central location. The residents have been set up for long-term success due to your efforts. You should be very proud."

"Thank you, sir."

Clearing his throat before continuing, I prepared myself for what seemed inevitable. I had a nagging feeling I wouldn't win this job, but I'd made peace with that. Returning to my position as Manager of Special Projects would still allow me to change the lives of families. Adding the creation of The Remington Family Center to my resume would be an asset, and if I ever felt pigeonholed here at the Foundation, I could seek a job at one of the many worthy charities in Hartford. Maybe I could even use my experience to help the residents of Belleston.

"Unfortunately, in light of recent events, we have decided to terminate your employment at the Hartford Family Reunification Foundation."

The words sank in as I was about to thank them for their consideration.

Terminated? That didn't make any sense.

"Excuse me?"

Undeterred, Mr. Greiner doubled down. "While we respect that your personal life is your business, we can't allow the bad press to cast a shadow on our work here. I'm sure you can understand."

I had no fucking clue what he was talking about. "I'm sorry, sir. I don't quite understand. What part of my personal life is an issue for the Foundation?"

Shifting in his seat, he reached for a manilla folder. Instead of opening it, he slid it across the conference table toward me. Cursing my shaking hands, I peeled open the folder, and my heart stopped. Staring back at me was a full-color spread of Liam and his ex-girlfriend, Penelope, together at the state dinner over the weekend. Pictures of Liam kissing her on the cheek, her grubby paw on his elbow as he escorted her, and most damning of all, Liam's face lit up with the smile he reserved only for me.

My heart was beating out of my chest as I processed what lay before me. This couldn't be real.

The headline read: *Rekindling the Flame? Prince Liam Remington and Lady Penelope Ward Cozy Up in Princess Amy's Absence. Is this the End for Belleston's Newest Royal Couple?*

Flipping to the magazine's front cover revealed it to be a particularly seedy tabloid. These publications were known for being unethical. How many untrue stories had been printed about Natalie over the years? Liam loved me. He'd never do this to me.

Seeds of doubt began to take root in my brain. Why hadn't he mentioned running into Penelope when he called every evening if it was an innocent encounter? There was a single spark of hope—maybe this was an old picture. Scanning for any proof that this was recent, my eyes landed on

Liam's tie. It was the same tie I'd bought him for Christmas, the one he had worn to the Center's grand opening.

This couldn't be happening.

Trying desperately to keep my composure, I held my head high as I addressed the board. "This is a tabloid. Most of what they print is clickbait—twisted tales at the expense of innocent people as they profit from lies."

Mr. Greiner had the good sense to look mildly remorseful. "Be that as it may, Ms. Michaels, we have an obligation to uphold our stance on strong family values. Perception is everything."

"So, I'm being punished for the actions of others?" I challenged.

"You chose to lead a life open to public scrutiny. This is where we part ways. We wish you the best in your future endeavors."

There was no use in arguing. They'd already made up their minds. My top priority now was getting out of this room before the full ramifications of these pictures hit me.

Standing, I left the room without a word, the manilla folder abandoned on the conference table. Panic began to set in as I waited for the elevator; the weight on my chest was so heavy it became difficult to draw air. The doors parted with a ding just as the first tears began to fall.

There was only one place I knew I could go.

Unlocking the side door to Natalie's house, I went straight to the living room, collapsing on the couch. As silent tears streamed down my face, I was grateful it was early enough that the kids were at school and wouldn't witness my unraveling.

Time stood still as I laid there wondering where the hell it had all gone wrong. A door closed in the distance, and I prayed it wasn't Jaxon who found me in this state. Emotionally wrung-out as I was, I couldn't even remember if he was on the road right now.

"Amy?" It was Natalie. Thank God. "What happened?"

My voice was hoarse from crying. "I lost my job."

"What?! That doesn't make any sense." The couch dipped as she sat on the edge.

I forced myself to say the words that had been bouncing around in my brain for hours. "He's cheating on me."

My declaration was met with silence. Daring myself to look at my best friend, she was staring at me, mouth hanging open.

Blinking a few times, she managed, "Why would you say that?"

Sitting up, I pulled my knees to my chest, hugging them tightly. My eyes were puffy, and there was a gritty sensation as if there was sand in them every time I blinked. "Look me up on your phone."

Warily, she grabbed her phone, typing in my name. Her eyes moved rapidly while reading whatever text accompanied the pictures of Liam and Penelope together. "Ames. You don't really believe this trash, do you? This is the same publication that Leo used to make me feel bad about myself for all those years. They're notorious for false stories. Liam would never do this to you."

Stifling a sob, I replied, "I tried to believe that. I did. I thought maybe it was an old picture, but he's wearing the tie I got him for Christmas."

Taking my hand, she countered, "How long did they try to sell the story of Liam and me sleeping together? You were here that whole time and know that never happened. This is a story, nothing more. He loves you."

"He's been hiding something from me. I've known it for a while but couldn't figure out what. It all makes sense now."

A strange look crossed her face, almost like she knew something I didn't, and I hated her for it. Liam was her brother-in-law, and she loved him, but we'd been best friends our entire lives. How could she choose him over me?

Squeezing my hand, she declared, "You need to talk to Liam."

"You know, don't you?" I accused.

"He's not cheating on you, Ames."

I wanted so much to believe her, but that dark cloud hanging over us for months finally unleashed its fury, and my heart was drenched in doubt. "Look at the pictures—that smile on his face. When else have you seen him smile like that?"

Natalie sighed as she resigned herself to what I already knew. "When he's looking at you."

"God, I'm such an idiot!" Tears fell freely down my face as old insecurities rushed to the surface. "Guys like him don't fall for girls like me. I should have known better. He played me."

"Don't say that."

"Do I have the words 'gullible girl' tattooed on my forehead in an ink only men can see? Or maybe it was my inexperience working against me—I never gave myself the chance to learn how to screen men properly."

She shook her head. "You didn't do anything wrong."

"How else do you explain the public humiliation that's come at the hands of the only two guys I've ever let get close to me? Once might be considered a fluke, but twice is a pattern."

"Liam isn't Chet."

"Stop fucking protecting him!" My sadness finally turned to anger, but it was directed at the wrong person. Remorse filled me for lashing out at my best friend. "I'm sorry, Nat."

Her warm brown eyes shone with tenderness. "You're hurting. I get it. I've been there, and you know that. Whatever you need, I'm here for you. I'm never going to choose him over you. Never."

Fresh tears were welling in my eyes as I asked, my voice barely above a whisper, "Can I stay here for a while?"

"Of course, you can."

Natalie hugged me as sobs shook my chest, realizing all I'd lost today. Liam had worked his way into my heart, only to rip it out of my chest once I'd let my guard down. I'd trusted him, and look where that had gotten me. I fell for his charm, for the man he pretended to be, but it was all an act. I'd believed Liam's guise of wanting to help me with my career, which had cost me everything. My reputation was ruined for the world to see, and I'd lost a job I loved as a result. I was left with nothing.

Our marriage was a contract, a harsh reminder that I was a fool to believe it could have evolved into something more—something real. Liam had broken the terms of that contract, thus proving how little it had meant to him in the first place.

My phone dinged in my purse on the floor. Breaking free of Natalie's embrace, I dug inside, half expecting it to be a text from my mother about how I'd embarrassed the family. When I saw the text staring up at me, I dropped the phone as if it had burned me.

Liam: *Wheels up in fifteen. Can't wait to see you and hear about your meeting. I love you.*

Liam's text had crushed me all over again. How could he say he loved me as if nothing had happened? Did he think I was that stupid? Of course, he did, or he wouldn't be running around with his ex behind my back, never expecting to get caught. The only silver lining was that his text gave me a nine-hour head start to move my essential items out of our house before he got home.

Evening rolled around, and I dreaded the moment when Liam returned home to discover that I had left. Would he even care? I thought back to the flight to Belleston when we sat on the floor in the middle of the night, combing through applications. When he told me how afraid he was to love because he'd only end up hurting me, and I would leave. Had he already been connecting with Penelope? Liam had seemed so confident that our relationship was doomed, and I was the sap who had been confident that he'd never hurt me.

Love had clouded my judgment, and I'd been blind to the warning signs. I only had myself to blame for falling for the fairy tale. If I hadn't, this wouldn't hurt so much.

"Dinner's here!" Jaxon's voice filtered through the house.

Dressed more comfortably for heartbreak in a tank top and leggings, I walked into the kitchen, where he and Natalie unpacked the takeout containers from our favorite Chinese food restaurant. Helping them fix plates for the kids, I fell right back into the role I'd held for years—live-in best friend helping to raise Nat's kids. It should have been comforting, but

I now felt out of place. This wasn't my home anymore, and neither was next door. There would be time to figure out my next move, but not today.

Pulling up a seat at the island with Natalie, I felt guilty for encroaching on this happy family unit.

"Thanks for letting me crash for a while, Jaxon. I'll try not to stay too long."

Jaxon surprised me by reaching across the island to grasp my hand, a soft smile on his lips. "You're family, Amy. Stay for as long as you'd like."

Squeezing his hand, I fought back the tears for what felt like the millionth time that day. Nodding, not trusting my voice, I let his hand go and began eating even though I didn't have much appetite. A few bites in, I gave up trying, pushing my food around my plate while everyone else enjoyed their dinner.

Once the kids were finished, Jaxon took them outside for playtime before bath and bed, leaving me and Natalie alone in the kitchen. All afternoon while we packed my things, I could see in her eyes that she wanted to tell me something, but whatever it was, she kept it to herself. What wasn't she telling me?

Gearing up to demand she tell me, I heard the front door slam open. My mind knew it couldn't be Liam, but I tensed anyway, anticipating the fight I had no energy for. I moved out because I didn't want to fight. I resigned myself to the end of my marriage, and fighting would only make this situation more painful.

Hannah burst into the kitchen like a tornado, a bottle of champagne in her hand. "Are we celebrating? Jaxon texted that you had food and Amy was here." Pausing, she must have seen the defeated look on my face because she softened. "Oh, shit. Is this a pity party instead? Did those fuckers give the job to someone else?"

Looking at Natalie, praying she would take the lead, she remained silent. How was it that Hannah hadn't heard? I'd been forced to turn off my phone as it had blown up with every news outlet under the sun asking for a comment or rebuttal. Those pictures and my shame were plastered everywhere at this point.

"I didn't get the job." Let's start with that.

"And why the hell not?" She threw her hands on her hips, poised and ready for a fight on my behalf.

"Because Liam's cheating on me." There, I'd said it. And it didn't hurt any less than the first time. If anything, it hurt more to repeat it, knowing it was true.

"No."

"No?" What did she mean, no?

She shook her head. "That's off-brand for Liam. He'd walk through fire to protect those he loves. Hell, he was willing to damage his relationship with Natalie to protect her from Jaxon when we all know that man is the best thing to ever happen to her. He's overprotective to a fault."

Hannah had never been Liam's biggest fan, so of course, she chose now to go to bat for him.

"I don't know what to tell you, Hannah. Pictures of him with Penelope are all over the internet."

"Tabloids," Natalie qualified.

Hannah wrinkled her nose in disgust. "And you believe that crap? Come on, Amy. You're the most level-headed person I know. A few days ago, Liam was talking about babies. No way would he throw that all away for a fling. Especially with *her*."

"That's what I've been trying to tell her." Natalie shrugged.

"Enough!" I shouted. "You two didn't see what I saw these past few weeks. I knew something was off, but I wasn't sure what. I asked for his honesty before asking a question, and he looked so panicked—a sure sign that he was keeping secrets from me. Then, I mentioned something about being grateful we weren't full-time royals, and his entire demeanor changed. It all makes sense now."

Natalie sighed. "I stand by my advice that you need to talk to him. Running away isn't the answer. You're married. You need to talk it out."

I flung my arms wide. "We did talk! Every single night while he was gone! The dinner those pictures are from was on Sunday. If it were innocent, why didn't he tell me? He's had plenty of opportunities."

Natalie tried to argue, "Ames. He loves you. We can all see it."

"No, you still don't get it! It was all an act. I was an easy mark, not having much relationship experience. I believed his bullshit about being scared to love." I rolled my eyes. "God, what a line. It's my fault, really. I shouldn't have gotten attached. I should have treated this marriage as intended—a business relationship, nothing more."

"That's why you're still wearing your rings," Hannah challenged.

Peering down at my left hand, I realized she was right. The heavy weight had been foreign months ago, but I'd quickly gotten used to it. Taking a deep breath, I twisted them, sliding the warm metal off my finger. There was a finality in removing them, and it ripped the heart out of my chest all over again.

Placing them on the kitchen counter, I held Hannah's stare. "Get them out of my sight."

When Hannah didn't move to take them, I let anger take hold and slapped them off the counter. The soft clinking as they bounced off the hardwood kitchen floor was deafening in the silence. Looking at my two best friends, I could see the shock on their faces. I was our group's calm, rational one, but I'd been pushed to the limit.

I should have left well enough alone. Why had I thought pushing Liam past the breaking point was a good idea? His resistance should have been a red flag. He'd never wanted me, but I practically threw myself at him. I brought this devastation upon myself.

Pushing off my stool, I had every intention of crawling under the covers of my bed and sleeping off this waking nightmare. Before I made it two steps, the heavy banging on the front door made me jump. All three of us turned toward the incessant noise, knowing exactly who it was.

Liam was home, and he was looking for me.

CHAPTER 28

Liam

THE FLIGHT HOME WAS long, and I hadn't been able to sleep. Keeping me awake was the fact that Amy hadn't texted me back. Had her meeting gone badly, and she didn't want to say? I tried a few more times while in the air, steering clear of the subject of her job, but was only met with silence. It was unnerving, and I found myself pacing for nine straight hours as I crossed the Atlantic.

I knew something was wrong the moment I entered the house. The energy was off, and I could sense Amy wasn't there. Exhausted, I chalked it up to sleep deprivation—it was the middle of the night in Belleston, after all. Climbing the stairs, my suitcase in hand, I walked into what was now our shared bedroom, and my blood ran cold.

The walk-in closet door was open, and I could see the empty racks from where I stood frozen in place. What the hell was going on? Forcing myself to step further into the room, I noticed her nightstand had been cleared, and upon inspection, the bathroom had been emptied of all her cosmetics and assorted beauty products.

It was clear that Amy had packed up and left. Everything she owned was gone from our bedroom, and not just for an overnight trip with the girls. There had to be a reason why she'd bolt without a word, and there was only one I could think of.

Fear coursed through my veins. Leo had essentially disappeared after our meeting, where the truth of his parentage had been revealed, taking several loyal bodyguards with him. No one had seen or heard from him since. He was unpredictable—especially when he felt threatened—but it was unlikely he was stupid enough to divulge the truth. He had the most to lose if the news ever leaked that he wasn't, indeed, a Remington.

With shaking hands, I pulled my phone from my jeans pocket, pulling up the search engine. For the first time in my life, I typed in my own name and held my breath, waiting for the results. The top of the feed was littered with pictures of Penelope and me at the state dinner and pages of articles discussing our rekindled love affair.

"No, no, no, no." Shocked, my legs gave out, and I collapsed onto the bed. Nothing was going on between me and Penelope. Amy was smart. She couldn't possibly believe this tabloid trash. She knew I loved her. I never let a day go by without saying those words to her. There was no way she left without confronting me.

Dialing Marcus, my heart hammered in my chest, waiting for him to answer. After two rings, his gruff voice filtered through the line, "Sir?"

I didn't mince words. "I need to know where my wife is."

"She's at the Slate residence, sir."

Of course she was. Hanging up on Marcus, I raced down the stairs, throwing open the front door before bounding across the path between our two properties. Out of breath, I bent over with hands on my knees, trying to calm myself. Getting my breathing under control, I straightened before pounding on the door.

When no one answered, I beat on it again, harder and harder, as my desperation grew. It opened suddenly, almost causing me to fall forward with the force used to throw my fists into the unyielding wood. Stumbling slightly, I righted myself as I leveled a glare on Natalie's small frame blocking my path to entry.

Breathless, I accused, "I know she's here."

"Who's here?" she asked calmly.

My irritation level was sky-high, and I didn't care if Nat was my little sister. I needed to get to Amy. "Cut the shit, Nat. I need to see my wife."

Natalie crossed her arms, leaning against the doorframe. "She doesn't want to see you."

"I didn't fucking cheat on her!" I roared.

Holding her ground, Natalie didn't flinch. "I know."

"Then let me see her!" There was compassion in her eyes. She knew the truth, but her loyalties were torn. Fine. I'd make this easy for her. "I'm going to count to three, Natalie. Then I will pick you up and move you. You're not going to keep me from talking to Amy."

"That would be a mistake." Jaxon's voice boomed from the hallway as he came into view. "Touch my wife, and I won't be held responsible for what happens next."

Fucking Jaxon Slate. "There won't be a problem as long as you let me in to talk to *my* wife."

Jaxon also knew the truth, but he would always take his wife's side over mine. "Amy doesn't want to talk to you right now. Let her cool down, and maybe she'll change her mind."

"Cool down. From what? I didn't do anything!" Realizing they wouldn't budge, a feral desperation clawed up my spine as I bellowed, "AMY! AMY! AMY!"

Jaxon stepped into the doorway, and in my frantic state, my first instinct was to charge him, forcing my way into the house. I was willing to risk life and limb to get to Amy.

"Liam. Go home. She's not going to change her mind. Not tonight. The only thing you're doing is scaring our kids."

My voice was hoarse from screaming, and emotion colored my words. "I can't go home without her. Jaxon, please." I wasn't above begging.

Sympathy shone in his eyes—he'd been there. "I know it's hard, man, I do. She needs time. It's not going to happen tonight."

Fuck. My mind was racing, but it finally cleared enough to realize what had happened. That dinner had been days ago, but that story was dated today. Leo was striking back. It had to be him. This was his version of the middle finger. If he couldn't have the life he wanted, neither could I.

Defeated, I turned on my heel and returned to my cold, empty house. How could I explain to Amy that this story wasn't true if she refused to see me? It wasn't like her to jump to conclusions, and I needed to see her and find out what really happened to cause this knee-jerk reaction. I wondered if I would ever get the chance.

Life was meaningless without Amy. Days turned into weeks, but they all blurred together. The only mark of time passing was the sun rising and repeatedly setting since I'd last gazed upon my wife's face—proof that the world kept turning even though mine had come to a grinding halt.

I couldn't eat. I couldn't sleep. Obsessively, I spent hours each day staring at my phone, willing for it to ring, for Amy to finally be ready to talk. When I finally gave up waiting for her to come to me, I dialed her phone, only to discover the number was no longer in service. She was right next door, and I couldn't reach her.

It was hopeless. I was hopeless.

Laying on the couch, I heard a key turn in the lock of the front door and sprang to my feet. Swaying slightly, I gripped the side table, trying to ward off the rush of lightheadedness that made my head swim. I was weak from lack of sleep and nutrition, but none of that mattered if Amy was home. I'd crawl to meet her at the front door if I had to.

The door opened slowly, and the light switch along the entryway wall was flicked on. I groaned against the blinding intrusion, throwing an arm over my eyes. I kept the house dark. It matched my depressed mood.

"Jesus. At least when Nat kicked me out, I had the good sense to shower." It wasn't Amy.

Slowly lowering my arm as my eyes adjusted to the light, I glared at Jaxon, who had apparently let himself into my house. He'd kept me from Amy, which wasn't an offense I would likely forgive or forget any time soon.

"Why do you still have a key?"

Jaxon shrugged, making his way further into the house. "For emergencies."

"This is not an emergency."

He walked into the kitchen, wrinkling his nose as he passed the trash I hadn't bothered to take out in weeks. "That's subjective."

Following him, I wanted nothing more than to throw him out on his ass. On a good day, I had a few inches and at least thirty pounds of muscle on the man, but he could easily take me in my weakened state. Maybe getting pummeled would make me feel something.

"Why are you here, Jaxon?" I said on a sigh.

"Addy called Natalie. You've skipped out on two weeks of work without a word, so I've been sent to check on you."

It had been two weeks? "Great. My mother and sister are conspiring. That's all I need."

"They love you and are worried about you. Seeing you now, I can't say I disagree with their concern."

"Don't talk to me about love," I snarled.

Placing a manila envelope between us on the kitchen island, he added, "I was also sent to bring you this."

I didn't need to open the envelope to know what it contained—divorce papers. Meeting Jaxon's eyes, they were filled with sympathy, but that was of little comfort. My wife wanted nothing to do with me. Worse, she wanted to sever any remaining ties.

"She has no grounds."

"I know," Jaxon said softly.

"You know, but you stood in my way when I tried to talk to her, to explain." My temper flared, and my voice rose.

"Natalie and I are in a difficult position. We can't choose sides," he explained.

"You've already chosen one! Hers!" There was a throbbing behind my temples, and I pressed my fingers against them to try and ease it. "You've been harboring my wife, and now you're bringing me divorce papers."

Jaxon sighed. "Nat is conflicted. She's trying to protect her best friend, who is hurting, but you know how much she cares about you. Hannah, on the other hand, does not share the same sentiment. There has been mention of burning things." He winced.

"Sounds about right." Inspired by that vision, I grabbed the papers off the island. Pulling a lighter from inside a drawer, I held it away from my body as I lit the envelope on fire before dropping it into the sink and turning on the faucet. "I'm not signing these." I dared Jaxon to challenge my decision.

"I didn't think you would, but that's not all she sent." Looking uncomfortable, he reached into his pocket, placing a small velvet box on the countertop. My knees buckled, and I collapsed to the floor. Papers I could fight, but she'd sent back the ring. Any hope I had of getting through to her vanished. It was over.

Jaxon rounded the island and sat on the floor, his back against the fridge opposite where I'd crumpled. "She lost her job over those stories."

Fuck. She didn't need me anymore. No wonder she could walk away so easily. "When?"

"The day you came home. She went into her meeting thinking she would find out if she earned the promotion she'd been chasing for a year, only to get fired because they didn't want the bad press. It didn't matter what the truth was. The image of one of their higher-level employees being publicly cheated on by her husband was bad for their image. That was enough to cause our rational Amy to spiral. She knew you were hiding something, so her mind believed the tabloid gossip."

"So, you just stood there and let her believe it? You and Natalie know that's not the secret I've been keeping from her. You could have told her!" It was easier to aim my anger at them than at myself.

"It was not our story to tell. It should have come from you months ago. We begged you to tell her. Maybe she'd have felt secure enough to know these rumors were false if you had. But you were a coward."

I hated that he was right. "Fuck off, Jaxon."

"No, you need to hear the hard truth. You did this to yourself. You did this to Amy. That woman has been our rock, and it's killing me to hear her cry herself to sleep every night."

"Are you trying to make me feel worse about it?" If he was, it was working.

"No," he challenged. "I'm trying to force you to man up and fight for your wife. I can't do it for you, and neither can Natalie."

"How the hell am I supposed to fight for her when she's changed her fucking phone number and is serving me with divorce papers? Amy is right next door, and I can't even go over there because you won't let me past the threshold!"

Jaxon raised an eyebrow before asking, "Are you ready to tell her the truth?"

"If she'll give me the time of day, I'll tell her everything. I have nothing left to lose."

A tiny smirk graced his lips. "I was hoping you'd say that. I can't let you past the front door of my house without risking the wrath of my wife and breaking Amy's trust, but what if I told you I could get her into your house?"

"I'll take all the help I can get. I only want a chance at getting Amy back."

"Get your act together. This house is a mess, and you look—and smell—like shit. I'll be in touch."

With that, he pushed off the ground and left the house. How the tables had turned. A year ago, I came here to smack some sense into Jaxon when Natalie had kicked him out, and now, he'd come to return the favor. There was no room for error if I only got one shot at winning my wife back.

Something Natalie said months ago floated to the front of my mind.

"There's the brother I know and love. Ready to burn down the world to save someone he loves."

She was right. Amy was the person I loved most, and suddenly, it became crystal clear where my loyalties lie. Mother told me to go home and focus on my marriage. I had a feeling that if she knew what I was about to do, she would support me wholeheartedly—she believed in love.

I would beg Lucy for forgiveness later. Right now, I had a marriage to save.

CHAPTER 29

Amy

WHOEVER SAID THEY'D RATHER lose a great love instead of never having experienced it at all didn't know shit. I would have happily lived the rest of my life blissfully unaware of the heartbreak that came with losing the love of your life. The past few weeks and the gut-wrenching pain I experienced made me realize that was exactly what Liam had been—the love of my life. I had fallen hard and fast for a man I had known for almost half my life, giving him my heart. And what did he do? He'd stomped on it as if it meant nothing.

Three weeks had passed since that fateful day, and while the pain lingered, it lessened just a touch with each passing day. I prayed there would come a day when it wouldn't hurt anymore.

I'd spent long enough licking my wounds. It was time to take action and move on with my life. The first step was sending Jaxon next door with divorce papers for Liam to sign and returning my ring. Next, I needed to find a new job and a place to live.

I couldn't stay with Natalie and Jaxon long-term, but I would prefer the divorce to be finalized before moving. I didn't need Liam claiming marital property on my new residence. Too many nights, I had woken from a dead sleep due to nightmares about the night Liam had practically beaten down the door. I'd never heard him lose control like that—seemingly possessed in his need to get to me—and didn't need him finding me at my new place when I no longer had the protection offered by the Slates.

I went dark following the day my life changed. At the time, it had seemed like the only option to keep a fragment of my sanity intact. Staying off the internet, not watching TV, and cutting off service to my phone, I poured my focus into Natalie's kids.

Pulling out my laptop, I took a deep breath. It was a necessary evil to search for a new job. I hadn't updated my resume in almost a year, and reviewing it now, I cursed myself for putting all my eggs in one basket. I'd never worked anywhere other than the Hartford Family Reunification Foundation, and they wouldn't likely give me a glowing recommendation to a potential new employer.

My fingers hovered over the keyboard. I couldn't bring myself to type out my most recent body of work because that would mean attaching Liam's last name to my accomplishment—his infidelity and my gullibility had forever tarnished it.

Natalie found me staring at the screen, perched on a stool at the kitchen island. Taking a seat next to me, she glanced at what I was attempting to work on, sighing softly. "Oh, Ames."

"I can't do it. How can I move forward when his name is attached to my most important project?"

"I know how you feel about earning a job yourself, but maybe you could let me put in a good word at the Connecticut Comets Foundation? Between Ace, Jaxon, and me, we could get your foot in the door. It might not be much, but it would be something new to put on your resume, and then you can keep looking."

I could barely afford to have pride anymore—Liam had stripped me of that as well. "Thank you. I appreciate it, Nat." With that, I closed my laptop.

Before she could respond, Charlie's cries filtered through the baby monitor app on Natalie's phone, indicating nap time was over. Natalie glanced at it, asking, "Could you get her? I'll make a quick call to my contacts and see if they can find a place for you."

"Sure." Shoving off the stool, I trekked up the back staircase that stopped on the second floor outside the master suite, with the nursery next to it for easy access. Pushing open the door, I was met by a red-faced Charlie standing in her crib, screaming to be heard. Lifting her into my arms, I cuddled her, bouncing gently to soothe her. "It's okay, pretty girl. Aunt Amy's got you."

A month ago, the possibility of a family of my own had been real—I had begun to picture a life featuring children with Liam. He was incredible with our nieces and nephews, so imagining him as an incredible dad wasn't a stretch. Like the rest of our future, that vision had gone up in flames.

Charlie settled enough that I took her to the changing station against the wall and freshened her up with a clean diaper. Pulling her soft, warm body back into my arms, I noticed new pictures decorating the nursery walls. Upon closer inspection, they were all candid photos from Charlie's birthday party—with her siblings, her parents, her grandparents, and several of Jaxon's teammates.

Making it to the end of the row, my knees nearly buckled when I reached the last picture. It was the moment Liam and I had shared on the couch, our smiles bright as we looked at Charlie standing on my lap. Any progress I made in getting over him was instantly lost. How could we have looked this happy and had it all come crashing down less than a week later?

"You know what I think of when I look at that picture?" Natalie's voice filtered in from the doorway, but I couldn't tear my eyes away from the smile captured on Liam's face. Not waiting for an answer, she entered the room, coming to a stop beside me. "I see love."

My chest trembled as a sigh escaped. "Why would you hang this picture?"

"Because no matter what happens with you and Liam, you are her aunt and uncle, and she deserves to see the love shining through your eyes." Looking at my best friend, my heart was breaking all over again. Recognizing that I couldn't find the words, Natalie continued, "Ames, I've known you both for a long time. Right now, you don't believe him, but I hope you can believe me when I say that the two of you were merely surviving alone, going through the motions in your own lives. Together, you were thriving, becoming better versions of yourselves—this picture captured that perfectly. That love wasn't all for Charlie."

"I'd happily take surviving over broken. I don't want to feel like this anymore." My voice was thick with emotion. I wasn't sure I would ever get over Liam.

"Not too long ago, you threw me for a loop, suggesting that every little thing in my life had led me to Jaxon. I couldn't wrap my mind around that idea because it meant all the pain I suffered under Leo was part of some master plan. Why would I have to suffer first to find the man I was supposed to love for the rest of my life? Besides bringing me three children I can't imagine living without, I couldn't understand it. Now, I do. If I hadn't lived through the nightmare that was marriage to Leo, we would have never made it here. You and Liam would have never been living under the same roof, he wouldn't have been here when you needed a significant other for some stupid job, and you would never have gotten married. I can make peace with that part of my life now, knowing it helped my best friend find her true love. And I know you still love him. You wouldn't be this broken if you didn't."

"I don't believe in that crap anymore." The words were barely a whisper.

"I think you ran away because you were scared of how vulnerable that love for Liam made you feel. It's easier to make a clean break than to fight, for fear of getting hurt down the line. I get it. Marriage is hard, even when you have a good one. Trust is scary. Every time Jaxon gets on a plane, I have to trust that he will make the right choices."

"Jaxon would never cheat on you. He adores you." Our situations weren't the same.

Natalie didn't back down. "And *your* husband adores you. Deep down, you know that too."

"What do you want me to do? Take him back? Forgive him? So that he can do it to me all over again?"

"I think you shouldn't be making decisions about your marriage based on twisted tales spun by the tabloids."

"I just want to move on with my life." Changing the subject, I asked, "Any word on that job?"

Natalie's eyes betrayed that there was more she wanted to say on the matter, but she decided to keep whatever it was to herself. "Yeah. They can see you at the end of the week."

"Great. My schedule is wide open."

Handing her Charlie, I retreated to my room. Natalie was right—loving Liam was terrifying. I had been so naïve when he told me how scared he was to love me that I willingly jumped off the cliff, not bothering to check for a safety net. It turned out there wasn't one, and my heart had been smashed by the rocks waiting for me at the bottom. How anyone agreed to fall in love more than once was beyond me. I was never doing this again.

Crashing atop my bed, I began to cry over him yet again. I thought I had run out of tears over Liam. I was wrong.

Would I ever recover from him stomping on my heart?

———— �֍ ————

The interview with the Connecticut Comets Foundation resulted in a job offer on the spot, effectively crossing off one more item on my list of tasks required to get back on my feet. My first assignment involved going to the league office in Toronto for a summit of all the teams' foundations to work on collective projects. Now, if only I could find my passport.

Natalie found me tearing apart my room, muttering to myself, "I know I packed it."

"Whatcha looking for?" Not waiting for an invitation to enter—it was her house, after all—she sat on my bed, which was messy from packing.

Sitting back on my heels, I let out a sigh of frustration. "My passport. I could have *sworn* I grabbed it when we packed my things next door. You went to all this trouble to get my foot in the door with the Comets Foundation, and I will look like a complete joke if I miss this summit because I can't find my damn passport!"

Natalie scanned the room with her eyes. "Are you sure you grabbed it? Is there any possibility that you left it?"

"Maybe?" After all the time spent searching, I wasn't so sure anymore. "It's not like I can walk over there to check. Could you do it for me?"

"Sure," she offered. "Where do you think you left it?"

"I don't know! Crap. I can't ask you to spend hours searching every inch of the house."

"A little birdie told me Liam went back to Belleston. The house should be empty."

I was flooded with a mix of hope and despair at her words—hope that I could finally move on with my life, but despair that he'd given up on me. That's what I had wanted, wasn't it? For him to leave me in peace so I could rebuild what was left of my life—there would be no mending my broken heart.

"Are you sure he's gone?" I asked skeptically.

"Lucy said he landed yesterday and was wondering where you were."

Guilt stabbed at my gut. The Remington family—minus Leo—had been so welcoming and kind to me during my few visits as Liam's wife. While I felt bad for leaving without a word to them, they couldn't possibly condone his actions. Or was that part of the royal code? Did they think they were above the rules and could do whatever they wanted without consequences?

Rising to my feet, I made my decision. "Okay. I'm gonna pop over there real quick and see if I can find it. There are only so many places it could be. If I'm not back in an hour, come help me."

Natalie rose, walking out of the room with me. "You've got a deal. One hour."

Not wasting any more time, I bounded down the steps and out the side door that spit me onto the path next door. When I reached the front door, I took a deep breath. He wasn't here. I could do this. Turning the key in the lock and poking my head inside as I held my breath, I was thankfully met with an empty house.

Latching the front door behind me, I leaned against it as a wave of grief hit me. Everywhere I looked were reminders of moments shared with Liam that likely meant more to me than him. Pushing those thoughts aside, I raced upstairs to check my bedroom. The less time spent in this house, the better.

Pausing at the threshold of what had become *our* bedroom—no longer only mine during the final weeks before my world came crashing down—I steeled my nerves and stepped inside. Looking around, I saw it was clean. The bed was made, and there were no lingering traces of Liam anywhere. That had me wondering if he'd left for good. If that was what I wanted, why did it hurt so much thinking that I'd never see his face again?

Checking both nightstands, I came up empty. The dresser was my next stop—nothing. Next, the closet—yet another dead end. Then, I remembered the safe hidden in the living room. Going back downstairs, I crawled beneath the writing desk, revealing the secret spot in the wall where Liam had kept a safe for important documents, using my fingerprints to open it. Careful not to disturb anything that didn't belong to me, I looked through the contents, coming up empty once more.

"Looking for this?" A deep voice I knew all too well carried across the room, and I froze. Maybe he wouldn't see me if I stayed like this, silent and still beneath the writing desk.

Who are you kidding, Amy? He's not a freaking T-Rex. Even if he were, are you prepared to stay here until he gives up and moves on?

Resigning myself to the fact that I was caught and would now be forced to face the man who broke my heart, I backed out from underneath the desk. Standing slowly, I counted to three in my head before turning around and leaning my body against the desk.

My chest squeezed at the sight of Liam before me. He stood in the open space between the living room and kitchen, holding up my passport. It didn't take much to figure out that I'd been set up. Natalie knew he was going to be here, and if I were a betting woman, I'd bet that I had packed my passport, and it magically migrated back over here, creating the perfect excuse for me to step foot inside this house.

"You're not supposed to be here." My voice was barely above a whisper.

"I am exactly where I'm supposed to be."

Dressed in one of his custom-tailored black suits, paired with an open-collared white shirt, he looked as handsome as ever, but there were subtle differences. Dark circles underlined his eyes, and the suit fit him differently, almost as if he'd lost some weight. I should be thrilled that he was suffering—it was his fault, after all—but I wasn't a sadist. I wouldn't wish this kind of pain on my worst enemy.

I was exhausted, weakened from weeks of crying over this man, and I had no interest in fighting. "I need that. And I'll take the signed papers while I'm here if you have them."

Liam's blue eyes never left mine as he calmly stated, "I burned them."

Of course he did. Nothing was ever easy with this man. "Please, just let me go."

A muscle ticked in his jaw. "Over my dead body—or his."

I scoffed. "So, it was okay for you to sleep with someone else *while we were married*, but I can't move on?"

He'd held himself in check to this point, but his temper flared at the criticism of his hypocrisy. "For fuck's sake, Amy! I didn't sleep with her!"

Flinching at his raised voice, I held my ground, challenging, "Then why did I find out while getting *fired* that you were with her at all? I lost my job because you were keeping this secret from me. You had days and days to tell me, and you didn't. Not once."

Pocketing the passport—great, I was *not* going in there to get it if that was his plan—he ran a hand through his dark hair. "You want to know why it never came up? Because my interaction with her was of no consequence. It was forgotten moments after I escorted her to dinner. I didn't even sit next to her. We spoke for a total of three minutes, Amy. She asked about you and Natalie, and that was it!"

He was saying all the right things, and my bruised and battered heart begged my brain to believe him, but I'd seen him turn on the charm at the drop of a hat as easily as his brother. "I'm supposed to believe that? Because you got caught? You were hiding things from me long before that trip."

"You're right."

"Excuse me?" He had to have said something else. In my experience, men never admitted when a woman was right.

"I have been hiding something from you, and I was so damn scared of losing you when you found out that I kept it to myself longer than I should have."

My legs threatened to buckle, and I gripped the edge of the desk tighter, needing support. I *knew* he'd been keeping secrets, but it had been all too easy to believe he was cheating on me. What else would have him so scared to tell me? Whatever it was, if he couldn't trust me, how could I trust him?

Liam watched my body language like a hawk—he'd always been able to read me—and realized I was waiting for him to make the next move, so he took a deep breath before uttering the words, "I find myself in direct line for the throne. Leo will never be king."

"Say that again?" Of all the possibilities of what Liam could have been hiding, I did *not* see that one coming.

Clearing his throat, Liam clarified, "Turns out Leo is my half-brother—the wrong half. He has no Remington blood. That leaves me as the heir."

My mouth dropped open, but my brain was working overtime. The last piece finally fell into place, and the picture became crystal clear. Suddenly, everything made sense. Liam hadn't gone home to Belleston once since bringing Natalie back to Connecticut but had made four trips in the last eight months. He suddenly needed a wife—a wife I signed up to be without having all the facts.

"How long have you known?" Crossing my arms across my chest, I already knew the answer. I needed to hear it from his mouth. To see how committed he was to coming clean.

Liam shifted on his feet, his eyes drifting downward to stare at the floor. "I knew when I asked you to marry me."

CHAPTER 30

Liam

MY CARDS WERE LAID on the table, and now my fate rested in Amy's hands. When she'd backed out from beneath the writing desk—and I laid eyes on her for the first time in a month—my heart had stopped. The woman staring back at me was a shell of the vibrant Amy I fell in love with. Her green eyes were dull, devoid of their usual sparkle, and her entire posture sagged in defeat.

My compassionate, determined redhead had lost the will to fight.

I'd done this to her. I'd stolen her spirit. If I had summoned the courage to tell her the truth months ago, I was sure she'd have been upset—she'd have been angry as hell—but I would gladly take that anger over this sadness radiating off her in waves.

"When do you leave?" Amy's soft voice snapped me out of my thoughts.

Had I missed some part of this conversation? Because I had no idea what she was talking about. "I'm not leaving."

"Of course you are. You have a role to fulfill and are no longer needed here. No holier-than-thou foundation board, no need for a fake marriage. I don't need you to stay here out of some misguided sense of obligation toward me. I appreciate the truth about both Penelope and your family drama, but it's probably best if we make a clean break—forget the past six months ever happened."

Amy was putting up her walls. She'd been burned in the past and was trying to protect herself from future pain. I'd battled my own demons and roadblocks when opening my heart and loving her, so I understood her reluctance. I had learned that falling in love was simultaneously terrifying and exhilarating. Still, I was willing to live with those conflicting emotions—while stepping outside my comfort zone—if Amy was by my side. She was my light, and my world would be dark without her.

"You might not need me anymore, but I still need you," I declared, allowing my vulnerability to seep into my tone.

She scoffed. "Yeah, because it's a bad look for a bachelor king, right?"

There it was. A tiny flicker of that fire hidden deep within the woman I loved. Knowing it hadn't been entirely extinguished gave me hope.

I needed her to know that she was the most important person in my world.

"I'd like to believe I wouldn't have asked you to marry me if I hadn't found out that Leo and his children would be scratched from the line of succession. But I would be fooling myself. I wouldn't have been able to deny you help if it was within my means to do so. It's in the very fabric of my being. We would have fallen in love no matter what, so I'm not going to give it up." Amy's gasp at my words spurred me on. "I'll be here waiting. You're it for me, Amy Michaels. I will love you today, tomorrow, and every day after that."

Silence descended the room as she processed my words. Finally, she asked, "What about what I want?"

Shoving both hands into my pockets, I went for broke. "I've made my decision. I will spend every day of the rest of my life trying to make up for the mistakes I've made these past six months. We'll have plenty of time. I'm giving it all up—Lucy can take my place. You said you wanted to burn with me, so here I am, returning the sentiment. I choose you."

"Shut up." Amy's voice was loud and clear for the first time since she'd crawled out from under the desk, and I was compelled to obey.

Slowly, she walked toward me, and I couldn't break her hypnotizing green gaze as she closed the distance between us. Stopping before me, Amy was close enough that I could get a hint of the floral smell that had long since dissipated from the pillows in our bedroom. Fighting the urge to close my eyes and savor it, I kept them trained on hers as I held my breath, waiting for her response.

"You haven't learned anything. I've spent months trying to teach you that marriage isn't about one person taking control. It requires balance—working together as a partnership. Now you go and make this major life decision without consulting me first?"

Stunned, I stared at Amy as I processed her words. What was she saying? I already told her I was giving it all up for her, so what was the major life decision she was referring to? Everything would be like before. We'd live here, she wouldn't be forced into a working royal role, and she could continue pursuing her career.

A thought pushed forward from the back of my mind. Amy was methodical, always carefully constructing her words. Did that mean she wanted our marriage to work? If I wasn't so blinded by the fear that she might still walk away after I bared my soul, I might have even thought she was baiting me. Our banter was something I'd missed the most in her absence.

Taking a leap of faith, I decided to answer as if she had been baiting me. It was a risk, but the reward would be huge if I was right. Meeting her eye, I shot back, "Like when you filed for divorce?"

Studying her face, watching for a sign of whether I hit my mark or failed miserably—that was when I saw it. That sparkle was back in her green eyes, and my breath caught in my throat as a corner of her mouth turned up.

Dropping to her knees, Amy peered up at me from the floor. "Is this the part where I get down on my knees for my future king?"

Was she saying what I thought she was saying? Gripping her wrist, I pulled her back onto her feet, feeling her warm body slide against mine. Taking her chin in my hand, I searched her eyes. "I want an equal. Do you understand me?"

Her plump lower lip pushed out. "But what if I want to get down on my knees?"

"Ames, don't tease me," I begged.

She smirked in response, and fuck if I didn't want to kiss that smirk off her face. "Who said I was teasing?" Dropping her hands to my belt, she unbuckled it and sank back onto her knees before me. Amy paused as she was about to unzip my pants, looking up, adding, "On one condition."

A rush of air flew past my lips, and my chest ached from the breath I'd been holding. "Anything," I breathed.

"Never, and I mean *never*, do you keep something so big it impacts both our lives from me ever again."

My head moved from side to side. "Never. No more secrets. I love you, Amy."

"Good. Was that so hard?" Proceeding to slide my pants zipper down, I groaned as Amy reached inside, freeing my aching cock. "Mm, guess it was hard."

Before I could respond to her teasing—just so damn glad she was back in my life—she took my length in her mouth, taking as much of me as she could handle.

I groaned. "Fuck, Amy."

She hummed around my dick, and it took every ounce of strength not to buck my hips and shove myself down her tight little throat. Reaching back, I gripped the barstools behind me to steady myself as my knees threatened to buckle. Her mouth was so hot as she sucked and bobbed along my length that warmth began to spread outward to my extremities.

As incredible as it felt, after a month apart and wondering if I'd ever see her face again, I needed to be inside her. Tugging her hair gently, I pried her mouth off my cock, pulling her back to her feet. "I need you, sweetheart. So fucking badly."

Amy snaked a hand into my hair, pulling my mouth down to hers, taking control, and kissing me deeply. Her tongue slid into my mouth, and she moaned against me as our mouths became as frantic as our bodies rubbing against each other.

Breaking our kiss, she whispered against my mouth, "Then fucking take me, Liam."

Growling, I lifted her effortlessly into my arms, spinning us around and depositing her on the kitchen island. "I don't think I can be gentle, baby."

"I won't break. Claim me. I'm yours."

Fuck, this woman. How did I get so lucky? Pulling at the hem of her tight tank top, she raised her arms so I could remove it before I practically ripped her shorts down her long legs. Her hands went to work, shoving off my suit jacket and tearing at the buttons on my shirt. My pants were already undone and fell down my legs, allowing me to kick them aside.

Amy was laid out in our kitchen like a feast, waiting to be devoured, and she was all mine. Forever. I was going to spend the rest of my life ensuring her happiness. My heart—my body—belonged to her, no matter what our future held.

Removing my boxer briefs, I stepped between my wife's legs, jerking as my cock brushed against her wetness. God, I already knew I wouldn't last long, and I wasn't even inside her yet. Looking at where our bodies would soon be joined, I froze.

Shit. I hadn't seen this going quite so well and was unprepared. There had to be a condom hidden in this kitchen somewhere from when Amy had been ambushing me months ago. Leaving the cradle of her thighs, I went to the drawers next to the stove, then the other side of the island. Each place I checked turned up empty. "Fuck."

Looking over her shoulder, Amy's brows drew down. "What are you looking for?"

"I don't have a condom. Stay here."

This would kill the mood of the moment, but I knew there were some upstairs and was halfway out of the kitchen when her voice stopped me in my tracks. "We don't need one."

Turning, I faced Amy. What did she mean we didn't need one? Charlie's birthday seemed like a lifetime ago when I blurted out that she looked good with a baby, but we hadn't discussed the possibility of kids since signing our marriage contract. Our relationship had changed since that day, but children might still be off the table. I'd never force her into something she didn't want. Did this mean she wanted to start a family with me?

Then, another thought crossed my mind. Maybe we didn't need one because she was already pregnant. We'd been careful, but that wasn't always enough—Charlie was living proof of that. A vision of my life flashed before my eyes—running around our backyard with a tiny redhead replica of Amy, bath time giggles, kissing scraped knees, late nights cuddling a soft body against my chest. I wanted it all.

"Are you—did we . . ." I gestured toward her as my words trailed off.

Catching my meaning, her green eyes grew large as saucers, and she shook her head violently. "Oh, God no." I'd be lying if I said a wave of disappointment didn't rush over me. "I got an IUD."

Considering she'd served me divorce papers, and I hadn't seen her in a month, that statement had me seeing red. All these months married, and she waited until we split up to get on birth control?

Gritting my teeth; my voice was lethal. "What's his name?"

Amy rolled her eyes. "Get over yourself, Liam. I had it put in a day before I got fired. It was supposed to be a surprise for *you* when you got home, but then everything went to shit."

Relief rolled over me, and I crossed the room in three strides, pulling her back into my arms. "Look who is keeping secrets now." Dipping my head to the side of her neck, I nipped playfully, causing her to arch against me.

"Are we talking or having makeup sex?" Amy teased, reminding me just how much I'd missed her.

Gripping her hips, I pulled her ass to the edge of the island, lining my cock up with her entrance and thrusting home. Amy's resulting moan as she dug her nails into my shoulders was almost as good as the feeling of being bare inside her. Almost.

She clung to me as I set the pace—hard and fast—desperately trying to make up for lost time. I wanted to do this for the rest of my life, making this woman happy, or at the very least, providing an unlimited stream of orgasms. Speaking of which, she was getting close, judging from the change in pitch of her moans and the flush of her skin. Holding her still, I took control, pumping my hips just right to create friction on her clit with each pass until she strained against me, screaming out my name as her release was ripped from her body.

Her tight heat clamped down on me, and I was lost as my own orgasm tore through me, spilling myself deep inside her. Amy clung to me as the waves rocking her body subsided, and I held her just as tight, never wanting to let her go.

I was man enough to admit when my wife was right—we needed to lean on each other if we were going to have a successful marriage. My life had been spent taking care of others, protecting them, but it was long past time that I allowed someone to take care of me. Amy was my person, and there was comfort in knowing she would constantly challenge me to be better.

Once our breathing slowed, Amy pulled back, reaching up to run her hands through my sweat-dampened hair. "So, did you already pass on your role to Lucy? And if so, is it too late to take it back?"

I raised a brow. "You were serious?"

"You're not only a stubborn man but also a stupid one."

"Ouch." My tone was playful.

"Do you really think I could stand by and be the reason for depriving Belleston of arguably the most loyal, caring king they've ever had?" Determination glittered in her dazzling green eyes.

"Ames, you can't go into this half-cocked. Once I take this job, it's for life. There is no early retirement. I can't ask you to do that for me—give up your life, your plans for a career. If we're lucky, we will get twenty, or maybe thirty years to be us, but there are no guarantees."

"In case you haven't heard, I find myself in search of new employment."

"What about the job you took with the Comets?" I asked.

One corner of her mouth quirked up. "That was a favor to Natalie. They created a position for me. I have a business trip to Toronto in a few days, but when I get back, I'll put in my notice."

I protested, "You don't have to do that. Belleston will be waiting for us whenever you're ready. There's no rush."

Tilting her head, she asked, "Do you know what I was thinking about sitting in that conference room before I knew I was getting fired?"

Unsure of where this conversation was headed, I was wary. "What?"

"I had this gut feeling I wasn't getting the promotion, and I remember thinking that I could use my experience to help those Bellestonians in need."

My heart twisted inside my chest. I had been so scared that she wouldn't want to stand by my side all this time, but she had this knack for surprising me at every turn. My Amy was unpredictable, and I looked forward to all the curveballs she would throw my way for the rest of our lives.

Regardless, I needed to know that she was sure. "But what about what you said a few months ago, that you were glad it wasn't our full-time job?"

Amy sighed. "I was tired and, as you well know, my feet hurt. It's kind of like a woman in labor saying she never wants to go through that ever again, but once the baby is out, the memory fades, and they realize it wasn't so bad."

"You're comparing royal life to labor? That doesn't sound very promising."

She rolled those pretty green eyes at me. "I think we can work out a more manageable schedule, don't you think? We packed so much into that one week that it was overwhelming. Spreading out our engagements with longer trips over there, plus getting to choose some of my own causes, and I could be happy working by your side."

"I want you always by my side, even when I take the throne. We are a team, and they can take it or leave it if they want us to rule."

Her smile was so brilliant that I fell in love with her all over again. "You have yourself a deal."

"You really want to spend more time in Belleston as a working royal?"

Amy shrugged. "I could be comfortable with a 50/50 split. Just so long as when we are here, it's our time. No late-night calls. It's our time off."

"God, you're incredible," I breathed out in awe. "Do you know that?"

That smirk made my heart flip. "I do, but it wouldn't kill you to tell me daily."

As I was gearing up to tease her in return, there was a timid knock on the door.

Our heads swiveled toward the front door as Natalie's voice filtered through the wood. "It's been an hour, Ames."

"Go away!" I barked. I wasn't in the mood to share my wife now that she was back in my arms.

Undeterred, Natalie knocked again, calling, "Amy?"

Amy called back. "I'll call you tomorrow!"

"Have fun, kids!" There was laughter in Natalie's voice, and we both laughed once it was clear she had left.

Amy's cheeks were flushed as she asked, "She's known the whole time, hasn't she?"

Sheepishly, I replied, "Not the *whole* time. I told her in February."

"How did she take it?"

"She's relieved. We still don't know when the family will announce it, but her kids are free when they do. Once they are, Jaxon wants to adopt them."

"And it's all because of you." There were stars in her eyes.

"I'm no hero, Amy." Even if my mother thought I had a hero complex.

"Perhaps not, but you stepped up. You may have just saved Natalie and those kids for the second time. You're a good man, Liam. Possibly the best I've ever known."

While she was riding high, I decided to take advantage. Stepping out of her warm embrace, causing her to whine slightly, I reached into the breast pocket of my suit jacket. Turning back toward the woman who made my life worth living, I presented her with the open ring box in my hand. Recognition lit up her face when she gazed upon its contents—her engagement ring.

Dropping down to one knee in the middle of our kitchen elicited a squeal from her lips. "What are you doing?"

Looking up at her from my place on the floor, I smirked at her panic. "Finally doing this right."

"Liam! Get up! We're naked!"

Slowly perusing her stunningly bare form from head to toe with appreciation, I nodded. "I've noticed."

Jumping down from atop the island, she stood before me, trying to pull me up. "I'm serious. You can't do this like this."

"Then it's a good thing we're already married. This is symbolic, Amy. Let me do this."

Sighing, Amy stopped tugging on my arms, huffing, "Fine." She was so damn cute when she was annoyed with me.

"Amy, we got married for all the wrong reasons and in secret, but we fell in love anyway. I can't imagine my life without you in it, so what I'm *proposing* is a redo. Will you marry me—the right way this time—knowing the full scope of what marriage to a man like me looks like?"

Crossing her arms across her bare breasts, she stared down at me, her brow furrowed in thought. "Big, fancy state wedding?"

"I want the whole world as my witness to see what real love looks like."

Amy reached out her left hand. "Well, how can I say no to that?"

Sliding the ring onto her finger, it felt as if all the pieces of my life had finally fallen into place. Even the ones I promised myself I didn't want or need. This woman had worked her way into my heart and changed my life, and now she was prepared to stand by my side as we shaped the future of my—no, our—country together. What we found was better than any fairy-tale ending Natalie had read in her books. This was real, and it was ours. Forever.

Epilogue

Amy

Five Months Later

I COULD FEEL HIS eyes on me as I finished reading the story to the small gathering of children at my feet inside the library at Stonecrest Palace. Knowing that if I looked I'd lose all concentration, I decided to power through the rest of the illustrated book held in my hands. Today's story time was part of the literacy program I was heading up in Belleston. Once a week, a selection of local children enrolled in the program were invited inside the castle for a special reading from yours truly.

A dozen tiny hands clapped in unison as I declared "The End" before closing the book. The program's director took over the group, and I headed to where Liam stood, leaning against the doorframe of the library. He had a dreamy look in his eyes, and the smile on his face always had the power to light up my insides.

When I got close enough, I ran my hands up his chest, disappointed that there were too many layers of clothing between us. Now that we'd assumed our role as working royals, he was often dressed in a suit. I might be a little biased, but he wore them well, which made the times when he was dressed down more of a treat, something reserved for my eyes only here in Belleston.

"What's that look for?"

His brilliant blue eyes held a hint of mischief. "Oh, you know. Just picturing you reading to a tiny red-headed boy."

Sighing and rolling my eyes, I pushed past him into the hallway. He was relentless. "We've been over this."

Turning to face him as he followed me out of the library, he had that sexy, smug look on his face. At least once a day, he commented about how much he'd love to start a family, and my answer remained the same each time.

"Remind me again." Liam spun me around by the waist, putting my back against the wall before caging me in with his strong arms, a hand on each side of my head.

Finding it hard to breathe—or think—I struggled to form the words. Damn him. He knew what he was doing. He was playing dirty, trying to get his way.

Closing my eyes to clear my head, I repeated the same reasons I had cited for months on end as to why we couldn't immediately get to baby-making. "We have a wedding coming up."

My eyes popped open at his laughter. "Sweetheart, we're already married."

"That may be true, but a pregnant princess bride isn't a good look with the whole world watching. You can wait six months."

Dipping his head, he captured my mouth in a kiss, and I melted into him. Pulling back slowly, he leaned his forehead against mine. "Pretty please?"

Pushing gently against his chest, I shook my head. "It's a good thing I took charge of our birth control situation."

"Fine," he huffed. "Six months."

Teasing, I ran a hand through his perfectly styled black hair. "Come on, don't you want to enjoy being us first?"

"Baby, I spent years not realizing the woman I was meant to spend the rest of my life with was right there all along. I've wasted enough time."

"Liam. You got the girl. Now, we have all the time in the world. We don't need to rush into the next step. Live in the moment for once."

He opened his mouth to respond when his body was suddenly jostled from behind, and his first instinct was to cover me protectively.

"What the fuck?" he muttered before turning to see who had practically crashed into him.

Pulling back slightly, our heads turned toward the sounds of stomping muted by the rugs lining the hallway to the view of Lucy's retreating form.

Stepping back from where he'd been shielding me, Liam called out, "Geez, LuLu! Where's the fire?"

Stopping in her tracks, Lucy turned to face us, her blue eyes full of fire. "Stop fucking calling me that!" Then she turned on her heel and vanished around the corner.

"Shit." Liam's remorse shone on his face. "I should go talk to her."

Looking in the direction from where she'd fled, there stood a man, rubbing the side of his jaw over a short, neatly trimmed dark beard. Putting my hand on Liam's forearm, I stopped him from following his sister. "I think that outburst may have been misdirected at you."

"What?" I tilted my head toward the man at the end of the hallway. Gazing where I directed his attention, he squinted. "Is that Preston?"

"You know him?"

"Yeah, you met him, remember? New Year's Eve? We grew up together. What the hell is he doing here?"

Honestly, I didn't recall much from that evening. It had passed by in a blur—well, with one exception. The time Liam and I spent alone that night was a moment that would forever be etched in my memory.

Pulling his attention back to me, I raised on my toes, kissing his lips quickly. "I've got Lucy. You handle your friend."

Shaking his head, he walked toward Preston, throwing over his shoulder to me, "Never a dull moment."

I might not admit it, but I wouldn't have it any other way. Having spent too many years sleepwalking in my own life, afraid to take a chance and let others in, I was ready to live.

Who knew playing pretend with the prince would turn out to be the best decision I ever made in my life?

For a bonus scene where Liam takes on the Foundation board, you can find it under the Bonus Scenes tab on my website, https://sienatrapbooks.com/

The saga of the Remington Royals continues with Lucy's story in *Feuding with the Fashion Princess*

If you missed Jaxon and Natalie's story, you can catch up with *Scoring the Princess*

Acknowledgements

To my husband, thank you for giving me the pleasure of watching you go from loathing Liam to declaring that "he's the man."

To my family, both immediate and extended, for their continued support as I pursue my career in writing.

To Katie, my editor, for always pushing me to be a better writer, and for declaring that Liam and Amy are her favorite couple I've written.

To Nina, my proofreader, for polishing my words for publication, and calling Liam one of her Top 10 Book Boyfriends.

To Amanda, for saying "I told you so" when I realized how hot Liam was months after writing him.

To my readers, a giant THANK YOU for making my words have meaning.

About the Author

Siena is originally from Pittsburgh, Pennsylvania, where a love of sports is bred into a girl's DNA. Her love of romance novels came early as well. She would often accompany her romance reviewer mom to book lovers' and romance writer's conventions, where she sat in on workshops and met numerous best-selling authors. It wasn't long before she was filling notebooks with her own stories, which often starred herself and a certain real-life prince.

As luck would have it, she met and married a handsome athlete instead. After several temporary residencies in multiple states and Germany, they finally settled in Michigan, the land where youth hockey reigns supreme.

Her stories no longer feature herself, but draw from her past experiences as an educator, businesswoman, fashion consultant, and world traveler when creating her strong heroines. "Oh yes," she says with a wink and a smile, "There are bits of me in all of them." Now, she spends her days writing happily ever afters for fictional characters and her evenings at the local hockey arenas cheering for her three children.

Siena loves to hear from her readers. You can email her at:

siena.trap.books@gmail.com

Or find her on social media (FB, IG, and TT): @siena.trap.books

More Books By Siena Trap

Remington Royals Series

Scoring the Princess

Playing Pretend with the Prince

Feuding with the Fashion Princess

Connecticut Comets (Hockey) Series

Coming in 2024

Bagging the Blueliner

(Cal's story)

Surprise for the Sniper

(Benji's story)

Second-Rate Superstar

(Braxton's story)

Made in the USA
Middletown, DE
13 May 2025